VICTORIA WALTERS

Summer at the Kindness Café

SIMON &
SCHUSTER

London · New York · Sydney · Toronto · New Delhi

A CBS COMPANY

First published in Great Britain by Simon & Schuster UK Ltd, 2018
A CBS COMPANY

Copyright © Victoria Walters, 2018

The right of Victoria Walters to be identified as author
of this work has been asserted in accordance with the
Copyright, Designs and Patents Act, 1988.

1 3 5 7 9 10 8 6 4 2

Simon & Schuster UK Ltd
1st Floor
222 Gray's Inn Road
London WC1X 8HB

Simon & Schuster Australia, Sydney
Simon & Schuster India, New Delhi

www.simonandschuster.co.uk
www.simonandschuster.com.au
www.simonandschuster.co.in

A CIP catalogue record for this book
is available from the British Library

Paperback ISBN: 978-1-4711-8116-0
eBook ISBN: 978-1-4711-8117-7

This book is a work of fiction. Names, characters, places
and incidents are either a product of the author's imagination or
are used fictitiously. Any resemblance to actual people living or
dead, events or locales is entirely coincidental.

Typeset in Bembo by M Rules
Printed and bound by CPI Group (UK) Ltd, Croydon, CR0 4YY

MIX
Paper from
responsible sources
FSC® C020471

For Erika, who was always kind

Part One

Promises

Chapter One

The endless green countryside stretched out as far as Abbie Morgan could see from the train window. The urban blanket of London had transformed into the rolling Surrey Hills as she made her way to the small town of Littlewood. It had been a nightmare of a week and her head was still pounding. Her suitcases were wedged in beside her, another painful reminder that this wasn't a quick visit to see her younger sister, Louise, she was actually moving in with her. Hopefully not for long, but still ...

Abbie sighed and leaned her head against the cool window so that her shoulder-length dark curls fell across her cheek, screening her from her fellow passengers. She was relieved that her train carriage was relatively empty, save for a mother and daughter a few seats away, so she could dwell on recent events in glum peace. She had lived in London for five years since leaving university and couldn't believe she was being forced to part ways with it. But when she had been made

redundant from her job at City PR, where she had worked for the last two years, she knew there was no way she could stay in the city she loved. The worst part was that her ex-boyfriend, Jack, a partner at the company, had been the one to deliver the news.

Abbie's phone on her lap buzzed with a call. 'Hi, Lou,' she greeted her sister, forcing a smile into her voice, if not fully onto her face. She was grateful to her little sister for putting her up but wished she didn't live in such a tiny town. At least the train would be quite quick for getting back to the city if she had interviews to go to.

'I'm so sorry I won't be there to meet you from the train,' Louise said. 'I won't be much longer though. Do you want to meet me at the café near the station and we can go home together?' Louise was a nurse at a hospital in the next, larger town, and her shift would be over soon. Abbie agreed to the plan and got directions to Brew. Louise said she was excited to finally show her town to Abbie, who hadn't had any time since getting the assistant job at City PR to make the trip out of London. Louise had always come to stay with her when she had time off instead. To Abbie, London was the place that everyone should want to be, so she had been surprised that Louise had settled somewhere so quiet.

The train soon drew into the small station of Littlewood. Colourful hanging baskets adorned the platform. It made a stark change from the graffiti Abbie was used to seeing on her old commute. She heaved her two wheelie cases off the

train and rattled along the platform with them. She had sent the rest of her things to her parents' house in Cornwall.

After struggling through the barriers with her bags, she began to walk to the café, which turned out to be in the grounds of a grand stone house perched on top of a hill looking over the small town.

The uphill walk was not at all easy in her favourite four-inch-heeled boots, but when you were as tiny as she was, you needed the extra height at all times, so she dragged herself and her bags towards the stately home. Louise said the café stood at the beginning of the estate and was the best place in Littlewood for coffee. And, God, Abbie needed a large cup.

She heard a faint noise in the wind behind her, but she kept up her brisk London pace, thinking it was probably someone after money or something. That was usually why people tried to get your attention nowadays.

Finally, she made it to the top of the hill. The café was just through the imposing iron gates of the stately home. There was a green and gold sign proclaiming the house to be Huntley Manor – a luxury hotel, apparently. Abbie glanced at the tall, light-brown stone building as she made her way to the cute-looking café on the edge of the green. The hotel looked as if it could have been lifted out of a Jane Austen novel and Abbie resolved to explore it soon.

Abbie gratefully pushed open the door to Brew to escape the light drizzle of rain starting to fall on top of her shoulders, and she went up to the counter to order. The café was cosy and colourful with small, round wooden tables with a

vase of sunflowers on each and slate chairs in different shades of blue, a black and white tiled floor and a large counter at the back with a vast array of delicious-looking cakes. Abbie breathed in the fresh coffee smell that lingered on the air. She loved cafés and this one felt like home as soon as she walked through the door.

'Good morning!' said a lady with a messy grey-haired bun and big smile, leaning on the counter to greet her. Her apron was blue and white with 'Have a Brew!' written on it in big letters. 'What can I get you?'

'A large latte, please.'

The woman started making it immediately and glanced back at Abbie as she did so. 'I haven't seen you in here before, have I?'

Abbie shook her head. 'No, I'm here to stay with my sister.'

'Well, I'm Joy and I own Brew with my husband, Harry. He's in the back making sandwiches. Welcome to Littlewood,' she said cheerfully, sliding Abbie's drink across to her. She moved to the till.

Abbie reached for her bag, but her hands grabbed air instead. 'Oh no!' she cried, looking down at her cases in horror.

'What's wrong?' Joy asked, leaning over the counter to see.

'But I picked it up off the train, I'm sure I did,' she said out loud, shaking her head. She had kept her handbag balanced on top of one of the wheelie cases so she didn't have to carry it on her shoulder. 'I can't find my bag,' she explained to Joy.

'Oh, dear, I'm sorry,' Joy said, sympathetically.

Abbie checked around her again, a sinking feeling in her chest. 'What am I going to do without it?' she said. If living in London had taught her anything, it was to keep a tight hold of your belongings at all times. She'd have to cancel her cards immediately. Oh, God. Her phone was in there. She started to feel panicky at the thought of not having it with her. How would anyone get in contact with her?

'Look, try not to worry. You're in Littlewood now and everyone looks out for one another here. I'm sure someone will find your bag and deliver it back to you. Go and sit down and drink your latte; you've had a shock and you need your coffee.'

'But I can't pay for it,' Abbie admitted, her cheeks turning pink. She had never lost her bag before. This week was just going from bad to worse.

'Don't be silly, it's on us.' Joy grabbed a brownie and put it on a plate. 'This too.'

'Oh, no, I couldn't possibly accept . . .'

Joy waved off Abbie's protests. 'Sit down, I insist. You can pay next time, after you find your bag.'

Abbie wished she shared Joy's faith that her bag would be found. She carried the brownie and latte over to her table, hoping Louise would hurry up and get there so she could use her phone to ring the bank.

The door to the café banged open, making Abbie turn with a start. 'There you are,' a woman cried, waving something at her. 'I've been chasing you from the station.' A little girl followed her inside the café; both of them were pulling

suitcases. 'Your bag fell off when you went through the barrier,' she said, a distinct accent to her brisk tone, holding up what Abbie could now see was her lost handbag.

Abbie recognised her from the train carriage and breathed a huge sigh of relief. 'Oh, wow, thank you so much,' she said, amazed that the woman had followed her all the way to Brew to get it back to her. She took it from her. 'I'm so grateful.'

The woman, who looked a similar age to Abbie's twenty-eight years and had a sharp, blonde bob, smiled. 'Of course. I would be so upset if I lost mine.'

'See? I told you it would turn up,' Joy called from the counter. 'All's well that ends well.'

'It certainly wouldn't have got back to me so quickly in London,' Abbie said. She pulled out her purse. 'And now I can pay you.'

'No, this one is still on us,' Joy said, firmly. 'What would you like?' she asked Abbie's saviour just as a tall, round-bellied man came out of the kitchen with two plates of egg and cress sandwiches for an elderly couple sitting by the door. 'This is my husband, Harry,' Joy told them. 'And I can see you're new to Littlewood too,' she added to the blonde woman who had seated her daughter with their bags at the next table to Abbie.

'I'm Eszter. This is Zoe. We've just arrived in England from Hungary.'

'Well, we hardly ever get any newcomers and now we have three! Coffee?'

Joy took Eszter's order and brought her drinks to the table.

She glanced at Abbie who was marvelling at how delicious her brownie was. 'You look so familiar; have we met before?'

Abbie shook her head. 'No, but my sister Louise lives here.'

'Is that Louise Morgan?' Joy asked, her eyes lighting up.

'That's right, yes.'

Harry came over and put his arm around his wife. 'We know Louise well, lovely girl. Drinks too much coffee for a nurse, though.'

Abbie smiled. 'It runs in the family.'

'So, you're here to stay with Louise, and what about you?' Joy asked Eszter.

'We're here to see family too. Well, sort of family, anyway.' She sipped her coffee with a nervous look on her face. She glanced at her daughter, who had long, fair hair and the same sharp eyes as her mother. 'It was a bit of a rush decision to come here. We don't even know where we're going to stay.' She bit her lip, then smiled quickly when Zoe looked at her. Abbie suspected she was putting a brave face on things and was intrigued by their story.

'I'm sure we can help with that,' Joy said. Then she clapped her hands together. 'And, Abbie, I just remembered, you must put Eszter's kindness to you up on the board,' she said, gesturing to the large chalkboard that hung across one wall. It was filled with chalk scribbles in various styles of handwriting and colours.

'What's that?'

'This is our Kindness Board. If anyone has an act of kindness done to them, they write it up on the board. We started

it this summer and it's already filling up. Eszter finding your bag is definitely worthy of being up there,' Joy said, going back around the counter to make Louise's regular coffee for her arrival. She held out a piece of chalk to Abbie.

'A Kindness Board?' Abbie glanced at her, wondering if it was a joke, but Joy told her to go on up. Sensing everyone's eyes on her, Abbie went to the board and looked at some of the entries already up there. Feeling like she was back in school, she added Eszter's random act of kindness to the board.

My lost handbag was returned to me by Eszter. Thank you for your act of kindness!

She added a smiley face to it.

'And now you'll have to pay her act of kindness forward,' Joy said from behind her.

'Huh?'

'In Littlewood, if someone is kind to you, you repay their act by being kind to someone yourself.'

Abbie stared at Joy, wondering if she had walked into some kind of cult. 'That's a thing?'

Joy laughed. 'We are trying to make it "a thing", yes. Ever since Harry was in hospital, and the whole town rallied around us and helped us keep Brew going, we have tried to be kind to the community when we can. Harry thought having a board in here would encourage others to do the same.'

'Is it working?' Abbie was sceptical. She was certain no one had ever been what she would call 'kind' to a stranger back in London.

'You'll have to come back and tell me if it works for you.' Joy went to serve another customer and Abbie watched her go, wondering if she was really expected to pay Eszter's kindness forward.

Was kindness something that could be sprinkled around as if it was confetti?

Chapter Two

Louise Morgan checked her watch and began a last sweep of the paediatric ward she worked on before heading back to Littlewood to meet up with Abbie. At twenty-six, she was two years younger than Abbie, and just as petite, although her dark hair was shorter and layered into an easier style, as she hated having to spend time doing it in the morning. She was excited that Abbie had come to stay, although she wondered how her sister would fit into her small, close-knit town. It would be very different to London.

It had been a busy night shift so Louise hadn't had time to dwell on the amount of messages currently clogging up her phone. She loved being a nurse. She remembered making Abbie play 'doctors and nurses' with her when they were little. Their Barbie dolls had been struck down with a vast array of illnesses and accidents over the years.

The hospital was always busy; there was very little time to think about anything other than what was right there in

front of you. You couldn't dwell on your personal problems when you were faced with kids battling for their lives on a daily basis, but she knew when she left, it would all come flooding back.

Louise paused in front of her favourite cubicle and peeped around the curtain. 'All set for the afternoon?' she asked Hazel, who was six and had just come back to the ward. She had cancer and was in and out of the hospital, which broke Louise's heart, but somehow the little girl stayed positive throughout. Louise supposed she shouldn't really have favourite patients, but Hazel was definitely hers.

'Mum got me a new colouring book. She's gone home to try and find my teddy. We think we might have lost it when I went for tests the other day.' Louise remembered the cute bear that Hazel usually had with her.

'Oh, I'm sorry. I'm sure he'll turn up. Enjoy your colouring and I'll see you when I'm next in?' Hazel nodded and Louise left her alone, wishing she could do something more to help her.

Louise grabbed her things from the staffroom and walked out, passing by the charity shop at the end of the ward. The teddy in the window immediately caught her eye. It looked very similar to the one that Hazel was missing and it was a bargain at five pounds. She went straight in and bought it. Checking her watch, she walked briskly back to the ward and hoped Abbie had found Brew safely and would be okay having a coffee alone for a bit longer. When she returned, Hazel's mum, Sarah, was outside the cubicle talking to a tall,

skinny man Louise had often seen on the ward. She thought he might be Hazel's uncle. She nodded and smiled at them as she passed and ducked back into Hazel's cubicle.

'Now I know this isn't your bear, but I think this one will do just as good a job looking after you,' Louise said, handing it to Hazel who gasped.

'Really?' Hazel's face lit up as she looked at it. That smile made all the long hours and the thankless tasks she often had to deal with worth it. 'I'm going to name him Sam.'

'I think that's perfect.'

'Oh, who's that?' Hazel's mum appeared behind Louise.

'Look what Louise got me, Mum,' Hazel said, waving the bear at her.

'Oh, Louise, you shouldn't have,' Sarah said, smiling at her. The man who stood by her shoulder grinned as well, showing two dimples in his cheeks that made him look cute, but Louise quickly brushed off that thought.

'It's no problem, honestly. Right, I have to go. Look after Sam, okay?' she said to Hazel.

'I promise,' Hazel said, waving Sam's paw in her direction. Louise smiled at them and left quickly, hoping Abbie wouldn't be too annoyed at being kept waiting at the café.

Louise climbed into her car and checked her phone reluctantly. There was nothing from her sister, but there were more messages from people back home in Cornwall, some of whom she hadn't heard from in years. She sighed. News really did spread like wildfire nowadays. She drove back to Littlewood, knowing that if she looked at Facebook again,

she would get upset and Abbie would notice straight away. Louise wanted to welcome her sister to her town before she told her the news.

When Louise had parked outside Brew and walked in, she was surprised to see Abbie standing in front of the large chalkboard. Louise had taken to looking at the acts of kindness the town was doing when she popped in to grab a coffee on the way to the hospital, so she was quite familiar with how it worked.

'You've already experienced an act of kindness?' she asked Abbie, who was handing the chalk back to Joy. Abbie's face broke out into a warm smile when she saw her sister, and she gave her a big hug before telling her about how Eszter had returned the handbag to her. Louise was introduced to Eszter and her daughter, Zoe, before being handed her usual by Joy to take over to her sister's table by the window.

'How was your journey?' Louise asked Abbie.

'It was fine. I can't believe how quiet this place is,' she said, looking out of Brew's window at the drizzle coming down.

'You'll get used to it. You could do with slowing down a bit,' Louise said, sipping her coffee. She had told Abbie off many times for how wrapped up in her job she had been. It had left little time for family and Louise had really missed her sister.

'Joy told me that I now have to do my own act of kindness,' Abbie said in a low voice so the others didn't hear. Her expression made Louise laugh as she took a sip of her latte.

'Is the idea of kindness really that shocking?'

Abbie shook her head. 'I can be kind if I want to be.'

'When did you last do anything kind?' Louise asked, with a teasing smile. 'To a stranger, anyway. I bet never in London. But you're in Littlewood now; we do things differently here.'

'It's all right for you, you're paid to be kind,' she replied with a shake of her head. 'I honestly don't know how you do it every day.'

'Maybe it's just what city life does to you; there isn't really such a community feeling there as we have here, is there?'

'I guess. I can't think of an example of a stranger ever helping me out there, but everyone just looks out for themselves, don't you think?' Abbie said.

'I think everyone could do with being a bit kinder,' Louise replied.

'Although if you ask me, you're too kind to others,' Abbie told her. Louise knew her sister thought she often let people walk all over her. 'If anything, you need to be kinder to yourself.'

Louise shook her head. 'That's not what the Kindness Board is about.' She thought about what had happened a couple of years ago and how she had dealt with her broken heart by throwing herself into her work and new life in Littlewood. She supposed she had neglected herself as a result.

'Actually, Abbie has a point,' Joy chipped in as she came over to clear their table. 'We should all be kind to ourselves, my dear. The world would be a better place if we were all kinder, I really believe that. Everyone is so wrapped

up in themselves nowadays. That's why we love living in Littlewood – there is still a tight-knit community here. It's getting harder to find, for sure.' She moved to Eszter's table to take away their ketchup. She looked between the tables, the women all listening to her now. 'Being kind is good for you. To others and yourself.'

Eszter nodded. 'I am definitely going to need to try to be kind,' she said. 'I'm here to see someone who I really don't think will be at all pleased to see me.'

'Where are we going to stay?' Zoe asked her mother loudly, before Joy could respond to Eszter. Zoe's accent was less pronounced than her mother's and she cheerfully drank her milkshake, oblivious to the look of panic on Eszter's face.

'I wish I knew,' Eszter muttered. 'Is there a hotel nearby?' she asked Joy, who was cleaning the next table to theirs. 'I'd have to find work if we end up staying in one for a while though, I suppose. I don't know how long we'll need to be here.'

'Well, the only hotel in town is Huntley Manor, but it's quite pricey,' Joy admitted, gesturing out of the window at the stately home behind the café.

'I might be able to help with somewhere to stay,' Louise piped up. 'My landlord owns two cottages and the one opposite mine has been empty for a few weeks, he's been trying to find someone to take it for the summer so I reckon he'd be open to negotiating on price if you wanted it. If you were thinking of staying the whole summer?'

'I'm not sure, we have open return flights, so I suppose

we might stay that long,' Eszter replied, uncertainly. 'The cottage sounds promising. Could you tell me how to find your landlord?'

'I'll do better than that. I'm driving us home once we've finished this so you can come with us; he lives just up the road from my cottage.'

'Oh, thank you.'

'And I can help with your other predicament,' Joy said to Eszter. 'We always get so busy over the summer and the girl that used to help us has gone travelling this year so we were just saying earlier how we really needed to find someone. Have you ever worked in a café before?'

'I worked in one in Budapest for two years before I went into retail. Do you really need someone?' Eszter's blue eyes lit up.

Joy smiled. 'We really do. How about doing a week's trial and we can see how we go?'

'That would be so kind of you. Although ...' Eszter paused and glanced at her daughter. 'I don't know what I'd do about Zoe.'

Joy waved her hand. 'She would be no problem, I'm sure, if she came with you. If that would suit you both?' She looked at Zoe.

Her daughter nodded. 'Will I get free cakes?'

Joy laughed. 'I think I can stretch to one or two.'

'Thank you so much, Joy,' Eszter said. 'Really, I don't know how to thank you, all of you.'

'Wait to thank me until you see if you like it first. Why

don't you start on Monday? That'll give you the weekend to settle into the town.'

'That would be perfect.'

The women finished up their drinks and left together, grateful that the rain had eased off and they could make it to the car without getting drenched. They just managed to squeeze themselves and all their cases in and Louise drove them through the town to her cottage.

It was comforting having the others with her. Louise knew that as soon as she was alone she'd think about Peter and his news again and she wanted to put that off for as long as she could.

* * *

'My husband never said his home town was so pretty,' Eszter said from the back of Louise's car, gazing out at the countryside as they passed by. Littlewood was perched on top of the hill, Huntley Manor making up most of the skyline, and the surrounding hills provided stunning views from most vantage points.

Eszter couldn't believe she was actually in England after hearing so much about it. She wished she had asked Nick more about it, never dreaming that when she finally came here, it would be without him. She thought of the letter in her bag that he wrote to her before he died, begging her to come here, including two plane tickets for her and Zoe, and asking them to fulfil his dying wish. She had done what he asked and jumped on that plane and now she had no idea what to do next.

Eszter was pleased that her welcome so far had been friendly. She had been nervous about the trip, as Nick had always been against bringing them to the UK; he wanted their life to be in Budapest, but getting sick had softened him. He had seemed to think more and more about the past and his home town, which, in the end, had prompted him to write the letter to her. She just hoped she could do what he wanted her to do. She was so used to having him beside her, supporting her, that it felt as if she was missing another limb as she undertook this journey alone. She glanced at Zoe who at seven was growing up faster than she ever thought was possible, and now she would have to do all the parenting by herself. She squeezed her daughter's hand and sent a silent wish to Nick to look after them both here.

'Harry and Joy are really something,' Abbie said, breaking the thoughtful silence in the car. 'They seem to love helping people.'

'Honestly, everyone has been really nice since I came here,' Louise replied. 'But they definitely are the heart and soul of the place. Everyone knows them. What did you think about their kindness idea?' she asked Eszter as they pulled into the parking space outside the pretty little cottage and Louise turned off the engine.

'It's strange, you know,' Eszter said. 'My husband wrote me this letter asking me to come here. Before he died. He wants me to find his mother. "Be kind to her," he told me. "Be kind to each other." I just hope I can be.'

'I'm so sorry about your husband,' Louise said.

20

'Thank you. It's been a difficult time but coming here has made us think about something else, hasn't it, Zoe?'

'We got to go on a plane,' her daughter told them proudly, which got a smile from her audience.

'I hope you can find his mother. Harry and Joy will know her, I bet.'

'I'll ask them, thank you.'

They climbed out of the car, with Louise letting Abbie into her cottage before taking Eszter and Zoe to see her landlord a few doors away. 'Make yourself at home,' Louise called to her sister as she pulled her bags out of the boot. 'Right, let's find you a place to stay,' she said to Eszter, who followed her hoping that she had made the right decision in coming to Littlewood. She supposed that she would find out soon enough.

Chapter Three

Abbie walked through the door into Louise's home. It was as cosy as you'd expect a cottage to be, with low ceilings, wooden beams and her sister's pretty belongings matching their surroundings. It was a home.

Abbie thought of the flat she had shared with Kate with its rented furniture, none of it really hers, and envied her sister for creating this for herself.

Abbie took her bags up to the spare bedroom that would be hers for the time being. She had known her redundancy money wouldn't last long in London, so after losing her job she had reluctantly swallowed her pride and asked Louise if she could stay while she looked for a new job. Louise had been excited by the idea straight away, Abbie less so. She hated leaving London, but looking around the cottage, she had to admit this wasn't really a hardship. There was three times as much space as she had in her city flat and she wouldn't even be paying any rent as Louise had refused to

accept anything. Abbie would definitely have to treat her to a few nice things to make up for it.

It would be fun living with her sister again, Abbie thought as she unpacked her things. They hadn't lived together since she had left home for uni ten years ago, and they hadn't spent a lot of time in each other's company since then. After uni, work had become Abbie's focus and it had never seemed the right time to leave London for a visit to Littlewood. Even at Christmas, she had chosen to stay with her ex, Jack, and had ended up regretting missing out on a family celebration.

If she really thought about it, she might even enjoy living here, if she could shake off this feeling of being an utter failure at being both out of a job and, essentially, homeless.

* * *

When Louise returned from helping Eszter, Abbie had finished unpacking and was sitting in the living room, looking at jobs on her laptop.

'He was so excited they wanted the cottage, Eszter was already hammering down the price for it when I left. She's strong-willed, that one. So, what do you think of my place?' Louise asked her.

'It's really homely.' Abbie closed her laptop as her sister sat down in the opposite armchair.

Louise yawned. 'Sorry. I'll have to head to bed soon. I'm knackered.'

'That's okay. I can do some exploring. I'll get us some dinner later, if you're up?'

'Can you cook?'

Abbie grinned. 'No, but I can order us something. Um, do you even have takeaways here?'

'We're not completely in the back of beyond! We might not be able to get sushi delivered at four in the morning or something but, yes, we have pizza and curry, and a really nice Chinese on the high street.'

'Thank God for that then. I need my spring rolls.'

Louise agreed before saying, 'I hope Eszter stays. I can't believe she lost her husband. She's not much older than us, I would think.'

'I know, it's crazy. I can't imagine being married, let alone having a daughter and then losing your husband and coming to another country on your own like that.'

'When I left, she promised she was going to repay my kindness. I think Harry and Joy got to her.'

'That means I'll have to do the same. And you. You're meant to be kinder to yourself, don't forget.'

Louise got up, ready to head to bed. She shook her head. 'If I see you do a random act of kindness for someone, then I promise I'll do something kind for myself. Deal?'

'Are we actually making a kindness pact?' Abbie grinned as she shook her sister's offered hand. 'Okay then, deal. I shall walk the streets of Littlewood looking out for someone in need.'

Louise laughed. 'You do that. I'm going to bed. Call me for dinner, okay? We can watch a film or something?'

'Perfect.' Abbie watched her sister go upstairs, regretting

that she'd never come to see her here before. Louise had fled Cornwall two years ago and Abbie was ashamed she hadn't really been around to support her through it all; she'd been too focused on working her way up the ladder and falling for Jack. Both things that turned out to be a complete waste of her time. She was determined that the next thing she decided to do would be worth her while. *Oh God*, she realised. *And now it had to be kind too.*

* * *

Louise listened as the cottage door shut before pulling on her pjs and closing the curtains to try to block out the blazing July afternoon. She hadn't had the energy to tell Abbie just yet, and she needed some time to process it all. Now she was alone, she looked at her phone again. Another message had appeared.

OMG I just saw the news Are you okay, hon?

Louise sighed. She hadn't been in touch with this girl for ages. Everyone was really crawling out of the woodwork after the news. She supposed it was no big shock; after all, she'd been the talk of the town for months. Which was why she had run as soon as she could.

With a groan, Louise stuffed her phone into the bedside drawer and lay down on top of the covers. It was too warm up there to get under the sheets. She wasn't sure if she'd be able to sleep anyway when all she could think about was Peter's news.

Two years ago, her childhood sweetheart had broken off

their engagement just two weeks before they were due to get married. Louise had applied for the first nursing job she could find that was far away from her home town in Cornwall, and that's how she had ended up in Littlewood.

She'd been with Peter since they were fifteen and couldn't have even conceived of a future without him by her side. She had been heartbroken and humiliated when he told her over the phone that it was over. He said she had pushed him into the wedding, when in reality it had been him who had surprised her with a proposal and a desire to get married that summer. But then suddenly, out of nowhere, he no longer wanted a future with her.

Unable to bear all the pitying looks she received every time she stepped out of her front door, she had left and hadn't looked back.

No one in Littlewood knew she was a jilted bride – except for Abbie now – and that was just fine with Louise. She had thrown herself into her new job and made friends and created a cosy home for herself. And she had resolutely stuck to her vow not to let another man get close to her. She couldn't take that kind of pain again.

She closed her eyes, willing sleep to block out her thoughts of the past. It was impossible, though. Ever since she had seen his news the night before, the words had been playing over and over in her mind on a loop like a slide show. They weren't Facebook friends anymore but they had so many mutual friends that her notifications had been ablaze with the news: Peter had got engaged to a girl he'd only been seeing for a few months.

Louise's heart threatened to break all over again, but she doubted she had enough of one left for it to do that. How was it that he had fallen in love so quickly and was now suddenly ready to commit the rest of his life to someone else? But the main question, the one she wished she could stop herself asking silently over and over again, the one that made her hate herself for being so pathetic, was – why wasn't it her?

Chapter Four

Eszter couldn't help but feel satisfied with a job well done. She glanced around the pretty cottage she had just secured for the summer. She had a job starting on Monday. Zoe was unpacking in her new room and had been excited by the sloping roof, wooden beams and pretty garden, as far removed from their city apartment back in Budapest as they could get. She had managed to do what had felt impossible when she had looked at the plane tickets that Nick had bought for them. Now all that was left was to find Mrs Harris and do what her husband had begged her to do.

That could wait until the new week though. She would find out all she could about Mrs Harris first. Nick had always been so cagey, so she really had no idea what she was about to face. Eszter was prepared for the worst, though – she had to be. Nick hadn't seen his parents for years. He had never really explained why, but she knew it couldn't be good.

She sat in her new kitchen at the small pine table and

phoned her own mother back in Hungary. Her parents lived out in the countryside but Eszter and Nick had spent many holidays with them; they had both got on well with Nick, welcoming him into their family as soon as she had brought him to meet them. They had been as devastated as she was when he was diagnosed with cancer.

Her mother hadn't wanted her to come to England so soon after his death. She wanted them to stay with her, but Eszter knew that the longer she put it off, the less likely she was to do it, and besides, the tickets were there ready and waiting to be used. And it meant she could shove her grief aside even for a brief time and focus on something else instead. Their apartment had become claustrophobic with memories of their life together. Without Nick, it just didn't feel like home anymore. Her mother had asked them to move in after Nick died but her parents lived miles from anywhere, which would make school and work difficult, if not impossible, to organise.

'You got there okay, then?' her mother asked when they greeted each other in their native Hungarian. Eszter's parents could speak some English but were nowhere near as fluent as she and Zoe were after being with Nick for so long, as well as learning in school and living in cosmopolitan Budapest.

'It was actually an easy journey.'

Eszter told her mum all about arriving in Littlewood and how she had already found a cottage and a job. 'I thought I'd have to survive in a hotel for a while and live off our savings, so we've been really lucky.'

Back in Budapest, Nick had worked as an English teacher and Eszter had worked in a clothes shop. Rent on their city place had been high, so they had never had lots of money when Nick was alive, and neither of them had even thought about getting life insurance at their age, so Eszter needed to work as much as she could even if they were just in Littlewood for a few weeks. She had sublet her apartment for the summer to a friend of a friend.

'It's really pretty here. I don't know why Nick didn't talk about it more.' To Eszter, it looked like a charming place to grow up, reminiscent of her parents' community in rural Hungary. She had never really wanted Zoe to grow up in a city, but there were so few opportunities for them anywhere else back home.

'What do you think your mother-in-law will be like?'

'Honestly, I'm terrified. But then, she produced Nick, so surely she can't be that bad?'

'Their rift went on for so long, she will be shocked to see you, I'm sure. You'll take care, won't you?'

Eszter assured her mother she would and promised to tell her as soon as she and Mrs Harris met. Her mum wished her good luck for her new job and then asked to speak to Zoe. The little girl came hurtling down the stairs to speak to her grandmother, chattering away as usual, telling her all about her new room. At least Zoe was bearing all the hallmarks of resilience. Eszter just hoped her excitement over their new house would last. It had been a tough few months; Zoe hadn't understood when her mother had told her that her

father wouldn't get better. The hole Nick had left in their lives would be felt for a long time yet.

After the phone call, Eszter suggested they walk to the local supermarket to find something for dinner. The landlord had directed them to the local shops before he had left and they weren't far to walk to. 'And tomorrow we can do whatever you want, okay?'

Zoe's eyes lit up. 'Can we go to the park?'

'If it doesn't rain.' Eszter had heard a lot about the British weather and it had already shown her rain and sunshine in just one day, so God only knew what it would do tomorrow. 'Let's go.'

They pulled on light jackets and shoes and headed out towards the high street. Littlewood was so sleepy compared to where they lived. Just one car passed them, and a man walking a dog waved at them from across the road. The small high street atop the hill had a supermarket, Post Office, a butcher's, a bakery, a small florist and a charity shop that Eszter resolved to have a good look in – Zoe was growing at an alarming rate and she always needed new clothes and shoes.

'Hi, neighbours,' a voice called from outside the bakery. Abbie waved at them. 'What are you up to?'

'Finding something to eat,' Zoe replied as they came nearer.

'I'm exploring our new town,' Abbie said. 'Thought I'd head over to Huntley Manor next. What are you going to have for your dinner, then?'

'I like pizza,' Zoe told her.

She laughed. 'Don't we all. Are you settling into the cottage okay?'

'It's lovely,' Eszter said. 'I can't thank your sister enough for telling us about it.'

'Louise is always making me feel bad for how helpful she is. I've promised her that I'll do an act of kindness, and I have no idea where to start.'

'You'll know it when someone needs your help,' Eszter said.

* * *

Abbie watched Eszter and Zoe go into the supermarket, and carried on her walk through the town. She wasn't sure who could need her help here. She didn't think her skills would be much use in Littlewood at all, which was why she had to move on as quickly as she could.

She walked down the length of the high street and then turned towards the Manor, passing Brew and making her way up to the large oak door. She'd always had a fondness for stately homes and hadn't been able to indulge in looking around one for ages.

Abbie walked into the lobby and saw a small, abandoned reception desk, so she carried on into the lounge area. There was an impressive fireplace with a painting of Littlewood hanging above it, but the room was dark, the curtains faded, the carpet looked a bit threadbare and the furnishings were clearly in need of a clean. It was elegant, but it looked as if

it needed some TLC. She couldn't help but cast her critical eye over it after spending many a meeting inside London's top hotels and a few nights in them with Jack.

She shook her head as thoughts of him invaded. He had bowled her over when she joined his company. It had felt illicit to start seeing one of the bosses and the fact that he was a partner there at the age of thirty-eight had impressed her. She felt like she could learn a lot from him; plus his good looks and smooth talking had charmed her on the first day they had met. Abbie wasn't sure what had gone wrong, but quite suddenly he lost interest and stopped arranging dinners and nights out, didn't text her good morning and, at work, become colder, more professional, all seemingly overnight. It all seemed so obvious now, that he had known she was on the redundancy list, and it had hurt to know he hadn't warned her or chosen their relationship over work.

Jack had looked nervous when they called her into the boardroom to tell her the news. He told her that as one of the newest staff members there, it was first in, first out. What had hurt the most was that Jack had had the nerve to offer his hand to shake, along with the other two partners, when she stood up to leave.

It had taken all of her willpower not to break down and cry right then in front of them. She had instead fled to the loos and broken down in privacy there.

Forcing herself out of her misery, Abbie looked around once more before moving on to the dining room. It was an impressive, long room with chandeliers hanging from the

ceiling and French windows displaying views of the vast estate. In front of the sloping green lawns was an outside dining area that had chairs and tables all covered up, which struck her as strange at the start of the summer season. Abbie noticed that the door was open slightly, so she stepped outside into the grounds. The sun was peeking out through the clouds, and the promise of warmer days seemed to be on the horizon.

Abbie couldn't see any guests around, or staff for that matter, as she strolled around the outskirts of the house. It was in need of a paint job and the garden could do with a tidy-up too, or at least some colourful flowers and hanging baskets. At the back of the house were stables, albeit empty of horses. She heard a noise and stopped.

'Look, I know I asked for more time before, but it's the summer – our busiest time – so . . .' a harassed voice sounded out from behind one of the stable doors. It was man with a cultured lilt to his frustrated voice. 'John, you know I would pay if I could. I just need another extension. A couple of months? Okay, a month then? Yes, I know you think I should sell. Well, yes, I might have to, but please, just give me this summer.' The stable door opened and Abbie jumped, her cheeks flushing at being caught eavesdropping. She stood there like a lemon as a tall, dark-haired man in a suit and wellies strode out. He didn't even notice her as he walked towards the house, talking on the phone. 'Okay, I'll come and see you next week. Thank you. Goodbye, John,' he said, shoving his phone into his pocket.

Abbie found herself following him. She knew she should act as if she hadn't heard any of that, but this man and his hotel were definitely in trouble, and she could see why. She could also see what a shame that was, as this place had a lot of promise.

She thought of Harry and Joy in Brew; when they were doing so well, how was it that the hotel whose grounds their café stood in wasn't reaping the same benefits? Curiosity got the better of her and she spoke up before she could stop herself.

'Excuse me,' she called tentatively.

The man stopped and finally noticed her behind him. 'Can I help you?' he asked.

Face to face, Abbie saw that he was younger than she had thought, only a couple of years older than she was. Yet this was the man in charge of Huntley Manor. She was intrigued.

'Are you the manager here?'

'I'm the owner actually. Well, and manager. Thomas Huntley.'

'Oh.' No wonder his accent was so posh, he owned this vast estate. Abbie was intimidated, but she wasn't going to let that scare her away. She thought of all the times she hadn't told Jack what she really thought and she didn't want that to happen again. Abbie thrust out her hand, thinking she had nothing to lose at this point. 'I'm Abbie Morgan and I think I can help you.'

Chapter Five

Thomas Huntley cut an imposing figure, especially as he was over a foot taller than Abbie, but it helped that he had wellington boots on as it made him seem a little more down-to-earth.

He raised his eyebrows. 'And how can you help me?'

'I couldn't help but overhear that the hotel isn't doing that well.'

'You mean you listened to a private phone call?' Disdain dripped from every word.

'Well, I certainly didn't mean to, but you do have a loud voice and it's very quiet around here.'

Thomas started walking again with a shake of his head and Abbie hurried to keep up with him. 'I suppose you want me to sell like everyone else? Another estate agent, are you? You really are all vultures.'

'I'm not an estate agent. Actually, I work in PR. Well, I did until very recently, and I think I can help. This place could be amazing, but I can't see any guests and, could you

slow down a bit, please?' Abbie was almost panting as her much shorter legs tried to keep up with his strides. They made their way into the dining room. 'I get that you don't know me, but I love coming up with ideas to help businesses and I happen to be free this summer.'

Thomas stopped and faced her again. 'Let me get this straight – you were sacked from your job but you think I need your help?'

This time, it was Abbie who raised her eyebrows. 'I wasn't sacked, I was made redundant and not because I'm not good at my job.' Why was she bothering to try and convince him? This place had drawn her in. It reminded her of the house her grandparents had owned in Cornwall, but she didn't think Thomas Huntley would be persuaded by sentimentality. 'I haven't been in Littlewood long, but imagine what it would be like if this house was left here empty, or worse if it wasn't standing here overlooking the town at all? Is that what you really want to happen?'

Thomas sighed. 'Unfortunately, I might not have any choice but to sell. The mortgage ... well, I'm very behind and, as you rightly pointed out, we have hardly any guests.' He sighed. 'Why would you want to try to help? Even I'm not sure there's anything left to save.'

'Isn't it better to say you tried to keep it going than to always wonder what might have been? Why regret not trying?'

'I can't pay you.'

She smiled. 'That's not why I offered to help. I promised someone that I'd pay their act of kindness forward so that's

what I'm going to do. I have skills that you need and while I'm here this summer, trying to find another paying job, you might as well put me to use. We can try and save Huntley Manor together. What do you say?' She held out her hand.

Thomas shook his head. 'Abbie, was it? I have never met anyone quite as forceful in my life before, and you should have seen my father. He would turn in his grave if I gave up on this house. So, okay, let's try. But I warn you, we're going to have our work cut out for ourselves.'

As Thomas shook her hand, Abbie grinned, feeling hopeful for the first time since she walked out of her office in London. 'I managed to get a disgraced client of ours to star in, and win, *Strictly Come Dancing*. This will be a piece of cake in comparison.'

'I have no idea what you're talking about, but okay. I'm guessing it was Harry and Joy who put this mad kindness idea into your head, wasn't it?'

'I knew it! It's a cult, isn't it?'

This time, Thomas laughed. 'I don't think Littlewood would ever be hip enough to have a cult, but they are passionate about being kind, and it has rubbed off around here.'

Abbie could understand why. As Thomas introduced her to the small staff, she felt good about herself for what she was doing. She liked that she was able to help out Thomas and the team, and that she had lived up to the pact she had made with Harry, Joy and her sister.

Eszter had been right: Abbie had known instantly that Huntley Manor needed her, and she was determined not to let it down.

* * *

They spent the remainder of the day looking around, with Abbie seeking out all of the hotel's nooks and crannies she could find. The upstairs rooms were similar in that they were elegant but in need of sprucing up. Though they had lovely views of the grounds, they lacked the amenities guests would expect from a luxury hotel.

'I'll start by making a list of things we need to look at,' she said decisively.

'We have no money for improvements.'

'There are still things we can do while keeping the cost down. We might be able to get a company to give away toiletries, for example, in return for promoting them. Oh, how is your online presence?' Abbie asked as they walked back through the lobby. The receptionist had at last appeared and looked thoroughly bored at her desk. Thomas and Abbie stepped outside. The day was drawing to a close. She had somehow spent hours there.

'Um . . . we have a website, I think.'

She gave him a withering look. 'You think? Thomas, your online presence is one of the most important things. I'll look at it tonight. That is something we can do something about, easily and cost free. Right, I'll talk to you on Monday then?'

'I'll be here.' Thomas shifted on his feet, 'Abbie, I do appreciate this, but I'd rather the town didn't know how much trouble the house is in.'

'They may want to help, though.'

'I suppose I'm not used to asking for help.'

'Well, now you have me, and I have no shame at all if it gets us where we need to be. But don't worry; I'll keep it to myself, if that's what you want.' She wondered why he felt the need to be so reserved, considering the trouble he was in. She supposed it was hard to change the ways of a lifetime. Huntley Manor must once have been the life and soul of Littlewood, and it must be so hard for Thomas to accept that the house was barely clinging on by its fingertips now. 'What was this place like when you were growing up?' she asked before she turned to go.

'It was ... thriving.' She could see he was remembering that time as he smiled and looked at the house rising behind them.

'Then it can be again.'

She hoped the same was as true for people as it was for places.

Abbie walked back to her sister's cottage, her heels almost bouncing off the pavement. A project already, it was just what she needed. She checked her email as she walked and there were a couple of rejections to her applications. There was also an email from a client she had worked with saying how sorry they were to hear she had left and they wished they knew of any opportunities for her. She tried not to feel disheartened. She hadn't been job-hunting for long. There was no rush. She needed to find the right thing anyway. And as she searched for the perfect place, she could throw herself into helping Thomas make Huntley Manor thrive again.

* * *

Louise was in the kitchen in her pjs pouring out wine for the both of them when Abbie returned with a Chinese takeaway. She had taken off her make-up after causing her mascara to spill everywhere as she let herself have a cry over Peter.

'I have news!' Abbie trilled as she walked in. Louise forced a smile but she couldn't match Abbie's beam. 'I have also bought enough to feed about six people. Are you okay, Lou?'

Abbie was staring at her and Louise knew she wouldn't be able to pretend everything was fine any longer. Wordlessly, she handed Abbie her phone with Facebook open on the screen. She turned to get out plates and cutlery while her sister absorbed the news.

'This has nothing to do with you,' Abbie said, firmly, turning off the screen and putting the phone down on the counter. 'Peter was always selfish. You got out just in time. You would never have been happy married to him.'

'He said he didn't want to get married, that everything was happening too soon, that commitment scared him. We were together for years, Abs. And now he's marrying someone he hasn't known for more than a minute! So, you're wrong. It has everything to do with me. I wasn't good enough for him to want to marry.' Louise hated how her voice wobbled as she spoke and she hastily took a long gulp of her wine, pleading with herself not to cry again. Abbie never cried over anything, she seemed to be able to handle whatever was thrown at her, whereas Louise felt like she was forever struggling.

Abbie grabbed her sister's hand. 'That's complete crap. You were, and always will be, good enough for whoever you fall in love with. The point is, whether they're good enough for you. You fell in love with him too young; you couldn't see his faults. You loved him unconditionally, that's how big your heart is. But trust me, you are much better off without him.'

'Let's get the food out. I am in dire need of some comfort eating.' Louise busied herself plating up the food, aware of her sister's gaze on her the whole time. 'I really thought I was over it,' she said in the end as they carried their over-full plates to the living room, curling up in an armchair each. 'What was your news? I'm sorry, you seemed excited when you came in and I ruined it,' Louise said, trying to inject some enthusiasm in her voice. She shovelled a spring roll into her mouth. When in doubt, eat, was their motto for most moments.

Abbie launched into an enthusiastic speech about Huntley Manor. 'It really reminded me of Nan and Granddad's house. I feel like I can help him, even though I don't think he believes it can be saved.'

'I've met Thomas a few times. He's always intimidated me. He's so tall and rich,' Louise admitted. 'But he definitely cares about Littlewood; he's on the board of some local charities and is a school governor, I think. Maybe he has just run out of ideas. You're brilliant at them, so I think you'll make a great team, and I'll be especially happy about it if it keeps you in my little town a bit longer.'

Abbie smiled. 'Small-town life doesn't really appeal to me

like it does to you, I'll still be trying to get back to London, but it'll do me good to get stuck into a project here. Maybe Harry and Joy are right about this kindness lark as I feel pretty good about trying to save Huntley Manor.'

Louise held up her glass of wine. 'Well, you've stuck to your end of the pact, so I suppose now I have to try and be kind to myself. Does this wine and the box of chocolates I have in the cupboard count?'

'For now, but you need to think a bit bigger. Like putting Peter behind you once and for all.'

Louise's smile faltered as she took another sip of her wine. She realised she had still harboured some hope that Peter would show up on her doorstep and beg her to take him back, even after all this time. Didn't everyone fantasise about that when someone dumped them? Louise hoped so, but she didn't dare tell Abbie about it.

It was hard to realise that all the plans she had made with him, he was now making with someone else. Abbie was right, though, she knew that deep down. Peter had clearly moved on. He wasn't going to show up now or ever. He was marrying someone else.

It was time for her to plan a very different future, but quite how she was meant to do that, she didn't know. Perhaps kindness started in small steps anyway. So, for tonight, she would chill with her sister, eating and drinking, and try to ignore that tiny voice that always piped up at her lowest points.

The one that told her no one would ever love her again.

Chapter Six

Eszter walked to Brew for her first shift on Monday morning with Zoe by her side. Her daughter was armed with a bag full of things to entertain herself with and Eszter wished she were armed with something equally useful. She was nervous. She was working in a different country and there was no one to give her support as she went into the café where Harry and Joy were opening up. It was moments like this when she missed her husband Nick the most. They had been best friends and he would have wished her luck this morning and given her a big hug before she stepped out of the door. She wondered when missing him might hurt just a little bit less.

Harry and Joy welcomed her enthusiastically and they seated Zoe at the table by the window and brought her an orange juice and a brownie and assured her that there would be lots of local kids coming in so she would easily make some friends there. They showed Eszter the ropes – she would be serving not cooking, which was good as she rarely cooked

anything more complicated than pasta at home. She had used a similar coffee machine before and the till was easier than the one in her shop back home. She picked things up quickly, thankfully, as then the morning rush began.

Eszter had been worried that Harry and Joy had given her the job because they pitied her but her fears were soon put to rest as Brew was really busy all day. In the morning, people picked up coffees to go as they walked to the train station and at lunchtime all the families on their summer holiday break came in for treats. Abbie popped in for a sandwich on her way to Huntley Manor and told them how she was giving Thomas some free PR advice. It seemed that Harry and Joy's kindness idea was really spreading through the town. Eszter just wasn't sure how to start her own kindness mission.

In a lull around four o'clock, with Zoe happily colouring, Eszter took the chance as she and Joy cleared and wiped the tables to ask about her mother-in-law.

'All I really know about her is that her name is Mrs Harris, and that her husband died a few years ago. Nick was always very vague about his family. It was a touchy subject, and it wasn't until he died that I realised how much it must have played on his mind all these years.' Eszter didn't even know if Mrs Harris was aware she had a granddaughter. She had already decided to make the first visit to her alone, just in case.

'I imagine that will be Anne Harris. I knew her better when we were younger – like me, she's lived here all her life. We went to the same school, although we were never close friends. When she married Frank, I saw her less and less. After

we opened Brew, they would come in occasionally, but I got the feeling their tastes ran to more elegant establishments. Frank was a private doctor in London and would commute in every day before he retired. His death was sudden. Anne was devastated, and after that, she seemed to retreat from the town. I haven't seen her in a long time. She still lives in their marital home, as far as I know.' Joy wrote down the address for Eszter and explained how to walk there from Brew.

'And do you know why Nick left all those years ago?' Eszter asked her tentatively. She couldn't imagine not speaking to her parents, even with them living far away.

'It seemed quite sudden when we heard he'd left Littlewood. He never came back and no one really knew what had happened to him. I understand that if anyone ever asked Anne or Frank, they were shut down pretty quickly. He was training to be a doctor, I know that.'

Eszter was surprised. 'Really? He was a teacher in Hungary; he never told me he had once wanted to be a doctor. He told me he did an English degree at university in Scotland and then decided to travel around Europe teaching English, which is how we met. When we fell in love, he decided to stay in Budapest. It was only when we got married that I realised how big the rift was with his parents. Neither of them came, and I found it strange at the time, but Nick put a brave face on it.'

'I think sometimes people don't realise how precious little time we get to make things right.'

Eszter nodded. 'When he got sick, it happened so quickly,

and we were told he wouldn't have long. I asked him if I could ring his mother but he kept putting me off. By the time I told her how ill he was, it really was too late, and she said she couldn't face the trip on her own. The funeral though . . . I was shocked she didn't come, but I know she's old and didn't have anyone to bring her. I think if he had realised how fast he would go, he would have come back here. But instead, he has left the task to me.'

'You'll do him proud, I know you will.'

Eszter hoped she could live up to Nick's faith in her. As Joy said, time was precious, and she only had the summer. She needed to see Mrs Harris before they missed another chance.

When Louise came in to pick up Zoe at closing time, having offered to look after her as she had the evening off, Eszter was a bag of nerves. She looked at her outfit of black trousers and shirt and smoothed down her blonde hair, hoping she looked respectable, like someone worthy of being Nick's wife. She told Louise she wouldn't be long. For all she knew, Mrs Harris wouldn't even be in, but it sounded like she didn't go out often. Louise told her she'd take Zoe to the Italian restaurant a short drive away and to text her when she was finished and they'd meet at the cottages. Eszter felt her kindness debt to Louise building up and up.

Eszter walked to Mrs Harris's house after Brew had closed. The sunshine of the day was still in full force. She was surprised at how light the evenings stayed here. Her feet ached after standing all day. After Nick had taken a turn for the worse, she had handed in her notice at her shop so it had been

a couple of months since she had worked and her feet needed to get used to it again.

Mrs Harris lived on the edge of town in a large house set back from the road, surrounded by trees. Eszter walked through the open gates, her shoes crunching on the drive-way. The three-storey house loomed large in red brick with ivy creeping over the door, which looked as if it needed cutting back.

Nick had shown her only a few photos from his youth and Eszter now remembered seeing one of him as a baby with his mother outside this very house. She wished he was looking down on her at this moment, and she tried to believe he was sending his strength to help her. Taking a deep breath, she marched to the door and knocked twice. The sound echoed in the stillness around her and she began to regret not having Zoe there to lighten the mood.

There was a long time until the door opened, as if Mrs Harris was slow in her movements. Which was likely, Eszter thought. She opened the door with a frown. 'Yes?' she asked with immediate suspicion. She was a tall, bony lady with a neat, grey bun and narrow dark eyes, which immediately reminded Eszter of Nick.

'Mrs Harris?' she asked. 'I'm Eszter Harris. Nick's wife.'

The woman stared at her for a long moment. 'Eszter?'

'I've come to Littlewood. To see you. Nick asked me to.'

Mrs Harris kept her hand curled around the door. 'What do you want?'

'Could I come in and explain?'

'What is there to explain? You come over now when my boy is gone? Why would I want to see you? It's Nick who I want to see,' Mrs Harris cried, her voice trembling with emotion.

Eszter's heart tugged. 'I'm so sorry. It all happened so fast. He wanted to come but it was too late . . .'

'If it's my money you're after then you can think again. I know what your sort are like.'

Eszter's mouth fell open. 'My sort?'

'You trapped him over there, and now you think I want you here? Go back to where you came from!' The door shut abruptly in Eszter's face, leaving her in stunned silence.

'Well, that went well,' she said aloud before turning slowly, shaking her head as she stumbled out of the driveway and headed towards home. Thank God she hadn't come with Zoe. There was no way she would have wanted her daughter to witness her grandmother like that.

The unfairness stabbed at her; after all, Eszter had been the one who had always encouraged Nick to heal the breach between him and his parents. Now she was here honouring his dying wish, and this was the reception she got. She tutted to herself and found herself pounding out her annoyance on the pavement as she marched towards her cottage. She couldn't believe she had come all this way to be treated like that. *Go back to where you came from.* Eszter had known that Nick's mother would be surprised to see her but she hadn't quite been prepared for such anger towards her. Maybe Littlewood's warm welcomes before this had been unusual, and this small town was more narrow-minded than she had thought.

For the first time in her life, Eszter felt like a complete outsider.

She called Louise to meet at her cottage with Zoe. Eszter had never been happier to see the friendly face of her beloved daughter and gave her a big squeeze until Zoe complained and she was forced to let her go. She invited Louise in for a coffee.

'So, it didn't go well?' Louise asked as Eszter made them both a cup. Zoe begged to watch a film and Eszter settled her on the sofa with some sweets, grateful she wasn't alone there.

'She basically slammed the door in my face.' She carried their coffees over to the kitchen table and glanced at her daughter happily watching Disney. 'God knows what she would have done if she'd seen Zoe. It's clear she holds me responsible for her not seeing her son. Maybe even him dying.' Eszter felt a lump form in her throat and hoped she wouldn't start crying in front of Louise. It felt far too early in their friendship to start crying on her.

'It must have been a huge shock to see you, I suppose. I'm sure she didn't mean what she said.'

Eszter tried to see if from her mother-in-law's point of view for a moment. 'I guess I should have called her first. I was just in such a rush to do what Nick wanted. I didn't think she would react like that though.'

'You were doing what your husband asked of you, so don't blame yourself. But you can't give up. She'll come round in time, won't she?'

'I honestly don't know.' Eszter took a sip of the strong

coffee. She had no idea quite where to go from here. How to get her mother-in-law to listen to her and believe that she didn't want anything from her.

'Does she know about Zoe?'

'I don't know. Nick invited his parents to our wedding but they didn't come. I don't think he had any more contact with them after that. He didn't tell me about it anyway.'

'Maybe seeing Zoe would soften her up a little?'

Eszter glanced at the blonde head of her daughter giggling at the film. She really didn't want Zoe anywhere near that cranky old woman, but then she tried to remember why she was doing this. Her pride made her want to stay away – she couldn't believe Mrs Harris actually thought Eszter was after her money – but then she thought of Nick and how much he wanted her to do this. She couldn't do anything else for him now. How could she look at herself in the mirror if she didn't at least try again?

'Maybe you're right. I can't leave it like this.'

'You'll get through to her, I'm sure of it.'

Eszter wished she had Louise's confidence. She remembered how stubborn Nick was and now she knew where he got that from. He hadn't wanted to break the estrangement with his parents and neither had they, so the years had passed and now they were lost to each other for ever. Eszter was determined that Zoe and Mrs Harris wouldn't suffer the same fate. Eszter was going to break Mrs Harris down. She just needed to work out how to do it.

Chapter Seven

Abbie found Thomas Huntley waiting in his office, his head in his hands. He looked up quickly and smiled when she entered but not before she saw a flash of genuine despair on his face. 'What's happened?'

'I've just been looking at the bookings for the rest of the summer – we're not even at half occupancy when it should be one of our busiest times.'

Abbie had spent the last couple of days getting to know Huntley Manor as much as she could. She had taken another in-depth tour, had a look at all their social media, and researched the house through the ages online. She had even checked out a book on local history from the library. She couldn't help but be fascinated by the house.

Built in the 1700s for the then Lord Huntley, a distant relation to royalty, it had been in the Huntley family for generations. As running a large estate became more costly, the family first opened up the house to paying visitors and

then Thomas's grandfather had turned it into a hotel. It had thrived for years and, under Thomas's parents, had done pretty well, but bookings had dropped as newer hotels had opened up in the surrounding area and the house became in need of repairs. When his parents died, Thomas was left to run the estate alone with no siblings or family of his own; the strain of that was clearly showing on both him and the house, Abbie thought.

'I spent yesterday updating your website and creating new accounts for the estate on social media. I can't believe you weren't on Twitter or Instagram. There was no opportunity for guests who enjoyed their stay to talk about the place so new customers would know where to find you. The website was really out of date as well. It talked about horse-riding weekends,' Abbie said, sitting down opposite him across his large, dark wood desk. 'But you don't have any horses.'

'I sold them last year to pay off some debts. We rarely had anyone who wanted to ride.'

'The stables are now just wasted space then. You could do something else with them.'

'It would cost a lot to convert them, though.'

'Well, we could put that on a long-term project list. One thing I was surprised that you *don't* offer here is weddings.'

'My parents never saw the need. It's a lot of work, isn't it? We'd need an event planner and I can't afford to take on any more staff. Another long-term project maybe?' He smiled weakly. 'Abbie – is creating a Twitter account really going to bring in some more guests before the end of the summer?'

'Every little helps,' she said, trying to keep her voice bright. It seemed like Thomas was already giving up. She opened up the book she had borrowed on the page that had caught her eye. 'Look what I found in the library.' It was an article in the local paper from years ago about a summer garden party the estate had thrown. The picture was taken outside in the grounds. There were people everywhere. The party looked like the kind of event people she knew in London would love to attend. 'Surely the reason you come and stay somewhere like this over a newer, flashier hotel is that you love history? You want to feel like you could be lady of the house, wearing a long dress, welcoming guests, and falling in love with a lord? You should be doing events like this again.'

'I was never any good at entertaining, I suppose. So, that sort of fell off my to-do list when I took over the hotel.' He looked sheepish. 'I don't even like going to parties.'

'You can't just avoid doing something because you personally don't like it; events are really important for a hotel,' Abbie said, a little impatient with his continuing negativity. Didn't he want to save his family home? Just because he'd never organised an event before wasn't a good enough reason not to try in her book. 'You need to try, Thomas.'

He regarded her coldly. 'If you think I haven't been trying, then you should just walk away now.' He stood up gracefully considering his anger. 'I didn't ask you to come here and criticise me. You have no idea how hard it's been running this place by myself. You wouldn't know anything about

54

the weight on my shoulders that this house produces. It's my family that I will be letting down if this fails. My history I'll be walking away from. My legacy.' He strode out of the room, leaving Abbie unable to come up with a response before he departed.

She sighed aloud to the empty room. She knew that Huntley Manor couldn't be easy to be in charge of alone but that's why she wanted to help. She thought of her grand-parents' house and how her parents hadn't thought they were up to the job of restoring the property. She had lost her legacy back then. She understood how Thomas must be feeling. This place was steeped in a far deeper, and grander, history than theirs had been but her heart had been broken when it had gone up for sale. She realised then that she was too invested to walk away. It didn't matter that Thomas was resisting her help. She could see his defences were up because he was scared. If he could start to see a difference then surely he would get stuck in too?

Abbie went down to reception where Amy was sat behind the desk doing nothing as usual. Abbie decided to show her the social media accounts she had set up as that would get her involved and give her something to do in between dealing with guests. 'I think we want to talk about the history of the place, play up the grand elegance of the house and things that have happened in the past. We want to draw in fans of BBC period dramas. We want people to think of romance when they come here. We want to appeal to city types looking for a traditional English country house experience.'

'I think it's a great idea. Whenever I take a photo here for my Instagram, it always gets loads of likes. Lord Huntley has a very old-fashioned view sometimes, despite his age; I think it's good you're showing him a new way of doing things.'

Lord Huntley? Abbie felt stupid for not realising that if his grandfather had been a Lord then obviously Thomas now had the title. She was glad she hadn't treated him any differently than she would any of her other clients.

Abbie's mind suddenly flashed back to what she had said about women who would want to stay in the hotel for the fantasy of snagging a lord for themselves and she blushed. What if he assumed she wanted that too? *God, how embarrassing,* she thought. She tried to shake off the mortification and concentrate on how she could get Thomas on board with all her ideas. If he could see just how passionate she was about the hotel then surely it would rub off on him and he could get over this defeatist attitude of his.

She decided to leave the library book about Huntley Manor for Thomas in the hope that it would provide similar inspiration for him. So before she left for the night, she walked to the private wing of the house. She had only seen it quickly on the grand tour he had given her. It was an apartment within the house, more modern than the hotel part, with things you'd expect in modern houses that would jar in other parts of the estate like flat-screen TVs, laptops and Ikea furniture.

She knocked on the door but there was no answer, so she pushed it tentatively. It led into a small hall and then

the open-plan apartment opened out before her. She saw Thomas sitting at his small, glass kitchen table with a ready meal in front of him, the TV on, and a beer beside him. He was staring into space, holding his fork in mid-air. Abbie looked at him for a moment. He looked so small in there. And lonely. She wondered if she should go in and ask him to have dinner with her. She hated the thought of him sat here in this massive house every night by himself.

Her phone buzzed in her bag, making her jump. She didn't want Thomas to think she was intruding, so hastily she left the book on the table by the door and softly walked out, pulling her phone out as she made her way to the front door. She looked at the screen in surprise. It was Jack. What could he want?

'Hello?' she answered, as she made her way outside. Brew was shut for the night and Littlewood was quiet as the sun set behind her.

'Darling, how are you?'

Darling? Abbie thought back to their last meeting when he told her she would be leaving the company. There had been no use of 'darling' then.

'I'm good. What's up?' she said shortly. She had no clue why he would be contacting her now. She strolled towards Louise's cottage, marvelling at how her pace had slowed down being here compared to how she had moved around London. She hadn't been able to abandon her heels, though, despite the hill she had to walk up to Huntley Manor. There were some things she just couldn't leave behind.

'The office isn't the same without you,' he said then, his smooth voice affecting her more than she thought it would. She closed her eyes briefly, remembering how he would tell her how beautiful she was, as they lay side by side in those crisp white hotel sheets. 'Nothing is the same without you.'

'You didn't think that when I was right there in front of you.' She hated the hard edge that came into her voice, knowing it showed she was still hurt, but she couldn't let that comment pass. He'd had lots of time in London to rekindle their relationship before dropping the redundancy bomb. Now she was miles away he suddenly realised he missed her?

'Things just got so intense at work. I was put in a very difficult position. I didn't want you to think I was involved in your redundancy. The other partners put pressure on me to keep things strictly professional between us. But I want you to know our time together was very special to me.'

Abbie wondered why he had never made her feel that way. She thought back to their months together. They had rarely spent time with each other's family or friends; their relationship had been restricted to dinners out and nights in.

'Jack, I don't know what you want me to say. I'm staying with my sister, trying to find work. I want to come back to London but it won't be for a while.'

'Our clients miss you as well. And at the last team meeting, we missed your ideas. I think some of the partners are wondering if we made a mistake,' he said in a low voice. 'Maybe I did too.'

Abbie couldn't believe what she was hearing. 'Maybe you

should have all thought about that before you sacked me then. Look, Jack, I have to go. I am trying to get back on my feet and that's my focus right now.'

'Maybe I could help? I'll have a think. I want you back in London with me. If that's where you want to be?'

'Of course it is,' she replied, meaning the city, but she realised too late he might take it to mean back with him too.

'I knew you missed me too. Talk soon, darling.' He hung up before she could clarify what she had meant. She put her phone away, as Louise's road came into view. Oh, well, what did it matter? If Jack wanted to help her get back to London then she wasn't going to stop him. She still blamed him for not giving her a heads-up that she was about to lose her job. She could have been looking for another one weeks ago and might have even been safely in a new position by now. Plus, quitting would have looked so much better to potential employers than the redundancy, but no, he had done what his colleagues had asked and pulled away from her. Now it seemed like he regretted it and Abbie wasn't quite sure how to feel about that.

Chapter Eight

Louise was in the middle of a night shift and the ward around her was dark and far quieter than in the daytime, which meant it was harder to focus on the tasks in hand. Thoughts of Peter kept invading her mind, especially when she went to say goodnight to Hazel. Watching the little girl clutching her teddy and falling asleep brought that familiar ache for a child of her own. She knew as soon as she started her nursing training that she wanted to work with children. She had always loved kids and she had been so sure that she and Peter would end up with a large family. Why was it so hard for her to let go of that fantasy when he had moved on to someone else?

Louise sat down later to check everything had been done that needed to be. Julie, one of the other nurses, was trying to persuade one of the kids that it was bedtime, but the noise was finally dying down around them. She pushed a strand of her hair behind her ears and then touched her earlobe. It was empty. She felt the other one, which still had an earring

in. She checked around her chair. The diamond stud must have fallen out somewhere that evening. She had had both in when she left the cottage. The earrings had been her twenty-first birthday present from her grandparents and she had always treasured them as it felt like the last piece of them, particularly after they had sold their beloved home in Cornwall. And now that had gone.

'Ugh, can I have any worse luck right now?' she murmured as Julie came over. 'You haven't seen my earring, have you?'

'No. Have you checked the ward?'

Louise walked down it, peeking into cubicles and checking the floor, but there was no flash of the diamond. She thought back to where she had walked that day. She had grabbed a coffee from Brew on her way in but that was it. She decided she would go and ask Harry and Joy if they had seen it after her shift, and in the meantime she would text Abbie to look around the cottage for her. Louise wasn't at all hopeful that something so small would turn up, but she carefully took out the remaining stud and zipped it up in her pocket, just in case.

Louise walked back to her desk with a heavy heart. She knew it was silly to be so upset about a lost earring, but after Peter's news, it felt like the universe was against her, and uncharacteristically she felt hard done by and just wanted to go to bed and shut out the world.

But with six hours left of work to get through first, she had to pull herself together and focus on the children who needed her care.

* * *

The sun was rising in a haze of orange sky as Louise drove back to Littlewood from the hospital in the early hours. She checked the time and was relieved that Brew would be opening soon. She needed a coffee before she headed home and wanted to see if she had dropped her earring there.

There had been a voicemail from her mother while she was on her shift. The news about Peter had reached her and she had wanted to check Louise was okay. She knew her mother meant well, but she couldn't face having to pretend that the news hadn't affected her when it had made her question everything, so she was putting off calling her back. Parking outside Huntley Manor, Louise got out of her car and called out to her sister who was strolling across the grounds.

'Blimey, you're up early,' Louise said when Abbie turned back to greet her.

'It used to take me an hour to get to work so I'm used to getting up early, and I wanted to speak to the staff I haven't met yet, not that Thomas has anywhere near enough to run the place properly.'

'You're really taking this seriously, aren't you?' Louise was a little surprised that Abbie was throwing herself into saving Huntley Manor when she was so desperate to get back to the city.

'This place deserves to be saved,' Abbie said firmly, gesturing behind her. The sun was peeking out from behind the grand building, casting a glowing light down on top

of it. It did look particularly special that morning. Louise couldn't imagine Littlewood without it watching over them. Someone could end up tearing it down if Thomas did lose it and Louise knew the town would suffer if that happened.

'I think it's great. Is Thomas open to your ideas though?' Brew was opening up so the sisters walked slowly over to it. Louise knew that Abbie was always enthusiastic about her ideas and couldn't quite picture Lord Huntley being as thrilled by Instagram posts or being retweeted by someone famous.

'He will be.'

Louise laughed. 'He doesn't know what's hit him yet, does he?' She waved at Joy who was unlocking the door.

'You two are keen,' Joy said, as she opened up.

'I just got off my shift and spotted Abbie heading to Huntley Manor. I think we both deserve a coffee and a croissant.' She turned to Abbie. 'You didn't find my earring, did you?'

'No, I'm so sorry. I looked all around the cottage but there was no sign of it.'

Louise looked at Joy. 'You haven't seen a diamond earring, have you? I've lost one.'

'I didn't spot one cleaning up yesterday, no, I'm sorry,' Joy said, starting up the coffee machine.

Louise's heart sank. 'Then I think it's gone for good.'

'Why don't you put up a message on the Kindness Board in case someone finds it?' Harry suggested, putting a croissant into a bag each for them. 'It's worth a try at least.'

Louise nodded and went to the board to put a kindness plea up there asking for people to look out for her earring. She noticed an act of kindness written up there in sloping writing.

My boyfriend John for looking after me when I got out of hospital – I couldn't have got through my operation without you!

Louise tried not to feel jealous of this girl – she'd had an operation, for God's sake, no need at all to wish she could swap places with her, but then she thought back to her relationship with Peter. Louise had always wanted to help people, and Peter was no exception. She would help him revise for his exams; she helped him apply for university and then for jobs. She didn't even think about it at the time. It was automatic for her. She loved him; they were partners, so she naturally wanted to help him. But seeing this simple thank you up on the board, Louise wondered if he had ever really thanked her for anything she had done. And she wondered if his new fiancée was now doing all the things she used to do. Or maybe now he was with someone he really loved, he was doing them for her instead.

Louise turned away from the board, hating that he still had the power to make her feel so hurt. She took the coffee and pastries from Harry and then she and Abbie left Brew. Outside, the morning sunshine was in full force, promising a lovely day.

'I hope someone finds your earring,' Abbie said. She looked at her sister. 'Are you okay, Lou?'

'Just tired,' Louise replied, not wanting to admit how much the news of Peter's engagement was still playing on her mind. She was sure Abbie would have put it behind her by now. 'I better get home and to bed. I'm off tomorrow, so we could do something?'

'Sounds good.' Abbie waved to her cheerfully and Louise headed back to her car, weary from her shift and thinking about the past. She wished you could just put your feelings into a box and seal them tightly up inside and never have to deal with them again.

Chapter Nine

Eszter held Zoe's hand as they walked to her afternoon shift at Brew. She had spent the last couple of days going over and over her first meeting with Anne Harris. She was still angry and upset, but acknowledged that her mother-in-law must have been shocked to see her and was a grieving mother who deserved compassion. Eszter knew she had to try again but had been clueless as to how to approach her. That morning, however, inspiration had struck as she had sat watching the sunrise with her coffee, her husband's letter in her hands.

Who better to tackle Mrs Harris than Nick himself?

'Who lives here?' Zoe asked as they paused at the top of the driveway.

'Your daddy's mother,' Eszter replied, knowing she couldn't lie to her about this. 'I'm just going to give her a letter.'

'Shouldn't we knock and say hello?'

'We will, but it's going to be a big surprise to her, so I think

we should tell her we're here first.' Eszter wished she had done this before turning up on her doorstep, then maybe she wouldn't have had such an unwelcome first meeting with her mother-in-law. She slipped up the driveway and thrust the copy of the letter through the letter box. She didn't trust Mrs Harris not to destroy it so had taken a copy of it at the library, just in case. She couldn't bear to ever lose the last thing that Nick wrote to her. She looked up at the second floor of the house and swore she saw the curtains twitch. She wondered if Mrs Harris was watching them. And what she would think of Zoe.

'Is it Daddy's letter?' Zoe asked when her mother returned to her side.

'Yes. I think she should see it and then she'll know we're here to see her.'

'I hope she's nice.'

'I'm sure she will be,' Eszter replied, glancing nervously back at the house as they carried on walking. She hoped that her daughter would get to meet her grandmother this summer and that it would go well. Zoe didn't deserve any more upset in her life. 'I think we need a slice of cake when we get to Brew, don't you?'

'Sometimes I think all we do at the moment is eat cake.'

Eszter was always surprised when Zoe made an observation like that, but she didn't know why; Zoe was as sharp as her father, even at her age. Eszter knew she was overcompensating for Nick being gone. She didn't think she'd gone as far as to make her daughter sick of cake though. 'Well, if you'd rather not have any . . .'

'I didn't say that,' Zoe replied cheerfully, making her mother laugh.

Thank goodness for Zoe; if Eszter was by herself right now she wouldn't be able to stop thinking about what Mrs Harris would make of the letter. Nick had made Eszter swear not to open it until he was gone. It had sat there for days burning a hole on the table, but she had kept her promise, and when the time had come to open it, she had ended up putting it off, unable to accept his death; opening it seemed to acknowledge he was gone. Eventually, though, curiosity had become too much and the need to hear her husband's voice again, even if just in the form of words, had been too strong to ignore.

My darling Eszter,

You're reading this, so it must mean that what we both wished would never happen, has. I never wanted to leave you or my lovely Zoe and I can't believe that this is the hand we've been dealt. The only thing that has made it bearable is knowing that I had the most wonderful life with you both and that you'll look after each other when I'm not there. I love you both so much.

This last week I've been thinking a lot about the past. I know that you never understood why I was so reluctant to talk about where I came from, and you were shocked when I told you I was estranged from my parents. The truth is, I let my pride stop me reaching out to them. When they didn't reply to our wedding invitation, the one you rightly pushed me to send, I was done with them. I suppose I always

presumed that we had time, to talk, to face the past, to heal. Then my father passed. I didn't tell you, but I phoned my mother when I heard the news. She asked me to come to the funeral and I said no. I wish I had gone now.

I have always wanted my mother to meet you and Zoe. I know she will love you as much as I do. I should have done more when I had the chance, but now I must ask you to do it instead. I'm sorry, Eszter. You're going to have so much to cope with after I've gone, but please do this one last thing for me. Enclosed are two plane tickets to England for you and Zoe. I want you to go to my home town of Littlewood. I want you and Zoe to see where I grew up. And to meet my mother. I want you to give her the watch back. I shouldn't have kept it all these years. I should have gone home to see her, to say I was sorry for cutting off contact with her, and to tell her I should have gone to my father's funeral. For her sake, if nothing else. But I let the past hold me back. And now it's too late.

Please do this for me, Eszter. And then hopefully we can all rest in peace.

You and Zoe are my world. I am so sorry I have to leave you. Please forgive me. Know that I will love you both always and forever and I will watch over you and be there for you whenever you need me.

Tell my mother I love her too.

Be kind to her. Be kind to each other.

Do what I was unable to do.

All my love, Nick

Eszter was sure that Nick would never have expected his mother to actually read the letter, but she hoped his words would soften her. It would show her at least that Eszter had no ulterior motives in trying to contact her; that she was there only to fulfil her husband's last wishes. She remembered talking late into the night with Nick after he had learned of his father's death from a family friend. He had told Eszter that he couldn't face the funeral.

'It just feels hypocritical. I walked away from them, I walked away from him, and if I turn up at his funeral and pretend to the world that I'm sad that he's gone, then I would feel worse than I would not going at all.'

'But he was your father.' Eszter hadn't understood. She couldn't imagine not being there for her mother if, God forbid, anything happened to her father. 'Besides, funerals are for the living, not the dead. Won't your mother need you?'

'She didn't need me when she let me leave all those years ago. They didn't come to our wedding, Eszter. That was their opportunity to make things right. I invited them and they didn't even bother to RSVP.'

'I just think you might regret not going,' Eszter had said. She knew now she had been right. Although he had never told her, he had obviously regretted it. When he realised he wasn't going to survive the cancer, it had been on his mind more than she had even known, causing him to write that letter and book her the flights. She felt a small prickle of anger at Nick for making them deal with this by themselves.

Eszter had put in a small note with the letter explaining

that she thought Mrs Harris should see it to know why they were here, and that she would come back to visit her in a couple of days. Eszter hoped her mother-in-law would understand why she was really in Littlewood after reading it.

And this time not slam the door in her face, she added to herself.

But she wasn't all that confident about that.

Eszter arrived at Brew and took over from Joy and Harry who stopped for a welcome break with Zoe, sitting down at a table by the window with drinks and sandwiches. Joy had checked that Eszter was happy to keep on working there after her trial had gone so well and Eszter had eagerly accepted. The job suited her and it was lovely having Zoe there as well.

Eszter served a couple of customers, then noticed a man reading the Kindness Board and furrowing his brow at it.

'Can I help you with something?' she called over the counter to him. He was tall and lean with scruffy hair, and stubble around his chin.

'I was looking at that note up there,' he said, pointing to Louise's plea for someone to find her earring. 'I know where the earring is. My sister found it. Actually my niece did. It was caught in the ribbon around one of her teddy bears.'

'Louise would love to have it back. I can give it to her?'

'My sister has it. She's at the hospital; I'm going to see her later though, so I can tell her. It's best to bring it here for this … Louise, then?'

'Well, actually, she works at the hospital. She's a nurse there – Louise Morgan.'

71

'Oh, great, I'll find her there later then. Can I have a coffee to go, please?'

Eszter made him a coffee, pleased that Louise would be reunited with her earring. She deserved something good to happen to her after how kind she'd been to Eszter and Zoe.

Eszter watched the man carry his coffee out and wondered if Louise might just be as pleased with him as she would be with the earring. Eszter could hear Nick in her head telling her to quit trying to matchmake. She couldn't help it though. She had always wanted to help people be as happy as she and Nick had been. And Louise was definitely someone she wanted to see happy.

Chapter Ten

Abbie was nervous to see Thomas again after their previous rather strained conversation. She met him in the grounds of Huntley Manor, as he was about to climb into the green jeep she had seen parked by the stables before.

'The gardener said there's a problem with the fence. Want to come with me to take a look?' he asked as he opened up the driver's side.

'Sure.' Abbie had to jump up to climb into the car and Thomas stifled a laugh as she half fell into the seat beside him.

'You try doing that in heels,' she said.

'You really should be in wellies, not heels.'

'I'd rather die.'

Thomas shook his head. 'I thought you said you grew up in Cornwall. You wore heels on the beach too?' he asked, starting up the jeep and driving away from the Manor. The jeep bumped along the grounds, heading for the woods on the edge of the estate.

'I started wearing them when I moved to London,' Abbie said, remembering how she and Louise used to scamper about on the sand growing up; she couldn't imagine doing that now. 'At my interview, they told me I needed to wear them. The men had to wear suits, the women heels.'

'And you call me old-fashioned.'

She smiled. 'I didn't really question it at the time, but you're right: it makes no difference to how you do your job, but impressions count, don't they? Our clients expected it and I like the extra height – without them I'm often mistaken for a child.'

Thomas chuckled. 'Well, just don't fall over while you're here – I can't afford a lawsuit right now.' They exchanged a wry look. 'Actually, I googled you last night.'

Abbie's eyebrows shot up.

'Um ... did that sound creepy? I mean, I looked at the company you worked for. They did a great job at making that new restaurant successful – what was it called – Let's Eat?'

Abbie nodded. 'I came up with the ideas for the launch party. But one of the partners, Jack, it was his client and so he got the credit.' She wished she could stop the frustration from showing on her face. She had put in so many hours on that restaurant and Jack was the one who was nominated for the best launch event award at the PR awards – and he won, of course, and didn't even mention Abbie in his acceptance speech.

'That doesn't sound fair. By the way, I looked at the book you left for me and, you're right, we had some great events

here in the past. Do you think something like that launch could help us here?'

Abbie was thrilled he was thinking along those lines. 'Definitely. We could relaunch the hotel at the end of the summer with a big party. I'm convinced you need to put this hotel back into people's minds. A relaunch would be the perfect opportunity to get everyone talking about it again.'

'Wouldn't we need to do a big renovation to justify a relaunch though?'

'Not if you had a new theme or, well, just something new to display? I'm sure we can think of something that doesn't involve going too crazy.'

'This is what has been missing – new ideas. I can see that. I thought Huntley Manor needed to stay the same as it was when my parents ran it, you know? But times change and the hotel needs to change with them, I suppose, if we're going to stay popular.'

'For sure.' She was pleased he was starting to believe that there was a chance to save the business; they just needed to think outside the box a little bit. Abbie loved this aspect of PR – working with someone to boost their business. She was an ideas person. She had loved coming up with plans at her old company. That's why it had stung when Jack had taken the credit without even thinking about all the effort she had put in. She had wanted to call Jack out on it but something held her back. Sometimes she had felt intimidated by her boyfriend. He acted as if she had such a lot to learn and it made her think he was right, but now she wasn't sure. Her

work had won an award – surely that meant she had been good at her job?

Being made redundant had knocked her confidence further, but she had to believe that she could do it. Jack certainly wouldn't let anyone tell him he couldn't. He always did exactly what he wanted to do. And that attitude had made her keep quiet at times when she knew she shouldn't have. Jack had been the one she ran all her ideas past, the one whose opinion had mattered the most, and now he wasn't here so she was relying on her own instincts again. And she was rather enjoying it.

'Here we are.' Thomas pulled the jeep over by a patch of trees and climbed out.

Abbie watched him walk through the trees to look at the fence and decided against following him in her shoes. She pulled out her phone. She had a message from Kate telling her she'd found a new flatmate. Abbie was glad she had found someone to help pay the rent but her stomach plummeted, as it meant if she did find a job in London she wouldn't be able to go back and live in her old flat.

'Right, so we need to get it repaired, which means another cost I could do without,' Thomas said as he climbed back in. 'This place just needs so much work doing to it.' He sighed. 'I honestly don't know where to start.'

'Do you have a list of what needs doing and a plan for when you can do it against your budget?'

Thomas just looked at her.

'You need to get some spreadsheets on the go, my friend. And, guess what? I love a spreadsheet.'

'I thought you were crazy when I first met you and now I know I was right.'

She elbowed him in the ribs and the jeep swerved. 'Can you not kill me, please? I don't want to have to sue you twice.'

'First she criticises my management skills and now my driving.' Thomas drove them back up to the house. 'You really don't go easy on me, do you?'

Abbie shrugged. 'We won't save Huntley Manor if we're not tough about it. So, you're on board then? We are going to have a party at the end of the summer and save the hotel?'

'I still don't really understand why you want to help so much.'

'My grandparents had a lovely house in Cornwall. Growing up, I spent so much time there, running through the house and playing in the grounds. It always felt special. Huntley Manor reminds me of it, I suppose,' Abbie told him, her mind flashing back to playing hide-and-seek with Louise and lying on the grass in the sunshine, her grandmother bringing them home-made lemonade and cookies. It had been idyllic. She sighed.

'When they died, my parents decided to sell the house, even though I begged them not to. They felt the house was a noose around their necks. It did need a lot of work doing to it that they couldn't afford, and they just didn't see any way to save it for our family. I was too young to be able to help.' Abbie looked at Thomas who was watching her. 'It was knocked down and turned into flats. I don't want that to happen here.'

'I'm sorry, Abbie. I can see why you're so passionate about this place. I think I've been so caught up with all the problems that I lost sight of what this house means to me. I feel the same way about it as you did about your grandparents' home,' Thomas said gently.

'I haven't been in Littlewood long, but I can't imagine the town without this house.'

'Nor can I,' he said softly, looking out at the place where he had grown up. 'I know you think I've given up, but the truth is, I've been trying not to be sentimental about the house in order to do what makes sense financially. But you've made me see that it's okay to be sentimental, that houses like these are special. Owning Huntley Manor is a privilege and I need to remember that, and fight to keep it, like I know my family would want me to.'

'What was it like growing up here?'

'It's hard to answer that as this was my normal. But I know that I was very lucky to have my childhood somewhere like this. I just remember lots of running around the estate, I was always outside, and the house was always full of people so I was never alone.' He sighed and Abbie realised how much things had changed for him and the estate. She really wasn't seeing it in its prime, but she hoped she would one day soon.

They got out of the jeep. The morning sun was in full bloom now and it bathed Abbie's shoulders. 'There was a room mentioned in that book that I haven't seen yet, I think. The Huntley Room?'

Thomas laughed. 'My family were not the most

imaginative of name-givers, were they? I'll show you.'
Thomas led her through the building. She still didn't think
she could find her way around it all yet, it was so vast – full
of twists and turns – so it was of little surprise to her that she
hadn't seen this room before. They walked through the grand
hall and to a room off to the side. Thomas opened the double
doors and stood back to let her walk in first. She hated the
fact that she liked this gentlemanly way of his; she supposed
it shouldn't register with her, as a modern woman, but maybe
chivalry wasn't actually dead. Just hidden out here in Surrey.

The ballroom was mentioned in the history of Huntley
Manor as being central to events on the estate – the room
that showed off the house and that everyone wanted to see
and talk about. Abbie found it hard at first to see that. The
room was long, and narrow, with a wooden floor and a floor-
to-ceiling window at the end, displaying the grounds. She
looked up and gasped at the high, ornate ceiling. Thomas
walked over and pulled back the drapes so the light streamed
in. In the centre of the ceiling was a massive chandelier that
looked as if it had seen better days. The whole room needed
a bloody good clean, but Abbie turned around, looking at
it, trying to picture it gleaming and imagine people milling
around in their finest. It could be special again, couldn't it?

'This is where we had evening parties when my parents
were alive,' Thomas said, his voice echoing around the room.
'But they dwindled with the guests and people didn't seem to
want lavish parties anymore, just a quiet stay here. It's been
closed up for about ten years now, I think.'

Abbie shook her head. 'This is it, Thomas. This is the reason we throw the end of summer party. You need to open up this room again. I know so many companies that would hire this out, if not for parties, then for work events. It could be stunning. And if you added French doors at the end to lead into the gardens, then the summer party could happen right here. What do you think?' She turned to face him, smiling at the thought of this room getting its groove back.

He looked at her for a moment. 'You really think so?'

'Trust me on this. This is going to put Huntley Manor back on the map. We just need to find you a budget to get it looking good and start organising the event.'

He looked around the room dubiously. 'I don't know. It sounds like a lot of work and expense.'

'You are going to have to invest a little bit if you want the hotel to be successful again, but I think we can do it without spending a fortune. Won't it be worth it if you save your house?' Abbie couldn't remember feeling as passionate about her work as she did right now. She could feel it in her bones that this was the right thing to do. Maybe it wasn't as important to be ambitious in your career progression as it was to work on things you actually believed in. Maybe that's where she had been going wrong in London. If she thought about it – losing her job there hadn't felt nearly as crushing as the idea of not saving Huntley Manor felt right now. She crossed her fingers. 'What do you think?'

Thomas nodded. 'I think we should do it. I trust you. But

I'd need your help. And it's too much work, too much to ask of you when I can't pay you.'

Abbie's heart was in this too much for her to walk away now. She thought about how to convince him. 'As long as you give me a killer reference then it's okay. You're giving me something to do whilst I'm in Littlewood, plus it will look great on my CV.'

'If we pull it off.'

'When we pull it off.' She closed the gap between them and held out her hand. 'So, we're doing this then?'

He shook her hand with a grin. She found herself smiling right back at him. It felt like they were a team already and she was excited to see what they could do there together. 'You, Abbie Morgan, are very difficult to say no to.'

'Maybe I should put that on my CV too.'

Chapter Eleven

'Excuse me – Louise?'

She swung around on her chair to find a man by her desk. She recognised him as Hazel's uncle. He always looked kind of scruffy and as if he could do with a few big meals, but she couldn't help notice again his big, deep brown eyes and the dimples in his cheeks when he smiled at her. 'Can I help?' she asked, hoping Hazel was okay.

'Actually, I think I can help you,' he replied and held up a sparkling stud. She gasped. 'I saw your plea on the Kindness Board in Brew. Hazel had found it on the bear you gave her.'

'Oh, I looked on her cubicle floor, I didn't even think about checking the bear! Thank you so much.' Relieved it had been found, she took out the one she'd been carrying in her pocket, slipping them back into her ears again. 'I can't believe you saw my note on the board. It actually works!'

'I always look at it when I'm in there; I love reading about all the acts of kindness in the town.'

Louise nodded. 'Me too. Harry and Joy will be thrilled it worked.' She realised she was smiling a bit too much at him and looked away. 'Well, I was really upset that I had lost it so thank you again for bringing it back to me.'

'Of course. Hazel says you're her favourite nurse, so I'm glad I could do something for you, no matter how small. I'm Alex, by the way.' He held out his hand and Louise shook it quickly. Warmth spread through her at the brief contact. 'Do you live in Littlewood too then?'

'Yes. I'm always in Brew,' she said before realising she shouldn't have said that as it looked like she was hinting to see him there or something. 'Well, not always, I mean, I get coffee there sometimes,' she amended quickly, feeling her cheeks turning pink. She stood up abruptly. 'I should go and check on something.'

'Sure. Well, maybe I'll see you here again or in Brew. I have to get coffee before work or I can't function. It's worrying really, isn't it?'

'Okay, bye,' she trilled as she grabbed her clipboard and rushed away, wondering why he was making her feel the need to flee so badly. She glanced back to find he was watching her and gave her a little wave. She ducked out into the corridor and took a deep breath.

There was no way that a man should be making her feel so panicky. 'Get a grip,' she muttered to herself, remembering that all men were just like Peter, so there was no need to even think about Alex again. She was ashamed that his smile, complete with dimples, popped into her head and she shook the thought

away fiercely. Alex was just the man who returned her earring to her. He was kind. Peter had never been kind. But that didn't mean he wouldn't crush her heart into pieces just like Peter had. It was much safer to assume that you were going to get hurt and avoid the prospect than end up heartbroken again.

When she got round to Hazel, she was nervous that Alex would still be there but the cubicle was empty apart from her young patient. Hazel said her mum was getting some dinner. It must be so tiring for her always going back and forth to the hospital; Louise felt so much sympathy for the family. She hoped they would get some respite soon.

'Did Uncle Alex give you your earring?' Hazel asked. She still clutched the bear Louise had given her.

'Yes, thank you. Your bear had been keeping it safe for me, he said?'

She nodded. 'My mum said we had to look after it until we could find who it belonged to, then Uncle Alex said it was yours.'

'He comes to see you a lot, doesn't he?'

'Not as much as I wish he could. He often works late, Mum says.'

'Where does he work?' she asked casually, wondering why she was grilling a little girl about a man she'd just met.

'He's a vet.'

Oh, great, Louise thought. He was an animal lover too. 'In Littlewood?'

Hazel nodded.

Louise wanted to feel relieved that she didn't have a pet

that might need his attention, but she wasn't totally sure that's what she was feeling. She hastily left Hazel in case she felt the need to ask her more questions about him.

She texted Abbie on her break to say her earring had been delivered safely back to her. By the local vet.

Is he good-looking?

Louise groaned at Abbie's reply and put her phone away.

* * *

Abbie and Louise went to have lunch at Brew before setting off on their shopping day. Louise wasn't working today and Abbie was leaving Thomas to speak to contractors about sprucing up the ballroom.

Louise went to the counter to order and told Joy she could wipe off her kindness plea. 'It's been found,' she said, showing off the matching pair of diamond studs safely back in her ears.

'Did he give it back to you? He was cute, wasn't he?' Eszter asked, coming over with a stack of plates for the dishwasher.

'Who was cute?' Joy asked.

'The man who found her earring.'

Louise rolled her eyes. 'His name is Alex, he's a vet apparently.'

'Alex?' Joy said, her eyes lighting up. 'We love Alex. He saved one of our dogs last year; he stayed all night at the surgery with him. He's always on the Kindness Board, and a very eligible bachelor.'

'Just because he's single doesn't mean he's eligible,' Louise said, cross that they were both so excited about him. This wasn't a romance novel, for God's sake. 'Two coffees and two Welsh rarebits please.'

'Speaking of,' Joy hissed as she typed Louise's order into the till. The bell on the door jingled and Louise couldn't help but glance at it as Alex walked in. Louise felt all their eyes on her as Alex came up to the counter. 'Morning, Alex,' Joy greeted him with a smile as she turned to make the coffees.

'Hi, everyone,' Alex said, waving his hand at them all. 'Nice earrings,' he said to Louise. 'I'm glad they haven't gone walkabout again.'

Louise felt her cheeks heat up and pleaded with Joy's back to hurry up with their order. Alex asked for a coffee and pastry to go.

'Just heading to the surgery. You're not at the hospital today?' he asked.

Louise shook her head. 'I'm having a day out with my sister, Abbie.' She pointed her out. Abbie was staring with blatant curiosity. Louise knew she'd never hear the end of this. She grabbed their coffees as soon as Joy slid them over.

'Enjoy your coffee,' she said and Louise hurried over to her sister.

'Who is that?' Abbie hissed, taking her coffee from her.

'God, he's just the guy who found my earring: Alex.'

'I knew he was good-looking!'

'Stop staring at him,' Louise hissed, hoping he wouldn't

notice. She wished he would hurry up and leave Brew. He was making her nervous being there.

Alex walked past their table with his cup and paper bag as he made to leave. 'Well, it was nice to see you again,' he said to Louise, who suddenly found that her coffee looked very interesting. 'I'm off to neuter a cat.' Then his face fell. 'That was too much information, wasn't it?'

Louise couldn't help but chuckle. 'It was a bit.'

'Well, maybe I'll see you when I next visit Hazel?'

'I'm not on nights for a while so probably not,' she replied, shortly. Eszter came over then with their cheesy bread.

'Ah, okay. Well, bye then,' Alex said, stuttering a little. He glanced at Eszter and Abbie. 'Enjoy your food,' he said and then ducked out of the café quickly.

'Lou, that poor boy,' Abbie said with a shake of her head.

'He was hoping he'd see you again,' Eszter added, watching him walk away out of the window. 'He's good-looking, isn't he? Don't you think?'

'And he's a vet,' Abbie said, starting to eat. 'Ooh, this is good.'

'Why would I care if he's cute and a vet?' Louise said, annoyed with all of them. She started eating and refused to say anything more on the subject but she didn't miss the look that her sister shared with Eszter, before she walked away to check on Zoe, who was reading in the corner.

Abbie sighed. 'I know the news about Peter has hit you hard, but it's been two years,' she said gently. 'Don't you want to put him behind you?'

'It's not like Alex asked me out or anything.'

87

'He would have done if you'd given him any encouragement.'

'What do you know, Abs? You've never been in love. That guy you were seeing in London didn't even have you round to his flat. You never met his family and friends. It was like you were having an affair with a married man. You know nothing about a real relationship or how it felt when Peter left me, so just drop it, okay?' Louise immediately regretted her words as Abbie's face dropped. 'I'm sorry,' Louise said quickly. 'I know you really liked him.'

'You're right. I've never been with anyone as long as you were with Peter, no one has asked me to marry them, but that doesn't mean I can't see that you deserve to move on. It doesn't have to be with Alex, but you did promise to be kinder to yourself, didn't you? I just wish you'd let someone in, a little bit. I want you to be happy.'

'I want you to be happy too. You deserve more than what Jack gave you, you know.'

Abbie sighed. 'We're a right pair, aren't we?'

Louise looked over at the Kindness Board and saw Eszter rubbing off the plea to find her earring. She touched her ear. She wished it was that easy to be kind to yourself. Abbie had jumped enthusiastically into their kindness pact and was doing a great job of helping Huntley Manor, and Eszter was persevering with her mother-in-law, but Louise just felt stuck.

Chapter Twelve

'What are you doing?' Thomas asked when he walked into Huntley Manor's library and found Abbie on her laptop in there.

'I was just drawing up a list of people to invite to the relaunch. We'll need to send out the invites soon or people will be busy. How did the meeting with the builders go?'

'It went okay. We've worked out a payment plan. Now I just need to speak to the bank about a second mortgage.'

'You'll convince them, I know it. Oh,' she paused as her phone buzzed in her hand. 'Jack has sent me a job link.'

'Is this the same Jack that stole all the credit?'

'Yes, and my ex,' Abbie admitted. She checked the link. 'Who seems to have forgotten I can't drive and this job needs someone who can.' She sighed. It was typical of him to not look at the fine print on anything. It was the third job he'd sent her that week. He was clearly trying to help, but she was still confused as to what had prompted him to get back in

touch so regularly. Plus all the jobs he was sending had something wrong with them. It was making her feel despondent about her prospects. Louise had said the job market went stale in the summer and Abbie shouldn't worry until September, but she was getting nervous about the gap on her CV.

'I could teach you.'

She looked up at Thomas, confused. 'Huh?'

'To drive. Come on, no time like the present.'

'Don't you have to speak to the bank?'

'They're shut. It'll have to wait until the morning. Come on; let me help you for a change.'

Sensing that he wasn't going to take no for an answer, Abbie got up and let Thomas lead her by the hand outside towards the jeep.

'Can I drive in these?' she asked, pointing down to her shoes.

'I'd rather you didn't on your first try. Here.' Thomas grabbed a pair of trainers from the stables. 'They look about your size.'

'Whose are they?'

He shrugged. 'Been there years.'

'You're a hoarder, you know that?'

'Shut up and get in,' he replied with a grin. She suddenly felt nervous. She hadn't needed to drive in London and whenever Louise suggested learning, she came up with an excuse. She liked to be good at things and something told her driving was going to be hard. On top of that, Thomas would be sitting very close and judging her the whole

time. She hung back, but he opened the door for her and gave her a stern 'no excuses' look, which she quite liked, to be honest.

Abbie was miles out of her comfort zone as Thomas went through all the gears and pedals with her, leaning over to show her things and making her more frustrated than she wanted to admit. Thomas was patient with her though and when she finally turned on the engine, his calmness helped her not to freak out when the car moved with a lurch.

She managed to make it move a little smoother as she drove across the field and tried to change gear a couple of times.

'There you go – you're driving,' Thomas said with a smile.

She couldn't help but beam back at him. 'I really am.'

They drove around the field a couple of times and then she pressed a bit too hard on the brake when he told her to pull over.

'Did I do okay?'

'You'll be passing your test in no time. Shall I drive us back?'

'Yeah, I don't want to try parking just yet.'

They swapped and Thomas took the jeep back to the stables. The car came to a stop and Abbie got out and started changing back into her heels right away. Aware that Thomas was watching her, she hopped about unattractively until he held her arm steady as she put her heels back on.

'Thanks,' she said as she straightened up. 'I just don't feel like me unless I'm in them.' She was now a tiny bit nearer his height and they looked at each other for a moment before

he released her arm. 'Thanks for the lesson; I think my sister would have made me too nervous.'

'That's the least I could do for ... oh, crap.' He broke off as the jeep started to roll back out of the stables. Abbie watched as Thomas leapt to the car door and leaned in to put the handbrake on. The jeep stopped with a jerk. 'And the next lesson is remembering to use the handbrake,' he said, looking wide-eyed at her. Abbie couldn't help it – she burst out laughing, and after a second he joined in too.

* * *

Eszter and Zoe went round to Louise's that night for a movie. Eszter was grateful to get out of the house and have some adult company. She was nervous about the letter she had left with Mrs Harris and she needed to follow through with her promise to go round there soon – the longer she put off seeing her mother-in-law again, the more nervous she was getting about it.

Louise opened the door and ushered them in after receiving the delicious chocolate cake they'd brought from Brew.

'I need this after today,' Eszter said, gratefully accepting the glass of wine Abbie gave her. 'Brew was so busy. There was a coach party who stopped on the way to a theme park and they all wanted bacon sandwiches. My hand actually hurts from frying.'

'The whole café smelt of bacon all day,' Zoe complained, taking her orange juice from Louise. 'But I finished my colouring book.'

'You two sound like you had a better day than me,' Louise replied. 'I got shouted at by a parent because their child didn't like their lunch.'

'Well, this will cheer you up,' Eszter said as they went into the living room. 'Alex came in today.'

'Why would that cheer me up?' Louise asked with a pointed look.

The doorbell rang and Abbie went to get the pizzas they had ordered, trying not to smile at her sister's defensive remark.

'He asked how you were. I think he was disappointed that you weren't around.'

'Food's up!' Abbie said, saving Louise from having to reply as she laid the pizzas out on the table – extra cheese for Zoe and Louise, and pepperoni for Abbie and Eszter. 'Well, my day beats all of yours then – I had my first driving lesson and Thomas almost killed us by forgetting to put the handbrake on in his jeep.' She pulled out a slice. 'Come to Mama.'

'I think my day was the best,' Zoe disagreed, taking a plate with two slices on from her mother.

'I think you're right, Zoe,' Louise agreed and they all smiled. 'Have you decided when you're going to go back to see your mother-in-law, Eszter?'

She nodded. 'Tomorrow. I can't put it off any longer.' She leaned behind her daughter who was picking out a DVD. 'I just don't know what to do if it goes as badly as last time.'

'Just kill her with kindness,' Abbie said in the middle of chewing her pizza.

Eszter looked shocked. 'You're suggesting I do what?'

Louise chuckled. 'It's one of our weird sayings. It just means you should be overly kind to her so she can't be rude or mean to you again.'

'But if she is, I think you just need to get the hell out of there,' Abbie said. 'Eszter shouldn't have to put up with that.'

'I think the letter will have helped, don't you?' Louise asked her.

Eszter shrugged. 'Honestly, I don't know. She was pretty vicious when I first met her, but if anyone can calm her down, it's Nick. I could never stay angry for long with him around,' she said as Zoe presented her with her film choice for the evening. 'What's another of your sayings here? Oh, yes. I'll just have to cross my fingers.'

'Then you won't be able to use them,' Zoe said, confused by that idea.

Eszter laughed. 'That's a good point.'

Chapter Thirteen

Eszter smoothed down her hair nervously. She had left Zoe with Harry and Joy in their flat above Brew. She was still too anxious about Mrs Harris to introduce Zoe to her yet. She hoped Nick's letter would have paved the way for a better welcome this time, but she certainly wasn't going to count on that being the case. She knocked on the door to the house, wondering if Mrs Harris would pretend not to be inside. She had a cake in her hand that Joy had made her take. If nothing else, it might be a peace offering. Joy was firmly of the opinion that cake could solve most things in life.

The door opened a crack and there was a sigh. 'It's you.'

'Did you read his letter?' Eszter asked, getting straight to the point. There was a silence, which she took to mean the woman had read it. 'Can I come in? Just for a minute? I have a cake from Brew, and could do with a cup of tea.' Eszter preferred coffee, but she knew what the English were like with their tea and she was certain Nick must have got

his five-cups-a-day habit from somewhere. There was more silence, then another sigh and the door opened. Mrs Harris walked away, which Eszter assumed was an invitation and followed her inside, closing the door behind her.

The house Nick grew up in was large with high ceilings and neutral carpet throughout. It was tidy and clean and smelt of lavender. Mrs Harris put the kettle on and pulled out two plates. Eszter handed her the cake and sat down, as she clearly wasn't going to be asked to. The kitchen had wooden cupboards and lemon walls and the patio doors opened out on to the wide garden. Eszter could see that the grass was slightly overgrown, but on the patio there were pots full of colourful flowers. It was evident that Mrs Harris took pride in her house. Eszter tried to look for any mementoes of Nick, but there were no pictures that she could see or any sign that anyone other than Mrs Harris had ever lived there.

They were silent as her mother-in-law made two cups of tea and brought them to the table with a small slice of Victoria sponge each. It looked very civilised, but Eszter saw Mrs Harris's hand shaking slightly as she put them down on the table and realised she was as tense as Eszter was.

'I know why you're here now,' Mrs Harris said as she sat down opposite Eszter. 'But that doesn't mean I am happy about it. I wanted my son, not you.'

'I understand that.'

'I hadn't seen him for nine years when he died. Nine years. He was playing happy families with you and forgetting all about me.'

'He didn't forget about you,' Eszter said. 'You read the letter – you were on his mind, even at the end. He regretted not trying to heal things between you. He didn't tell me much about what happened between you but it's clear he wished things had turned out differently. His letter was his last chance. I had to do as he asked.'

'Well, you've done what he wanted. You don't owe him more than that.'

'But I'd like to get to know you a bit more, and I'd like Zoe to meet you. Wouldn't you? I can tell you about Nick . . .'

'He was my son, you can't tell me anything about him that I don't already know,' Mrs Harris snapped.

'As you said, you hadn't seen him for nine years – I can fill in that time for you.'

'I suppose you blame me for not seeing him for all that time. He was the one who ran off to Europe; we didn't even know where he was for years.'

Eszter felt the woman's anger radiating across the table. 'I know. He did invite you to our wedding though.'

She shook her head. 'That's what he said in the letter, but I never saw an invitation so I don't know about that.'

Eszter was surprised. She knew how nervous Nick had been sending that and how eagerly he had checked the post for weeks until he realised that no RSVP was coming. 'I saw him send it. He wanted you there.'

'And then he didn't even come back for his father's funeral. I had to deal with everything alone.'

'And then you didn't come to his,' Eszter said quietly, only

then realising how angry she was that her mother-in-law didn't support her.

'It was too far. And I wanted to remember my son as he was.'

'I didn't have that luxury. I had to stand there and receive all the sympathies from his friends and colleagues. I had to look after our devastated daughter.'

'How old is she?'

'Zoe is seven. She looks just like him.' Eszter took out her phone and showed her a picture. Mrs Harris glanced at it briefly before looking away.

'I don't understand why he sent you here. It was a long time ago that he left Littlewood. I think the past is better off left buried.'

'Really? I think that's the last thing it should be,' Eszter said. 'My daughter has no connection to her father besides you. She needs her family now more than ever.'

'I told you that I have no money. All I have is this house and you'll have to move me out of here dead,' Mrs Harris snapped.

Eszter closed her eyes for a moment to try to control her temper. 'I keep telling you that I don't want anything from you. How could you read Nick's letter and still think that's why I'm here?'

'You have no idea what it was like when Nick left.'

'No, I don't, but I know how much I love Zoe and how I'd feel if I lost her. Nick didn't tell me why he left. He didn't talk about the past much at all. Like you, he wanted to bury

it, but his letter proves that he wasn't able to do that. He sent me here because he couldn't come himself. I think we both owe it to him—'

'I don't owe him anything,' Mrs Harris interrupted. 'He left me. I moved on. And now, so should you.'

'Nick asked me to give this to you.' Eszter hated how this second meeting was going, but he had asked her to give the watch back to his mother, so at the very least she was going to do that. She took it out of her bag and held it out for her. Nick had worn it every day and for some reason it had been important enough that he wanted his mother to have it now.

Mrs Harris stared at it, then stood up abruptly. 'Nick took that from us,' she said, her voice hard and bitter. 'It belonged to Frank. His father.'

'Maybe he wanted something to remind him of you both?' Eszter put it down on the table but Mrs Harris pushed it back to her.

'I don't want it.'

Eszter sighed and took the watch back, standing up. 'I'm staying in Littlewood for a while. Won't you let Zoe come and see you? Let her meet her grandmother?'

'You think I want anything to do with your daughter? You two stole my son from me.'

'You know very well that's not the case. Nick was the one who stayed away. I tried to persuade him to talk to you. I don't know what happened, but I'm starting to see why he left here.' Eszter started to walk away, fed up with her attitude.

'You have no idea what it was like!' Mrs Harris cried and followed her.

Eszter stopped and faced her. 'No, you're right, I don't. If you want to tell me, then that's fine. I'm trying to do what my husband wanted, but none of this is my fault.'

'If he hadn't met you then he would have come back.'

Eszter raised an eyebrow. 'Really? Or would you have never heard from him ever again?' They stared at one another. In the silence, Eszter heard a noise from upstairs and wondered if there was someone else there. 'I know that I'm not a substitute for your son, but you have a granddaughter who would love to meet you.' She saw then on the table in the hall a photo of Nick when he was at school, one of those posed ones that look formal and stiff. She recognised his smiling eyes though. It showed Mrs Harris had some feeling, surely? 'Wouldn't you want that?'

It seemed for a moment that she was softening, that she might come around, but then she shook her head with a stubbornness that made Eszter want to scream. 'I don't want anything to do with either of you,' she said coldly.

Now Eszter could see why Nick had walked away from his parents all those years ago. 'Fine,' she said.

I'm sorry, Nick, she thought, *but what else can I do here?* She flung open the door and walked out. Her mother-in-law obviously had no desire at all to heal the past.

Eszter wished her husband was there to help her know what to do but was also glad that he wasn't. At least he had died with the hope of reconciliation and would never have to know what had just happened between them.

Then suddenly behind her there was a loud crash, which made her jump and turn around. A cloud of dust spread out of the front door and she heard Mrs Harris cry out. Instinctively, Eszter hurried back to see what had happened and from the doorway she saw that the ceiling had collapsed and water was pouring down into the hall from upstairs. Mrs Harris was clutching the table in horror, her clothes covered in dust and a piece of the ceiling sat on her shoulder like an unwelcome parrot.

'I forgot the bath was running!' Mrs Harris broke the shocked silence with a wail and started to cry. Eszter looked up to see the underside of the bathroom now visible from the hall.

'Come on, it might completely collapse on us,' she said, leading the distraught Mrs Harris out into the driveway. She stood there wondering what to do as Mrs Harris sobbed, and suddenly she saw that this was a frightened, lonely old woman. Be kind to each other, Nick had said. Well, this woman was going to get her kindness now whether she liked it or not.

Chapter Fourteen

Abbie and Louise walked around the supermarket together, sharing the task of food shopping for the first time since they were kids. Abbie waved to someone down the frozen aisle and explained it was someone working at Huntley Manor.

Louise grinned. 'You've settled right in to Littlewood, haven't you?'

Abbie thought about it as she added a whole chicken to the trolley. It had only been a couple of weeks, but she did feel as if she'd been in the town for a lot longer than that. 'I suppose I have.'

'So, it's not proving too dull for you after London life?'

'I do miss having an H&M on my doorstep and there's no cocktail bar, but it's not as bad as I thought,' Abbie admitted. 'I can see why you've stayed here for two years.'

'You thought I was mad moving to a small town.'

'I didn't understand it, no, but I can see why you like the community here. It's much slower paced than London. I

suppose I do feel a bit more relaxed. I should be worrying that I haven't had any interview offers, but all this work I'm doing at Huntley Manor makes me wonder how I'd have the time if I did get one.'

'The job market is always slow over the summer, and you are working, just not getting paid. Voluntary work always looks good to employers.' Louise threw in the two types of bread they both liked.

'I hope so. I can't afford to keep working for free, or sponging off you.'

'It'll all be okay, I know it.'

Abbie wondered how Louise could be so positive when it came to her sister but not for her own life. Then her phone started to ring, so she walked away to answer it, leaving Louse to grab the milk. She was surprised to see the name on the screen, especially after talking to Louise about how settled she was feeling in Littlewood. London seemed very far away but now it all came rushing back.

'Abbie, darling,' Jack said warmly when she said hello. 'I've been thinking about you all morning. We had a meeting with Let's Eat and they asked where you were. I think they were disappointed you'd left the company.'

'You mean, been forced out,' Abbie replied. She was sure the client would be missing her; it was her ideas after all that had helped them become a success, not Jack's. Not that Jack would ever admit that, of course.

'Let's not dwell on that. I miss you. Can I come and see you?'

Abbie looked around her in surprise. The idea of Jack

strolling through the streets of Littlewood was far too strange to imagine, but then two weeks ago, she would never have pictured herself here either. 'Why?' she asked, wondering why he wasn't breaking off all contact between them as she assumed he would once she left the company.

'I just said – I miss you.'

'You can see why I'm confused though – you broke things off.'

'I have a proposition for you. We can't keep talking over the phone; we need to see each other again. There's still something between us, isn't there?'

Abbie thought for a moment. She really hadn't felt the urge to get in touch with him since leaving London, but she thought about how much passion she had felt for him just a couple of months ago and it was hard to know if that had been extinguished completely or not. Seeing him would make that decision for her, she was sure.

'Honestly, I don't know, but it would be good to see you,' she said, cautiously. She had been hurt by Jack, but Louise had been right that she hadn't completely fallen in love with him. And she was sure he hadn't loved her either, but maybe she had judged him too harshly.

'Thank you. So, can I come and see you next weekend? Where can I stay?'

'Huntley Manor,' she said immediately. She didn't want him at the cottage confusing her more, and Thomas needed the guests. Jack knew a lot of people in London and he could easily spread the word. 'I think you'll love it there.'

'If I get to see you then I definitely will.'

Jack hung up after telling her he'd call her when he'd made the reservation. She stood still for a moment, unsure if she was more excited or nervous at him coming. Louise was right that she hadn't been pining for London as much as she had thought she would, but thoughts of her previous life there now flooded in. What would Jack be offering her next weekend? A chance to rekindle their relationship? An opportunity to come back to the city?

Abbie didn't know what she wanted his visit to bring but she felt that change was on the horizon, whether she wanted it or not.

Louise was ducking down low by the jars of marmalade when Abbie came back. 'What are you doing?'

'Shh,' Louise hissed, pulling Abbie down beside her as Alex, the vet, walked along the supermarket aisle next to them, basket in hand. They watched as Alex disappeared out of sight and as he did, Louise's phone buzzed in her bag. She answered Eszter's call, standing up slowly.

'Hello?' she said in a low voice to make sure he didn't hear her. She could feel Abbie giving her a pointed look and her cheeks turned red.

'Louise, are you near Littlewood? There's been a slight disaster . . .' Eszter said in a frantic voice.

'What's happened?' Louise listened as Eszter told her the ceiling had just collapsed at her mother-in-law's house, and they needed help. 'Stay put, we'll be there as soon as we can.' Louise hurried to the checkout, telling Abbie what was going

on as they walked. They hurriedly paid for their shopping and got into the car to head back to town.

'What was that all about?' Abbie asked as they drove.

'What?'

'Hiding from Alex back there!'

Louise avoided her sister's gaze. 'I just didn't want to have to make small talk. I mean, look at me,' she admitted, gesturing to her old jeans and hoodie. She'd left off her make-up that morning and had been planning to wash her hair that night.

Abbie smirked. 'Didn't want to see him when you're not looking your best? And you told us you didn't care that he was attractive.'

'I don't!'

'I think the lady doth protest too much.'

Louise shook her head, wishing her sister would stop talking about him. Something about Alex made her feel nervous and she didn't want to analyse the reasons why.

They soon arrived outside Mrs Harris's house, and found Eszter and her mother-in-law standing in the driveway. The front door was open and as Louise and Abbie jumped out of the car, they could see the debris all over the floor.

'Are you okay?' Louise asked as they approached them.

'It was quite a shock,' Eszter replied, looking pleased to see them. She gestured for them to have a look at the mess. 'She can't stay here,' she hissed in a low voice as they stood in the doorway to assess the damage.

'Definitely not,' Abbie agreed.

'I turned the water off from the cupboard under the stairs; it looks too dangerous to go up there.'

'I know a builder at the Manor who can take a look. Does she have insurance?'

'I hope so,' Eszter said. She sighed. 'I'll talk to her.'

* * *

Eszter walked over to Mrs Harris, who had perched on a log in the garden. She looked much older suddenly and far less formidable than she had been when they had been arguing just half an hour ago. 'You really can't stay here, Mrs Harris. I'm taking you back to my cottage with me,' Eszter said firmly. She saw Mrs Harris was about to protest. 'No arguments. Is there anything you need which I can try to get?'

'My bag,' Mrs Harris said weakly, wiping her eyes and looking unsteady on her feet.

Eszter picked up the handbag from the hall table and locked the door with Mrs Harris's keys. Abbie and Louise got in the car to wait for them. She looked at her mother-in-law, who was gazing at her house shaking her head in disbelief. Eszter knew that Mrs Harris had no one else to help her so she would have to step in, but she doubted the woman would be happy about that.

'Right, Louise is going to drive us to my house, and we can sort out everything there. And have a cup of tea. Don't worry; it will all be okay,' Eszter promised. Eszter had always been good in a crisis and she ushered Mrs Harris into the car before she could stop her. Mrs Harris seemed to be in shock anyway.

Eszter looked back at the house as they drove away. She certainly hadn't planned for any of this when she stepped onto the plane Nick had booked for her. She was determined now to find out what had happened between them in the past and to heal the divide between them.

Which was definitely not going to be easy. But if there was one thing Eszter had always relished – it was a challenge.

She watched the town stream past the window as Louise drove them back to their cottages and she was sure for the first time since arriving in Littlewood that she was where she was supposed to be.

Notes from the Brew Kindness Board:

Someone left a copy of a book on the train with a note saying, 'This is my favourite – hope you love it too!' and it kept me gripped all weekend. I'm now going to leave it on the train so someone else can enjoy it.

* * *

Thank you to my friend Alice who saw I was exhausted and picked my son up from school and looked after my new baby so I could have my hair done. An hour alone being pampered was the best!

* * *

I was struggling to lift my shopping bags out of the trolley and into my boot at the supermarket after breaking my arm and a kind man walking past stopped to do it for me. Thank you for helping me!

* * *

My neighbour Steve – for looking after my cat for me so that I could go on my friend's hen weekend. A paws up from Whiskers and me!

Part Two

Making Friends

Chapter Fifteen

Eszter watched the sunrise outside the cottage. Her hands were wrapped around the mug of strong, black coffee she had just made, and she was relishing the bitter caffeine hit and having a few minutes to just think. Upstairs it was silent, but soon her daughter Zoe would be up and they'd both have to deal with their unexpected new houseguest.

Eszter had had to practically drag her mother-in-law Anne to their cottage the day before. Due to the shock of what had happened, Mrs Harris had retreated to bed early, leaving Eszter to sweep into action, phoning builders and the insurance company.

It had all happened so quickly that Eszter hadn't really had time to process much, but now, in the light of day, she was nervous about what would happen when the woman awoke. Relations between the two of them had been more than frosty and she wasn't sure what she could do to smooth things over.

Her phone vibrated beside her. It was Louise.

'I thought you'd be up,' Louise said when Eszter answered the phone. 'I'm just on my way to work and I wanted to see how you are?' Eszter had been very glad of Louise and Abbie's friendship over the past twenty-four hours. After taking them back to Eszter's cottage, they had both stayed until late to help Eszter sort everything out.

'I didn't sleep very well, to be honest, so I'm downing coffee as we speak.'

'I'm not surprised; it was all so dramatic. You dealt with everything so well, though, and I know that Mrs Harris will be grateful to you, even if she doesn't show it.'

Eszter had told Louise all about her argument with Mrs Harris, so she knew how difficult Eszter was finding the task of building bridges with her. 'I'm so grateful you were around to help. We need to go back to the house today and start sorting it all out. I'm nervous for her to wake up, to be honest.'

'I think it will be fine. Just focus on the tasks in hand and everything else will sort itself out. If you need me, just text me, okay?'

'Thanks, Louise.' Eszter said goodbye, wishing that she didn't have to deal with all of this on her own. Eszter was still struggling with how hard things were now without her husband to lean on.

A noise made her shake off her impending melancholy. She had to cope with things on her own now. Mostly because of the small, blonde girl who was shuffling into the kitchen and rubbing her eyes.

'Hi, darling,' Eszter greeted her daughter. She'd been up later than usual in all the drama. 'Are you hungry?'

'Of course, it's breakfast time,' Zoe said with her usual deadpan expression. Eszter hid a smile. Zoe was a real character sometimes. Eszter gave her a bowl of cereal and a glass of juice but didn't think she could face eating herself. 'How long is she going to be in my room?'

Eszter followed her daughter's gaze to the ceiling where there was some definite movement happening. 'Until it's safe for her to go back to her house.'

'Do I call her "grandmother"?'

'I'll get back to you on that one.' They both fell silent as they heard footsteps on the stairs and in walked Mrs Harris, wearing her clothes from the day before. 'Morning, Mrs Harris. Would you like a cup of tea?' Eszter asked, getting up to switch the kettle on.

'Yes, please,' she said as she sat down stiffly at the table and eyed Zoe. She had spent much of the previous afternoon glancing at her granddaughter and Eszter knew she could see the resemblance between Zoe and her son. Sometimes even she was startled by it. She liked it, though – it meant Nick was still part of her life through his daughter.

'Did you sleep well?' Zoe asked her grandmother as she ate her cereal.

Mrs Harris looked even more shocked at being addressed by her. She accepted the tea from Eszter, who rejoined them at the table. 'Not really, I haven't slept anywhere but my own house for a long time.'

115

'We can collect some more of your things when it's safe to go in. They're sending an assessor round to look at the damage,' Eszter said.

'I do appreciate what you did yesterday, but it's really unnecessary for me to stay here any longer,' she replied.

'It's not safe for you to go home at the moment, not until they check the whole ceiling won't collapse. And it's fine for you to stay here until then,' Eszter said, cutting in. 'You're family,' she added, to remind herself more than anything.

Mrs Harris looked at her and then at Zoe before taking a sip of her tea, apparently at a loss as to what to say.

'It'll be good for us to all get to know one another,' Eszter said, hoping her voice sounded more cheerful than she felt. She glanced at a rather nervous-looking Zoe, but she thought of her beloved Nick and how much he wanted them to do this and she knew they had to see it through. 'Zoe, show your grandmother where the towels are. I'm sure she will want a nice relaxing bath before we go back to her house.' Neither Zoe nor Mrs Harris dared to contradict her and she watched them go upstairs. She sent up a silent plea to Nick for help in bringing the three of them together.

Chapter Sixteen

Louise walked into her morning shift at the hospital, taking a big gulp of the takeaway coffee she had picked up from Brew. She greeted Julie in the staff room as she stored her things in her locker.

'I saw Hazel and her mother on my way in. They think she'll be going home later today,' Julie said. Louise turned around in surprise and smiled.

'That's such wonderful news,' she said, glad that the day was starting off so well. Hazel had been on the paediatric ward for a long time, suffering with cancer, but her latest treatment had gone well and the doctor was obviously confident enough to let her become an outpatient again. Louise made her way straight to Hazel's cubicle when her shift started.

Hazel was in bed clutching the teddy Louise had given her and her mum Sarah was beginning to pack up her things.

'Guess what?' Hazel cried when she saw her.

'What?' Louise asked, not wanting to ruin the little girl's excitement at telling her the news herself. She exchanged a smile with her mother, though. The woman looked so relieved that Louise's heart swelled for her.

'I get to go home today!'

'That is brilliant news!'

'Will you miss me, though?'

'Of course I will, but I'll be happy that you're getting better at home.'

'We can't thank you enough for looking after Hazel so well,' Sarah said.

'No thanks needed, this is my job.'

'You went above and beyond,' she said, enveloping her in a hug.

This is what she got into nursing for, Louise thought as she went back to the nurses' station. She was so happy that Hazel was on the road to recovery and that she might have helped in some small way.

* * *

The morning went quickly as Louise moved from cubicle to cubicle, helping her patients. It was with a sigh of relief that she walked outside on her break, desperate for some fresh air, only to bump straight into a tall man who was hurrying into the hospital.

'Ouch,' Louise said as her shoulder collided painfully with his.

'Oh, I'm so sorry,' the man said as he steadied her arm,

then stepped back and looked at her. 'Louise! Just the person I was coming to see,' he said when he recognised her, a charming smile spreading across his face.

Louise found her cheeks immediately started to burn up as she realised it was Alex the vet, Hazel's uncle, and the rescuer of her lost earrings. She didn't know why he seemed to make her both curious and nervous.

'Why was that?' she asked, when she realised she had been staring at him in silence.

'To give you these,' he said, pulling a large bouquet of flowers from behind his back with a flourish. 'I had to get them to say thank you for looking after our Hazel so wonderfully.' He handed them to her and she breathed in the scent of the yellow roses. Her favourites.

Louise was taken aback. 'You really didn't need to do that. I was just doing my job.'

'It's not a totally selfless act,' Alex said then, running a hand through his hair. 'I did wonder if you might want to grab a coffee together sometime soon?'

'Why?' she asked without thinking.

'Well, it would be, uh, nice to get to know you better,' he stammered, blushing, which annoyingly made him look cuter.

Louise wished she didn't find him attractive. She turned even redder along with him and she looked down at the flowers, for a second wishing that things were different. If only she could just say yes to getting to know him better, but the past wouldn't let her.

'Um, look, Alex, thank you for the flowers, and for finding my earring, but I'm not really looking to date. Anyone.' Louise had checked Facebook before she left for work and had seen more congratulations pouring in for the man who had broken her heart who was now engaged to someone else.

The thought of putting herself 'out there' again just wasn't something she felt even remotely keen on doing. Although she'd be lying if she said she wasn't flattered that Alex was interested in her, or that a tinge of regret hadn't accompanied her words.

'I'm sorry, Alex,' she said, hating to see the look of disappointment on his face.

He forced out a smile. 'I understand. As you know, I'm always in Brew, so if you ever change your mind . . .' He trailed off and gave her an awkward wave, before he quickly walked off into the hospital, his head down.

Louise's heart sank as she looked at the yellow roses he had given her, amazed that he had chosen the flowers she liked the most.

Someone pushed past her and she realised she was standing right in the way of everyone, so she turned to head to the canteen, wondering why she couldn't be a hundred per cent sure that she had made the right decision in saying no to Alex.

Chapter Seventeen

'I think that should go over there,' Abbie said to the men, pointing to the corner of the reception area and watching as the chef and gardener from the Huntley Manor Hotel moved the new plant she had found at the local garden centre into the bare space. 'Perfect!'

She looked around the reception, which it was her mission to spruce up today.

'Wow, it looks so much better,' Amy, the receptionist said, twirling around to take it all in. They had started early and the room was already looking so much more inviting. They didn't have much money to make changes so Abbie had been bargain hunting. She had found two leather armchairs at a second-hand shop to replace the threadbare sofa and, as well as the plant, had put up a couple of beautiful old paintings she had found in the attic. The room had been cleaned thoroughly and the final touch was a vase of flowers, freshly picked from the grounds, on the now polished and shiny reception desk.

'I think we can call this a job well done,' Abbie agreed, smiling at them all. The phone rang and Amy told her that Thomas wanted to see her in the ballroom. Abbie was pleased that when the phone rang again straight away, it was someone calling for a room.

Since setting up social media accounts and giving Amy responsibility for updating them regularly, they'd already taken a few more bookings over the summer. People were actually starting to hear about the hotel.

Abbie walked from the reception to the ballroom, which was currently being renovated for their planned relaunch party at the end of the summer. Abbie was confident their work would pay off. Even now, with the room no more than a building site, she felt a thrill of excitement. This ballroom had been the scene of some grand parties in years gone by and she was sure it would be again.

'I have good news,' she called out as she walked through the door.

Thomas turned and smiled, holding out a hand to help her step around a pile of scaffolding on the floor. He wore a suit, as usual, paired with his wellington boots. He was still so much taller than her, even though she was wearing her high-heeled shoes, and she had to look up to meet his gaze.

'What's the news?'

Abbie had to remind herself that he was actually a lord. It seemed so strange, when he was only thirty, that he owned this vast estate and was trying to run it single-handedly after his parents died. It had been a tough couple of years for him and the

business, and she hoped that she was making things easier for him. 'I got a company to agree to fit our bathrooms with toiletries in return for us promoting them and selling the products.'

The bedrooms at the hotel were stunning but they lacked amenities that guests now expected of hotels. Abbie's next task was to get working Wi-Fi for the hotel and, when they had enough money, persuade Thomas that the rooms should all have flat-screen TVs, but one step at a time.

'That is good news,' Thomas replied, his dark eyes twinkling at her. 'We are well on our way. And see how much better the ceiling looks already.' He pointed above them, where workers on scaffolding were cleaning the ceiling. The chandelier had been sent away to be refurbished and Abbie was certain it would be a glittering centrepiece again soon.

'It is really starting to take shape. We'll need to get our guest list sorted for the party today; the invites need to go out, as we only have six weeks.'

He ran a hand through his dark, floppy hair, then gestured to her. 'Lead the way, boss.'

Abbie laughed and they walked out of the ballroom and to Thomas's office in what was the former library. She showed him the list of people she had started to invite – past guests at the hotel, press, both local and national, people she knew in London who needed to use hotels a lot, and names she had found on old event lists that he had given her. Thomas also had lots of family and friends who would want to support the event and he reeled them off as Abbie added the names to a spreadsheet on her laptop.

When they had finished, Thomas suggested they have a second driving lesson. 'We could head out to Littlewood this time?'

Abbie shook her head. 'The estate is fine for now,' she said, instantly nervous about getting back behind the wheel.

'Okay. One step at a time.' They walked out to his jeep, parked by the stables, and ran through the controls again.

Abbie took the car gently down the track that ran round the perimeter of the vast grounds. The windows were all rolled down to let in some of the July breeze.

'What are you doing on Friday?' Thomas asked as they drove bumpily through a clump of trees. Abbie was pleased for once that there weren't many guests around. She would rather no one witness her attempts at driving. Thomas was smiling though, so hopefully she wasn't too much of a danger.

'Nothing, why?' Abbie still hadn't mentioned to him that her ex – Jack – was coming to visit, but she knew she'd have to as he would be staying at Huntley Manor; Thomas was bound to see them together. She wasn't sure why she was hesitating in announcing it, maybe because she had told Thomas that she felt Jack hadn't appreciated her enough at work and had taken credit for some of her ideas. She wished she hadn't let her hurt loosen her tongue so much.

'I thought we could have dinner together. If you'd like?' Then he gasped. 'Look out!'

Abbie swerved at the last moment to avoid a massive oak tree. She quickly slammed her foot on the brake and the car stopped as she sucked in hasty breaths. Beside her, Thomas

had gone pale. 'That was close,' she said, putting her hand on her heart.

'Was it something I said?'

Abbie blushed. The dinner invite had thrown her and she hadn't noticed the tree until the scary last minute. 'My foot slipped,' she lied weakly.

'Well? Providing we live until Friday, will you let me cook for you?'

Abbie loved how polite he always was, his cultured voice making most things he said sound as if they were coming from one of her literary heroes.

'You can cook?' she asked, trying to lighten the tense atmosphere in the small space between them. She was suddenly eager to get out of the car and into the fresh air.

'I'm no Jamie Oliver, but hopefully I won't poison you. Is that a yes?'

She nodded and found she couldn't look at him. 'Yes, please.'

'I'll see you at seven then. Now, can you drive us back in one piece, do you think?'

She elbowed him firmly in the ribs, making him laugh, and she was relieved the tension between them had broken.

Chapter Eighteen

When Abbie returned to the cottage that night, Louise was in the kitchen making dinner for the two of them. 'What a day!' Abbie said, dumping her bag on the floor and climbing up onto the kitchen stool.

'Wine?' Louise slid a glass over to her.

'Lovely.' Abbie took a sip, then her eyes fell on the vase of yellow roses next to Louise as she made a salad. 'Who are they from?'

'Oh,' Louise said, her eyes flitting to the flowers then back to the salad. She looked a little flushed. 'They're from Alex.'

'Alex? The Alex who found your earring? The dishy vet?'

Louise rolled her eyes. 'Yes. He came by the hospital to thank me for looking after his niece.'

'And?' Abbie could always tell when Louise was holding something back.

Louise sighed. 'He asked me to go for coffee,' she said in

a rush, but before Abbie could get excited, she told her she had turned him down.

'You said no?! Why?' Abbie was confused. She was sure she had seen a spark in her sister's eyes when she looked at Alex. And who could blame her? He was good-looking and seemed really nice, plus he looked after animals, and Louise was all about caring for others. To Abbie, they seemed like a perfect match.

'Abs, I hardly know him!'

'That's the point of having coffee with him. I knew he liked you – it was written all over his face when we saw him in Brew.' She watched her sister add chicken to the salad. She hated that Louise had become so closed off to the opposite sex. 'Is this about Peter?'

Louise shook her head. 'No . . . well, not exactly.'

'What is it then, exactly?'

Louise ducked her head a little. 'I don't want my heart broken again,' she replied in a small voice.

Abbie wished she could take her sister's pain away. 'Lou, it's been two years. You can't let Peter destroy any chance you have of being happy. Everyone is nervous at the start of a new relationship, no one wants their heart broken, but it's about taking that leap. It's a chance we all have to take, isn't it?'

'I'm not ready,' Louise said stubbornly.

'I don't think anyone is ever ready.' Abbie decided to tell her that Thomas had asked her over for dinner. 'I don't want to get hurt again either,' she told her. 'I was really hurt when Jack distanced himself from me; it had felt like the start of

something special. And then he told me I'd lost my job. It's not easy for me to trust a man again either.'

'But seeing you get hurt just makes me more scared,' Louise confessed. 'I'm happy on my own.'

'Are you?' Abbie asked her pointedly. She knew that Louise had a big heart; she had so much love to give, and she deserved to be loved in return. 'Don't forget our Kindness Pact,' she reminded her. They had promised each other at the start of the summer to add some kindness into their lives. Abbie had done her part by helping Thomas Huntley, and Louise was meant to be acting more kindly to herself. 'You should give Alex a chance.'

'Are you going to give Thomas a chance? What about Jack?'

Abbie was confused as to how she felt about Jack coming for the weekend. She had been enjoying staying in Littlewood, and it felt worlds apart from her life with Jack in the big city, but she was curious to find out why he wanted to see her. She was enjoying working with Thomas and had definitely felt a spark between them in the car, though.

She shook her head at her sister. 'Fine, it's going to be complicated, but I'm going to see what happens. I'd rather be open than close myself off to the both of them.'

'Even if one of them isn't good for you.'

'Well, I hope I'd realise that before I got too hurt.'

'I didn't, and that's what worries me.'

'Peter wasn't the right man for you.' Abbie really hoped that Louise would one day realise that Peter actually did her

a favour by leaving her before they got married. 'Will you think about Alex for me, please?'

'Dinner's ready so let's change the subject,' Louise said, grabbing two plates for them.

'Lou,' Abbie said sternly. She didn't want her sister to miss out on a chance with Alex but was at a loss as to how to show her that love didn't have to be something to be scared of.

'Fine, I'll think about it,' Louise muttered.

* * *

Abbie stopped by Brew on the way to Huntley Manor in the morning. There were two people in bright pink T-shirts at the counter talking to Joy and handing her a bunch of leaflets.

'This is Abbie,' Joy said when she saw her. 'Abbie, this is Jenny and Martin. They work for Littlewood Animal Rescue.'

'We're having our annual fete this weekend,' Jenny explained, handing Abbie a leaflet. 'We always need volunteers, in case you'd be interested.' She turned back to Joy. 'I don't know where we're going to find another vet at such short notice.'

'Their vet is having to go to London to help with a surgery,' Joy explained to Abbie, who was looking at the leaflet with interest. The fete was to raise funds for the charity and encourage people to adopt their animals.

'What about Alex?' Abbie said, looking up. 'Have you asked him?'

Joy beamed at her. 'What a great idea, I'm sure he'd be willing to help out.'

'Is that the vet in the high street? We haven't had much to do with him, but I've heard good things,' Jenny said.

Abbie's mind started whirring. 'I could ask him for you,' she offered, wondering if she could use the opportunity to put in a good word for Louise. She didn't want her sister to have completely discouraged him.

'Really?' Martin said. 'That would be great.'

'And you need more volunteers, did you say? Leave it to me.' Abbie got a coffee and left, practically skipping along the pavement towards the vet surgery. She was sure she could persuade Alex to help out at the fete and hoped she could also do some matchmaking while she was at it.

Abbie felt like a wannabe spy as she checked over her shoulder before opening the door to Littlewood Vet Surgery to make sure Louise was nowhere to be seen.

Abbie approached the reception desk. 'Is Alex in, please?'

'Do you have an appointment?'

'No but . . .'

'That's okay,' Alex himself said, appearing behind them. 'How can I help, um . . .'

'Abbie,' she said quickly. 'Louise's sister. We met briefly in Brew?'

He nodded. 'Of course. Come on through,' he said, looking curious as to why she was there. He led her into the consulting room. 'Do you have a pet you need help with?' he asked her after she shut the door.

'No, actually I came to ask you a favour.' She showed him the Littlewood Animal Rescue Fete leaflet. 'It's going to be

an important day for the charity, but their vet has had to go to London, and they really need someone there to answer any questions people might have about adopting one of their animals.'

He took the leaflet and nodded. 'That sounds sensible.'

She smiled. 'And we wondered if you could be that vet?'

Alex raised an eyebrow. 'Oh, right. Do you work with them, then?'

Abbie thought quickly. 'Well, actually, I will be volunteering there too, and Louise told me what a good vet you are, so when they said they needed one, I thought of you,' she said in a rush, hoping flattery would help and that he'd like the fact Louise thought highly of him.

Alex did in fact smile at that. 'Oh, well then, how can I say no?'

'Really? Oh wow, thank you! I'll get Jenny, the organiser, to call you with all the details then.'

'Great. And I'll see you there then. What about Louise? Is she volunteering too?'

'She is,' Abbie replied, firmly. She was certain that she could persuade Louise to help out, then she and Alex could bond over animals in need. It was right up Louise's street. She wouldn't be able to say no if she thought the charity needed her; Abbie knew her too well. And if she spent the day with Alex, then surely she would see that there was nothing to be scared of, that she should take a chance on him.

Alex grinned. 'Oh, well, that's great. We'll all be there, then.'

'Yes, yes we will.' They stared at one another, smiling. Abbie was thrilled he seemed excited to see Louise there; she knew that if her sister just gave him a bit of encouragement, he would forget about her rejection at the hospital. She clapped her hands together. 'Excellent. I'll let you get on then, and thanks again for giving your time. I know they'll really appreciate it.'

'It's no problem; it's for a great cause.'

'Plus, if you get people to adopt animals, you'll get more customers here.'

Alex laughed. 'That's a good point.'

Abbie waved and left the vet's, thrilled Alex had agreed to volunteer. Now all she had to do was persuade Louise to go along as well. Abbie realised as she walked away that she couldn't be there, as that was when Jack would be arriving. But maybe that was a good thing. She could tell Louise she had volunteered before Jack had told her he was coming and beg Louise to take her spot instead.

If only it was as easy to sort out her own love life.

Chapter Nineteen

'I'd say a week at least.' The builder sent by the insurance company gave his verdict to Eszter and her mother-in-law as the three of them stood in her hall looking up at the collapsed ceiling. 'You'd better stay elsewhere while we do the work; the bathroom will be out of use, as will down here, and there will be a lot of dust.'

'It's no problem, you can carry on staying with us. Do you want to pack a bag?' Eszter asked Mrs Harris, who was looking at the mess in her house with a stricken expression on her face. Eszter touched her arm for a moment, then withdrew it, sure that her mother-in-law wouldn't appreciate it. 'I know it looks a real mess, but they will get it looking as good as new, won't you?'

The builder nodded. 'Don't worry, it will be fine.'

'Do you want me to help you?' Eszter asked.

Mrs Harris started climbing the stairs carefully and didn't object, so Eszter followed her up into the older woman's

bedroom. It was strange for Eszter to think of her late husband Nick climbing these very same stairs. She tried to picture him growing up here, but she had only known him in her own country, their city apartment, walking the streets of Budapest hand in hand, and Littlewood was very far removed from that world. The Harris house was large and clean, but it lacked warmth somehow. Perhaps because the family it had once nurtured was gone; only Anne now remained.

'Do you have a bag?'

'At the top of the wardrobe.' Mrs Harris began opening drawers and pulling out clothes as Eszter pulled down the large holdall for her.

Eszter noticed two photographs in frames on the bedside table and bent down to look at them. One was of Anne on her wedding day and the other was of her holding a boy's hand – he was in his school uniform and they both beamed at the camera.

'Zoe has his exact smile,' Eszter said, looking at it and thinking of her daughter, who was with Joy and Harry at Brew.

'I noticed that as soon as I saw her,' Mrs Harris said.

'Nick would be so pleased that you got to meet her,' Eszter said carefully. She didn't want to start another argument, but she needed to know about the past if they had any chance of building a future relationship with one another.

'He didn't even tell me about her.' She kept her back to Eszter as she packed her bag.

'After you didn't come to the wedding, he thought that

was it as far as any contact between you went. I suppose he didn't think you'd want to know,' she replied, gently.

Mrs Harris's shoulders sagged. 'I keep telling you that he didn't invite us to your wedding. I would have come. I would have.' She stopped and turned around. 'Are you really sure he sent us an invitation?'

'I promise you. I saw him write it and posted it myself.'

'Oh.' She turned away again.

Eszter walked over to her. 'Mrs Harris . . .'

'I suppose you can call me Anne.'

Eszter nodded. 'Anne – is it at all possible that your husband saw the invitation but didn't tell you about it?' She knew that their estrangement had had a lot to do with Nick's father, and she could see the truth on Anne's face – she would have come to the wedding if she had known about it. Maybe her husband had known that and made the decision for them both.

There was a long silence as Anne kept folding clothes, and Eszter wasn't sure she was going to answer her, but finally she did. 'Nick's father was not always an easy man, and Nick disappointed him. I tried to make peace between them, but Frank, Nick's father, disowned him when he left us. Perhaps I should have been stronger, but it was different in my day. You respected your husband, you took vows to obey. I had nothing of my own, do you understand? It's not like I could leave him.' Sadness welled in her eyes until she looked away. 'So, yes, if we received the invitation, he could have decided not to show me because he knew I'd

want to go. No wonder Nick was so cold when he spoke to me after Frank died. He thought that I hadn't wanted to see him get married.'

'When I told Joy, at Brew, who I was when I first got here, she told me that Nick had trained to be a doctor. Is that true?'

Anne nodded. 'It was all Frank ever wanted for him. He was strict, I won't deny that, and he wanted Nick to be the best. Nick didn't really want to be a doctor, but he went to medical school to please us. I was proud of him. I wanted him to be as successful as his father.' She shook her head. 'Did I make mistakes? Yes. We both did. But I never thought that Nick would leave and never come back.'

'He was a teacher in Hungary; he really loved it,' Eszter explained.

'I'm glad of it.'

'So, Nick decided he didn't want to be a doctor and that's what the last argument was about? He told me that there was a great divide between you all and he couldn't see how to cross it.'

Anne nodded, and carried on folding clothes as if it was too painful to look at Eszter.

'He didn't plan to stay away, he told me. He wanted to travel, and then he met me, and couldn't imagine coming back home. But as the years passed, he thought about you both a lot; he wanted to build a relationship again. That's why he invited you to the wedding.' Eszter could see how painful talking of the past was for Anne, but she knew they had to do it. 'Do you have everything you need?'

She sighed. 'Yes, I think so.' She zipped up her bag. 'Eszter, I know that I was very unwelcoming when you first arrived.'

'I understood.'

Anne nodded. 'I am glad Nick had a family. That he was happy. I am glad of that.'

The two of them left the house and walked slowly to Brew to collect Zoe. As they strolled through Littlewood, Anne was looking around the high street in interest.

'I have lived here all my life, but I haven't been out and about in the town as much as I used to. When Frank died, it was hard being on my own and then perhaps I got too used to it.'

'I felt really lonely after Nick died, being in the apartment without him, but thankfully I had Zoe. Coming here has been good for us, I think. Seeing where he lived, I feel close to Nick but also not trapped by memories of our old life. Does time really heal, do you think?'

'Some things you never get over, but you learn to live with them.'

Eszter was sure that Anne was thinking of her own life as they went into Brew. She couldn't imagine what kind of man her husband had been; it sounded like he had been strict and controlling with his wife and son, pushing Nick away with his demands. She could tell that her mother-in-law bitterly regretted the past and she was full of sadness that she and Nick never got the chance to reconcile. Eszter just hoped she was helping them both in some way by being there in his place.

'Mum!' Zoe called when they walked into Brew. Eszter smiled to see her at the table with Abbie and Joy, tea and cake served for the three of them.

'Look what's happening on Saturday. Can we go, please?' Zoe pointed at a leaflet that Abbie had.

'An animal charity is having a fete on Littlewood Green,' Abbie explained, showing her the leaflet. 'Louise is volunteering,' she added with a smile.

'Let's all go,' Eszter agreed readily, pleased to see Zoe so excited to go and happy to get involved in more of Littlewood's activities.

'You'll have to tell me all about it,' Abbie said. 'A friend from London is coming to stay for the weekend, so I can't make it.'

'Will there be a lot of animals there?'

'I'm sure there will be,' Eszter said to her daughter, hoping to avoid the 'can I have a puppy?' conversation if at all possible.

'It's good to see you in here again, Anne,' Joy said, getting up. 'I'll get you both some tea, you look like you could do with it.'

Eszter wondered if there was anything that happened in Littlewood that couldn't be helped by having tea at Brew, and very much doubted it.

Chapter Twenty

Abbie slid the Littlewood Animal Rescue Fete leaflet across the kitchen counter to her sister. 'I have a massive favour to ask you. Now that Jack is coming to stay this weekend, I can't volunteer for this anymore. I don't want to let them down, though, and since you're off work that day, I thought you could go instead.'

'Oh, you did, did you?'

'Please, Lou, the animals need you!'

'I thought you said I needed to be kinder to myself? I was planning to veg all day in my pyjamas and watch Netflix.'

'You can do that when you get home. Please, I feel really bad about letting them down. And, if you think about it, it's really your fault for encouraging me to do these acts of kindness. I just couldn't say no when they asked me to volunteer, but now Jack will be here.'

Louise rolled her eyes at her sister's attempt at a puppy-dog look. She sighed. 'Fine, but I'm ordering a curry afterwards, and it's on you.'

'I'll get you some ice cream too.' Abbie beamed at her. 'You're a star.'

'And how are you feeling about Jack coming, anyway?' Louise wasn't at all convinced this visit was a good idea. She was trying to keep her thoughts about Jack to herself, but it seemed strange to her that after breaking up with her sister and letting her go from the company they worked at, now suddenly he realised he missed her. She hoped he was genuine and wasn't messing with Abbie's head.

'I told Thomas earlier that Jack would be staying at Huntley Manor for two nights.'

'What did he say?'

'Not much, just asked me why he was coming, and I said I wasn't sure. It's going to be very strange having them both in the same place.'

'Especially now that Thomas has asked you out.'

'It's just dinner, no need to read too much into it,' Abbie said, looking a little unconvinced herself.

'Be careful, Abs. I don't want you to get hurt.'

'I'm a big girl. I can take care of myself.'

Louise watched her get up and walk into the living room. Maybe this fete would be a good thing. It would beat sitting in the cottage on her own all day worrying about Abbie, with inevitable thoughts of the past leaking in as well. She couldn't help but see the pictures of the animals on the leaflet and think briefly of Alex. She hadn't seen him since he asked her out, now that Hazel had gone home. She had found herself glancing around Brew when she went today, but they

obviously got their coffee at different times. She told herself that it was for the best anyway, because if they saw each other again, it was bound to be awkward.

If only Abbie was as sensible when it came to men. Louise had turned down a date, while her sister had somehow accepted two, and she didn't even seem to grasp the fact. Louise hoped it wouldn't all end in tears, but when was anything to do with romance ever plain sailing?

* * *

Eszter watched as Anne prepared dinner for them in the kitchen. She had insisted on making them a cottage pie to say thank you. Now that she was staying with them for a week, she wanted to make herself useful. Eszter was happy to let her take control in the kitchen, and the smell coming from the oven was making her stomach rumble. Zoe was reading a book at the table, and the radio was playing softly in the background. Eszter sipped her glass of wine as she sat opposite her daughter. Anne had refused the wine. She seemed to live on cups of tea.

'Have you read this?' Zoe asked her mother, showing her the book. In the spare room of the cottage, they had found lots of books on a large bookcase and Zoe was eagerly delving into them. She was an avid reader – something that Nick had instilled in her. The two of them had always been reading together, either aloud or curled up on the sofa with a book each, making Eszter's heart sing. Zoe held up *Anne of Green Gables*. Eszter shook her head, but Anne turned around.

'That was my favourite book when I was young,' she said, looking at it. 'My mother bought it for me because I had the same name as the main character, and I loved it from the first page.'

'It's very good,' Zoe said, nodding.

'Do you have a favourite book?' Anne asked, leaning down to look at the pie in the oven. Eszter was pleased to see her chatting to her granddaughter and gave Zoe an encouraging smile.

'I like *Matilda*. I asked Mum if I could change my name to that, but she said no.' She gave her mother a disparaging look.

Anne chuckled. 'Quite right too, Zoe is a lovely name. Now, the cottage pie should be ready. I'll dish up,' she said, briskly attending to the food.

Eszter was surprised to be complimented on her daughter's name. Anne couldn't know, but Eszter had chosen it because her own grandmother, who had died when she was just a teenager, had been named Zoe and her daughter was turning out to be just as much a force of nature as her namesake.

Anne piled their plates with steaming cottage pie and they all tucked in eagerly. 'This was your daddy's favourite meal when he was your age,' Anne volunteered then, smiling fondly at the memory.

'I like it,' Zoe declared after tasting it.

'It's delicious, thank you,' Eszter said. It reminded her of her own mother's stews – comfort food to sit down to as a family. 'You'll have to give me the recipe.'

'You wouldn't be able to make it as good, Mum.'

'Well, I can try, darling.' Children really kept your self-esteem at bay sometimes.

After dinner, once Zoe was tucked up in bed, Eszter joined Anne downstairs as the sun finally began to set. Anne put on her favourite soap on TV and told Eszter all about it as they watched it together.

'Zoe is really looking forward to the fete on Saturday,' Eszter said when they had turned off the TV and were preparing to head to bed themselves.

'I haven't been to a local event in a very long time. I was always part of them when I was younger. I used to love the community spirit here,' Anne said.

'It's definitely still alive,' Eszter told her. 'We would have been stuck if it hadn't been for the help of the people who live here. It's a real contrast to living in a city.'

'That's why I never wanted to leave Littlewood. I was born here, and so was Frank, and it has always been home. I suppose after he died, I found it harder to be involved in things without him.'

Eszter nodded. 'I know what you mean. Without Nick, everything has seemed more difficult. I sometimes can't believe we actually made it here. But I'm glad he pushed me to bring Zoe over. I think we're going to have a lovely summer here.'

'You really loved Nick, didn't you?' her mother-in-law asked her quietly, looking down at her hands.

'I did, and I always will.'

Anne turned to smile at Eszter. 'I had a lovely evening,

thank you. You didn't need to take me in, especially after everything I said, so I am very grateful.'

Eszter smiled back. 'It's our pleasure. We came here to get to know you, so I'm really pleased that you're staying with us.'

Anne went into the bathroom and Eszter ducked into her room to pick up the watch that Nick always wore, which she now knew to have been his father's. Anne hadn't wanted to accept it before, but Eszter was sure it had been a reluctance to acknowledge just how much it meant to her.

Eszter went softly into Anne's room and laid the watch on her bed. She had been sent to Littlewood to give it back to her and she was happy to have done what her husband had asked of her. She went into her own room again and closed the door, looking forward to climbing into bed after a long day. She knew it would always be sad that Nick hadn't been able to come with them to Littlewood and make peace with his mother himself, but she felt a sense of pride that she had been able to do it for him.

Eszter was determined to bring Anne back into the community so that when they left, she wouldn't be so lonely and isolated anymore. She couldn't imagine living in this town and not being a part of it; she already felt as if the people here had embraced her and Zoe, and she wished she could return all their kindness. Anne needed to remember just why she was so lucky to live in Littlewood, and Eszter couldn't wait to show her.

Chapter Twenty-one

As Abbie got ready for her meal with Thomas, Louise watched her from the chair by her bed. 'Are you nervous?' Louise asked, as Abbie sprayed even more perfume on herself.

Abbie sighed. She had been playing this meal down, but she was nervous, and wanted to look her best. She had chosen a floral tea dress with wedges, her dark hair loose over her shoulders, and her favourite lip gloss on her lips. 'I don't know. Maybe. Is this okay?'

'It's perfect, Abs. I'll drive you so you don't have to walk in those,' Louise said, giving her shoes a disapproving look. Abbie laughed but accepted the offer and they walked downstairs together.

'I can't believe Jack will be here tomorrow,' Abbie said, grabbing her bag and following Louise out to her car. 'It will be strange to see him here in Littlewood. When I think of Jack, I think of London and vice versa.'

'That's how I used to think about you,' Louise said with a

smile as they climbed in and set off for Huntley Manor. 'And now you're part of the furniture.'

'I'll try to take that as a compliment!' Abbie couldn't ever picture Jack fitting in in Littlewood.

The sun had started to dip slightly in the sky. It had been a stunning summer's day and the evening was continuing the same way.

Louise pulled up outside the stately home, which looked magical in the fading light. 'Enjoy,' she said, winking at Abbie as she got out of the car. Abbie just rolled her eyes at her sister and walked away.

She headed through the oak front door and towards Thomas's apartment, hoping she looked cool and calm. Her phone beeped as she made her way there, and she checked it quickly. It was a message from Jack.

Just packing. Can't wait to see you tomorrow, J x

She stuffed the phone back into her bag and knocked on the door that led to Thomas's self-contained flat within the stately home. She wasn't sure which was giving her the biggest butterflies right now – her date with Thomas or the impending arrival of her ex. Perhaps Louise had a point about avoiding all romance.

The door swung open and Thomas stood there, smiling, in dark jeans and a shirt, and her nerves began to melt.

'You look lovely, Abbie,' he greeted her, standing back to let her walk inside.

The apartment was a stark contrast to the rest of the hotel, being much more modern, decorated in simple cream with a wooden floor and functional furniture. Abbie could see why Thomas had decorated it so differently, but she secretly thought that if it had been hers she would have made sure it was in keeping with the rest of the house. A delicious smell took her mind off the décor though as she followed Thomas to the open-plan kitchen and living room. A small glass table was set for two, complete with lit candles and wine ready to be poured.

'Take a seat. I've made an old family recipe from the archives. You've encouraged me to start digging into my past more,' Thomas said, passing her a glass of wine and sitting down with her.

'I'm pleased. I think it's wonderful this place has been in your family for generations. It must make you feel proud?'

He nodded. 'Although, there is a weight of responsibility that comes with it too. I don't want to let my family down and I've been struggling more than I wanted to admit, even to myself.'

'I think you've done really well trying to run it all by yourself, but as I said to you before, there's no shame in getting some help too. It's a massive place and there's so much to do.'

'I'm glad you came along, Abbie Morgan.' He lifted his glass and met her eyes across the table, making her feel more of a glow than could be blamed on the wine and candles. Abbie raised her glass and they clinked, both taking a sip and smiling at each other.

Thomas got up then and served up two plates of salmon

en croute with minted new potatoes and vegetables, drizzled with a parsley sauce. 'I hope you like it,' he said as he sat down.

'This is really good,' Abbie said, as she tasted the salmon. 'I am a pretty rubbish cook myself. I've become reliant on takeaways and eating out in London. Louise keeps trying to get me to cook more but, beyond pasta, I'm a bit hopeless.'

'I'm fine following a recipe, but I couldn't come up with anything of my own. I found it quite relaxing today, although I rarely bother when I'm alone.'

Abbie looked at him and decided to ask a question that had been on her mind for a few days. 'Can I ask – why are you on your own? You could easily qualify for the most eligible bachelor pages in *Hello!* magazine,' she said with a small laugh. She drank more of the wine; it was definitely helping to relax her.

Thomas chuckled. 'Well, as for being an eligible bachelor, I can't comment on that,' he said with a grin. 'But as for why – I was engaged once to a girl called Annabelle. We became a couple at university; she was the daughter of an old family friend so we were encouraged to be together for years really. But she didn't want to run Huntley Manor with me.

'After my parents died, she told me to sell it if we were going to have a future together; she wanted us to live in London and for me to work for her father at his bank. It was pretty clear to me then that we wanted different things. I couldn't see myself working or living anywhere else.' Thomas sighed. 'Although this year, I have wondered several times if she was right.'

Abbie shook her head. 'You would have never forgiven

yourself if you had agreed to what she wanted,' she said. She couldn't picture him in the city at all. He belonged in his jeep, bumping along the track around the estate, wearing his suit with his wellington boots, and living in this house.

'What about you? You haven't thought about settling down with anyone yet?' he asked.

'No. They were a few flings in London, but the scene there, I don't know, nothing ever felt like it could be permanent.' She hesitated, wondering whether to tell him more about Jack or not.

They were both being honest and she didn't want Thomas to think she was keeping anything from him. She trusted him, she realised, and wanted him to trust her in return.

'Jack was probably my longest relationship. I suppose I thought we could have a future.'

'Do you think he is coming here to try to win you back?'

'I don't know about that. I think it might be work related, but he did say that he misses me.'

'And . . . do you miss him?'

Thomas's gaze was unrelenting. She bit her lip, unsure how she felt. 'I don't know.' She was desperate to move the subject off Jack; it was all too complicated. 'I miss my life in London sometimes, but Littlewood has surprised me. I like the community and being with my sister. I feel like I'm making connections here. Everything is so fast and impersonal in the city sometimes. I feel like you can really get to know people here. And I'm really enjoying working at Huntley Manor.'

Thomas smiled. 'I'm happy about that. I think we needed an outsider with some good ideas. I know that I did. I just thought I should run things exactly as they always have been run, but I see now that we need to make changes if we are going to survive. I just hope I can keep the bank at bay while we do.'

'I think we've managed to make some good improvements already.'

'You are really changing this place, for the better.'

Abbie felt her cheeks glow. She was pleased Thomas thought that. She couldn't help but hope Jack thought so too when he arrived. It had knocked her confidence when City PR had let her go and she couldn't help but wonder if she and Jack might still be together if that hadn't happened. She wanted to show him that she could do well without him, but also she wanted him to be proud of her. He had always told her how good she was at her job and she wanted him to see she still was. It was hard to shake the habit of wanting his approval.

'I think this summer will turn both our fortunes around,' she said firmly. She was hopeful a great new job was on its way, and maybe Jack even had some news on that front. And she was sure that Huntley Manor was willing them to be successful. The house wanted to be saved, she could feel it, and she was determined to make that happen.

'I think we deserve some chocolate cake now, don't you?' Thomas said when they had finished the main course.

'I could kiss you for that suggestion,' she said, her tipsiness stopping her from keeping her mouth in check. She gasped at her words as Thomas looked surprised, his cheeks turning red.

'Oh, well, I hope it lives up to expectations,' he said a little awkwardly. He grabbed her plate and disappeared into the kitchen, leaving Abbie feeling a little foolish.

Pull yourself together, she told herself sternly as Thomas dished up dessert. She had obviously thrown him with her flirtatious remark. Clearly this dinner was merely a thank you for all her help, and he saw them just as colleagues. She blamed Louise and all her talk about this being a date.

'Abbie,' Thomas said as he came back and slid a slice of cake towards her. He cleared his throat. 'I wanted to say that—'

A buzz from his phone made them both jump. Thomas looked at it with a sigh. 'It's the night manager; I'd better get it, hang on.' As he listened, Abbie soon got the gist that a guest was being awkward. 'I'll be there in five minutes.' Thomas hung up and looked at her, full of regret. 'I'm so sorry, but I had better go and deal with this.'

'Of course.' Abbie suddenly felt sober. 'I'll head off, it's getting late.'

'Oh. Are you sure?'

She grabbed her bag, suddenly desperate to be out of there. She was certain that Thomas just wanted a business relationship with her and had been about to awkwardly tell her that. It was clear that she had been letting the wine and candlelight carry her away to thinking there could be something else happening between them. 'Goodnight,' she said. 'Thank you for dinner.' She took off before he could stop her and was relieved when she reached the cool air outside.

Chapter Twenty-two

Louise got up just after dawn on Saturday, grumbling to herself that she had let Abbie talk her into helping at the animal charity fete, though she knew that her heart would melt as soon as she saw the animals.

After her shower, Louise pulled on old jeans, sneakers and a vest top and made a cup of strong coffee in the kitchen, where she was joined by a yawning Abbie. They had chatted for a while the night before when Abbie had returned much earlier than Louise had expected. Louise had been disappointed, hoping that Thomas might have been planning to tell her sister that he liked her, but Abbie was adamant he only saw them as colleagues.

Louise poured her a cup too. 'I can't believe I'm doing this,' Louise said as she put some bread in the toaster. 'You owe me.'

'I know, I know. Thank you,' Abbie said, sipping her coffee on the stool by the kitchen counter.

'Hopefully there will be lots of cute puppies to make it worthwhile. What have you got planned with Jack?'

'I don't know really. He texted last night to say he'd come for lunch and that he wants me to show him around town. It's going to be so weird to see him in Littlewood.'

'Maybe I'll finally get to meet him.'

When Louise had gone to London to see Abbie while she was living there, she had never got even a glance at Jack. He was too busy to take time out to see her, she had read between the lines, and she had worried he wasn't in it for the long haul with Abbie.

'I'll make sure of it,' Abbie promised.

'Right – I'd better go, the animals need me.'

'Have a good day!' Abbie called as Louise grabbed her bag and left the cottage, missing the wink her sister had added to her words.

The bright and sunny morning cheered Louise up as she made her way through Littlewood to the large green on the edge of town that was useful for outdoor events like the fete. She was pretty sure parking would be a nightmare and, as it was a lovely day, she made the most of it and walked slowly over there.

The green was already a flurry of activity by the time she arrived. There were tents set up, all emblazoned with the logo of the animal charity, plus several food vans, a bouncy castle and a face-painting area. A lady wearing a Littlewood Animal Rescue T-shirt met Louise and she ticked off her name on the volunteer list, gave her a T-shirt

to put on and directed her to the tent she would be helping in for the day.

'We're going to put you in with the vet – he'll be taking questions from people thinking about adopting an animal. We'll also be doing a raffle, a training exhibition and a dogs' and owners' race, so it should be a good day,' the lady said, hurrying off to greet the next person walking across the green.

Louise slipped the T-shirt on over her vest top and walked across the grass to the tent she would be working in. She stopped in the entrance and stared, confused, at the person already in there.

'Louise!' he said, equally surprised, pausing in arranging leaflets on the table to look at her. 'Can I help you with something?'

She swallowed. 'I'm volunteering. They told me this would be my tent,' she said, looking at Alex awkwardly. She couldn't believe her luck – they would be spending the whole day together. She wasn't sure who looked more embarrassed.

'Ah, well. Excellent. Come on in, then,' Alex said, letting out a nervous cough. There were two fold-up chairs behind the table and Alex gestured for her to sit down next to him. 'Abbie said you'd be taking part as well today,' he said, breaking the silence after a few seconds. 'But I didn't know we'd be in the same tent.'

'Abbie?' Louise asked, confused.

Alex nodded. 'She came to my surgery and asked me if I'd

volunteer today, as the charity needed a vet. She said she'd be here too. Where have they placed her?'

Louise's mind started whirring. 'She was meant to be here, but a friend from London has come to stay so she had to drop out.' He nodded and she thought this was too much of a coincidence. Had her sister engineered this? Louise was almost certain she had.

She glanced at Alex who was pouring them cups of tea from a plastic flask he had. He didn't seem suspicious, but she was embarrassed to think he might believe she was the one who had planned this. Why had Abbie done this?

The answer came to her suddenly: the kindness pact. Abbie clearly thought Louise should be giving Alex a chance and had decided to force her into doing just that.

Louise looked from Alex to the entrance, panicked, but then her decision was made as a volunteer arrived with a dog for their station and her heart melted. This was for a good cause; she would grin and bear it. She just hoped Alex didn't think she had schemed to spend the day with him.

Alex got up from his chair then to greet the dog, who jumped up eagerly as he ruffled his fur, laughing when the dog tried to lick his face.

Louise looked away, hating that the scene had made her smile. She loved it when people were kind to animals; she was sure you could tell a lot about someone by how they treated them. She remembered asking Peter if they could have a cat, only to be told they couldn't because he was allergic; she discovered later on from his mother that he had

lied – he just didn't like animals. Louise wondered if she should have taken that as a red flag right there and then.

The volunteer left the dog with them and went off to organise the raffle. It was a Labrador called Ben and he lay down at Alex's feet, looking perfectly content there.

'Do you have a dog of your own?' she asked Alex as they waited for someone to come into their tent.

'No. I did growing up and I would like one now, but I'm at work six days a week so it wouldn't really be fair. At least I get to see so many in the surgery.'

'I keep thinking about getting a cat.'

'You should. Animals are great company, aren't they?'

'Yes, I suppose it can get lonely living on your own. It's been nice having my sister to stay,' Louise said, although she wasn't so happy with Abbie right now.

Alex nodded. 'If I didn't have such a demanding job, I think I'd get lonely too. I used to live with my ex before I moved to Littlewood. It's the little things you miss, like having someone to cook with or watch a box set with, you know?'

She nodded, a lump forming in her throat. She lifted her eyes to meet his. A look passed between them, but then a family came into the tent and Alex got up to greet them. Louise leant back in her chair, realising she had been absent-mindedly leaning towards him.

She pulled her phone out to text Abbie.

Your matchmaking needs to be more subtle!

Abbie replied immediately:

> I just wanted you to see the possibility. He's a nice
> guy, Lou, why not give him a chance?

Louise fired back:

> Why not let me make my own choices?

Louise sighed and put her phone away at Abbie's response:

> I just want you to be happy xxxx

She knew her sister's heart was in the right place, but why did Abbie always think she knew best?

Okay, so maybe she was a bit lonely; the news of Peter's engagement had hit her harder than she cared to admit and left her longing for someone to love, but the thought of having her heart broken once more just made her want to run out of the tent and hide in her cottage. How were you supposed to take a chance on love again?

Ben the Labrador padded over to her then and she patted his head as Alex explained to the family how they would need to take care of a dog like him.

Louise wondered what his instructions might be for taking care of a human, because she really didn't have a clue.

Chapter Twenty-three

Eszter, Zoe and Anne walked across the green later that morning to check out the fete for themselves. Anne had been quiet on the walk there and Eszter realised she was nervous as they weaved their way through the throngs of people.

'Would you have always gone to this sort of thing with Frank?' Eszter asked her. She wondered why, after living all her life in one place, Anne didn't seem to have any close connections with anyone there. Surely after Frank died, people would have rallied around her like they did for Joy when Harry was ill?

'Frank liked to come to community events,' Anne said. 'But obviously he was very busy and often we had to be in London, especially when we were younger. He was a very successful doctor.' Anne looked around nervously. 'There are a lot of people here.'

'We don't need to stay long if we're not enjoying ourselves,' Eszter said gently. Zoe let out a squeal as a volunteer

approached them with a black poodle. 'Although how we're going to drag Zoe away from all the animals, I don't know,' she said with a laugh.

Anne smiled. 'Frank was allergic to most animals, so we never had any pets when Nick was growing up; he would have loved a dog.'

'We couldn't have a dog back at our apartment in Budapest, which is a shame,' Eszter said, watching her daughter patting the dog carefully. 'It would be lovely to have a dog here though, there are so many beautiful places you could walk one.'

'Anne Harris?' called a voice from behind them. They turned to see a small lady walking towards them, her grey bob bouncing with her steps. She smiled. 'I thought it was you; it's been so long since I last saw you.'

Anne nodded. 'Hello, Jane. This is Eszter, my daughter-in-law.'

Eszter smiled, pleased that Anne had introduced her as family so comfortably.

'I run the community centre,' Jane said, shaking Eszter's hand firmly. 'And who's this?'

'This is my granddaughter Zoe,' Anne said, gesturing for Zoe to come over. She left the dog and went to Anne's side, who wrapped an arm around her proudly.

'We're staying for the summer,' Eszter told her. 'How do you two know each other?'

'We actually went to school together,' Jane said. 'I'm always trying to persuade Anne to come along to the centre;

we have so much going on. And for all ages. There's a kids' club too.'

'That might be good, Zoe, maybe you could make some friends in Littlewood?' Eszter said.

'Here, take a leaflet,' Jane said, pulling one out from the stack in her hand. 'There's a list of all the activities we run. You should all come and see us.'

Eszter nodded. 'Sounds great.' She glanced at Anne, who was looking away, distinctly uncomfortable with the conversation. 'It was lovely to meet you.'

Jane walked on, ready to hand out more leaflets, so the three of them made their way down the green. When Zoe spotted the face-painting station, Anne and Eszter stood by while she sat down and was turned into a cat.

'I think Zoe might enjoy the kids' club,' Eszter said, looking at the list. 'Do you know, I've always fancied taking a drawing class, so maybe I should go along too. You've never fancied it before?'

'Jane and Frank didn't get on,' Anne replied, then walked over to look at Zoe being painted.

Eszter watched her go, frustrated. Anne seemed to have really cut herself off from Littlewood when there was so much there for her, and it all seemed to come back to her husband and the shadow he still cast, years after his death. She spotted Louise then in her tent and waved to her; pleased to see she was in there with Alex. Surely Louise would come to agree with her and Abbie that the vet was worth a date?

Perhaps everybody needed a helping hand in the right direction. They'd all be so much happier if they would just open up their hearts a little bit.

* * *

Abbie's heart was beating faster than normal as she walked through town towards Huntley Manor to meet up with Jack. It felt as if two very different worlds were colliding as she walked in and waved to Amy, spotting Jack sitting on one of the leather armchairs in the lounge, glued to his phone. She glanced around but there was no sign of Thomas and, if she was being honest, she felt relieved. She wasn't sure she wanted to introduce them to one another.

'Abbie, darling,' Jack said when he saw her, putting his phone in his pocket as he got up from the chair. She smiled as he gave her a big hug and kissed her on the cheek.

'Hello, Jack,' she said, looking at him when he pulled back. He was wearing his usual dark suit with his fair hair gelled back and she breathed in the musky scent of his expensive aftershave. 'Have you settled in okay?'

'All unpacked. I was expecting you to be working somewhere a bit more five-star,' he said, looking around the room.

'Well, admittedly, it needs some polish, but it has a lot of charm, don't you think?'

Jack raised an eyebrow but then took her hand. 'It's really good to see you. Come on, I've booked us somewhere for lunch and I have something that I want to ask you.' Taking her by the hand, he led her outside to his car. 'You look

gorgeous, Abbie,' he said as he opened up the door for her. He pushed back a strand of her hair. 'I've really missed you.'

Abbie smiled. It was good to see him again.

She glanced at Huntley Manor as she climbed into the car beside him and saw Thomas walking across the grounds, looking at them. She lifted her hand to wave, but he turned and disappeared.

'Come on,' Jack said, so she hurriedly got in.

They drove through Littlewood to a gastro pub a few miles away, up high in the Surrey Hills. Jack had always known how to find good places to eat. As they had passed the green where the fete was in full swing, Abbie wondered how Louise and Alex were getting on together. She hoped Louise would forgive her matchmaking.

They got a table outside in the sunny beer garden, Jack bringing out a beer and glass of wine.

'What's been happening in London?' Abbie asked.

'Oh, the usual,' he replied with a wave of his hand. 'But I want to hear all about you. Are you surviving in this backwater town?' He grinned and brushed her fingertips with his.

'I'm not missing the city as much as I thought I would. It's lovely around here.'

'Well, London is certainly missing you, and surely you want to get back to it? I was thinking about that time we stayed up all night in the office because we had so many ideas for that restaurant opening. Do you remember?'

Abbie smiled. She did. They had spent the night in his office coming up with ideas, eating a takeaway and drinking

wine, and then they had ordered a taxi back to his flat, tumbling into bed and staying there all day. 'We made a good team.'

'We really did, and we could again.' He reached for her hand, but the waiter arrived so they ordered lunch. When he left, Jack leaned in closer again. She had forgotten how he focused in on her when he spoke, his eyes fixed on hers, and his attention one hundred per cent hers. She had loved that about him. So many men in the past had pretended to listen, but Jack always did. 'Tell me about the work you're doing at the hotel, then. I want to hear all about it.'

So Abbie told him about Huntley Manor and how she was determined to help save it from closure. 'It's such a beautiful place, and I love that Thomas has been on board with all my ideas. That's what I've really enjoyed about being here – I have creative freedom.'

'You were always brilliant at coming up with ideas. Honestly, we've really missed that at work. I think all of the partners are starting to regret letting you go.'

'Really?' Abbie was pleased that her hard work hadn't gone unnoticed, as she'd thought. She wondered if that was the reason Jack was there.

He took hold of her hand, and Abbie was surprised that his touch could still warm her skin so quickly. 'Of course. Abbie, you have so much talent. I hope this Lord Huntley realises that. You could charge him a fortune for the help you're giving him. I don't want anyone taking advantage of you.'

Abbie smiled. 'I can take care of myself, Jack.'

He shook his head. 'I know that. But that doesn't mean I don't want to take care of you.' He squeezed her hand and looked at her fondly. 'I have really missed you.'

'Is that why you came?'

'I do want to talk to you about something, but let's just enjoy lunch. I'll get us more drinks.' He went off to get her another wine and she leant back in her seat, the sun on her face, and smiled.

Abbie had forgotten what good company Jack could be. She was still hurt by how he had treated her, but he had clearly missed her and it was flattering to know she was missed at the office. She was intrigued to know what he wanted to talk to her about, but when he came back with a story of a couple having a row at the bar, it slipped her mind and they spent the rest of the afternoon chatting about London and all the people they knew. Abbie soaked up all the news he had of their mutual friends, and wondered why she had been so nervous about him coming. Jack was a master at putting people at ease; she had seen him charm the prickliest of clients. Abbie was soon having a much better time than she had told herself she would have.

Chapter Twenty-four

Louise flopped down in her chair in the early afternoon and pushed her hair back off her face. 'This place is crazy,' she declared. She had been in the tent with Alex all morning, with a constant stream of people coming in to ask him questions and to meet the dogs that the volunteers kept bringing in. There was a tiny lull, so she had slipped out and got them both drinks and burgers from the nearby food van and they sank into their fold-up chairs gratefully.

'I didn't expect to have to work this hard today,' Alex admitted, taking a big bite of his burger.

'It looks like the rescue centre is going to be inundated with people wanting to adopt.'

'I hope so. Thanks for all your help today, especially when that little girl started crying because her parents wouldn't let her take the sheepdog home. They live in a flat and she just couldn't understand why the dog wasn't suitable for them. I'm sure I can still hear her having a tantrum out there.'

'I'm used to kids at the hospital; we see a lot of tantrums there, bless them.' She sipped her Coke.

'I definitely don't have your patience. I prefer dealing with animals, much less stressful, and far quieter.' He grinned and she chuckled. 'So, what brought you to Littlewood two years ago then?'

Louise wondered how honest to be. If she was going to keep things from being awkward between them, and she would like to be friends with him, then it was best to be honest so he would know why she didn't want to date him, or anyone else. She swallowed her mouthful and sighed. 'Well, I wanted to get away from my home town in Cornwall really, and this was one of the first vacancies I applied for. I had just broken up with my fiancé and it seemed far enough away but also a small, community town like the one I grew up in.'

'So a broken heart brought you here?'

'I suppose you could say that. It was a huge shock; he left me just before we were going to get married, so yes it really hurt me and I needed a change of scene pretty desperately. So, that's how I came here, and I loved it straight away. I think you said you had recently broken up with someone too?'

He nodded. 'I already had the job here, but she decided she didn't want to come with me. We lived together, but I think we both knew that we weren't going to get married, so it made sense to part ways when I came here. She stayed in our old place. It's hard isn't it? After a break-up, thinking

about moving on? You spend so much time with someone, then suddenly you're on your own again.'

'I just haven't felt ready,' she admitted then, thinking he deserved her to be completely truthful about it. 'My sister keeps telling me to move on, but I think I'm still hurt.'

'I imagine it would be hard to trust anyone again. You planned a future with him and he walked away from that. He must be crazy.' He smiled at her. 'You just have to go at your own pace. I'm sure Abbie understands that, she just wants the best for you.'

'I know. She keeps telling me to be kinder to myself but it isn't easy, is it?'

'Well, your sister definitely has good advice there. You should. After we're done today, you need to go home and put your feet up. Vet's orders.'

Louise laughed and then a family came into the tent and their brief lunch break was over.

The rest of the afternoon moved quickly and when the lady who ran the rescue centre came by at four o'clock to tell them everyone was packing up, Louise was pleased they had done so well, albeit relieved to be going home. 'You'll end up with loads more customers after this, I bet,' Louise said to Alex as they helped clear up the tent.

'It would be great to see some of the animals from today find a home. I just hope everyone realised that it's a lot of work adopting an animal.'

Louise hid a smile at his serious face. She liked how he took the animals' well-being so seriously. 'You gave them

great advice,' she assured him. After a quick look around the tent, she said, 'Well, I think we're all done here. I can just hit Brew before it closes and then collapse on the sofa.'

'I'll join you, if you don't mind? I need a large coffee after today.'

'Sure.'

They left the green together, walking through Littlewood towards Brew. Lots of people were still milling around in the sunshine. Louise felt conscious that after all her protests she was having a coffee with Alex, but she hoped now it was clear they were just friends. She had enjoyed hanging out with him in the tent; he was polite and kind to everyone and clearly loved all animals with the same kind of passion that she felt towards her patients in the hospital.

She glanced across at him as they strolled casually and she had to admit that Eszter and her sister had been right: he was good-looking. Not that it mattered or changed anything, but it felt okay to admit it to herself. She had set the boundaries between them and she could relax a little bit more in his company now.

'How's Hazel doing?' Louise asked, breaking their companionable silence.

'She's doing really well; it's been lovely for my sister having her back home. They were the reason I applied for the job in Littlewood – I wanted to be close to Sarah and Hazel again, especially with everything they've been going through.'

'I'm sure your sister was grateful. I can't imagine how hard it's all been for her. Watching your child go through that.'

'I'm just hoping she's on the road to recovery finally.'

'What happened to Hazel's dad?'

'When she was diagnosed with cancer, the cracks began to appear. He started drinking a lot and staying out all hours. I guess he just couldn't cope, but I'll never forgive him for walking away from the both of them.'

Louise nodded. 'I can't believe someone would do that.' Then she thought about Peter – when the going got tough, would he have stuck around? She had her doubts now, whereas before she thought he was her everything. But she knew now that your partner should be someone that you could count on, someone to get through the difficult things with, someone you could trust.

They reached Brew and Alex held the door open for her; she couldn't help but think to herself that Alex would be that kind of man. She dismissed the thought quickly though.

'You just caught us open,' Joy greeted them cheerfully. 'We're tidying up. What can we get you?' she asked from behind the counter. Harry was starting to stack up chairs and waved to them both.

Alex and Louise ordered coffees to go and Louise added a brownie to her order, so Alex got a Danish pastry, both of them agreeing they deserved it after the day they'd had.

'How was the fete?' Joy asked as she prepared their orders.

'It was hectic,' Alex said.

'But I really enjoyed it,' Louise added. 'And if I ever want a pet I now know exactly how to look after them. Alex was very strict with everyone.'

Alex laughed. 'I just want people to be responsible pet owners.'

'The animals will appreciate it,' Louise told him with a smile.

'Well, I'm glad it went well. We were pretty quiet in here, so I think a lot of the town must have popped by. Here we go.' Joy held out a coffee and paper bag to each of them.

'I'll get these,' Alex said, quickly handing Joy a ten-pound note. Louise started to protest but he shook his head. 'Honestly, you were a star today, sitting there listening to me droning on, so please, let me get them. You can get the next ones.'

Louise felt her cheeks glow warm as she took her coffee and brownie. She found herself hoping there would be a next time and she wished the idea of seeing him again didn't make her want to smile quite so much. 'Well, thank you.'

'Have a lovely evening, you two,' Joy said. 'I can't wait to put my feet up and have a cup of tea.'

'You enjoy yourself too,' Louise said. 'Goodnight,' she said to Joy and Harry and she followed Alex out, Harry closing up the café door behind them. They walked to the top of the hill together and paused on the corner where they would walk their separate ways to their homes.

'Thanks for helping today,' Alex said.

'No problem. I'll see you soon.' She wished it didn't sound like a question.

He nodded. 'You will,' he said and, with a wave, strolled off towards his flat above the vet surgery.

Louise watched him for a moment before turning towards her cottage, an extra spring in her step, although she tried to ignore it.

Chapter Twenty-five

Eszter, Zoe and Anne made their way back to their cottage after the fete late in the afternoon. Zoe carried a cuddly cat that they'd won on the raffle, and was chatting away about all the animals they had met, and how she wished she had one of her own. Eszter glanced across at her mother-in-law – she looked tired but was smiling at Zoe, and Eszter was certain the day had been good for her.

When they got home, Zoe took her cat and curled up on the sofa with a book but soon fell asleep. Anne went into the kitchen to prepare the meal and Eszter sat at the kitchen table chopping vegetables for her. It was strange how easily they had formed a routine in the house, with Anne taking over all the cooking and Eszter able to relax after her shifts at Brew, more than she usually would have done. It was an arrangement that was suiting all of them. Zoe especially seemed to be enjoying having her grandmother with them. Eszter was pleased to see a bond forming between the two of them,

something she could never have imagined when she arrived in town, particularly after their disastrous first meeting.

'I'm glad we bumped into Jane,' she said as she chopped an onion. Anne was making pasta, her back to her as she stirred the saucepan over the hob. Eszter felt more confident in speaking up when they weren't making eye contact. She was still a bit nervous of her mother-in-law and didn't want to do or say anything that might disrupt their shaky truce. 'I think the community centre is such a good idea. I definitely want to take Zoe over there. Do you feel like doing a class with me too? It'd be nice to meet some more people here.'

'I'm not sure it's really for me, to be honest,' Anne replied, keeping her back towards Eszter.

'But wouldn't you like to meet some people too? I mean, don't you ever get lonely in that house all by yourself? I know since Nick died, I've felt that way, especially when Zoe is in bed and I have the evening all to myself.'

'I suppose I'm used to it. Frank didn't really want me being too involved in community things without him,' Anne said quietly.

'Anne,' Eszter said, before getting up and going over to her. 'Was Frank quite ... controlling?' she asked, tipping the onions into an empty saucepan. She was sure that Nick wouldn't have walked out on his family if there hadn't been a good reason for it. Their falling out over his career didn't seem like enough of a reason to cause such a rift for so many years. 'I had a boyfriend when I was younger,' she carried on when it was clear that Anne was hesitating to answer her. 'He

was very controlling and he started to tell me how to dress, who I could be friends with, even that I should go on a diet, but I didn't really realise what kind of effect he was having on me until my mother stepped in. Once I had some distance from him, I realised how toxic the relationship had been.'

Anne sighed. 'Frank was a man who liked to have his own way, yes. He wanted our family to be respected in the community. He was strict with Nick, as you know, and really wanted him to be a doctor. He liked me to be at home, that's true, and we rarely went anywhere without each other. But that's marriage, isn't it?'

'Come and sit down a moment.' Eszter led her to the table. 'I'm trying to understand why Nick left you for such a long time. I know that you were both disappointed when he didn't want to carry on training to be a doctor, but would that have really caused you all not to have any contact for so long?'

Anne looked down at her hands folded on the table. 'I wish you would let the past be the past, Eszter. It's hard enough dealing with the loss of my husband and my son. I don't want to rake over everything that happened.'

'I'm sorry, but I can't go back to Hungary and think of you alone in your house not seeing anyone, not being part of this town. You must be lonely.'

Anne's eyes glistened. 'I am sometimes, but in the past I was more involved, I had friends, I had Jane, and it all got very complicated so it was easier to, well, step back.'

'Is it because you were worried people would find out what Frank was like?'

'He didn't encourage me to have friends that weren't his. We used to just go out as a couple. He didn't like me going out without him,' Anne admitted, her head lowering. 'I loved him and I wanted to make him happy, so slowly, yes, I drew back from people, and after he died, I just didn't know how to change that.'

'Anne, did Nick leave Littlewood because of his father?' Eszter asked, reaching over to touch her hand.

A tear escaped Anne's eye and ran down her cheek. 'Nick told us he didn't want to be a doctor and there was a huge row about it. Nick said he was tired of his father controlling his life and he was leaving. Nick asked me to go with him, he said I needed to get away from Frank, and he'd look after us both. But you have to understand, I had been with Frank since I was a teenager, he was my husband, my everything. I couldn't just leave him. Nick told me I was letting Frank control both of us. He was angry with me for not standing up to his father. I think he blamed me for Frank being so strict when he was growing up; he thought I should have done something. That I should have left him.' Anne started to cry in earnest then and Eszter wrapped an arm around her shoulders.

'I can't imagine how hard that was for you.'

'Despite it all, I loved Frank. I couldn't imagine living without him. Nick just didn't understand. He thought I was a coward. When he left, I knew I had lost my son and no matter how much I begged Frank to reach out to Nick, he said he had gone and that was the end of it. I should have tried harder, I know I should.' She sniffed loudly.

'I'm so sorry, Anne,' Eszter said, everything now becoming clear. She knew how black and white Nick could be. He'd clearly had enough of his father controlling him, and once he was old enough to make his own decisions, he couldn't understand why his mother didn't feel the same way. He'd walked away and all of them were too stubborn to reach out to one another and piece their family back together. 'It must have been very hard to know what to do; you were caught between your husband and your son.' She thought of Zoe in the living room, knowing she couldn't have let her daughter walk away, but it was easy to judge and she knew that Frank must have been so much in control of Anne's life, she hadn't known what to do. 'It's okay.'

'But it isn't. I lost Frank and I lost Nick. I thought when Frank died ... but then Nick didn't want to come to the funeral and it felt like I would be going against Frank's memory to come to Hungary. I should have done, though. And when you told me he was sick, if I had known how serious it was, then I would have tried to come.'

'I know. We didn't know either and by the time we did, it was too late. I'm so sorry.'

Anne wiped her eyes and looked at Eszter. 'I never thought that Nick would stay away so long. Every day I thought there would be a knock at the door and there he would be. We didn't know where he was for a long time. And as I said, I never got your wedding invitation. The more I think about it, the more I'm sure Frank kept it from me.'

Eszter nodded. 'It looks that way, yes.'

'Will you show me pictures?'

'Of course.' Eszter went upstairs to get her laptop and when she came back down, Anne had dried her eyes and put the pasta bake in the oven. Zoe was awake too, so Eszter loaded up the laptop and the three of them looked at the photos from the wedding and then Zoe's christening.

It was painful for Anne to see them, Eszter was sure, but she was also glad that Anne was getting the chance to see how happy her son had been. They couldn't do anything about the mess that had been made in the past, but Eszter hoped that now they were in each other's lives, they always would be.

'How about tomorrow we go and look at this community centre?' Eszter asked Zoe and Anne as they moved the laptop away and served up dinner.

'I think we should,' Zoe readily agreed, trying to eat while still clutching her cuddly cat. Anne nodded too, eating quietly, still wrapped up in thoughts of her lost family.

Eszter smiled at them both, pleased the day had been a success. She felt as if she knew Anne a lot better now and she was hopeful she could help her this summer and maybe some of the past wounds could heal for them all, if they only let them.

Chapter Twenty-six

Abbie was definitely drunk. Jack had stopped drinking after his first beer as he was driving but had kept buying her more wine and, as lunch stretched into early evening, they finally climbed back into his car and Abbie half fell into the seat. 'You're a bad influence,' she told him sternly as she tried, and failed, to put her seatbelt on.

Jack laughed and did it for her. 'You looked as if you needed to have some fun. Being here has made you a lightweight.'

'Well, we don't go out drinking every night like we did in London.'

He started up the car and drove away from the pub and back towards Littlewood. 'Sounds boring.' He winked at her, turned the music up, and drove too quickly around the country lanes.

Abbie laughed and sang along, thinking it had been a while since she had cut loose. Jack had always been hard to

resist when it came to going out and having fun. He was always the last to leave, the one to buy all the drinks, and the life and soul of the party.

They pulled up outside Huntley Manor in record time. 'I still have something I need to talk to you about. Why don't you come up to my room for coffee and we can chat? I think you could do with a cup,' he said as he parked up outside.

'I'm not going to your room, Jack,' she said firmly. She wasn't that drunk.

He put his hands up. 'I just want to talk, and you need to sober up a bit first. I promise. Come on, we don't want everyone in the lounge listening to our conversation. I swear, no funny business. Just coffee.' He raised an eyebrow. 'Don't leave me hanging here, Abs.'

She shook her head. Why was it so hard to stay angry with Jack? She tried to remember him avoiding her eyes as she was told she was being made redundant, but then she saw how hopeful he looked right now. It wouldn't hurt just to find out what he wanted to say, would it? She sighed. 'Okay, one coffee.'

He beamed at her. 'You won't regret it.'

Abbie really hoped she wouldn't.

Jack rushed around to help her out of the car, and she was annoyed that she needed his help. He put a hand on the small of her back as they walked inside. She looked around, hoping that she wouldn't bump into Thomas. She didn't want him to see her this drunk and having to put her arm through Jack's so she could walk straight and not stumble. She was sure he wouldn't approve.

Thankfully, there was no sign of him as they walked up the wide staircase to the bedrooms.

Jack let them into his room and went to the phone to order coffee from room service while Abbie flopped down into the armchair. She looked out of the window onto the grounds below and kicked off her heels, beginning to regret drinking so much wine. Her head felt fuzzy and she had to admit Jack had been right about her needing coffee.

'Are you okay?' Jack asked, pulling off his tie and throwing it onto the four-poster bed.

'I'll be fine.'

Jack smiled. 'It's never dull with you around, Abs, that's for sure. My flat has been really lonely without you in it.'

'Jack, why did you cool things off because I was being made redundant?' she asked in a blunt rush. She had dwelled on this for a long time; it had been upsetting to think that he had walked away from their relationship just because she was losing her job. It had made her think he had only been with her because it had been convenient and they worked well together.

Jack perched on the edge of the bed and leaned towards her. He sighed. 'Because I'm an idiot? I am so sorry, Abbie. When the partners said you were on the list, I tried to talk them out of it, but they said it had to be first in, first out. It was the fairest way. And they made me swear not to tell you. How could I go on seeing you while keeping something like that from you? I felt like I'd let you down. I thought you'd be better off without me.' His shoulders slumped. 'I thought that once you found out about the redundancy, you wouldn't

179

want to go near me. I suppose I broke things off before you did. I didn't want to hurt myself more than I already was. I was a coward. Can you ever forgive me?'

She looked at him, amazed at his honest response. She could see what he meant. She wasn't sure if she could have stayed with him, watching him going off to work, living off him. She probably still would have come to Littlewood. 'It hurt, Jack, you cutting me off, then losing my job. Not even giving me a heads-up so I could have found something else.'

'They made me swear. I would have lost my job. I'm sorry.'

She could understand how torn he must have felt; she wouldn't have known what to do either. She sighed. 'What a mess. We were over before we had even begun.'

Jack shook his head. 'Not true. We were very much begun. The truth is I was in love with you. I love you, Abbie.' He hadn't told her that at the time. 'I should have made sure you knew.'

A knock at the door broke the tense silence and he got up to get the coffee. He poured them both a strong, black cup and moved to the armchair opposite her to drink it. She was still trying to absorb his words. She had been infatuated with him ever since they had first met; he had swept her off her feet but she hadn't given herself time to think about love. Jack had certainly never uttered those words before. They had been about fun, living well, having it all. It had been a whirlwind. She could barely take in what he was saying. 'Is this what you wanted to talk to me about?'

He nodded. 'Yes, but there's more too. I miss you and I'd

like us to try again. You and me, but I also know that I hurt you and you might not be able to get past that. It will suck,' he said with a small smile. 'But I'd accept it. I can't lose you from my life. All I thought about while you were gone was how much of a great team we were, in and outside of work. So, I had an idea.'

Abbie sipped her coffee, hoping she could sober up quickly as Jack made his offer.

'As I said, the company isn't the same without you. I just can't see a future for me there. With my business skills and your creative ideas, why would we join another company that probably won't realise just how special we are, when we could set up our own?'

Abbie stared at him. 'Are you serious?'

He grinned. 'Deadly. You and me. What do you think?'

Abbie's mind reeled. 'But I thought you loved working at City PR?' When Abbie thought about the company she had worked in for two years until just a few weeks ago, it was impossible to separate the place from Jack. He was the company to her. Jack had been the one who had interviewed her, who had introduced her to all the clients, and who had encouraged her ideas, and then, of course, the one who had won her heart.

'I did. But there would be so many more opportunities if I had my own business, and I want to work with you again. We could do something great, I just know we could.'

His enthusiasm was infectious. She tried to process what he was offering her. It was hard not to feel a flicker of excitement.

They had been a good team, although she still wished that she had been given more credit for her ideas. Mostly, the clients assumed the whole project was run by Jack, and he had never corrected anyone. She didn't want that to happen again. Working at Huntley Manor had shown her she could manage a project by herself.

'When you say you want us to set up a business together, do you mean as partners? Business partners?' Abbie clarified hastily, not sure what to say to his other offer of them trying again. She had to think long and hard about that. But she liked hearing that he'd missed her, that he loved her. Who wouldn't? She just needed to work out how she felt. But working together . . . Well, that was different. It was an opportunity. One that she had been craving since she left London.

'Of course,' Jack said. 'You haven't found a new job, so this is perfect. Can't you just see it, Abs?'

And she could. She allowed herself a smile. 'But won't we need money?'

'I can find us investors, no problem,' he replied, waving her question away with his hand. 'I haven't been the same man since you left, I just don't work as well without you by my side. I was such a fool not to realise it until you came here. What do you think?'

Abbie put her coffee down, wishing again that she hadn't drunk so much wine. 'This is a lot to take in, Jack. I didn't think I'd ever see you again.'

'Of course, I understand. You need to think about it, I know that. But it's not a straight no, is it?'

She shook her head slowly. 'It's not a straight no.'

Jack clapped his hands. 'That's all I needed to hear. I'll persuade you, I know I will. Let's start brainstorming!'

'Now? It's getting late.'

'Have you got anywhere to be? Because I haven't.'

She watched him grab a notebook and pen, and refill their coffees, and she had to laugh at how happy he seemed. It reminded her of the old times, and she ended up helping him to come up with ideas.

The sun set outside the room but Abbie didn't notice. Time with Jack had so often stopped still, and here it was doing it all over again.

* * *

Abbie opened her eyes and groaned as her head started to pound immediately. A patch of light hit her face from the window and she rolled over, coming face to face with a sleeping Jack. She started, and then it all came flooding back to her. They had stayed up planning until the early hours and had fallen asleep side by side as they had done so many times before.

Jack's eyes opened and he smiled. 'Good morning, gorgeous.' He leaned in and she found herself closing her eyes as he kissed her. 'I've missed waking up with you,' he said, looking at her. He reached for her again, but she drew back.

'Last night was ... I still need to think,' she said, sitting up. 'Ouch,' she complained, rubbing her head. God, so much wine.

'I understand. Let's get you some painkillers, a long shower and some breakfast, okay?'

She found herself nodding. Why was it so easy for her to get swept away by Jack?

She felt a bit more like herself an hour later as they left the breakfast room at Huntley Manor. She'd had a lot of coffee, bacon, eggs and pancakes and was now looking forward to going home and putting on clean clothes, and speaking to her sister about last night.

Jack had been in a buoyant mood over breakfast, chatting about his ideas, and seeming really confident that she would go into business with him. Abbie was desperately trying to sort out her thoughts on it all. Everything seemed to be moving at breakneck speed and she couldn't quite catch her breath.

Walking through the hotel, she was struck by the thought that she might not be there much longer. If she did agree to set up a business with Jack, she knew that they needed to be in the same place, and that meant going back to London. She had been enjoying her summer in Littlewood, more than she ever thought she could, but the plan had always been to get back to the city, she reminded herself. She'd feel bad though about leaving Huntley Manor before the end of the summer relaunch, but maybe she could still help remotely.

Abbie jumped as Thomas rounded the corner and stopped in front of them. He smiled at her, then looked at Jack and back again, his smile fading. Abbie knew she looked worse for wear after staying up half the night, and she blushed when she realised what Thomas would think. She knew

that nothing had happened, but he wouldn't. Abbie didn't want him to think badly of her, and found herself babbling. 'Thomas, oh my goodness! Fancy bumping into you. Um, yes, this is Jack. Rogers. My, um, friend from London.'

'A bit more than that, I hope,' Jack said, smoothly shaking Thomas's hand. 'Good to meet you. I can see why this place has been keeping Abbie so occupied, it needs a lot of work to compete with some of the hotels I've stayed in,' Jack continued. 'But I'm sure you'll get there.'

'We shall do our best,' Thomas replied dryly.

'Well, you'll have to manage without this one as I'll be taking her off your hands again soon,' Jack said, grinning at Abbie.

'Oh?' Thomas raised an eyebrow and looked at her.

Abbie wondered why she felt so guilty suddenly. 'Well, nothing's been decided yet.'

'I've asked Abbie to set up a PR company with me. She'd be brilliant at it, wouldn't she?' Jack threw an arm around her shoulder and pulled her close to him.

Thomas was still looking at her and Abbie was uncomfortable with his scrutiny. 'She would,' he said shortly. 'I must go, they need me in the ballroom,' he added quickly and strode away without looking back.

'Jack, I haven't made any decisions yet,' she told him, cross that he'd said all that to Thomas without checking with her; she had wanted to talk to Thomas herself. She ducked out from under his arm. 'I told him I would help this summer and . . .'

185

'You are working for free, Abbie. The man can't expect you to turn down an actual job offer. Come on, I'll take you back to your sister's.' He leaned down and brushed her lips with his. Abbie hated how she found herself leaning towards his kiss. It was all so easy with Jack, and he seemed to be offering her everything she had wanted just a few weeks ago. She didn't know what to do; she hoped Louise could help her.

She glanced back before following Jack out and saw Thomas standing in the doorway at the end of the corridor before turning and disappearing from view; he had been looking right at them. He must have seen the kiss and she wasn't sure how she felt about that. She thought she'd seen a flicker of anger in his eyes, but that was crazy because their relationship had only ever been about saving Huntley Manor. Hadn't it?

Then she realised that he must be angry with her for leaving; after all, she had promised to help the hotel until the end of summer.

But Jack was right, she needed a job. A paying one. She didn't want to upset anyone. She would just have to make sure Huntley Manor would be okay without her. Abbie wished she could avoid letting anyone down but it seemed impossible. All she could do was follow her heart, and hope that everything would be okay.

Now she just needed to work out what the hell it wanted.

Chapter Twenty-seven

Louise was sitting on the sofa drinking coffee, with a plate of peanut butter on toast beside her, the sun pouring into the living room, when the front door opened and Abbie came in wearing yesterday's clothes. 'And here comes the dirty stopout,' Louise said when her sister sheepishly shuffled into the room and plonked herself down in the armchair.

'Jack just dropped me off,' Abbie said, trying to smooth down her hair. 'We were up most of the night talking. And I drank a lot of wine. I feel like crap.'

'Up all night *talking*?' Louise raised her eyebrows, completely unconvinced. She was surprised her sister had got back with her ex so quickly, knowing he had hurt her a lot before she came to Littlewood. It made Louise thankful once again for her permanent single status.

'I promise. We had a lot to talk about.'

'And there was I thinking you'd stayed out to avoid my wrath!' Louise said.

Abbie leaned forward and looked regretful. 'I'm sorry I didn't tell you Alex was going to be there ...'

'You set it up! What, did you think that by putting us together for the day, I don't know, that I'd change my mind about dating him?' Louise tried not to think about his cute smile as she gave her sister a hard look.

Abbie shrugged helplessly. 'I'm sorry, Lou. I just thought you two could be good together. I won't interfere again. I was obviously wrong.'

Louise didn't want to admit that Abbie may have been right, because it didn't matter – she wasn't ready for anyone. Even Alex. 'I can make my own decisions, okay?'

Abbie nodded. 'Okay. I'm not sure the same can be said for me, though. Jack made me an offer, and I don't know what to say.'

'What kind of offer?'

'He's suggested that we set up our own business together.'

Louise's eyes widened. 'Wow. That's a big leap from breaking up with you, isn't it?'

'I know. I'm still shocked. He wants me to go back to London straight away, and get started on it all.'

Louise listened as Abbie explained how he had apologised and told her how much he had missed her, and how he knew he had acted badly at the end of their relationship. 'Wow. And how do you feel about what he said?'

Abbie groaned. 'I just don't know. I thought we were over, you know? But it's a great opportunity, and we did make a

great team. It's all very confusing. And I'd feel bad about leaving Thomas in the lurch.'

'Surely you don't need to rush into making a decision? Maybe you should take some time to think about it.'

'I know you've never been Jack's biggest fan.'

'I just don't want you to get hurt again. It's a big commitment you'd be making. What if he let you down again?' Louise was nervous about this. She understood that Jack had realised he missed Abbie, and he obviously knew what a great businesswoman she was, but it felt so rushed, she didn't want Abbie to make a hasty decision and then regret it. Plus, the thought of her going back to London and hardly ever seeing her again meant she couldn't be as enthusiastic about the plan as Abbie seemed to want her to be.

'It will be hard to trust him again,' Abbie said slowly. 'But it's a chance for me to be my own boss. I've always had so many ideas; I know that I could do it.'

'Of course you could. But that doesn't mean you have to do it with Jack, does it?'

Abbie groaned. 'It's too much to think about with this hangover. I'm going to go and have a lie-down.'

'Maybe it would help if I actually got to meet Jack?' Louise wanted to finally see this guy for herself, and judge if he was too good to be true or not.

Abbie stood up and thought for a moment. 'Okay, maybe we can all have lunch at Brew then? I'll text him.' She paused. 'And I'm sorry about Alex, but did it go okay?'

'It actually was fun helping out,' Louise admitted.

Abbie smiled. 'I'm pleased. Alex is a good guy, Lou.'

She nodded. 'I know.' She hoped this Jack was too, but she wasn't so sure.

* * *

Louise and Abbie walked into Brew later, which was pretty busy, but Eszter had reserved a table for them. She waved from the counter, where she, Joy and Harry were busy serving the customers. Louise went up to order and Abbie sat at the table, jumping up when Jack walked in. He gave her a kiss on the cheek and Abbie called out to Louise to get him a coffee too.

'Who's that?' Eszter asked as she prepared their order.

'That's Abbie's ex-boyfriend from London,' Louise replied in a low voice. 'He's here to try to persuade her to go back with him.'

'You're not a fan?'

'This is the first time I've met him, so I'll let you know later.'

'I hope she doesn't go,' Eszter said, sliding the tray of coffees to Louise across the counter.

'She never planned to stay though,' Louise said sadly before taking the drinks over. Abbie introduced her to Jack, who kissed her on the cheek and sat down, wrapping his hand over Abbie's.

'So, this is where you've been getting your caffeine fix, then?' he said, looking around Brew. He took a sip of his drink. 'You must be missing Starbucks like mad.'

'I love the coffee here,' Louise said, annoyed at the slight against Brew. As if a chain like Starbucks could hold a candle to somewhere as warm and welcoming as Brew.

'It's all right,' Jack said after tasting his. 'It's what you get used to, really, isn't it?'

'I like both,' Abbie said tactfully. 'The cakes are definitely better here, all home-made.'

'I'll take your word for it,' Jack said. He watched as a woman walked up to the Kindness Board and started to write on it. 'What's that?' he asked, straining to see.

'Oh, it's such a lovely idea,' Abbie said. 'The owners, Joy and Harry, set it up so people in the town could write down random acts of kindness that people have done for them. They've been encouraging everyone to be kinder to each other and to themselves.'

Jack looked at her with a smirk. 'Seriously? A Kindness Board?' He chuckled. 'Can you imagine that in London?'

'I think that's the point,' Louise said. 'We like to be different here in Littlewood. People actually talk to each other and care about one another, unlike Londoners.'

'I was sceptical too at first,' Abbie reminded her. 'But it's a cute idea, and we've all tried to get into the spirit. That is how I got involved with Huntley Manor actually.'

Jack looked at Louise. 'I really think this Lord Huntley should be paying Abbie instead of getting all her talent for free.'

'I think he would, if he could,' Louise replied, not warming to Jack at all. 'The hotel was almost closed down.'

'Well, maybe it should be, you know. That's what business is all about. If he can't run it properly ... Anyway, at least you won't be there much longer, and you'll soon be reaping all the rewards for your work.'

'I'm still thinking about it,' Abbie reminded him with a smile.

'Louise, it's a no-brainer, isn't it? Abbie would be amazing running her own company. Plus, no more having a boss, we'll be our own bosses. That's what everyone wants, isn't it?'

'I don't know about that,' Louise said slowly, acknowledging that at least he thought highly of her sister. 'I love being a nurse, and I'm not my own boss. But if it's what Abbie wants, then she'll do a brilliant job. She just has to be sure it's the right move to make.' She gave her sister a reassuring smile, hoping to let her know that she didn't have to say yes to Jack. 'She has a place to stay here if she needs more time to think about what she wants to do.'

'But if she stays out of the London game much longer, she won't be able to get back into it. Everyone is so fast-paced there, Louise; you wouldn't really know about that out here in the country, but Abbie needs to remind people she's still here before they forget all about her.'

'I don't think my sister is easily forgotten,' Louise told him loyally.

He grinned and squeezed Abbie's knee. 'Well, that's true. I couldn't stop thinking about her after she left.'

'This is all very flattering,' Abbie said with a laugh. 'But Jack is right, I haven't been able to stay in the game, no one

has had any job prospects for me since I've been here, and my contacts will forget what I can do if I don't show them again soon.'

'I just don't think you need to rush into anything. You've only been here for a month after all.'

Abbie sighed. She looked torn. 'I do miss London a lot. And I have always wanted to set up my own business.'

'I am going to make it impossible for you to say no to this.' Jack beamed at her, then drained his coffee cup dry. 'Right, I need to make a couple of phone calls. Dinner tonight, Abbie? My last night in Littlewood then I'll be heading back to London tomorrow,' he reminded her. 'Hopefully not alone,' he winked and stood up. 'Great to meet you, Louise,' he said with a charming smile before striding out of Brew again.

Louise felt a little stunned by him. He certainly was a smooth talker but was he sincere? She flopped back in her chair and looked at Abbie, who had watched him go thoughtfully. 'He's very confident that you're going to go with him.'

Abbie sighed. 'I have really enjoyed it here, but it was never meant to be a long-term thing. Just until I found a new job,' Abbie said. 'And it's been really hard. I haven't had a flicker of interest from anyone. Jack is offering me a great opportunity.'

'Can you trust him, though?' Louise asked. She still felt nervous about him.

'I don't know. He is sorry for what happened. At least he's admitted he made a mistake. I want to trust him. And

I think he's right, we would be a great team. We could be really successful, Lou.'

'I have complete faith in you, but I am worried,' Louise said, deciding to be honest. 'It's such a turnaround from you guys breaking up, and you leaving London, to this. He not only seems to want you two to be business partners but to get back together too,' she said, thinking about how affectionate he had been with Abbie.

'He kissed me this morning,' Abbie admitted. 'And it was nice. It was unexpected, but I do still have feelings for him, Lou.'

'Even though he hurt you?' Louise bit her lip, thinking about Peter and how she didn't want Abbie to become as scared as she was of having her heart broken again. Surely going back with Jack was just asking for trouble?

Abbie let out an exasperated exhale. 'Life's too short to keep dwelling on the past, you have to look forward, Lou. I know that you can't get over Peter hurting you, but if Jack wants a second chance then maybe I should give it to him. He's offering me everything that I wanted just a month ago, how can I walk away from that?'

'I thought you wanted different things now,' Louise said, feeling tears start to well up in her eyes. She didn't want to lose her, but it felt like Abbie had already gone.

'I just want to be happy. Don't you?'

Chapter Twenty-eight

Louise's gloomy mood lingered as she went into work after lunch and all through her shift until it was time to leave. Abbie texted to say she was staying with Jack again, and the prospect of going home to an empty cottage wasn't as enjoyable as it had once been. She would miss Abbie more than she cared to admit. She had spent two years convincing herself she was happy being alone, but now Louise wasn't so sure.

She went to grab her coat and bumped into Julie in the staffroom, also finishing her shift.

'Are you okay?' Julie asked her, looking concerned.

'I'm fine. I think I just need a large glass of wine when I get home.'

'I'm with you on that,' Julie agreed. Then she stopped packing up her handbag and looked at Louise. 'Why don't we get a drink together? There's quite a nice pub close by.'

Louise was surprised but she smiled, pleased she wouldn't

have to go home and dwell on what was going on with Abbie. 'That's a great idea.'

The pub was close enough for them to walk to so they left their cars at the hospital and headed straight there. It was a warm night still and the beer garden was full to bursting when they got there, so they went inside and straight to the bar.

'I'll get these. See if you can find anywhere to sit,' Julie told her, walking up to the bar. Louise looked around. It was a pretty pub with beams on the ceiling and lots of polished wood. It was very popular too and she couldn't see an empty table as she walked around.

'Louise?' called a voice from behind her. She turned around to see Alex at a table behind her with two other men. 'Do you want to join us?'

She hesitated, but there wasn't anywhere else for them to go. 'Okay, sure, thank you.' She squeezed in next to him, making room for Julie as she returned from the bar. Alex introduced his work colleagues Mike and David, and Louise introduced herself and Julie.

'Oh, I recognise you from the hospital,' Julie said to Alex. They had to talk loudly over the thrum of the pub and everyone was leaning in towards one another. Louise was very aware that Alex's knee was just touching hers, and wondered if he realised it too. She couldn't quite bring herself to move away though.

'That's right, I was visiting my niece Hazel,' Alex said with a nod. 'She's home now, thankfully.'

'That's how you know each other, then?' Julie said to Louise.

'Yes, and we both live in Littlewood.'

'Poor Louise had to suffer through an animal charity fete with me yesterday, hearing me lecture people about how to choose a pet responsibly; she deserves a medal really.' They all laughed.

'It was for a good cause at least,' Louise replied, taking a gulp of her wine. Her cheeks were glowing and she wasn't sure if it was from the warm pub, the wine or Alex. 'Alex is a vet,' she explained to Julie.

'Oh, really? Wow. I have two cats; I hope you'd think I'm a good cat owner,' she said to Alex with a smile.

'I'm sure you are.'

'Are you both vets too?' Louise asked the other men. One was a veterinary nurse, the other a vet who mostly worked on farms and was training Alex to deal with some of the horses in the surrounding areas.

'I think we need more drinks,' David announced then, getting up.

The evening passed far more quickly than Louise could have imagined, with lots of laughter, and she began to forget that Alex was sitting so close to her and just enjoyed the company.

When she and Julie went to the loos together, her friend was just as flushed and beaming as she was.

'Okay, tell me honestly,' Julie said as soon as they were in the ladies. 'You and Alex, you're just friends, right?'

'Why?' Louise asked, glancing in the mirror and wishing her cheeks weren't quite so red. She reapplied her lipstick as Julie fluffed her blonde curls beside her.

'Why do you think?' Julie laughed. 'He's gorgeous, don't you agree?'

'You like him?' Louise wasn't sure why her stomach had just dropped.

'I think you'd have to be blind not to like him, but he seems really sweet too. Is he single? You're not dating?'

Louise shook her head slowly. 'We're not dating, no,' she replied. How could she say otherwise?

Julie disappeared into one of the stalls. Louise looked at her face in the mirror. Julie was very pretty and there was no reason for Alex not to like her.

'Do you think he's a nice guy?' Julie called through the closed door.

Louise closed her eyes briefly. 'I think so, yeah,' she said, knowing that he was. So, why was she so scared to let him in? She thought of her sister's words back at Brew, about how she wasn't able to trust or move on from Peter. It had hurt because it was true. She still thought that Abbie was making a mistake in going back to Jack; something wasn't quite right about his offer, she was sure, and he was definitely full of himself. Wasn't Abbie endangering herself by letting Jack back in? And wouldn't the same be true for Louise if she did open up to Alex?

Julie came out then, happy that Louise appeared to be giving her blessing for her and Alex, and they went back to

the table, where more wine awaited them. Louise found herself draining her glass dry quickly, wanting to block out how low she was feeling. It wasn't something she usually did, but tonight she didn't care; she wanted to get drunk, and forget about everything. It was hard to numb all her emotions, though, because since coming back from the loos, Julie had managed to take her seat next to Alex and the two of them were sitting very close together, laughing and talking quietly so she couldn't hear what they were saying.

'Another?' David asked her when he saw her glass was empty. She nodded, wanting to drown out the loneliness that seemed to have overcome her now, and which was being made steadily worse every time she looked over at Alex and Julie.

The night began to pass in a blur and suddenly the bell was being rung for last orders, and the room appeared to be spinning around Louise. She got up, unsteadily, and Alex had to grab her arm to stop her from falling over.

'There's no way we can drive home,' Julie said with a laugh.

'Louise, you can share my taxi back to Littlewood and you can get your car in the morning,' Alex said to Louise, who was finding it tricky to stay upright. It was decided that Julie would share with the other two and they could drop her off en route to their flats outside of town.

'It was great meeting you,' Julie said to Alex when they all stepped outside the pub. 'Maybe we can all do this again sometime?'

'I'd like that,' Alex replied with a smile. He was still holding Louise's arm. 'Right, let's get you home.'

'I don't need babysitting,' Louise said crossly, shaking him off and stumbling to the taxi.

'That's going to hurt tomorrow,' she heard Julie say behind her.

'I'll get her home safely, don't worry,' Alex said.

They all waved and called out goodbye as Louise half fell into the taxi and leaned back against the seat. She closed her eyes, and prayed she wasn't going to be sick and completely embarrass herself in front of Alex.

The taxi started the short journey back to Littlewood. Louise couldn't wait to climb into her own bed. She glanced at Alex. 'I think I had too many,' she said.

He chuckled. 'I think maybe you did, but it doesn't matter. You deserve to let your hair down. And it was a fun night. Julie is really nice, isn't she?'

Louise nodded. 'She is.' She wondered if he was interested in Julie as well and the thought made her throat feel thick.

'Is she . . . is she seeing anyone right now?'

Louise turned her head to look out of the window in case he saw anything on her face that she didn't want him to see. 'I have no idea,' she found herself lying. She desperately wanted to change the subject. 'Oh, look, here we are,' she said, relieved to see Littlewood come into view.

Louise leaned forward to direct the driver to her cottage. Her heart had plummeted when Alex had asked about Julie. But what could she say to him?

Thankfully, the taxi soon pulled up outside Louise's cottage. Alex got out and came round to her side to open her door. She was embarrassingly unsteady on her feet and Alex had to grip her arm to lead her to the door. Then she couldn't seem to unlock it, so Alex did it for her, pushing it open and turning on the hall light. He told her to wait there and nipped back outside for a couple of minutes. She managed to stumble into the kitchen.

'Right, I sent the taxi away. I can walk from here. I wanted to make sure you're okay first.'

She found herself wobbling, so he told her firmly to sit down. She flopped on the sofa and kicked off her shoes and threw her bag onto the floor. She wished the room would stop spinning.

'Drink this,' Alex said, handing her a large glass of water. 'All of it.'

She did as he said and the water did feel pretty good.

'Right, come on, I'll help you up to bed.' He saw her shake her head. 'No arguments.' He helped her off the sofa and they went up to her room. She felt her face turn red at the sight of him in her bedroom.

He pulled back the covers on her bed and turned to her. The room was dark and it was just the two of them. Louise had followed him right to the bed, so now they were only inches apart.

For one crazy moment, she wanted to lean towards him and press her lips against his. She found herself darting forwards, but instead of meeting Alex, she tripped and stubbed her toe on the side of her bed. 'Ouch!'

Alex chuckled and grabbed her arm to steady her again. 'You need to lie down.'

Mortified, she half fell down onto the bed, still in her clothes. She certainly wasn't going to take them off in front of him. 'I'm sorry,' she said.

'We've all been there, don't worry,' he replied. He thought she had meant about being drunk. 'Get some rest, okay? Goodnight, Louise.'

Louise watched him go, wishing she could call him back. She had to say something. 'Stay,' she said.

He stopped and turned. 'Huh?'

'Stay. Please,' she found herself murmuring. 'I don't want to be on my own.'

Her eyes closed. She suddenly felt so sleepy. She wasn't sure if he replied or not. Everything was hazy. She curled up into a ball and everything went dark.

Chapter Twenty-nine

Abbie was in Jack's room again. They'd had a lovely meal together in a small Italian restaurant in the next town and then they had come back to the hotel and Jack had ordered them champagne and strawberries. Abbie had been firm that she had come back just to talk more about Jack's offer, but sitting next to him on the luxurious four-poster bed, the room lit only by two candles, with a glass of champagne in her hand, the lines were starting to blur.

'Abbie, darling, I wish you'd put me out of my misery,' Jack said in a soft voice. They were facing each other on the bed and it felt like the past few weeks in Littlewood hadn't happened. Abbie knew she could erase the humiliation of losing her job, the hurt of Jack turning his back on their relationship, the confusion she felt over her future, with one move. All the choices she needed to make seemed to be spread out in front of her, taunting her. She could just give in and kiss him. She wished she didn't want to, but she had

to admit it would make everything so much simpler. She wouldn't be uncertain anymore.

'I think we have something really special together. Don't you?' He reached out and touched her cheek. 'You look incredible tonight.'

'Jack, do you really think working together and getting back together is a good idea?' Abbie's heart felt as if it was being torn in two. She had started to love Littlewood and the thought of leaving Huntley Manor, its future still up in the air, was making her want to pull away from Jack, but she felt safe in the familiarity of him and their life back in London. She could go back to it as if the past month had never happened. Wasn't it what she had wanted? To go back to the city, back to her career, back to the man who could give her all of it? Why couldn't she be sure, then?

Jack smiled. 'Abbie, we belong together. You know it, and I know it. Why are you still pushing me away?'

'I don't want to get hurt again,' she said, realising she sounded like her sister. She didn't want to be like Louise. She wanted to trust people, to give second chances, to do what would make her happy. But would this make her happy? She just didn't know, but if she didn't try then wouldn't she always wonder?

'I don't want to hurt you ever again. I want to make all your dreams come true.' He leant in then and kissed her.

Abbie was happy to lose herself in the moment, and forget about all the choices she had to make. She found herself hungrily kissing him back, her body responding to him

as it always had. She only hoped that she wasn't making a huge mistake.

* * *

Abbie walked into Brew as soon as it opened the following morning. She had left Jack sleeping and slipped out of the hotel, hurrying in case she bumped into anyone, but, if she was honest, she was mostly nervous about seeing Thomas. She knew that she needed to talk to him, but she wanted to put it off until she was one hundred per cent sure. She had walked outside into the fresh morning, dew dancing on top of the grass, birds singing in the trees around her. She had to admit that last night had been fun. Jack had a way of making everything seem special. And she could say that it had all been down to him, but she admitted that she'd wanted his attentions, and she'd enjoyed waking up with him.

Everything seemed back in order again. Littlewood was a blip in her big plans. She had to stick to what she had mapped out for herself ever since university: being a success in London. And Jack was the key to that. He was offering her the dream again. Only a fool would turn it down.

'Good morning,' Eszter said cheerfully as Abbie walked up to the counter in Brew. 'You're up early. And you're smiling. Something happen last night?'

Abbie laughed. 'You're too intuitive for your own good. I stayed over at Huntley Manor, with Jack.'

'Ah,' Eszter said knowingly. She started making Abbie's

coffee. 'Two coffees to go then?' Abbie nodded and leaned against the counter to wait for them. 'And so, you've made your decision?'

'I think so. I need to go back to London. That was always my plan.'

'Plans can change though, look at me.'

'I know, but I love my job. I want to get back to it, and setting up my own business is something I've always wanted to do.'

'And you need Jack for that?'

'I want him for that,' Abbie admitted. 'He's so successful, Eszter. This is going to work, I know it.'

'Well, as long as this is what you want, then I'm really excited for you.' She slid the two coffees over. 'They're on me. I'll be sorry to see you go, Abbie, but if this is your dream then you should go for it.'

'I think I'll always wonder "what if", you know, if I don't try it.'

'That's true. And you know that we're always here for you, if things don't work out.'

Abbie frowned. Why was everyone so unsure that it would work out? 'Well, thank you, but it will work out. I can do it.'

'Oh, I know you can. I meant with Jack.'

'Why wouldn't it?'

Eszter put her hands up in surrender. 'I'm not saying that it won't. I just wanted you to know that we're all here for you. You can leave Littlewood, but I don't think it ever leaves you, right?'

Abbie picked up the coffees. 'I guess I'll let you know about that.'

'Good luck, Abbie. Honestly, I wish you every success.'

'I know,' Abbie said, letting her defensiveness slide. She smiled. 'Thanks, Eszter. And this isn't goodbye.'

'It better not be.'

Abbie walked out of Brew, looking up at Huntley Manor as she strolled back to Jack. The sun had started to appear and the building looked lovely in the morning light. She would miss this place. More than she ever thought possible before this summer. But she had made her decision.

No going back now.

Now she just had to tell her sister, and Thomas, and she really wasn't looking forward to doing either.

Chapter Thirty

Louise couldn't remember the last time she had felt this hung-over. Not since university, she was sure. She managed to climb out of bed, but her head was pounding, her eyes sore, and her body ached. She was still in her clothes from the night before, and her mouth felt like she had swallowed sandpaper. Ugh. She had no idea why she had done this to herself.

She got out of bed and changed into pyjamas, knowing she wouldn't want to get out of them all day. She tied her hair back and went into the bathroom to wash off the remnants of her make-up and to brush her teeth. She then stumbled downstairs, in need of painkillers and coffee, and possibly a bacon sandwich. The cottage was still and quiet, and she remembered Abbie had stayed at Jack's last night. She was alone again.

Louise walked into the living room and stopped in horror. 'Oh,' she said with a start. Lying on the sofa was a man, his

arm hanging towards the floor. She walked forwards as he grunted and rolled over. Louise stopped again in horror.

Oh God. Alex was asleep on her sofa.

'Alex?' she said tentatively, walking up to him.

He opened his eyes and groaned again. 'What time is it?' he asked, his voice gruff. Louise leaned over to see the clock on the cooker. 'Almost eleven. Um, what are you doing here?'

Alex sat up slowly, looking as rough as she knew she did. It looked like they had all overdone it at the pub. He met her gaze and smiled. 'Well, you asked me to stay last night, so I slept down here.'

Louise felt herself blush from head to toe. She had asked him to stay? How embarrassing. 'I should never have drunk that much.'

She turned quickly and went into the kitchen, unable to look at him any longer. She hurried to the coffee maker. She couldn't believe she had asked Alex to stay. What else did she do or say to him last night?

'How are you feeling?' Alex had followed her in.

'I'm fine,' she trilled, keeping her back to him. 'Well, a little bit hung-over. Look, I'm so sorry I asked you to stay. I shouldn't have done that.'

'I didn't mind,' he replied. 'I've got the day off today anyway.'

She glanced at him quickly over her shoulder. He was watching her closely. She looked away quickly. 'Coffee, or do you need to get home? I bet you have lots to do on your

day off,' she babbled. She poured a coffee and took a deep gulp even though it scalded her.

'Um, yeah, maybe I should go then.'

Louise turned around slowly. 'Of course, yes, you should get going. I'll show you out!' She hurried past him, registering the look of surprise on his face. She just wanted him gone. She was so embarrassed about her behaviour and she was suddenly worried that he might have read something into her asking him to stay. Why had she done it? She was so annoyed at her drunken self. She walked into the hall and yanked open the front door.

Alex shuffled past her. 'Well, I guess I'll see you soon, then?' he said awkwardly, stepping down onto the path. He looked back at her.

Louise wished she could turn back time and stop herself after that first glass of wine. 'Sure. Thanks for looking after me,' she said. 'I promise it'll never happen again.'

He smiled slightly. 'Honestly, I didn't mind at all. I'll see you later.' He lifted his hand in a wave and walked off, his hands in his pockets, head down.

'Alex!' Louise found herself calling out. He paused and turned around. She hurried out of the house and reached for him. She felt him tense up, surprised, but then he returned her hug. She made sure it was quick and pulled away before she could sink too deeply into him.

When they pulled back, they looked at one another and it seemed as though he was about to say something so Louise got there first.

'You're a really good friend,' she told him, forcing on a smile.

Alex kept on looking at her and she was both desperate and terrified for him to stop. Finally, he nodded. 'Take care, Louise,' he replied, and carried on walking.

She watched him go, wishing she could have done more than hug him. But she knew that she couldn't. She had made sure he knew that they were friends, and that was it.

She closed the door slowly and then sank against it. She wasn't ready to start anything with anyone, even if the sight of him on her sofa had made her knees wobble, and her stomach had come alive when he had held her for that brief moment.

It was better for them both if she stayed away from him.

Even though she really didn't want to.

Chapter Thirty-one

After lunch, Eszter headed with Anne and Zoe to the community centre. The morning had become grey and drizzly and they wanted to see what was on offer there for them to do in the afternoon.

The centre was in a low, red-brick building off the edge of the high street, with lots of colourful posters stuck around the walls of the hallway, which led to two large rooms used for activities, a small kitchen and an outside area complete with playground, vegetable patch and sandpit. Everyone was inside today, though.

Jane met them near the entrance. 'I'm so glad you came by,' she greeted. 'We have two classes on today – painting for adults, and drama club for kids.'

'Sounds perfect,' Eszter replied with a smile. Zoe hung by her side looking nervous, which was most unlike her. 'You love being in plays at school, this will be really fun,' she reminded her daughter, remembering how she and Nick

had watched with pride as Zoe starred in her school musical just a year ago.

'Come on, let me show you what we're doing,' Jane said kindly to Zoe, taking her hand. She led the way to the kids' room, and Eszter anxiously watched them go.

'Do you ever stop worrying about them?' she said out loud.

Anne shook her head. 'Even when they move away, no.'

They shared a look of understanding, then headed off down the corridor. The art class was just starting when they walked into the long, narrow room. There were twelve other people waiting for the class to begin and a teacher at the front in an apron, ready to go. Everyone had their own table and chair and there were paints, paper and brushes all set up ready. At the front, next to the teacher, was a small table with a bowl of fruit on it.

'Welcome to Watercolour for Beginners,' the lady at the front greeted them with a smile. 'I'm Lisa and I'll be your teacher today. We're going to start small with this bowl of fruit and see how we get on. Has anyone painted before?'

Eszter was surprised to see Anne's hand join the four in the air. 'When did you paint?' she asked Anne as the teacher walked around to get a better idea of everyone's competency levels.

'A thousand years ago. When I was a teenager, I loved art, especially painting, and I used to annoy my parents by talking about making it a career. Of course, then I met Frank, and other things got in the way.'

Eszter didn't like the way Frank seemed to have shaped the whole of Anne's life. A partner should complement you,

not control you. She thought about Nick and how she used to tell him how much she envied him for being so happy as a teacher; he was passionate about it. She now knew he had been so passionate he had given up a medical career and left his family because of it. Eszter had never had any inkling what she wanted to do, so she had drifted from job to job and she wasn't sure even now what work would make her happy. She liked working at Brew, but it didn't particularly challenge her. She had no idea what she would do after the summer.

They started sketching the fruit, with the teacher walking round to give pointers. Eszter didn't think her messy pencil scratchings resembled anything close to the bowl of fruit and she swallowed the urge to start giggling. She glanced at Anne who was engrossed in her drawing and was doing a much better job.

'Sometimes I think I'll never find anything I'm really good at,' Eszter admitted aloud, thinking that her pear looked more like an egg.

'You're a brilliant mother, don't ever underestimate that.'

Eszter was surprised and touched to hear that praise from her mother-in-law. 'That's really kind of you to say.'

'I could never have coped without Frank, I'm sure.'

'Honestly, you would be surprised with what you can cope with when you have to.'

'Right,' the teacher announced. 'Why don't we start putting some colour into our pictures?'

Eszter looked up in horror.

* * *

The two-hour class ended up moving surprisingly quickly and at the end of it Anne had a pretty painting of fruit, whereas Eszter had some coloured splodges on her paper. She promptly threw hers away and decided the painting class wasn't for her, but she encouraged Anne to sign up for the six-week course and was really happy to see her do just that.

They walked to the kids' area to collect Zoe, who hurried past them, head down, straight for the door.

'What's going on?' Eszter went after her daughter, the rain still floating down from the grey sky. She pulled the hood of her parka up and looked around frantically, spotting Zoe standing on the pavement, her hair getting soaked.

'Zoe, what's happened?' Eszter rushed to her daughter. She heard Anne hurrying to catch up with them. Eszter was horrified to see tears in her daughter's eyes.

'I just want to go home,' Zoe said, trying to pull away from her. 'Back to Hungary!' She started walking again and Eszter and Anne hurried to catch her up.

They walked back to the cottage with Zoe refusing to talk and Eszter and Anne sharing worried and confused looks.

Once in the warm, dry cottage, they shed their shoes and coats and Anne went into the kitchen to make tea.

Eszter led Zoe to the sofa and wrapped an arm around her daughter. 'Zo, you need to tell me what happened at the community centre. I'm worried about you.'

Zoe nestled in closer to her mother. 'We all had to read

215

some of this play out loud, and when I read my bit, the other kids laughed. They said they couldn't understand me because of my accent. They said I didn't belong here.' She started to cry.

Eszter felt like her heart was breaking and that she wished she could go back to that community centre and shout at all the kids. Instead, she pulled her daughter into her arms and stroked her hair. 'It's okay. They've just never met anyone from Hungary before. When people are faced with something different, sometimes it scares them a little and instead of being welcoming and kind, they choose to attack.'

'But I'm not different to them. Am I?'

'You just come from somewhere different, that's all. You're special, and they didn't know how to handle that.' Eszter was shocked after having had such a warm welcome in Littlewood that Zoe had faced this kind of hostility. 'I'm sorry, darling, but once they get to know you, they won't notice that you have an accent, they will just love you for the person that you are.'

'I'm never going back. Why can't we just go home?'

Anne paused in the doorway with a tray of mugs and biscuits. 'Is everything all right?' she asked hesitantly.

'Zoe is just a little bit upset.' Eszter told Anne what had happened.

'I don't like it here,' Zoe said.

Anne handed Zoe a mug of warm milk, coffee for Eszter, and a cup of tea for herself and they each had a chocolate biscuit. 'Well, I'm really glad that you're here.' Anne told her. 'Listen, Zoe, your dad was born here and this was where he grew up, so

you belong in Littlewood just as much as those other kids do.'

Eszter's phone rang and she saw it was Anne's builder. Eszter picked up and he told her that after a week's work it was okay for Anne to move back into her house whenever she wanted. When Eszter hung up, she looked over at Zoe, who had gone to sit next to her grandmother to show her some pictures on her phone. It was a shame that Anne would be moving out when they were really just getting to know each other. Eszter decided not to say anything until the morning and hopefully they could salvage the evening.

* * *

Eszter made her way to Brew in the morning, relieved that the day had dawned bright and dry. She had managed to cheer Zoe up with an evening of playing board games, and she had left her and Anne planning to go to the park while she was at work. She was worried about both of them.

Eszter had told Anne before she left that her house was ready for her to go back to.

'That doesn't mean that you and Zoe will be leaving soon, does it?' Anne had asked in a low voice as she made their breakfast.

Zoe had seemed slightly more cheerful in the light of the new day, but she had told Eszter before she fell asleep that she missed Hungary. Eszter thought about their life back there – she had no career to go back to, her parents lived far away, and the flat they had shared with Nick no longer felt like home, but they did have friends there, and it was

familiar, so she understood why Zoe was missing it. Life had been easy and happy for them there before, but Eszter also knew that without Nick, everything would be different when they went back to Hungary, and she was in no rush to face a new life without him. She told Zoe they had planned to spend the summer in Littlewood, so they would see it through; her daughter hadn't looked too happy about it, but Anne had visibly relaxed when Eszter reassured her that they would help get her settled back in her home. They wouldn't be rushing to get on a plane anytime soon.

Eszter felt the burden of responsibility for making all the decisions now herself. She missed having a partner to discuss the future with. What would Nick say they should do?

She pushed open the door to Brew, her mind still agitated. Joy immediately noticed her preoccupation as she and Harry worked with Eszter to get the café ready for opening.

'Has something happened?' Joy asked her as she switched the coffee machine on. Eszter had been wiping the same spot on the counter for the past five minutes without realising it. 'A problem shared, and all that.'

Eszter smiled at Joy, grateful that there was someone she could unburden herself to. She told her what had happened at the community centre. 'I was nervous before coming here, after hearing all the news about Brexit, you know. I wasn't sure we'd be welcome, but you were all so lovely to us, I thought how lucky we were to be here. I certainly didn't think Zoe would have any trouble. She wants to go home, but I know Anne would be devastated if we did. I just don't know what to do.'

Joy sighed. 'Gosh, kids can be so unkind sometimes. I agree with you, I just think they aren't used to having anyone here from another country, and change can be scary. I think once they get to know Zoe, they will make friends with her.'

'I don't want Zoe to be faced with something difficult and choose to run away, but also she's young and doesn't deserve to go through this after losing her father. Maybe I should just take her home.' Eszter sighed. She wasn't sure going back to Hungary was what she wanted at all, though.

'Why don't you see if you can encourage Zoe and the other kids to come together? We could do something here. Maybe a cooking class? We could get Jane to bring them in for a lesson and have Zoe lead the class with us. I think they would all have fun, and see that Zoe is very much part of Littlewood.'

'I suppose that might work,' Eszter said slowly. 'We've been having such a lovely summer, I don't want this to ruin our memory of Littlewood.'

Joy nodded. 'I think you should talk to Jane about it, tell her what's happened, and she can talk to the other parents. Littlewood is a welcoming place, no one wants to see the two of you leave under a cloud, I know it.'

'I hope you're right. I just want Zoe to be happy.'

'I know, but she has been so far, hasn't she? It's just kids being kids. We will bring them all together, I promise you. Who can be unkind when surrounded by cakes?'

Eszter laughed despite herself. 'Joy, the world should really think more like you.'

'My thoughts exactly!'

Chapter Thirty-two

Abbie took a deep breath and knocked on the door of the library at Huntley Manor. She was nervous about telling Thomas her decision to go back to London. She had spoken to Louise earlier, who had seemed resigned to the news if not overly enthusiastic about it, but she knew that her sister just wanted her to be happy and that she would miss her. She wasn't sure how Thomas would react at all, but she couldn't avoid him any longer.

Thomas's deep voice told her to come in, so she pushed open the door and smiled tentatively at him. He was at his desk, buried in paperwork, the sleeves of his crisp white shirt pushed up, his hair tousled as if he had been running his hands through it.

Abbie stepped into the room and found herself taking a mental picture of him, wondering if she would ever see him again. She was sure of her decision, but seeing him made her waver. She had loved working here with him. The thought

that she wouldn't be any longer was harder to comprehend than she had realised. 'Do you have a minute?'

'Of course. Take a seat.'

Abbie sat down on the other side of the desk and crossed her legs. 'I wanted to talk to you, to tell you that I've made a decision. As you know, Jack's been here all weekend and he's presented an opportunity to me, and I feel that I need to accept it.'

He nodded and put his pen down. 'You're going back to London.' His face showed no sign of what he felt about that.

'I have to, Thomas. Setting up my own PR company is something I've always wanted to do. And I haven't had any hint of other job prospects so far this summer. I can't turn this down. But I am sorry to leave here.'

Thomas nodded, avoiding her eyes. 'I'm sorry that you'll be going,' he said softly, then he cleared his throat and spoke more formally to her. 'It sounds like a good opportunity, and I'm aware it wasn't ideal working here for free. I appreciate all you've done.'

'You know I was happy to help,' she said, wishing he didn't sound so businesslike. Wouldn't he miss her at all? 'I'm so sorry I won't be seeing out the summer here, but I know you'll make a big success of the relaunch and I will definitely . . .'

'We'll see,' Thomas cut her off before she could say that she wanted to come back for the party. 'I'm just looking at the books, and even if I do the relaunch party at the end of the summer, I just don't think I can hold the bank off much

longer. Perhaps you leaving is the sign I need that this place is finished.'

Abbie stared at him. 'No, you have to keep trying! The party is all set up, the ballroom is almost ready. Please don't give up just because I'm going.'

'It has nothing to do with you.'

Abbie was stunned by his coldness. She thought they had become close, and that he might be happy for her. She was at a loss as to what to say.

'Look, Abbie, I appreciate your enthusiasm for this place, I really do, but you're going and it's up to me what I do next.' He picked his pen up and looked down at his paperwork; apparently the conversation was over in his mind.

Abbie was furious with him. 'Why won't you try?'

'This is no longer your concern, Abbie,' he said, not even bothering to look up.

Abbie stood up. She couldn't believe their partnership was ending like this. She thought back to their dinner together and how she had thought there was something in the air between them. That all seemed like it had happened to two different people. 'Goodbye, Thomas,' she said, matching his cold tone, and hoping that she didn't start crying in front of him.

'Abbie?'

She paused in the doorway, hating the hope that sprang up as she turned around. She wasn't sure what she wanted him to say, but she waited, with bated breath.

He looked at her for a moment, then nodded. 'Good luck.'

Abbie was annoyed that tears started to well up behind

her eyes. She couldn't understand why he was being so distant after all they had shared since she arrived in Littlewood. She didn't know why he couldn't be happy for her, or why he was so willing to give up on Huntley Manor. There was nothing left to say. Everything between them seemed dissolved for ever.

Why did that hurt so much?

She spun around and marched out, her heels echoing down the hall. She left as quickly as she could, yanking open the front door and stepping out into the morning light.

Abbie pulled out her phone and typed a message to Jack.

I'm coming to London tomorrow.

His reply was instant:

You won't regret this!

Abbie was relieved that she had made the choice she had. It was clear that Thomas didn't care what she did. She marched back to Louise's cottage and decided that the sooner she was back in London, the better.

'What's happened?' Louise said, looking up as Abbie flounced into the kitchen. She was making a sandwich for lunch.

Abbie sank down onto a stool and sighed. 'I just told Thomas that I'm going back to London, and he was horrible about it. He acted as if he didn't care at all, and then he

said he was going to give up on the hotel, after all the work we've done!'

Louise carried on slicing up some cheese. 'Maybe he's upset you're going? You know how reserved he is, maybe he couldn't show how much he's going to miss you.'

Abbie snorted. 'Honestly, he didn't care at all. And now he might just sell up, what was the point?'

'Do you think he's just worried about doing it without you?'

Abbie felt a flash of guilt, but she shook her head. 'It didn't seem that way. I think he's glad I'm going. I thought we were friends, you know? Well, it just proves that I'm doing the right thing, doesn't it?' She wondered why Thomas not caring that she was going was upsetting her so much.

Louise looked at her. 'Thomas cares about you, I'm sure he does.'

'He's got a funny way of showing it. I'd better get packing, I suppose.'

'Are you really sure about this, Abs? You want to go?'

'There's nothing here for me.'

'You know that's not true! We're all going to miss you.'

Abbie forced a smile. 'I'll miss you, Lou, but I'll see you soon. I have to do this. And you don't need me; you've been fine here for two years without me.'

Louise sighed. 'But who will push me to do things that scare me?'

'The Kindness Pact still stands,' Abbie said, climbing off

the stool. 'You still need to think of yourself more, and I'll expect lots of progress reports. Especially about Alex.'

'There's no progress report there. I told you, we're just friends.'

'But he stayed over.'

'He probably thought I might choke in my sleep or something.'

'Or he cares about you.'

Louise sighed and looked away. 'I think seeing me that drunk is enough to put anyone off for a lifetime.'

Abbie didn't want Louise to sink back into her shell when she was gone. 'Just think about it, Lou, for me? I think the two of you could be really happy together.'

'I don't want you to go,' Louise admitted then.

Abbie felt tears prick in her eyes again. Why was it so hard to leave this place? She'd only been there for a few weeks but it had crawled under her skin. She should be excited about going back to London, but part of her was resisting the pull back to the city. 'Please be happy for me,' she said, a lump rising up in her throat.

Louise rushed around the counter to hug her. 'I am happy for you. I want you to do what you want to do. If this is what you want, then I'm really excited for you.' She pulled back to look at Abbie, tears welling up in her eyes too. 'It is what you want, right?'

Abbie nodded, wondering why she didn't feel as sure as she had a few minutes ago. The meeting with Thomas had shaken her more than she cared to admit. She didn't like the

thought of that being their last ever conversation. But he had made it clear that it was. She had to look to the future now. She needed to jump into this new challenge, and not look back. She pulled back from her sister. 'This is what I need to do.'

'I really hope it works out for you.'

Abbie walked up to her room and looked at her things, ready to be put back into her suitcases. This was only ever meant to be a short-term visit, just until she got back on her feet. And she had. Jack was offering her everything she had ever wanted. She just needed to grab it with both hands. But she found herself perching on the edge of the bed, not quite ready to start packing just yet.

Abbie told herself she was making the right decision. That she belonged back in London. That Jack was her future. That Littlewood wasn't her home.

But still a slither of doubt ran under her skin.

She wondered why her head was telling her she was doing the right thing while at the same time it felt as though her heart was trying to pull her in the opposite direction.

Notes from the Brew Kindness Board:

The kind stranger who paid for my coffee in here when he was buying his — an unexpected treat!

* * *

Thank you to the woman who let me go in front of her at the post office, seeing I was struggling with two kids crying to go home, her kindness really helped rescue the situation.

* * *

My next-door neighbour for bringing me and the kid's dinner every night while my wife was in hospital for a week. You saved us from beans on toast!

* * *

Thank you to my niece for walking my dog every morning in the holidays to save me struggling with my arthritis. We both appreciate it darling.

Part Three

Crossroads

Chapter Thirty-three

Louise stomped over puddles as she walked through the town, her head covered by the hood of her parka. Usually she loved Littlewood but today, soaked by rain even though it was the end of July, she felt decidedly grumpy with it. She had planned to spend her day off under a blanket on the sofa, but Eszter had begged her to have breakfast at Brew. Louise knew that the real reason Eszter was so keen for her to go there was because she thought Louise would spend the whole day wallowing, and annoyingly she was right.

Louise was still upset that Abbie had gone back to London with Jack a few days ago. She was trying to be excited for her but she couldn't shake the feeling of doubt she had deep in her bones that Abbie had made a mistake in going.

As Louise got closer to Brew, her bad mood started to lift as she thought about the delicious breakfast she would get there and the very strong cup of coffee she was craving. Maybe it was better to spend the morning with her friends

rather than worrying about her sister. The sofa would still be there waiting for her that afternoon anyway.

She reached the cosy, welcoming café, and walked in, pulling down her hood, and shaking off the rain. Harry and Joy waved from behind the counter as Eszter called out 'Good morning!', and Louise smiled despite herself.

'It's horrible out there,' she said, unnecessarily. If you couldn't comment on the weather when you were British, then what could you do? She walked over to the counter and noted that the café was particularly quiet. Obviously everyone else in Littlewood had decided not to leave the shelter of their cars to stop off for coffee on the way to work.

'How are you?' Eszter asked her. 'Have you heard from Abbie?'

Louise shook her head. 'No, nothing since she texted to say they had arrived, but I guess she has to settle in.' Louise bit her lip. She wanted Abbie to tell her how well things were going so she could relax a little bit more.

'Abbie will be fine; she can make a success out of anything,' Eszter said. 'I just wish she could have stayed here longer. We'll all miss her.'

Louise nodded. 'It was all very sudden. I hope you're right and everything will be okay. I can't help worrying. Plus, selfishly, I didn't want her to go. I liked having her here.'

'We all did,' Joy said. 'Abbie knows what she's doing. If she needs help, she will call you. Now, what can we get you? You look in need of sustenance!'

Louise smiled. 'Yes, please. A very large coffee and a full English today, I think.'

'Eszter, why don't you take your break, and I'll bring you some breakfast too?'

Eszter and Louise went over to a table by the window and sat down, Louise removing her many layers now she was in the warm café. She looked out at Huntley Manor standing tall through the sheets of rain still coming down. 'I just thought she had settled in so well here,' she said. She knew that Abbie had been enjoying working at the hotel and thought it was a shame she had left it.

'But she'd always planned to go back to London,' Eszter said, gently. 'And running her own business is a great opportunity, right?'

'I know, I want to be happy for her, but I just can't shake the feeling that Jack isn't right for her.'

'And you thought Thomas was?'

'They were getting on so well. She was so excited about helping the hotel be more successful; I was surprised she was so eager to give it up and rush back to London with Jack, that's all.'

'I think Thomas was surprised too. He came in yesterday and seemed very down.'

'They had an argument before she left, she told me,' Louise said. 'I think he was upset she was going and told her that he might just give up on saving the hotel; Abbie was furious with him.' Louise sighed. She hated to think of her sister leaving town on such bad terms with him. 'I thought there might have been something between them.'

'But she still loves this Jack?'

'Seems so. I just hope he pulls his weight and doesn't leave everything to Abbie.' She smiled at Joy then as she brought over two coffees and two large, steaming plates of eggs and bacon. 'This looks amazing.'

'I hope it will cheer you both up,' Joy said, giving them a stern look. 'You'll frighten away our customers with those serious faces.'

'What's on your mind?' Louise asked Eszter when Joy left to serve someone who had just walked in. 'The cookery class?'

Eszter nodded. 'I just want it to go well.' It had been Joy's idea to run a cookery class at Brew to try to help Zoe make friends with the local children after they had upset her at the community centre.

'Who can resist Joy's cakes?'

Eszter smiled. 'Anne has been really worried since Zoe said she wanted to go home. She's only just getting to know her granddaughter, so it would be a real shame to leave now. Hopefully once the kids get to know Zoe, and they all have fun in the class, she'll stop saying it. It was a real surprise, I think, to both of us. We'd only been made to feel welcome here before.'

'Zoe is just a bit different in the kids' eyes, that's all. As you say, once they all have a chance to get to know each other, then they'll forget that she doesn't come from here. Joy will bring everyone together, she always does.' Louise smiled over at the café owner who was bustling about behind the

counter. Behind her was the Kindness Board, full up with acts of kindness that locals had been writing on it. 'Kindness will always win out.'

Eszter nodded. 'Joy's philosophy is a good one. Let's hope it works on children as well as adults.'

Louise looked out of the window then and saw Thomas Huntley walking past, wrapped up in a coat, hands in pockets, with his head down. He cast a subdued figure as he strolled past Brew and walked towards his family home. 'I hope he's okay,' she said, frowning.

Eszter followed her gaze. 'He won't really give up on the hotel now that Abbie's gone, will he?'

'Maybe I should talk to him?'

'It can't hurt. I hope Abbie realises how much we all miss her.'

'I wonder if she misses us too.'

Chapter Thirty-four

Abbie smiled as Jack walked into the open-plan kitchen-living room in his riverside flat in London. She hadn't slept well again so had got up before him and started to make them breakfast. 'Are you hungry?' she asked, holding up a spatula. 'I made pancakes and eggs and there are still loads of pastries left from the weekend.'

Jack came over in his suit to kiss her on the cheek. 'Darling, I can't. I'll be late if I stop to eat all this.' He grabbed a muffin from the plate. 'I'll take this to go. Shall we have a takeaway tonight?' He moved away to pick up his briefcase and phone.

'Sure,' she said, trying not to be disappointed. 'What time will you be home?'

'Hopefully not too late. Decided on a name yet?'

She shook her head. 'But I'm almost there.'

'I know you are. You'll think of something perfect. See you later!' He left in a whirl, shutting the door to their flat with a bang.

Abbie sighed. She had been back in London for a few days and had spent most of that time in Jack's flat watching him go to work, trying to start planning their company on her own. He obviously had to stay in his job for the time being, as they needed some income coming in, after all, but she was feeling the pressure of coming up with all the ideas on her own. They needed a name and a business plan so they could approach investors. Jack had suggested the night before that they put the company in her name for now, as he still worked at City PR and didn't want anyone there finding out he was planning to jump ship until he was ready to go. It made her even more nervous to think that this would all be hers.

If she was completely honest with herself though, the real reason she hadn't slept well was because she kept thinking about Littlewood.

She grabbed her phone to text Kate, her former roommate and university friend, asking if she fancied breakfast before work. Kate replied straight away to say she would pop in. It was on her way and they'd barely had time for a proper catch-up. Abbie was relieved she wouldn't have to spend the whole morning alone with her thoughts. She didn't want to end up eating all the food by herself either.

Abbie sat down at the glass table and poured herself a coffee. She looked across at the window that displayed a pretty impressive view of London. It was a grey, cloudy morning that promised rain on the horizon, but she'd thought that she would feel happier at being able to look down at her beloved city than she did. She put it down to

the fact that she had left Littlewood so abruptly, and that she had upset everyone by doing so. She thought of the look on Thomas Huntley's face when she told him she was going back to London. It was only there for a moment before they ended up rowing, but it was an expression of pure disappointment. She really felt as if she had let him down.

Jack had told her not to be such a walkover – that she had been giving Thomas her PR expertise for free and he needed to sort his own business out. But that went against the kindness pact she had made with her sister and Eszter, and she had been feeling really good about helping Thomas to save Huntley Manor. They had been renovating the ballroom after she suggested it was a room people would love, and they had been planning a big party at the end of the summer to mark its reopening.

Abbie had fallen in love with the hotel. Huntley Manor had reminded her so much of her grandparents' home in Cornwall that her family had sold, and she didn't want Thomas to have to go through the same heartache. But now that she had gone back on her promise to help him over the summer, she was worried he would do just that.

Abbie sighed as she sipped the coffee, willing it to make her feel slightly more human. She wished she could keep everyone happy, but it was proving impossible. Jack was so excited for them to have their own business, and she knew it was a great opportunity, but she wished she could feel more enthusiastic about it.

The flat doorbell buzzed and she jumped up to let her

friend in, pleased to have a distraction. Kate was a willowy blonde who worked as a journalist for a London paper. They had been firm friends since university, and she had missed living with her. They had often spent their Friday nights watching TV in their PJs, wine and snacks scattered everywhere, putting the world to rights.

'Hello, stranger,' Kate said, pulling her in for a tight hug. She leaned back to look at her. 'I think the countryside suited you – you look great.'

'It was a more relaxing pace of life, for sure. Come in and help me eat all this food please.'

Kate followed her into the living area and whistled. She had never seen Jack's flat before. 'He definitely makes more money than us.' She laughed. 'Blimey, you have a feast here.' She sat down at the table and Abbie handed her a plate and a coffee. She had gone a bit overboard with the tray of pastries, the scrambled eggs and bacon, pancakes and fruit basket, but that's what insomnia did to her. 'So, how is it being back in London? Did you miss us? Or have you become a country bumpkin?' Kate tucked into the food as she waited for Abbie to reply.

'I enjoyed it there more than I thought I would. It was lovely living with Louise, and I actually found a project to work on, which I'm a bit bummed about not being able to finish actually.' She told Kate all about Huntley Manor.

'It sounds like something out of Jane Austen! This Lord Huntley, is he an eligible bachelor? A Mr Darcy? Do I need to book a stay there?'

Abbie laughed. 'He's really nice. I feel bad for coming back here. I hope he'll be okay without me.'

Kate looked at her. 'But Jack made you an offer you couldn't refuse? I'm sure Thomas understands. I was surprised though. I thought you and Jack were over for good. Where is he anyway?'

'At work.'

'Oh, he's found something while you work on the new business then?'

'What do you mean – found something?'

Kate looked at her for a moment, then she frowned and put her fork down. 'Hang on, he has told you everything, right?'

Abbie suddenly felt nervous. 'Told me what?'

'About City PR?'

'What about them?'

Kate sighed. 'He was suspended, a week or so ago. They're investigating whether he's stolen money from the company. I heard it from Melanie,' she said, referencing the receptionist at Abbie's old office. 'She said the whole place was in uproar.'

'That can't be right. He's been going to work every day since I came back.'

'I don't know what to tell you; she was pretty definite about it. Do you think he was too scared to tell you?'

Abbie shook her head. 'This makes no sense,' she said, but then she thought about it. Maybe it *did* make sense. If he had been suspended, maybe that's why he came to see her in Littlewood. He knew he would need a new job, and that she didn't have one, so thought they could run their

own business together instead. 'Oh, God, is that the real reason why he suggested our company should be in my name? Because no one is going to invest in something run by someone who steals money.' She felt sick and pushed her plate away. 'I can't believe he would keep this from me. I've dropped everything to come back here for him.'

'Hang on; maybe it's not as bad as we think. Melanie does like to exaggerate, doesn't she? And you said he's been going to work, right?'

'Unless he's been putting on a suit and pretending to go. No, seriously, would anyone actually do that?' They stared at one another, trying to decide if Jack could be that person.

'There's only one way to find out!'

'I need to go to City PR,' Abbie said, jumping up. She had to know if Jack had been lying to her or not.

'I'm coming with you.' Kate grabbed a Danish pastry and followed Abbie towards the door.

As they left, Abbie couldn't help but worry that her sister had been right all along. Had she really made a huge mistake in coming back to London? With a sinking feeling that refused to leave her stomach, they flagged down a taxi and headed to her old office to see if her boyfriend was really there or not.

Chapter Thirty-five

Louise walked in to Huntley Manor through the large oak door. She asked Amy, the receptionist, where she could find Thomas and was directed to the ballroom. It had been a stunning space used for many parties and events through the years, both when it was just a stately home and when Thomas's parents ran it as a hotel, but it had fallen out of use and Thomas had left it locked up until now.

She had never taken Abbie for a romantic, but when Louise walked in and saw how the ballroom was taking shape, she thought that her sister must be one at heart. Even Louise, who was herself firmly against romance since her childhood sweetheart had left her at the altar, stood in the doorway, her mouth open as she took the room in. She could instantly picture people in years gone by floating around, the room lit by candlelight, the clinking of crystal glasses, soft music playing, the formal dancing and coy glances at beaus, the rustle of long dresses . . . it all seemed

to be happening right in front of her eyes. 'This room is beautiful,' she said.

Thomas turned around and smiled at her. 'There's a lot more to do, but it's starting to look like how I remember it again.' He gestured to the room. 'It brings back a lot of memories.'

'I bet. I just wanted to see it, after Abbie told me so much about it. I hope that's okay?' Louise hadn't spent much time with Thomas; she had always been slightly intimidated by him being a lord and he seemed to keep himself to himself. But she had only ever heard good things said about him in the town, and she wanted to make sure he was okay now.

'Of course. How is Abbie doing?' he asked, not quite meeting her eyes.

'I haven't heard much from her; I expect she's busy getting settled. There's a lot for her to do.'

'Of course.'

'I suppose I wanted to make sure that you were still renovating this room.' Louise looked at him. 'She mentioned that the two of you had words before she left.'

Thomas sighed. 'I've decided to wait until the ballroom is finished before I make any decisions about the future. I know that Abbie was convinced we could save this place from closing, and I'd like to believe that she was right, but the debts are building. The bank tells me I can make more from a sale if the room is renovated, so at least I have some time to think it all over.'

'Well, I know she really wanted to help you keep this

place open. It's such a lovely building, and the history of it is really important to the town. I hope you can make it work. If there's anything I can do, just let me know. Please.' Louise felt guilty that Abbie had left halfway through the project, although it wasn't her fault, but it was her hometown and she didn't want anyone to be unhappy there.

'Thank you. Actually, I'm glad you're here. I have something to show you.' He led her out and they walked through the hotel.

They entered the grand library, which was now his office, and she could see why Abbie had been so captivated by the place.

'Abbie told me that this house reminded her of the home your grandparents had when you were growing up, and that it was sold and divided up into flats.'

Louise nodded. 'I remember it less vividly than Abbie, but she always loved that house, and I know she was upset that my parents let it go. I think that's why she was so determined to help you.'

'When she told me about it, I was curious, so I started to research it and I found something I thought she might like. I have no idea when I'll ever see her again, so I thought you could give it to her instead?' Thomas lifted up a large box and laid it on his desk. He opened it up and inside was a painting in a wooden frame of the house in Cornwall.

Louise let out a small gasp. She leaned over it and was pulled back to her childhood: summers spent running around the house with Abbie, lying in the grass under the summer

sun, feeling as if nothing bad could ever touch them there. 'It's amazing. Thomas, however did you get this?'

'It's a painting by a local artist, I found it on her website and she was still selling prints of it, but the original was hanging in a local gallery and they sold it to me. Do you think Abbie will like it?'

Louise looked at him. 'She will love it. What a wonderful gift.' She was worried that her heart, firm against anything to do with love, might be melting right then and there. She touched his arm. 'It's so thoughtful of you.'

'I wanted to repay her for all that she had done for me this summer. I had basically given up, and she changed that.'

'Are you sure you don't want to give it to her yourself?'

He shook his head. 'She's in London now. I don't want her to feel any obligation to me, I mean, this house. You give it to her, Louise, and I hope she's happy.'

Louise looked at the painting and wished they could go back to that simpler time. Everything seemed so complicated now. 'You need to keep this hotel open, Thomas; we would all help you with the reopening event. Think about it.'

'I will.'

* * *

Abbie and Kate climbed out of their taxi outside City PR's tall office block. Abbie looked up at the shiny glass building where she had worked for two years and took a deep breath.

She was glad Kate was with her when she took her arm as they walked through the doors and into a lift. Abbie

wasn't sure what was worse – the idea that Jack had been stealing from his work, or that he had been pretending to be going into the office every day. Either way, she was about to have confirmation that her boyfriend had either had his good name sullied for no reason, or that he was a complete and utter liar. She wished the lift would move slower, but they soon reached the right floor and were walking towards the reception desk. Abbie could see Melanie there, and she wanted to turn back around and run, but she knew that Kate would stop her. And she had to know one way or another.

'Oh my God, Abbie! And Kate! What are you guys doing here?' Melanie said with a big smile for them.

'We're here to see Jack,' Abbie said, her throat feeling like sandpaper. 'Is he here?'

Melanie looked confused. 'I haven't seen him for a week. He's meant to come in soon for a meeting, I think.' She looked at Abbie and saw the look on her face. 'Oh, you thought he was here?'

'He's been telling her he's still working here – he left the flat this morning in a suit,' Kate confirmed. Abbie wanted to sink through the floor.

'Oh my God! I always thought he was a twat, but that's so shady. No, they suspended him a week ago.'

'Why? What happened, Mel?' Abbie managed to ask. She wasn't sure if she wanted to cry or hit something really hard. Well, hit Jack, actually. He had made such a fool of her.

'They realised that his expense account was out of control, that he was claiming for things that had nothing to do with

work, including some of the rent on his flat. They don't want any bad publicity, so I heard they're planning to make him resign and leave quietly.'

Abbie couldn't believe that Jack was capable of that. Sure, he had always been a charmer, a little bit arrogant sometimes, but a liar and a thief? Did she really not know him at all? 'I have to go, I need to find him.'

'Shall I . . . ?'

Abbie shook her head at Kate. 'I need to do this alone. I'll call you.' She hurried back into the lift and flopped against the wall as it floated back down to the ground floor. Where the hell was he? If you were pretending to go to work, where would you go instead?

Then Abbie realised she knew exactly where he was, and she walked out into the pouring rain and into a waiting taxi, determined to track him down and confront him.

She watched the city float past the window, and the place that had always filled her with energy and excitement now felt strange to her. Suddenly, she longed to be having a cosy cuppa in Brew with her sister, and it took all her effort to keep her anger alive, and not to dissolve into tears.

Chapter Thirty-six

When Eszter had finished work, she walked to her mother-in-law's house. Since Anne's ceiling had collapsed when she had left the bath taps running upstairs, she had been living with Eszter and Zoe in their rented cottage, but her house was all fixed now and they had moved her things back in over the weekend. Anne was looking after Zoe there while Eszter was working at Brew, and the two of them were in the kitchen, surrounded by baking equipment when Eszter walked in.

'We're practising for the cookery class,' Anne explained, looking up as Eszter appeared.

'We've made a bit of a mess,' Zoe said with a giggle. She had flour in her hair and her hands were covered in cake mixture.

Eszter laughed. 'I can see that, but I'm pretty sure that means the cake will taste twice as good.'

'It's ready to go in the oven. How about you wash up,

Zoe?' Anne picked up the cake tin and slid it into the oven while Zoe went to the sink to clean up. 'How was work?'

Eszter sat down at the table, relieved to be off her feet. She scooped up some mixture with her little finger and licked it off. Why was raw cake mixture so tasty? 'It was fine. Joy asked me to send her the list of cakes we'll be making in the class and she'll write them on a chalkboard at the front so everyone can see. Have you narrowed it down yet?' She looked at all the recipe books stacked on the table. It looked as if they had spent her whole shift studying up. She was pleased they were having so much fun with each other, and Zoe didn't seem as nervous about the class now that she was helping to organise it all.

'I want to do brownies and flapjacks, and Gran wants to do a Victoria sponge. We thought we should do cupcakes too,' Zoe said, coming back to the table. 'You can choose something too, Mum.'

Eszter smiled. 'Well, then, I vote for gingerbread – that's always been my favourite. I think five things sounds perfect. We can split up into groups and each group can make one of the cakes. I'll ring Joy tonight to tell her.'

'Do you think everyone will enjoy it, Mum?'

'Who doesn't enjoy baking?'

Anne put the kettle on. 'I remember my grandmother teaching me to make a cake when I was your age, Zoe. I think the whole class will have a great time. And Joy said you and I can wear Brew aprons for it too.'

'But we're not getting paid, are we?'

Eszter chuckled. 'Nice try, Zo, nice try.' She looked around the kitchen. 'So, you're all settled back in now?'

Anne nodded. 'It's quieter than I remember though,' she said as she started making tea. 'Strange, how new things strike you after being away.'

'It's because you've been living with this noisy little thing right here.' Eszter ruffled her daughter's hair and was pushed off. She didn't like the thought of Anne being in the house all by herself, though, when they went back to their cottage. It had been so nice having all three of them under the same roof.

'I'm not noisy!'

Anne laughed and passed Eszter a cup of tea, easing herself into the chair opposite them, a mug in her own hand. 'It's okay, Zoe, it's a comforting noise, I promise. Well, we have about an hour to wait for the cake. Are you two in a rush to get home? We could eat here if you're not?'

'And play a game?' Zoe asked eagerly, looking pleadingly at her mother.

'Sounds like a good plan to me,' Eszter agreed, not wanting to separate them for a while longer. She loved seeing the two of them becoming so close. It was such a shame that her husband never got to see his daughter and mother together but she knew that Nick would have felt the same. All they needed now was for Zoe to make a couple of friends and then the summer ahead would look bright for all of them.

* * *

Abbie got out of the taxi in front of the library that stood just a short walk away from Jack's flat. She didn't really think he was in there but she hoped he was. That meant at least he could be working on their business or clearing his name, something that would show her that he was trying to make things right.

She peered inside, but her chest quickly deflated because, as she had predicted, there was no sign of him in there. That meant he was in the other place Abbie had thought of back at the City PR office, and she was disappointed in him all over again.

Abbie left the library and walked briskly around the corner to Jack's favourite bar. They had spent many evenings in there either alone or with their workmates and friends, stumbling back to his flat afterwards late in the night, light-headed from the champagne Jack always ordered for them. Abbie had loved how generous he was on nights out, often footing the bill for everyone, and always paying for Abbie's drinks, but now it made her feel a little bit sick. How much of that had been stolen from City PR? How long had it been going on? Had she really known the man whose bed she had been sharing?

Abbie pushed the door to the bar open. It wasn't even lunchtime yet but a few people were in there, and she felt a wave of pity for them. She looked around and there in a booth at the back, his suit still on but with his tie cast aside on the seat next to him, was Jack, slumped over a pint of beer, his laptop closed on the table. Abbie took a deep breath and marched over to him.

'Hard at work, I see.'

Jack jumped, startled and looked up at her. She wondered how she had missed the tired look in his eyes. 'Abbie, what are you doing here?'

She slid into the booth opposite him, conscious of the barman looking over at them curiously. 'Me?' she hissed, leaning forwards. 'You told me you were going to work.'

'I just popped in for a quick drink before I meet a client,' he said so quickly and smoothly, Abbie was shocked. He really could lie so easily, it just dripped off his tongue, with no sign that he wasn't speaking the complete truth. She wondered what else he had lied about since she met him.

Her eyes narrowed. 'I've just come from City PR, so how about you finally tell me the truth. I know you've been suspended. Have you really been stealing from the company?'

Jack winced. 'It's not like that. It's just a mistake.'

'How is it a mistake?'

'I didn't realise that some of the things I was claiming for weren't allowed,' he said slowly, still avoiding meeting her gaze.

'Like rent on your flat?' Abbie asked, incredulously.

'That was only once! It costs a fortune, that place. I have been paying it back, I swear. Things just got on top of me, and I am a partner there. They don't pay me enough.'

'So, you thought you'd just take it instead?'

'Borrow, just borrow. I swear, Abs, you have to believe me.' He tried to reach for her hands then, but she pulled them on to her lap out of his reach.

'It doesn't even matter whether I believe you or not, you should have told me what was going on when you came to see me. Instead, you pretended you just wanted a new challenge and brought me back here, to do what, set up a company so you can steal from me too?'

'No! God, no. I thought it was a second chance for me, yes, but for you too. I knew you hadn't found anything, and I thought my days at City PR were numbered, so it made sense. I missed you, that wasn't a lie, and I knew we'd make a great team.'

'How could we when you were lying to me?'

'I thought it would all blow over, and then you'd never need to know.'

'But you knew that no one would support our company. You said to put it in my name because you knew how much trouble you were in. Even with it in my name, once people find out what you've done, who the hell is going to want to work with us? You were jeopardising my whole future without out even having the decency to tell me and let me decide for myself if I still wanted to do it.'

Jack shook his head and took a long gulp from his beer. 'I'm sorry, but I knew you wouldn't come back with me if you knew. And I do love you, Abs. That's the truth.'

'If you really loved me then you wouldn't treat me like this. I've been working ever since I got back with no help from you because I thought you were busy at work, but you've been in here, day after day, drinking, and not doing anything. We're supposed to be partners, in life, and in

business. How can I ever trust you again?' Abbie stood up, suddenly exhausted by her anger and how Jack seemed so defeated opposite her. This wasn't the man she had been attracted to. This wasn't someone she wanted to spend any of her time with, professional or personal. Everything had changed.

She started to walk away but then he called her name. Reluctantly, she paused and turned back, wondering what he could possibly say to make any of this better.

'What will you do without me?' he said, a sudden challenge back in his gaze.

He really thought that she needed him. That she couldn't be successful without him, that much was plain. It was written all over his face. He thought she would forgive him, that she could get over his lies, and his stealing, that she wouldn't be able to survive without him. She knew he was wrong, and she would prove it to him.

'Anything, and everything, that I want to,' she replied, spun on her heels, and left the bar. It was really over this time, and Abbie was surprised at how little sadness she felt about it. She had made a huge mistake in going back to Jack, and she vowed she'd never do that again.

She pulled out her phone to call Louise as she walked back to Jack's flat to pack up her things and hoped that Littlewood's kindness was still in full force because, right now, she had never needed it more.

Chapter Thirty-seven

Louise saw Abbie's name flash up on her phone and she grabbed it quickly. 'Abs?' She was so happy that her sister was finally getting in touch.

'Hey, Lou.'

'What's wrong?' Louise asked, immediately on alert at Abbie's distressed tone. She was in her cottage. After she'd had breakfast at Brew, she had gone for a walk, then changed into her comfiest clothes and curled up on the sofa for the afternoon, determined to make the most of her day off, by not doing anything. She sat up, waiting to hear what was going on.

'You were right about Jack.'

'What's happened?'

Louise listened as Abbie spoke in a rush, evidently upset, and told her that Jack had been lying about going into the office every day. He had in fact been suspended, Abbie told her – suspected of using company expenses for his own ends.

'No way!' Louise cried, shaking her head although she was on the phone. 'I can't believe it.'

'I just confronted him about it, and he confirmed it all. He's a liar, and a thief. I can't believe that I trusted him, and that I dropped everything to come back here with him.'

'I'm so sorry, Abbie,' Louise said, hating that she had been right about Jack. She had never trusted him, but even she wouldn't have thought him capable of that. 'Where are you now?'

'I just got back to the flat to pack up my things. He's in a bar drowning his sorrows. Turns out I didn't know him at all.'

'Ugh, Abbie, what an utter dick. Seriously. You are so much better off without him,' Louise said, her heart going out to her sister. After all, she knew exactly how much it hurt when someone you loved let you down. Abbie's experience with Jack made her feel better for sticking to her no-romance vow. 'You're coming straight back here, okay?'

Abbie sighed. 'I don't know, Lou. I do need to find a job and I couldn't when I was in Littlewood; maybe I should stay in the city.'

'But you were happy here. And you were working at Huntley Manor. Thomas still needs you. I was going to call you actually. He bought you something and he's given it to me because he didn't think he'd see you again. I'm going to text you a photo of it. I think it will make you see that you belong here. We all miss you.'

'I miss you too.' Abbie's voice broke a little. 'Listen, I'd better get packing. I don't want to see Jack again.'

'Then get straight on a train and I'll pick you up from the station?'

'I'll think about it.' Abbie hung up and Louise immediately went over to the painting of their grandparents' house in Cornwall that Thomas had given to her for Abbie. She snapped a photo of it on her phone and sent it to her sister, hoping that it would show her how much she meant to Thomas, and that she needed to help him save his home. She crossed her fingers and went back to the sofa to wait for Abbie's response.

* * *

Abbie threw her things into her bags, pleased that she hadn't brought everything with her from Louise's, so it wouldn't take too long. She really didn't want to have to deal with Jack again.

She texted Kate after seeing many missed calls from her and told her that Jack had admitted everything, and she was leaving him. Kate immediately offered her a place to stay and Abbie wasn't sure what to do. She missed Littlewood and was in need of all the friendly faces there, but she was also feeling embarrassed that she had dropped everything to follow Jack, and that had turned out to be a huge mistake. She wasn't sure she wanted to go back and admit that it had been such a disaster. She was okay with telling Louise everything, but the thought of going back to Huntley Manor and admitting to Thomas that everything had gone wrong really wasn't appealing to her.

Her phone vibrated again and she opened up Louise's message. Abbie stared at it in wonder. It was a painting of her grandparents' house in Cornwall, inside a beautiful frame. Abbie stared at it, remembering how much she loved that house. She couldn't believe Thomas had found a picture of it. And he had found it for her. She hadn't expected a good welcome from him if she decided to go back to Littlewood, but now she wanted to go there as soon as she could. Her heart was pulling her back there, she couldn't deny it.

Abbie replied to her sister and said she was heading to the train station. She didn't know what she was going to do, but she realised that being in London hadn't made her happy. She wanted to be back in Littlewood, and then she could plan her future.

She grabbed her bags and looked around Jack's flat one last time. It was spacious and modern with a stunning view; Abbie knew many would kill to live there, and now she realised Jack couldn't even afford it. He wanted a lifestyle that had started to seduce her as well, but no longer. Suddenly, the flat just felt empty. It wasn't cosy or comfortable; it wasn't a home, not like Louise's cottage. Abbie had always planned to build her life in London, but now she wasn't sure that was what she wanted anymore.

Abbie walked out of the building and flagged down a taxi to take her to the station. She was hurt by Jack's lies, but she wasn't as upset as she would have imagined. She was angry and humiliated but her heart was still intact.

The taxi pulled away and she turned her back on the

place she had planned to call home. She knew then that she didn't love Jack anymore, possibly never had. She had been trying to make it work, sure that the opportunities he was offering her were ones she should be grasping at, but she knew now they weren't what she wanted at all. Her future wasn't with Jack.

She leaned back against the seat and watched the city roll past. She had left it once in turmoil, desperate to get back there, but now she was leaving it willingly, and was hopeful about the future. Sure, she was single and had no job prospects, but somehow, she knew she would be okay.

'Where you heading off to?' the taxi driver asked her.

'Surrey. A little town called Littlewood.'

'Hmmm, I don't think I've heard of it.'

'You wouldn't have, but it's very special.'

'You off on a holiday?'

'Actually, I don't know, I might not be coming back.'

'I always dream of leaving the city.'

Abbie smiled because she never had before, but now she knew what he meant. 'I hope you get to do it one day.'

'Maybe you'll inspire me.'

'I'd like that.'

Abbie thought of all the people she had met in Littlewood and realised they had all inspired her. She had sneered at the little town to begin with, been confused about their passion for being kind, sure that she needed to be ambitious and selfish to be successful, but now she couldn't wait to get back there. She missed all of her new friends and knew that,

despite her earlier misgivings, they wouldn't judge her for coming back, and that's what she loved about the place. She felt like she could be herself there. She hadn't realised how different she had become working at City PR and being Jack's girlfriend; she barely recognised that girl now.

Abbie was ready for a fresh start. It was time to get her life back on track.

'Good luck!' called the taxi driver out of the window as she walked into the station, pulling her bags behind her. Abbie waved to him, hoping that her luck was as ready to change as she was.

Chapter Thirty-eight

Eszter was up just after dawn in need of a very large coffee. The cookery class was happening later in the morning and she was more nervous about it than she wanted to admit. She was putting on a confident and cheerful face for Zoe and Anne, though, as this was all her idea.

The three of them walked over to Brew early, where they were met by Joy and let in so they could all prepare. They had twenty kids from the town coming with Jane, who ran the community centre.

The first thing they did was clear all the round tables and chairs to the edge of the room and set up three long tables instead for them to do the cake preparations on. The kids could then stand around the tables to learn how to make the cakes, and take part too. They also had lots of decorations for the kids to use once the cakes were baked.

Joy had the ovens on already and, as promised, had written

down the cakes they were making on a chalkboard she had propped up on the counter.

The four of them were wearing their 'Have a Brew!' aprons – Zoe's looked a little too big for her, but they had tied it around her middle twice to keep it on.

'I think we're all ready,' Joy said as they stood looking around at their preparations.

Joy, Eszter and Anne would be supervising the cake-making, with Zoe as their helper.

'I think we are,' Anne agreed. 'I'm getting hungry already!'

They all hoped that the cosiness of Brew, coupled with the delicious smell of cakes, would ensure there was no hostility from the kids towards Zoe, but she grew quieter as the time drew near for them all to arrive. Eszter gave her a big hug and tried to think what Nick would say to put them at ease, which he had always seemed able to do. 'If all else fails – we can eat the cake we make.'

'I like that idea,' Zoe said, smiling a little.

'Here they are,' Joy called from the door. She had closed Brew to usual customers for the morning and opened up now to let the class in, greeting Jane, and smiling at the queue of boys and girls, all around Zoe's age. 'Welcome to Brew,' she said, shutting the door when everyone was inside and making the 'Closed' sign visible. 'Eszter – do you want to start?'

Eszter faced the class and smiled, trying not to wonder who were the ones who had picked on her daughter. She knew that kindness was better than giving them a telling-off, however much she was itching to. 'Welcome everyone. We

decided it would be fun to do a baking class today and rather than have it at the community centre, it made sense to use Brew's facilities, plus Joy over there makes the best cakes in Littlewood, so we wanted to steal her expertise. We're going to make five cakes today and show you all how to make them, and we're going to need lots of help. And at the end, we'll get to try all the cakes that we have made. Zo – do you want to tell everyone what we're going to make today?'

Zoe read out the cakes from the board and Eszter was relieved that everyone listened and she detected no obvious sniggering or whispering. Jane then separated everyone into three groups and Eszter, Anne and Joy stood at each table to start the baking.

Zoe stood next to Eszter. They were going to demonstrate how to make gingerbread. Jane came to watch with a few of the kids. One of the boys pushed his way to the front, arms crossed, and Eszter clocked him immediately. She saw Zoe shift a little bit nervously and resolved to keep an eye on him.

'Do you even have gingerbread where you come from?' the boy asked loudly after Eszter had read out the list of ingredients they needed for the recipe.

'Simon!' Jane cried, shaking her head.

'What? I'd like to know,' he replied, defensively.

Eszter raised an eyebrow. Why was there always one? She bet he was the one who had encouraged the other kids to pick on Zoe. He glanced at her daughter, whose head was down, cheeks flaming red. 'I think you just volunteered to help.' Eszter handed him the bowl. 'First you need to sift the

flour with the bicarbonate of soda, ginger and cinnamon.'
She passed him a sieve.

'This is stupid,' he muttered.

'Either do it or I'll call your mother to take you home,'
Jane told him.

'Fine.' Simon started to pour the flour into the sieve and
poured it too fast, resulting in a cloud of flour flying out on
to the table.

'Do you not have flour where you come from?' Zoe asked
him. The whole group burst out laughing.

Simon threw the sieve down. 'I'm not doing this anymore,' he muttered and moved to the back of the group,
looking humiliated.

'He's such an idiot,' one of the girls whispered to Zoe,
who beamed.

'Can we have another volunteer then?' Eszter asked,
relieved that the tension had been broken and everyone
seemed pleased Zoe had said something. They probably all
disliked this Simon but preferred it when he was picking on
someone other than them.

A girl stepped forwards and this time Zoe moved closer
and helped to show her what to do. Simon stayed quiet for
the rest of the demonstration thankfully, then the groups
swapped so Eszter and Zoe showed another set how to
make cupcakes.

Soon, everything was in the oven and they got the kids to
start preparing all the decorations. The gingerbread needed
to be turned into men and women, the cupcakes needed

icing and decorating with hundreds and thousands, the Victoria sponge needed jam, and the brownies and flapjacks needed cutting up and Smarties placing on top.

Brew was quickly filled with the delicious smell of baking cakes, and the kids gathered around the tables ready to finish the cakes off.

'This was a great idea,' Jane said to Eszter as she watched Zoe show a couple of girls how to use an icing piping bag. 'I'm going to have a word with Simon's mum. We don't want him being disruptive in every class. I'm sorry if he upset Zoe.'

'I think he did, but she's a tough cookie, she'll be fine. I think this has really helped her come out of her shell. She had a lot of friends in Hungary and I'd love her to make some here.'

'Mum!' Zoe appeared. 'Can Daisy come round for tea tomorrow?'

Eszter smiled. That was more like it. 'Of course she can.' She walked over to see how they were getting on with decorating the gingerbread. She saw that Simon was concentrating hard on piping a face on to his man. 'That looks great, Simon,' she said. He smiled. And she hoped that he'd realise he didn't have to be mean to get people to notice him. 'Don't forget, you take home anything you decorate,' she called out to the room. There were a few cheers at that, and she laughed. You couldn't deny the power of cake.

'Look who it is,' Joy called, waving out of the window. Eszter followed her gaze to see Louise and Abbie walking towards them. 'I think they're allowed in, don't you?'

She greeted them at the door and explained what they were doing.

Eszter walked to the door and gave Abbie a hug. 'It's so good to see you back here!'

'It's good to be back,' Abbie said. 'I have been dreaming about a Brew latte,' she said, looking hopefully at Joy.

Joy laughed. 'Come in, you two, I'll make you a coffee to go. And I'll pop in a couple of cakes – we've made far too many.'

'You, Joy, are a star!'

'Are you back for good?' Eszter asked her.

'For now, at least. London really didn't have the same attraction. I think Littlewood has got under my skin.'

Eszter nodded. 'It does that, doesn't it?'

'I'm so pleased you're back,' Louise told her sister. 'The cottage has been really quiet – and far too tidy.'

Abbie elbowed her. 'Hey, I'm not messy; you're just a clean freak!' She looked out at Huntley Manor. 'I wonder if Thomas will be as pleased to see me. I think I need to work up the courage to go in there, to be honest.'

'He will be pleased, don't worry,' Eszter told her. 'But you'd better not wait too long. I saw someone in a suit talking to him yesterday. He looked like he was from a bank, so I don't know what's going on.'

Abbie groaned. 'I hope he's not giving up on our relaunch idea. Littlewood needs Huntley Manor.'

'You can convince him, Abs, I'm sure of it,' Louise said. She smiled at Joy who handed them each a coffee and a paper

bag with samples of the cakes in. 'This is amazing, thank you. We'd better leave you guys to it, you have your hands full. It looks like it's going really well though.'

'We've had a great morning,' Eszter confirmed. She saw Anne looking for her. 'I'd better go, see you both soon. We need a proper catch-up, Abbie.'

'Can't wait!' Abbie and Louise left and Eszter went to help Anne finish off the Victoria sponge. She was relieved that the class had been a success. She was feeling more a part of Littlewood's community every day. And now, hopefully, Zoe would too.

Anne showed the cake off with a flourish to applause from the children. She looked as if she was having lots of fun too, which pleased Eszter. Her mother-in-law had spent so much time hiding herself away, and she needed to be part of the town again. And this was a great step in the right direction.

Anne walked over to the Kindness Board and picked up a piece of chalk to write with. Eszter watched, smiling as she saw her name appear up there.

Eszter and Zoe Harris for organising a baking class at Brew, and everyone who took part. We had such a fun morning!

Chapter Thirty-nine

Louise yawned as she made her way to work. She was tired after staying up late talking to Abbie and had left her sister in bed as she crept out of the cottage early in the morning. She was relieved that Abbie, although angry and hurt, seemed like she would be okay. Louise felt no smugness about being right about Jack; she wanted her sister to be happy, but was pleased that Abbie had learnt the truth before she had become too involved. Now, she was back where she belonged in Littlewood, and Louise was sure that she would be her old self again very soon.

Annoyingly, she was too late to stop off for a coffee at Brew, so when she arrived at the hospital, she was feeling sluggish and regretted staying up so late with her sister. Abbie had said she wanted to see Thomas but was very nervous about it. Louise hoped they would work things out as she had a feeling about the two of them. Why was it always easier to see what was good for other people but not for yourself?

She parked in the staff car park and walked into the hospital, heading for her ward.

Julie came into the staffroom as Louise changed into her nursing uniform, waving her phone at her. 'Alex just texted me,' she said.

Louise turned to put her bag in her locker in case her face betrayed anything. 'What did he say?'

'He wanted to know what we were doing later – said he's planning to have a barbeque and did we want to come?'

Louise wondered why he had texted Julie, and not her. Perhaps he thought she would say no, whereas Julie's eager tone made it clear she wanted to go. Or he had felt the same attraction to Julie as she clearly had to him. Louise hated the way that thought made her stomach plummet. She turned after organising her face into what she hoped was a natural expression. 'Oh, did he?'

'Are you up for it? It sounds fun; he's invited lots of people. We could head there straight after our shift.'

Louise hesitated. She did want to go. She hadn't seen Alex for a few days and she knew they would have a fun evening, but if she had to watch Julie and him flirting all night . . .

'Please, come. I can't go without you!' Julie pleaded, seeing her hesitation. 'It'll be fun.'

She sighed. She didn't want to let Julie down. 'Sure, okay. I can't stay too late though, my sister has just got back and I don't want to abandon her all night,' she said, pleased she had a get-out clause in case the night became too uncomfortable for her. Julie beamed and began to text Alex back. Louise

had no right to be annoyed but, for some reason, her heart was stubbornly ignoring that fact.

* * *

Her shift went far too quickly and all too soon, they were grabbing their things and heading out into the sultry evening. They drove separately to Alex's flat above the vet's surgery in Littlewood. Louise dropped her car off at the cottage and walked into the High Street, waving at Julie who was parked outside, waiting for her to go in together. They walked up the stairs and knocked. Music and laughter drifted through the closed door.

'Hello, you two,' Alex said as he opened the door and smiled at them. He was wearing jeans and a dark shirt with the sleeves pushed up and was holding a bottle of beer. His arms and face were glowing with a summer tan and Louise found her eyes going straight to his dimples, and then wishing they hadn't. 'Come on in.' He stepped back to let them walk through.

The flat was open-plan and the sliding doors that led out on to the balcony were flung open; the smell of the meat cooking on the gas barbeque made Louise instantly hungry. Alex took them into the kitchen and poured them each a glass of wine. They greeted Mike and David, Alex's friends who they had spent an evening in the pub with, and were introduced to the other people there – a mix of veterinary colleagues, a couple of Littlewood residents who Louise recognised, and Sarah, Alex's sister, who stood close to the balcony with a friend.

'Hi,' Louise said, going over to her. 'How's Hazel doing?'

'She's doing well. We're seeing her consultant in a couple of weeks, so fingers crossed. It's been so lovely to have her at home. Alex made me come tonight as I haven't really left her side. Our mother is watching her, but I'll probably sneak back early when he's not looking.'

Louise smiled. 'I understand. It's good to have a break though. You have to look after yourself too.'

'I'll try,' Sarah replied with a wry smile.

Louise knew how hard it was to focus on yourself sometimes. She remembered her sister telling her the exact same thing when they made their kindness pact at the start of the summer. Abbie had promised to help a stranger, and then she'd discovered the failing Huntley Manor. Louise had in turn promised to be kinder to herself but was finding it much harder. She watched as Alex went out on to the balcony to check on the food. She knew that by turning Alex down, she hadn't lived up to her side of their pact. But it had been two years of keeping her heart closed off, and it was hard to break the habit.

Louise took a deep breath and followed Alex out onto the balcony.

'Not burning the sausages, are you?' she asked, taking a sip of her wine. The heat from the day had barely cooled and the sky was still cloudless and blue above them.

Alex grinned. 'Hey, I'll have you know I'm an expert at cooking sausages.' He picked one up with a fork and showed her. 'See?'

'Looks good.'

'Almost ready to put everything out. I hope you're hungry.'

'Starved. I didn't get a chance to have lunch; it was crazy on the ward today. Sarah said that Hazel is doing great.'

'I really hope we've turned a corner,' he replied with a nod. 'And I heard that Abbie is back in town?'

'Yeah, London didn't work out for her. I think she's been surprised by how much she likes it here in Littlewood.'

'I wasn't sure I'd love living somewhere much quieter than where I was before but it just feels like home now, you know?' He looked at her and they shared a smile. She had very quickly felt at home in Littlewood as well. 'You must be happy she's back.'

'It's been fun living with her again. It would be great to have her close by permanently, but we shall see.'

'And what are you two plotting out here?' Louise jumped as Julie poked her head around the balcony. She felt instantly guilty, which was crazy. 'Is the food ready yet? We're all dying in here!'

'Yep, grab some trays, would you?'

The next few minutes were a flurry of laying out the food in the kitchen and everyone piling up their plates with bar-bequed meat and sweetcorn, salad and coleslaw, new potatoes and crusty French bread. Louise was impressed with the spread and found a chair to perch on while she ate. The flat was warm but a cool breeze had picked up outside and was drifting through the sliding doors. Alex had soft music on, and everyone was enjoying chatting to one another.

Louise couldn't help but watch Julie talking to Alex and David across the room from her, failing to listen to Mike and Sarah, who sat with her and were sharing embarrassing stories of their teenage years. She bit into a sausage and had to admit it was perfectly cooked. She saw Julie throw her head back with laughter and wished she knew what they were talking about. Alex caught her eye then and smiled, so she quickly looked down and focused on eating, her cheeks flaring up that he had seen her watching them. What was it about him that made her act like she was a teenager again?

'The things I could tell you about my brother,' Sarah said then, drawing Louise's attention back to their conversation. 'He always wanted to be a vet, and when we were younger he used to beg me to play vets with him. I'd have to pretend to be a sick animal, and he would heal me,' she said, laughing.

'I always made Abbie, my sister, play doctors and nurses with me,' Louise said, smiling at the thought of Alex pretending his sister was an ill cat.

'This is the problem with being an only child, I had no one to pretend to be an animal for me,' Mike said, laughing into his beer.

Louise glanced back over and saw Alex and Julie going out onto the balcony together, their plates of food abandoned. Louise put her own knife and fork down, her appetite fading. Why was she so bothered about seeing the two of them together? She had told Alex she wanted to just be friends, and she had told Julie to go for it.

She had no one to blame but herself.

Chapter Forty

Abbie stood outside Huntley Manor and looked up at the stone building, the sun starting to set behind it. She felt warm just being back there. The house had crawled into her heart and she hadn't been prepared for how much she had missed it in London. She was unsure of the reception she would receive inside, but she couldn't keep avoiding the place. She walked through the door and found herself heading in the direction of the ballroom, incredibly curious to see what progress had been made while she was away.

When she walked into the Huntley Room, she let out a small gasp. The room was almost complete. She turned around, taking in the freshly painted walls, the now shiny wooden floor gleaming under her feet, the new gold drapes by the door showing off the beautiful grounds, and the crowning glory – the chandelier – was up again in the centre of the ceiling, but it was covered in cloth so she couldn't see how it had been transformed. The new mirror had been

added on one wall, a large, gold-framed glass that made the room look even bigger. Abbie had found it on eBay and it had been refurbished to huge success. A couple of paintings that had been hanging elsewhere had been added on the other wall. That hadn't been her idea so Thomas must have done it. She was impressed. The room looked like the tasteful, elegant space it had been in the past, and now was again.

'What are you doing here?'

Abbie jumped to see Thomas in the doorway behind her. She smiled instantly at the sight of him and felt her heartbeat begin to quicken. She tried to hastily compose herself. He wasn't smiling, she realised, his arms were crossed and he frowned at her. She swallowed. 'I wanted to see how it looked. It's wonderful, Thomas.'

He nodded. 'I meant, what are you doing here in Littlewood?'

She wasn't at all sure if he was pleased to see her. 'I've come back. I've left London; it didn't work out. I'm back. Indefinitely.'

'Oh,' he replied.

She took her chance as he absorbed her words, wanting to show him how much she cared about Huntley Manor. 'So, how does the chandelier look?'

'I thought it could be unveiled at the party. Make the evening as dramatic as possible.'

'I love that idea!'

'You must be rubbing off on me.' He stepped fully into the room and they were now just a few feet apart. He looked

around. 'It's just how I remember it from when I was little.' His eyes came back to hers. 'What happened, Abbie? Why have you come back?'

'I should never have gone. I missed this place too much. And Jack ...' Abbie looked down, embarrassed. 'He kept things from me. We're not going to work together anymore. So, I'm back with my sister, and trying to decide what to do next. But I was hoping that you might have me back here? Let me help with the relaunch party?' She lifted her head slightly, nervous about his reaction.

'You didn't think I'd sold the place off then?'

'Well, I hoped you hadn't. You haven't, have you? Because this room is perfect.'

He nodded and started to pace, shoving his hands in his pockets. 'After you left, I talked to the bank again. I found out how much we could sell the house for. And there's so much land, it's worth a lot. But when I came in here, I saw the house as it used to be. I don't know if I can do it, Abbie, but I do want to try. I want to go ahead with the party and give it a couple of months. If there's no uplift in business, well, then, I'll have to sell it, but at least I'll know that I tried.' He paused and looked at her. 'I didn't behave very well when you left.'

'I promised I'd help you this summer, and then I just walked away. I was in the wrong.'

'You don't owe me anything, Abbie.'

'I shouldn't have gone back on my word. I'm sorry. I thought that I was a failure, living here with Louise, being

unemployed, so I jumped at the chance to get everything I lost back, but I realised that's not what I want anymore. I need to find something that makes me happy. I wasn't happy there, but I am here.'

Thomas smiled then, finally. Her chest sagged with relief. 'Well, then, I am glad to have you back on board.'

'Does that mean I get to see the chandelier?'

'No, you can see it at the unveiling like everyone else. But you can help me plan this party, because we've had a lot of people accept the invitations, and time is ticking on.'

She nodded. 'It'll be a great night,' she said firmly. She lifted her eyes to meet his and felt a little shy suddenly. 'I have to thank you, for the painting,' she said, a lump rising in her throat. 'My grandparents' house. It has been so long since I have seen it, it's such a beautiful picture and it just reminds me so much of my childhood. It was such a wonderful present, Thomas.' Abbie was suddenly worried she might start crying.

Thomas cleared his throat, looking a little emotional himself. 'When you told me about their house, and how it made you want to save mine, I really wanted to see it, and when I saw the painting, I knew you would love it. It felt like it belonged to you. It's a thank you for all you've done here. All you've done for me.'

Abbie smiled, flushing a little. 'Well, it was an amazing find. I can't wait to hang it in my room. It made me certain that I belonged here. It made me want to come back.'

Thomas touched her arm briefly. 'I'm glad it did. I'm so

pleased you like it,' he said, his voice soft in the large room. 'Do you need to rush off or can I offer you a drink?'

'Sounds good to me.'

She followed Thomas out of the room, glancing back at it over her shoulder as she passed through the door. She imagined herself in a cocktail dress, the room lit with candles, soft music playing, and Thomas in a suit, holding out his hand to her. She hurried out of there, embarrassed by her fantasy but secretly hoping that it might come true on the night of the party. She wanted to dance in that room. And she wanted to dance with him.

She went into the library and Thomas came in a few minutes later, carrying two glasses of wine he had picked up from the hotel bar. A definite perk of running the place, Abbie thought. They sat down opposite one another in the large, red armchairs, the fireplace in between them.

'I didn't think I'd see you in here again,' Thomas said then.

'I would have always come back for the party. I didn't realise how much I would miss this place though,' she said, taking in the library. 'This house gets under your skin.'

'I've had a lot of sleepless nights imagining selling it and never being here again.'

She regretted ever thinking that he didn't care about the house. She looked at him closely and saw the dark circles under his eyes, a few days' stubble on his chin when he was usually clean-shaven and the paleness of his face. 'You've been worrying a lot, haven't you?'

'I know, I wish I could stop,' he said, sipping his wine

and resting his head on the back of his armchair. He looked so tired.

'Thomas, I'm sorry that I was so harsh with you. I know how much this house means to you. You've had to deal with it on your own for so long, I don't think I realised how difficult that had been. So much responsibility, all resting on your shoulders. I know that if you do sell, it will be because you have no other option,' Abbie told him. 'I'll do all I can to help you in the meantime. At least we can throw one hell of a party, right?'

Thomas smiled. 'Deal.' He held up his glass, and she did the same, and they sipped their wine in the grand library of the stately home and it felt as if they had been doing just that for every evening of their lives.

Abbie couldn't help but hope it was something they could do for a long time yet.

Chapter Forty-one

At Anne's house, Eszter was on the phone to her mother in Hungary. Anne and Zoe were in the kitchen putting the leftover cake from the baking class into Tupperware boxes. They decided to pass them on to Louise to take into the hospital and give to the kids there. Eszter was in the garden, sitting on the stone steps which led down to the lush green grass. It was a perfect summer's day and she smiled as she told her mother about the class.

'Zoe has already arranged a playdate with one of the girls who came. She's much happier.'

'I'm pleased. And how are things with your mother-in-law?'

'She and Zoe are really building a good relationship. Anne said she has something to show me; she's been sorting through things from the past. I think she's finally ready to deal with everything that's happened.'

'I can't imagine how you would even begin to cope with

the death of your child. She is a brave woman, and strong too. Just like you are for being there.'

'I'm just doing what Nick asked me to.'

'Which took strength and courage. I wish I could see the place.'

'I think you'd like Littlewood, it reminds me of home sometimes. The peace and quiet, and the community here. We feel more settled here than I thought possible. I do wish we could have come with Nick, though.'

'Of course you do. But for whatever reason, the two of you were destined to discover it on your own. Nick is looking down on you both, I'm sure. Give Zoe a big kiss from me, okay?'

'Of course. I'd better go, she's waving at me.' Eszter lifted her hand to wave back to her daughter in the kitchen behind her.

'Take care, Eszter.'

'You too. Love to Dad as well.' Eszter hung up, missing her parents as she always did after she spoke to them and thinking of home back in Hungary. She hadn't been like Nick; she was content to settle in her home country, instead of travelling the world. She hadn't had his wanderlust. Though they had always planned to visit the UK one day, she could never have dreamed that she would end up making the trip on her own.

Eszter began to walk back inside, the sun warm on her back, and she realised that she did feel proud of herself. She had made this journey and had brought her daughter and her husband's family back together. She hadn't been sure of

how she would manage everything without Nick, but each day she was becoming braver and stronger and increasingly ready to think about a future without him.

'It's all ready,' Zoe said, gesturing to the boxes on the table.

'Great, I'll walk them over to Louise's later,' Eszter said. It had been Anne's idea to give the leftovers to the hospital and it pleased Eszter to see her taking an interest in the community again.

'I was looking through some things earlier,' Anne said. 'I thought you might both like to see them?'

Curiously, Eszter and Zoe followed Anne into the living room, which was filled with cardboard boxes.

'These were all up in the loft, I haven't looked at them for, well, years, but it was time to do a sort-out. There are a lot of Nick's things that I thought you might like to see, or even have,' Anne explained, hesitatingly. She took Zoe's hand and led her to one of the boxes. 'In here are some of your father's books from when he was young. I know you love to read, so why don't you look through them and see if there are any you want?'

Zoe knelt down and started to look through the box carefully, her face filled with wonder.

'This is a lovely idea,' Eszter said to Anne. She had found it so hard sorting out Nick's things in their flat in Budapest but it had also been good to be reminded of their happier times, and here were a host of memories that Eszter had never seen before. She was eager to know more of her husband's past.

She sat cross-legged on the floor with Anne in the

armchair behind her and opened up a box with some of Nick's school things in.

'His favourite subject was English. He loved telling stories,' Anne said as Eszter lifted up a notebook filled with Nick's childish writing. 'In hindsight, it shouldn't have been a surprise that he ended up teaching it.' She sighed heavily, the weight of the past still acute.

'He wanted to make you happy,' Eszter said, looking at a school photo of Nick. Her husband had been kind and loyal; she knew he would have wanted his parents to be proud of him, and that must have weighed on him growing up, when he knew he really wanted to do something vastly different to what they wished he would. She hoped she would always let Zoe choose her own path in life.

She glanced at her daughter, who was lost in the box of books, and smiled, knowing that she would always be proud of her, whatever she chose to do.

'Look at this, Mum,' Zoe said, holding up a copy of *The Lion, the Witch, and the Wardrobe*. 'This looks good.'

'Your father loved that one,' Anne said. 'Open up the first page.'

Zoe did and showed them that Nick had written his name there and the date he got the book. 'Can I add my name?'

'I think you should,' Anne told her and handed her a pen.

Eszter watched her daughter add her name and ask Anne for the date, and her heart swelled. Nick and Zoe would read the same pages of that book years apart. They would always be connected. The ones we love and lose never leave

us. They leave their mark on us, an imprint that stays with us even though we don't always know it's there. Eszter knew that she and Zoe would be okay because of the imprint Nick had left on them. They had had so much love and happiness in the years they spent together, she knew that they would always carry that with them.

'I'm going to start reading it tonight,' Zoe said, holding up the book so they could see her name below her father's.

'Will you read it to me? I'd like to hear the story too,' Eszter said, her voice breaking a little as she looked at how happy her daughter was to have Nick's book.

'We could have hot chocolate too!'

Eszter laughed. 'Sounds perfect.'

* * *

After dinner, Eszter left Zoe having a bath at Anne's and walked round to Louise's cottage to drop off the cakes for the kids at the hospital.

Abbie opened the door with a smile. 'Come on in,' she said, letting Eszter go on through. They went into the living room. 'Louise is still at work,' Abbie said, offering Eszter a drink, which she turned down, knowing that she couldn't stay long.

'I just wanted to drop off these cakes for Louise to take into the hospital,' Eszter explained, putting them on the kitchen counter.

'Oh, that's sweet of you, they will love them.'

'So, how does it feel to be back?'

Abbie smiled. 'Really good. I was surprised how much I missed it here. And all of you guys.'

'What happened with Jack?'

'It turned out he's been suspended from where we worked. They think he was stealing money, claiming things under expenses that weren't legit.'

Eszter let out a gasp.

'I know. I couldn't believe it. Needless to say, I no longer wanted to set up a company with him or stay living in his flat.'

'I can believe that. It's good you got straight out of there. I bet Lord Huntley was pleased to see you?' Eszter smiled, thinking that the two of them made so much more sense than Abbie and that horrible Jack. She knew that Louise thought there was chemistry between them too. After Louise and Alex seeming to fail before they had even begun, Eszter was keen to matchmake for someone else, and Abbie sure needed something good to happen after going through all of that with Jack.

'I'm not sure, to be honest. I think I hurt him by going away. He's happy for me to keep helping out, and we're planning the end of summer party together, but it's not quite the same.'

'But I thought he bought you a painting?'

Abbie pointed to it, now hanging above Louise's fireplace. 'That's it there. It's a picture of our grandparents' old house in Cornwall. It was such a thoughtful present, but he bought it before I left.'

'He cares about you, Abbie, that's obvious. You don't buy a sentimental painting like that for someone that you have no feelings for.' Eszter remembered Nick buying her a necklace that looked just like one she had had when she was younger soon after they first met. It had really touched her. Expensive gifts didn't mean anything compared to ones that showed the giver had really paid attention to things you had told them.

'Maybe.' Abbie shrugged and looked as if she was pretending not to be bothered when she obviously was. 'I need to start thinking about what to do after the end of the summer though. Once we relaunch Huntley Manor, I won't be working on anything.'

'I thought you were planning to set up your own PR company?'

'That's what I was going to do with Jack.'

Eszter raised an eyebrow. 'Why can't you do it without him?'

Abbie looked at her. 'Well . . . I don't know.'

'Seems to me that all he did was hold you back.'

'I guess I could,' Abbie said slowly. 'It would be scary, though, on my own.'

'Sometimes the scariest things are the ones most worth doing,' Eszter replied, thinking of her trip to the UK. 'Think it over. You can claim Thomas as your first client; I'm sure he'd give you a good testimonial.'

'Let's see if we can keep the hotel open first.'

'Well, if you need any help, just let me know. To be honest, I have no idea what I'm going to do at the end of the

summer either, so anything that takes my mind off that is a good thing.' She stood up from the sofa. 'I'd better get back to Anne's. It'll be Zoe's bedtime soon.'

Abbie followed her to the door. 'Thanks again for the cakes. And the career advice.'

Eszter chuckled. 'You're welcome. Think it over. I'm sure you can do anything you want to do, Abbie.'

Abbie gave her a hug. 'You too.'

Eszter stepped out into the darkening light and waved to Abbie as she started to walk back through Littlewood. She knew she couldn't put off thinking about what she and Zoe would do after the summer ended for much longer. August was in full bloom – before they knew it, the trees would start to turn and the nights would draw in, and it would be time to leave Littlewood. She would never have guessed how much that thought would sting.

She looked around the town as she strolled back to Anne's house, feeling more at home here than she ever thought would have been possible. She had to remind herself that this wasn't her town, she was just visiting. It seemed as if she and Abbie were both at a crossroads, not sure which turn to take next.

She hoped the answer would soon become clear to both of them.

Chapter Forty-two

A few days later, Louise felt as if she was dying. She was curled up on the sofa under a blanket. It was grey and raining outside and she blamed the cooling of the weather for the stinking summer cold she had suddenly come down with. That, and the snotty kid at the hospital a few days before who she was sure had passed on his lurgy. The perils of working in close contact with sick people and their visitors, she supposed.

Abbie had forced her to call in sick before setting off to Huntley Manor, which Louise really hated doing, but she had to acknowledge that she was in no fit state to look after anyone. At least Louise had two days off work after today so could get over it properly. It sucked, getting a cold in summer, and she was feeling really sorry for herself.

There was a sudden knock on the door, causing Louise to jump and then groan.

'Who is it?' she called out groggily from the sofa, not wanting to have to walk all the way to the door.

'It's Alex, can I come in?'

Louise's mouth opened in horror. Her nose bore a sharp resemblance to Rudolph's, her throat was dry and croaky, her hair was unwashed and limp, and she had come out in at least four spots around her chin. Plus, she was lying in her PJs having not even washed that morning, and there was a row of used tissues on the coffee table in front of her.

The door opened. 'I'm coming in!'

'Wait, I'm ill . . .' she started to protest, trying to sit up.

But there he was in the room. 'I know you're sick, that's why I came by. Don't get up! Please, lie back down.' He walked over and sat down in the armchair by her. 'I was just in Brew and Abbie was getting coffee, she told me you were having a sick day, and your cottage is so close to work, I thought I'd drop off a care package.' He held out a paper bag and a cup. 'Coffee and the biggest Danish pastry they had.'

Louise was stunned. 'Oh, wow, thank you.' She had been trying not to listen to her rumbling stomach as the thought of getting up and going into the kitchen to make something had zero appeal. She took the bag and cup gratefully. 'Thank you so much. It smells amazing.'

'I know I always fancy that when I'm ill and never feel like getting up to go to Brew. So now you won't have to,' he said with a smile.

'This is really kind of you, Alex.'

He stood up. 'No problem at all. Oh, Abbie gave me this for you as well.' He passed her a plastic bag. Inside were

two magazines, more tissues and a big bar of chocolate. 'Everything you need to survive, right?'

'You guys are brilliant,' Louise replied, feeling distinctly less sorry for herself.

'You'd do the same for us, Nurse Louise. Now, lots of fluids and rest, yes? Vet's orders.'

She smiled. 'Well, I'd better do as you say then, hadn't I?'

He chuckled. 'Anything else you need while I'm here?' He picked up the remote control to the TV and put it by her. 'In case you feel the need to indulge in daytime TV.'

'Does anyone feel that need?'

'Good point. Right, I'd better get to work and help heal more of the Littlewood sick. Take care, okay?'

'I will.' She watched him walk out. 'Thanks, Alex,' she called, wishing she didn't feel all warm and fuzzy inside about his visit.

She opened up the bag from Brew and felt like applauding the deliciousness inside. Alex had somehow known exactly what she needed.

Louise wished he hadn't seen her looking and feeling like such a mess but she knew it didn't matter; they were friends and that was that.

She bit into her pastry and opened up one of the magazines, thinking that a sick day like this she could almost actually enjoy.

* * *

Abbie's phone rang as she walked towards the library in Huntley Manor with the two coffees she had bought at Brew

on the way in. She put them down on a side table in the corridor and paused to answer, looking at the name on the screen with a smile. 'Hi, Kate.'

'So, are you all settled back in Littlewood?'

Kate was really the only thing she would miss in London, Abbie decided. 'I am. I've just arrived at the hotel to start work. We really want this party to be huge. You are coming, aren't you?'

'Of course. I even sent back my RSVP. Actually, a few people from my work were talking about needing a hotel for events so I told them about it. It's okay if I show up with a few more people, right?'

'Sure. Just try to let me know numbers as I'm terrified we'll run out of wine.'

'That really would be a disaster.' Kate paused. 'Listen, I have news but I'm not sure whether to tell you.'

'Is it about Jack?' Abbie was instantly worried about what she might hear. She hadn't had any contact with him since she left London, and she really didn't want to.

'Yes. Do you want to know?'

Abbie wished she could confidently say no, but she was still curious about what was going on. Even though she was furious with him, she was also worried about him; she had, after all, cared about him for a long time. 'Tell me.'

'I spoke to Melanie. They were talking about a tribunal, maybe even the police, so he did what he had to and resigned; they're dropping the investigation. But, basically, they all know that it was true – he was fiddling his expenses.'

Abbie exhaled. 'Wow. He's resigned. Well, he had no choice really, did he? He must be devastated.'

'Plus, there's no way he can keep his flat now, is there?'

'No, I guess not. Wow. He really has ruined everything.'

'Don't feel sorry for him, Abs,' Kate said sternly, hearing the concern in Abbie's voice. 'He brought all of this on himself, don't forget that.'

'I know, I won't. But we spent a long time together, you know? I just wish it had all turned out differently.'

'Do you miss him?' Kate asked then in a softer tone.

Abbie shook her head even though Kate couldn't see her. 'I miss what we had, what we could have had, if that makes sense? I did the right thing in coming back here. I don't think the London life is for me anymore.'

'I honestly never thought I'd hear you say that.'

'Me neither. I can't wait for you to come here and see it for yourself.'

'I'm looking forward to it.'

They said goodbye then, and Abbie picked up her coffees again and walked to the library.

She hoped Jack was okay. Maybe he could go and stay with his parents until all the furore died down. She supposed he wouldn't be able to work in PR again. When your own public image is worse than your clients', you have a pretty big problem.

'Morning!' she called to Thomas as she went in.

He was at his desk and looked up with a smile. 'That looks like a welcome delivery.'

'I had to stop off at Brew on the way in.' She passed him his coffee, then sat down opposite him. 'What are you working on?'

'I've been looking at local bands — it would be nice to have a local group doing the music at the party. Make it a real community event?'

'That's a good idea. Plus, they will hopefully be cheaper, or even free.' They grinned at one another. 'I did something this morning.'

'Oh God, what?'

'Hey!' Abbie said with a laugh. 'I booked a driving lesson. I thought it was about time I learnt for real, and I can't keep driving around here and narrowly missing trees, can I?'

'Look out, Littlewood.' Thomas smiled at her annoyed expression. 'I'm only joking, it's a great idea. If you're planning to stay out of London you'll need a car.'

'I've been thinking about that. Eszter had an interesting idea actually.' She told him what Eszter said about Abbie setting up her own business. 'I mean, do you think I could do it?'

'Of course you could. It won't be easy, as you've seen from my experience, but you have all the right ideas and skills to be able to make a success of it. All you need is the determination.'

Abbie smiled at him. His words warmed her. She liked how Thomas seemed to really see her. 'It's just getting started really, isn't it? I'll need investors and some cash flow before I can take on any clients. It's scary.' She bit her lip. She had

never shied away from a challenge, look at how she had got to work on Huntley Manor, but this would be her biggest challenge yet.

'I'll have a think if there's any way I can help. You should go for it though.'

'Maybe I need to wait to see how this party goes. If it all fails, it won't look good to new clients, will it?'

'I thought I was the pessimistic one,' he reminded her. 'We've already had some people book in to stay the weekend of the party. It appears people are looking forward to it, so that's a great start. We just need them to spread the word if they have a great time here.'

'Which they will.' She sipped her coffee. 'I'm going to start calling the local press; we need it to be covered as widely as we can,' Abbie said, pulling out her laptop and phone from her bag.

'I wish I could stay and hear you smooth-talk journalists, but I have guests to see to. We could have lunch together?' he suggested.

'Definitely.'

She stole a look as Thomas walked out, his long legs striding gracefully as usual, and then looked away quickly, feeling silly. They were work partners, that was all, she told herself sternly, but the thought of lunch together with him out on the terrace kept her smiling most of the morning.

Chapter Forty-three

Louise was having lunch with Julie in the hospital café. A rare opportunity, as they hardly ever managed to have a break at the same time. Louise picked at her sandwich, still not feeling a hundred per cent after her nasty cold. Julie was grinning at her phone, frantically texting someone. Louise didn't want to ask, but she was convinced it was Alex who she was talking to.

'Oh, he's so sweet,' Julie said, finally putting her phone down and picking up her sandwich again. 'He's coming to get me after work. We're going to see a film and have dinner. It's the first time I'll be seeing him since the barbeque. I'm kind of nervous,' she gabbled, her face unable not to smile.

Louise could barely remember that first flush of romance. It was so long ago that she and Peter got together, and they were so young they hadn't really dated, just become boyfriend and girlfriend from friends. But then she thought about how she felt when Alex smiled at her and she understood why Julie was so excited.

'That's great,' Louise managed to say, putting her sand-wich down, its taste suddenly sour. She didn't want to be one of those people who couldn't be happy for other people just because they're not, that wasn't her, but it had been easier to do it when she hadn't been remotely interested in love herself.

'I brought a dress to change into. I hate having a date after work, you always feel like a mess, don't you? But at least it stops you spending two hours changing outfits,' Julie said with a laugh.

'Two hours? I'm glad I'm not dating,' Louise said, trying to laugh as well.

'You really should. Don't you get lonely?'

Louise shrugged. 'No, not really. I wouldn't want to be with someone just because I was lonely, I'd want to be with them however I was feeling just because they're them. You know?' She knew that after Peter she'd never expect, or want, a partner to complete her. She was fine on her own, but she now conceded that having someone to share her life with, to be partners with, might be nice. If she could learn to trust someone again, that is.

Julie smiled but Louise could tell she didn't feel the same way; she wanted a boyfriend and it looked like she was about to get one. 'You'll find someone. If I can, then so can you!' Julie looked at her watch. 'Crap, we'd better be getting back. This afternoon is going to go so slowly.'

Louise got up and followed Julie out, telling herself to be pleased that Alex and Julie had found each other. If she did

decide she wanted to be with someone, she would find him. Alex wasn't the only man in the country, for goodness' sake.

It was just that he was the first one that made her think she could trust someone again.

* * *

The afternoon went too quickly for Louise, in contrast to Julie. She watched Julie get ready in the staffroom as she gathered her things and told her she hoped she would have a good time. In a way, she was glad Julie and Alex were having this date so quickly, as it meant she could now get over any interest she was starting to have in Alex. It was for the best anyway. She had been on her own for two years; she would just carry on the way she had before.

'I'll tell you all about it tomorrow,' Julie called as Louise headed out.

She waved back to her and walked towards the hospital entrance. She was looking forward to a night in front of the TV.

'Louise!'

She jumped as someone called her name and she turned to see Alex walking towards her. She smiled but it felt as if her heart was sinking. 'Hi, Alex,' she said.

'Are you heading home?'

'That's right. Julie won't be much longer.'

Alex followed her through the doors out into the late afternoon sunshine. 'Are you feeling better now?'

Louise wished he wasn't so thoughtful. 'I am, thank you.' She paused. 'Right, well, I'll see you then? Enjoy the film.'

Alex looked confused. 'Film?'

'Oh, I thought Julie said you were going to the cinema?'

He still looked confused. 'Julie?'

'On your date,' Louise said, wondering what was up with him.

'Date? You mean her and David?'

'Huh?' Louse stared at him stupidly.

He nodded. 'Yeah, David and Julie, they're going out together. That's why I'm here actually, David's car is playing up, so I dropped him off. Why did you think *we* were going on a date?' Alex looked amused.

Louise's cheeks were by now ridiculously red. She moved her bag on to her other arm to try and look casual. 'Oh, I guess I just assumed.' Her heart had just decided that now was a good time to beat furiously inside her chest. She couldn't believe it. Julie and David?

'After you left my party, the two of them were joined at the hip,' he explained. 'He has talked of nothing but her for days, so I'm glad they're finally going out, I couldn't take it much longer. Let me walk you to your car.' They started strolling across the car park.

Louise was stunned that she had got it all wrong and wished that she didn't feel quite so pleased. She stole a glance across at Alex, his hands were in his pockets and he was looking at the blue sky with a smile on his face. He radiated calm. She, however, felt like a nervous wreck. They reached her car quickly though. 'Thanks, Alex,' she managed to say, eager to be alone with her thoughts.

'No problem. Maybe I'll see you soon? I'll probably need to escape David talking about his date with Julie,' he said with a smile.

She let out a nervous laugh. 'I'd like that,' she said quickly, her cheeks turning even more red, if that was at all possible. 'I'd better go,' she said, opening up her car door.

'See you later,' Alex said to her back.

Louise climbed into her car and took a deep breath. She watched Alex walk away and slumped over the steering wheel. She felt like a silly teenager, but she was so relieved. He wasn't dating Julie!

As Louise drove home to Littlewood, she thought seriously about whether or not she might be able to let Alex into her heart one day. The problem was, how long did she have to decide? He wasn't going to stay single for ever. She knew that. Julie had been interested in him after all; she just happened to connect more to David. Louise wondered whether Alex had nudged the two of them together. Could that mean he was still interested in Louise? Even after she told him she just wanted to be friends? Surely that was too much to hope for. But if it wasn't, would she ever be brave enough to take a chance on him?

Chapter Forty-four

Eszter looked up from her laptop as Anne and Zoe walked into the cottage. 'Did you have a lovely time?' she asked her daughter, who bounded over for a hug. She had been at a friend's house and Anne had been to collect her. It was a warm afternoon and Eszter had the back door flung open to the small garden, letting in a stream of light as she sat at the kitchen table in front of her computer with a glass of chilled wine beside her. She'd had the day off from Brew and had been putting it to good use, searching the internet for a key to her future. But it turned out that Google could only really help if you knew what you were actually searching for.

'It was fun. Can I carry on reading my book now?'

'Sure. Why don't you go in the garden? Dinner's in the oven, I'll call you when it's ready.'

Zoe skipped outside with her father's book.

Anne sat down at the table with Eszter. 'Catching up with your parents?'

'I phoned them earlier, but I've been looking online for jobs. Which would be a lot easier if I knew what I wanted to do. I've never found anything I really loved, not like Nick,' she said with an apologetic smile as she knew Anne had hoped Nick would have ended up doing a very different career.

But Anne nodded. 'I never had a career either, and I always envied Frank for how much he enjoyed his job. What about Brew? I thought you enjoyed it there?'

'I do, mostly because Joy and Harry are so lovely, but coffee shops aren't quite as pleasant in Budapest, and as you say, it's not really a career.'

'You think you will go back to Budapest then?' Anne asked her.

'My parents live in too remote a place, they're retired now, so it's fine for them, but I'd struggle to find work, and the nearest school for Zoe is too far for her to go to every day. It just wouldn't work unfortunately.'

'I mean, you don't think you'll stay in the UK?'

Eszter looked at her. 'I suppose I haven't really thought about it,' she replied, slowly.

'I think you should consider it,' Anne said quickly. 'You said yourself you love living in Littlewood, there are some great schools nearby and you and Zoe are really settling in here. I'm sure you could find work easily, you could even work in London. Plus . . .' Anne's cheeks coloured, 'I would love you both to stay.'

'You would?' Eszter was amazed, given how shaky their

relationship had been at the start of the summer, that they had come to this point. She knew that Anne had been enjoying spending time with Zoe, and the three of them saw each other pretty much every day. She had been so helpful looking after Zoe so she didn't have to sit in Brew every day, but Eszter hadn't realised Anne had been dreading the end of the summer too.

'I would.' Anne smiled, and got up. 'I'll check on the dinner. Have a think about it, Eszter.'

She nodded, still a little taken aback. Eszter wondered what Nick would have said about his mother's offer. Then again, he was the one to send them to Littlewood when he knew he wasn't going to be there for their future. Perhaps he was already thinking further ahead than Eszter was and believed Littlewood might be the place they could start afresh.

Eszter got up and looked out of the door at her daughter sitting cross-legged on the grass, absorbed in her book, the summer sun brightening her hair. She had certainly cheered up since their cookery class, where she had made several good friends, and was blossoming now. It had been such a tough couple of months for the pair of them.

Eszter was unsure if she was up to making such a big, life-changing decision so soon after Nick's death, but then again, was there ever really a good time to make that kind of decision? Life usually pushed you into a corner, leaving you not much choice but to make a change, and life had definitely thrown them through a loop recently.

'It's ready,' Anne said gently behind her.

Eszter called Zoe inside and they sat down for their dinner with Eszter's mind whirling through the whole meal. There were a lot of advantages to Anne's suggestion – Zoe would be close to her English grandmother and Nick had always said she'd have a great education in the UK; Eszter could definitely make more money working once she decided what she wanted to do, and they would always feel a connection to Nick, living in his birthplace. But she would be far away from her own parents and living in a foreign country, having to get used to how everything worked. A place always felt special on holiday, but would they be happy to stay year after year? Eszter was unsure. There were only a few weeks left before their return flight back to Hungary so time was running out to pick a future out for her and her daughter.

* * *

The sun was only just setting outside Zoe's room when Eszter went in to say goodnight to her. She perched on the side of her bed and took away the book. 'You've almost finished it.'

'It's so good. Can I read the rest of the series afterwards?'

'Of course. We'll go book shopping at the weekend.'

Zoe lay down and Eszter pulled the sheet up, brushing back her hair.

'Are you enjoying your summer here, Zo?'

'It's fun,' she replied with a yawn.

'Do you miss home, though?'

Zoe considered that. 'I miss my friends, but we do more

things together here, which I like. And Gran's really nice. We have more cake here.'

Eszter laughed. 'That's a good summary. Sleep well.' She kissed her goodnight and left the room, walking back downstairs in the silent, darkening cottage. Anne had gone home after dinner and Eszter still found moments like this tough. It was just her and her thoughts. This was the time she and Nick had spent together, curled up on the sofa with wine, talking about everything and anything until bedtime.

She thought about how hard it would be to return to their apartment and resume their old life there without Nick. Would it be harder to be without him there or here? Or did it not matter? He would always be a huge missing piece in their lives. She supposed it was just about finding the right place for them to be while they attempted to carve out a new life without him.

She sat down on the sofa and pulled out her laptop again. She started looking for jobs around Littlewood out of interest, to see what she could do if she did stay. She had been content when she was with Nick to do whatever job she could find, just to earn money, eager to get home to him and Zoe at the end of the day. It didn't matter to her then, but now she was a single mother, she wanted to do something more challenging and make as good a life as she could for her and Zoe.

She just had to choose what she wanted that life to look like.

Chapter Forty-five

Abbie walked to Huntley Manor after having her first official driving lesson. It had gone pretty well, considering how nervous she had been, and thankfully there had been no near misses with the handbrake or a tree as there had when Thomas had taken her driving on the estate. He had called her to wish her good luck in the morning and now they were meeting up to continue their party planning. She had missed his calm presence in the car with her, although she had to admit that there had been no distractions as her instructor was a middle-aged woman, which she conceded was probably for the best if she was ever going to pass her test.

The afternoon was cool, a fresh breeze whipping through her hair, and she felt the end of summer drawing ever closer. She hadn't expected to still be in Littlewood, but she had never felt more optimistic about the future.

Her phone vibrated in her pocket and, when she checked

it, she was stunned to see Jack's name flash up on the screen. She took a deep breath before reading his text.

I'm sorry I lied to you. Can we talk? I miss you.

She put her phone away quickly. She had no idea how to process that or how she would even compose a response. He obviously thought she could forgive and forget. He didn't even seem to realise why she had upped and left. It wasn't just that he had lied to her: he had stolen money, he had tried to trap her into working with him, threatening her own future, and he had told her he loved her when it was clear he didn't care about anyone but himself.

She had been concerned when Kate had rung her, but that concern was rapidly evaporating. She decided the best thing would be not to reply and then hopefully he would realise that the bridge between them had been burnt permanently. Abbie knew they really needed to have a clean break. It was sad, but it was better he was out of her life for good.

'How did it go?' Thomas greeted her at the entrance to the hotel. He looked much better than when Abbie first arrived back, she was pleased to see. The sun had put golden streaks in his dark hair and his face had caught a tan, the circles under his eyes had gone, and he smiled at her. She could tell he was feeling more positive again about the future of the hotel, and she wanted that to continue.

'It was good – no crashes to report,' she said with a laugh. She slipped an arm through his as they walked through the hotel.

She could see a few guests in the lounge and dining area, which helped the house look much more alive than it had felt when she had taken her first tour of it. The place was cleaner and brighter after Abbie had made a checklist for the housekeeper to work from, and she had organised a thorough window clean by a local firm who were quite reasonable. The reception area was far more welcoming too, and the social media had put the hotel back on the map.

Now they just needed a relaunch that would get everyone talking.

'I had an idea,' she said as they went into the library, which had become relaunch headquarters for them. 'We could really make this party special by having a theme, and I thought what about doing the 1920s? It would be like the picture we found in that library book when I first arrived. I think it could make the room really feel as it did back in its heyday.'

Thomas grinned. 'I like it. We could have all the staff dressed up and we can use the 1920s dinner service we have.'

'Exactly! And serve 1920s cocktails and have the band play music from the time, if they will. We could even send out emails to everyone and say they can dress up too if they want to.'

'I love it.'

'I'm so pleased. Let's do it!' Abbie started googling ideas for a 1920s party immediately. This is what she loved about her job – the buzz that came with a great idea. She paused for a moment to look at Thomas across the desk, also typing on his laptop. 'This is what I want to do for my career.'

He met her gaze. 'Then do it, Abbie, I know you can. It wouldn't cost too much to set up your own PR business. As I've learnt recently, you just need a good website, and you'll have a great reference from me, and I'm sure your old clients would provide testimonials, and if you contacted them they might even hire you over City PR.'

'I did think about that. Especially if I was cheaper,' she said with a chuckle. 'But what about where I would work? I don't think home-working would look that good, would it, but renting an office would require money. I'd be nervous about getting a bank loan.'

He nodded. 'I know I'm having trouble with the bank, but they are behind new small businesses. There's no need to take the risk if you don't need to, though. Let me show you something.' He got up and nodded at her laptop. 'We'll come back to that.'

He held out a hand and she took it, standing up and enjoying the feel of his skin against hers. But he let go of her hand as he led her through the corridor and up the stairs into the wing where his apartment was. He didn't take her in there though but led her down another corridor, where there was an open door. They walked through and he stepped forward to show her the long, narrow empty room. Light flooded in from the large window which overlooked the grounds.

'What do you think? Our old events manager used this room as an office and, as you can see, it's just empty space right now.' He turned to face her. 'Why don't you take it?'

Abbie looked around the room in wonder. It was perfect.

Plus, it would mean she would still get to work every day with Thomas after the party. 'Are you sure?'

'No one is using it, I'd love you to have it, and that way you won't need to pay rent.'

'I couldn't use it for free,' Abbie immediately protested.

'After all you're doing for me, I absolutely insist,' Thomas replied firmly.

Abbie twirled, taking in the space from every angle. It would suit her perfectly. She was scared though. This would be a tough thing to do. She wasn't sure how she felt about trying it on her own. She had seen how stressed Thomas had been before she arrived, and at City PR she had liked being part of a team.

'Okay,' she said. 'I'm going to think about it. I want to be really sure this is what I want, but, Thomas, this room is wonderful. Thank you,' she said, giving him a wide smile. She had only known him a few weeks, but it felt like so much longer than that. 'It would really make a great office.'

'I can see you in here,' he agreed, giving a tender look that threatened to make her melt.

He walked towards the door, and she took another look at the room, already thinking about how she would transform it into her workspace. She didn't want to go into this full of nerves though, she wanted to be confident and determined. She wasn't sure why she was still hesitant, but she was learning to trust her gut, so she was going to listen to it, and trust that the right way forward would become clear soon.

Thomas and Abbie went back into the library and time

just flew as they planned out their 1920s party. So much so that the sun began to set outside before they thought about stopping.

'I should check on dinner, make sure everything is okay,' Thomas said, stretching after being slumped in front of his computer for so long.

'Oh, wow, it's late. I better get going,' Abbie said, realising she was hungry.

Thomas turned to go, then paused and looked back. 'Abbie, I was thinking, I know that this will be a work function. The party, I mean,' he began, sounding a little nervous. He cleared his throat. 'But I'd be honoured if you'd accompany me to it?'

If a heart could really skip a beat, Abbie was sure that hers just had. 'I'd love to,' she said, smiling at how formally he had asked her to be his date for the evening. She knew it would be a busy event for the two of them, but she loved the idea of them turning up to it together, and hopefully getting that dance in the ballroom.

'Wonderful.'

Thomas left to sort his guests, and Abbie couldn't resist a quick look on her computer at 1920s dresses. She really had to look the part for this event as it was her idea, plus she would be turning up with the most eligible man in Littlewood.

She wanted the night to sparkle in every possible way.

Chapter Forty-six

Louise was completely lost in her own thoughts as she left Brew with a takeaway iced tea. It was rare not to have her usual coffee, but it was a hot afternoon and she decided to make the most of it by taking a stroll through Huntley Manor's grounds and she needed a cool drink to take along for the ride. Then she heard her name and turned to see Alex waving to her by the door to Brew so she walked back to greet him.

'Where are you off to?' he asked after they had said hello. He was wearing a short-sleeved shirt and jeans, his hair wet and tousled as if he had just had a shower. Louise took a quick sip of her drink to hide her smile at the thought.

'Just going for a walk.'

'Can I join you? I've finished work for the day and it's too nice to go back to my flat.'

'Sure,' she agreed, pleased he wanted to spend time with her.

He went into Brew to get a drink and then they set off together, walking around the side of the house and into the grounds.

Louise could see her sister had made an impact on the hotel already. There were now tables and chairs outside arranged to provide a good view of the grounds, a pretty umbrella above each table to shield guests from the summer sun, and flowers as a centrepiece. There were also lots of pot plants on the patio, lending much-needed colour to the edge of the manor house. Even more of a bonus was the fact that several guests were actually seated at the tables having a drink, something that had become a rarer and rarer sight.

'I don't think I've actually ever walked around the gardens,' Alex said. 'It's lovely here.'

They headed across the lawn to where it sloped down towards the lake. Abbie had added several benches, which she'd found on eBay, so you could now sit and look at the water.

'It's really peaceful,' Louise agreed. 'I don't come here as much as I should.'

'Your sister has been working here, hasn't she?'

Louise told him all about Abbie's mission to save the hotel from closure. 'And it all started because I basically dared her to do an act of kindness for someone.'

'Brew's kindness mission is hard to say no to.'

'Well, you lived up to it when you found my earring.'

'And you're kind every day to the kids in the hospital. Hazel still talks about you. Shall we sit for a few minutes?'

They sat down on one of the benches. The sun was dancing across the clear blue water in front of them.

'Actually, Abbie dared me to do my own act of kindness,' Louise said, enjoying how comfortable she felt talking to Alex. 'Because I look after kids every day at work, she said that I needed to do an act of kindness for myself. Which is proving harder than I thought it would be. I don't know, I guess I just prefer looking after other people.'

Alex was silent for a moment before nodding. 'I know what you mean. In jobs like ours, when it's all about caring for others, you can forget to care for yourself. My mother is always checking that I'm eating properly, even at my age.' He chuckled, then looked over at her. 'I think being kind to yourself is about going after the things you want, and remembering that you can't look after others if you haven't taken care of yourself first.'

'It sounds so simple when you say it. But sometimes you don't know what you want, or if you do, it scares you, or you're not sure you deserve it,' Louise replied quietly. She didn't mean to let the words out but her mouth opened before she could stop herself. She was sure he would read between the lines and realise she was talking about him, and she couldn't lift her eyes from the ground.

Finally, he answered her. 'I'm certain you should have whatever you want, Louise, but it sounds like you need to learn to believe it yourself. No one else can help with that, unfortunately.'

She nodded. She knew that part of her aversion to a new

relationship after being so hurt by Peter was that she didn't feel she deserved to be loved. She thought there must have been something wrong with her for him to leave her as he had. She was scared, too, of feeling that way again. But perhaps Alex was right. No one, not even him, could help her get over that. She had to believe she could be loved and manage to push her fear aside to give someone a chance to love her. She wasn't sure if she was ready, but she also knew that she probably never would be. At some point she needed to take a risk, make a leap, all of those clichés, but not for anyone else, not even for the kindness pact she had made with her sister, but for herself. She had to allow herself to be happy.

'Let's walk a bit more,' Louise said, keen to focus on something other than the thoughts running amok in her head. She smoothed down her shorts and T-shirt as they stood up and took another refreshing sip of her iced tea.

They continued with their circle of the grounds, the sun beating down on their shoulders.

Alex started to tell her about a nervous dog he had in his surgery the day before. 'His legs were actually shaking, poor thing, but we managed to get him on the table and he calmed down after I gave him a few treats. He was in for a vaccination. I felt so bad for the poor chap,' he said, shaking his head. 'Makes me feel like a monster when that happens; they don't realise how much I love animals.'

'They just see you as a big, scary man with a large needle,' Louise said with a laugh.

'Me, scary?'

'You're right, you're as far from scary as a man can be.'

'Are you saying I'm not manly, Miss Morgan? I'll have you know that if I was threatened by an intruder ... I would run and hide, I've got to be honest.' They laughed, and Louise wondered when she had last felt this at ease with a man. Certainly not since Peter. And even with him sometimes she felt as if she was trying to be his idea of a perfect girlfriend. She felt that with Alex she could just be herself.

They finished the tour of Huntley Manor's gardens and walked back out of the gate and towards Littlewood's High Street.

'Thanks for letting me crash your walk,' Alex said as they approached the vet surgery and his flat above.

The sun was still high in the sky and Louise was looking forward to returning to the cool shade of her cottage and another cold drink, but she found herself slowing down her walking pace as they drew nearer, and Alex did the same.

'It was a lovely afternoon,' Louise replied, hoping that he would think the flush in her cheeks was due to the sunshine and not her sudden shyness. Despite the friendly nature of their walk, it felt weirdly like the end of a date, when you have that equally exciting and awkward moment wondering whether to kiss or not.

'It was. Well, uh, bye then,' Alex said, seemingly just as flustered. He gave her a goofy wave and tripped a bit as he walked to his door.

Louise waved back and hurried off towards her cottage. She made herself not look back, even though she really wanted to, as she knew she'd be upset if she didn't catch him doing the same thing.

Chapter Forty-seven

Eszter was getting ready to go around to Louise's cottage for drinks with her and Abbie. It was a balmy evening, the sun still out as she put some lip gloss on and pulled her hair into a messy ponytail. She put on jeans and a T-shirt and paired the casual look with a pair of sandals. Grabbing her bag, she went downstairs, where Anne and Zoe were just about to sit down to a pasta meal.

She was looking forward to a girls' night, something that she hadn't had for a long time. She was starting to feel more and more at home in Littlewood. She really liked Abbie and Louise and was excited when they suggested they make the most of the mini heatwave by having drinks and nibbles in their garden. She hadn't had a lot of close friends in Budapest; once she met Nick her time had been spent mostly with him outside of working and when she had Zoe, her life became all about family, but she missed that closeness she'd had when she was younger with her friends, and was happy to recapture that here.

'Have a lovely time,' Anne said as Eszter kissed her daughter goodbye. Her mother-in-law smiled at her but turned back around to face the cooker again quickly. Eszter knew Anne was on edge at the moment. Eszter told them she wouldn't be late and walked out of the cottage to make the short walk over to Louise's house.

Earlier, they had been out in the garden when Anne had raised the subject again of what was going to happen at the end of the summer.

'I've been thinking about how much I'd love for you and Zoe to stay in Littlewood,' Anne had said quietly, watching Zoe playing a few feet away from them on the grass. 'I have really enjoyed having Zoe around my house so much and if you both did stay, wouldn't it make sense for you to give up this cottage and come and live with me? The house is so big for just one person, and that would mean you wouldn't need to pay rent or anything,' she had said all in a rush.

Eszter had been taken aback. She had known how lonely Anne was at the start of the summer. She had spent years without her husband and her son, separating herself from Littlewood's community, but now she was blossoming, spending time with Eszter and Zoe, and taking art classes at the community centre. Eszter was so happy at how things had worked out. From such a frosty beginning, they now had a good relationship and she knew Nick would have been proud of all three of them. Joy had been right about the power of kindness.

Eszter had thanked Anne and told her she was still

thinking about their future. The weight of the decision rested heavily on her shoulders as she knocked on Louise's door. Anne had offered them a huge opportunity but Eszter was still nervous about making such a big choice.

'Come in!' Louise said with a big smile, giving Eszter a hug when she opened the door. 'We're already out in the garden,' she said, leading Eszter through the cottage to the living room where the patio doors were flung open.

They joined Abbie in the garden. There was a table and chairs on the patio and a small patch of grass with flowers dotted around the edge. The table was full of appetising-looking food and a jug of Pimm's, full of fruit and ice. Abbie handed Eszter a glass. Eszter took a cautious sip as she'd never had it before, but it was just the refreshing drink she needed.

'Here's to our summer in Littlewood,' Abbie said, clinking each of their glasses with hers.

'I can't believe how quickly it's gone,' Eszter said. August was already halfway over, and September was fast approaching. Zoe would need to be in school soon. But here or back in Budapest?

They sat down at the table and filled their plates with salad, marinated chicken, fresh bread, cheeses, olives, and new potatoes. Abbie kept their glasses topped up with Pimm's as the evening sun shone down and all three of them relaxed in their chairs, smiling at each other as they chatted. It was a perfect summer's evening.

'I'm so glad I came back,' Abbie said, taking a long gulp of her drink. 'I swear I never felt this chilled out in London.'

'You would have had to fight for a space somewhere outside on a night like tonight,' Louise said. 'I couldn't live anywhere without a garden.'

'I'm getting very spoilt on that front,' Eszter agreed. 'I didn't really miss a garden in Budapest, but Zoe really loves our one here, and at Anne's.'

'When we were kids, we seemed to be always outside,' Louise said. 'I think growing up somewhere like this is far better than a city; I've got to be honest.'

'I'm starting to agree with you,' Eszter said. 'But it's harder with work and things like that in a quieter place.' She told them that Anne was keen for her and Zoe to stay on in Littlewood and had even offered for them to live with her.

'What do you think you'll do?' Abbie asked her.

'I don't know. On one hand, it would be lovely for Zoe to be with her grandmother and grow up where her father did. She really likes it here, I know. She'll miss her friends back home but she is making new ones. I wouldn't particularly like being in a different country from my parents, but they lived quite far away in Hungary, we could only see them in the holidays, so that could still happen.' She sighed. 'I'd need to think about what I would do for work though, and make sure Zoe would get into a good school here.'

'I'm sure you could find work around here,' Louise said. 'I'd love it if you guys stayed. We all would.'

'I just don't know what I want to do. I've never really had a burning desire to follow a particular career path,' Eszter admitted. She was envious of how much Louise loved being

a nurse, and Abbie seemed so determined to set up her own business. 'It's hard making such a big decision on your own, you know? I have been used to having a partner to talk things over with, I suppose.'

'You just need to follow your heart,' Abbie told her firmly. 'Where do you feel it's telling you to be? Here or back in Budapest?'

'I think it's difficult for me to imagine going back to our old life without Nick.'

'Maybe it's time for a fresh start then,' Louise said. 'You'll always miss him, wherever you are, but maybe building a new life for yourselves will help you, I don't know, move on a little bit, I suppose?'

Eszter nodded. She just didn't know what the best thing to do was, but perhaps you never did.

'Thomas has offered me an office at Huntley Manor if I want to go ahead with my own business,' Abbie told them.

'Oh, has he now?' Louise turned to grin at her.

'What?' Abbie asked, trying to hide her smile.

'As well as being your date for the party?'

'What?' Eszter asked, looking at Abbie eagerly. 'You've kept that quiet.'

'He's only just asked me! I mean, it makes sense as we'll be there together, making sure it runs okay . . .'

'Abs,' Louise cut in, 'Thomas thinks the world of you. Why won't you just admit you feel the same? You're always telling me to be honest with how I feel.'

'I know. It's just happened so quickly and I really thought

I'd messed everything up with going back to London with Jack, but there's always been this spark between us. I just didn't think he'd felt it. Thomas is more reserved than I'm used to.'

'Probably a good thing,' Louise replied dryly.

'What do you think about his office offer?' Eszter asked her.

'I'm just nervous setting out on my own, you know? Like you say, Eszter, making that leap is so hard.'

'Once everyone sees what you've done for Huntley Manor you'll get loads of people wanting to work with you,' Louise said.

'I just want this party to go well. I've been speaking to the press, and we should get some good publicity for it. But only if it all goes to plan.' She pulled a face.

'It sounds really exciting. I haven't looked round the hotel yet. I'd like to see it.'

Abbie clapped her hands together, making the other two jump. 'I just had the best idea!' She spun round and grabbed Eszter's hand. 'I have been nervous about doing this business on my own, I've always worked well in a team, and something has been holding me back from getting started on it all. I wasn't sure what it was, but it's suddenly become clear. It's you!'

'Me?' Eszter asked confused. She glanced at Louise, who shrugged, also bemused. Eszter wondered if Abbie was drunk already.

'Yes, you. Why don't we set up the business together? We could be partners!'

'But I've never worked in PR,' Eszter pointed out.

'You've worked in retail, which is all about dealing with people and trying to sell things; it's the same thing pretty much. I know we'd work well together, and you are looking for something you can be passionate about. It's the perfect plan. What do you think?'

Eszter stared at her. 'Are you serious?'

'Look, come and see Huntley Manor with me tomorrow. I'll show you around so you can see all the changes we've made, and I'll tell you what we're doing for the party. Then I can take you to the room Thomas said I could have so you can see if this is something you might want to be part of. What do you think?'

'Why do I have so many decisions to make suddenly?' Eszter asked in despair. Then the other two laughed, and she found herself smiling too. Abbie's excitement was infectious.

'I'm loving this idea,' Louise said then. 'I think you should go for it.'

'Eszter?'

'I'll come and look around with you,' Eszter agreed, not wanting to promise anything. She hadn't even thought about working in PR, but the prospect of having her own business was exciting. She could really sink her teeth into it, and she liked Abbie and thought they could work well together. 'Are you sure though, Abbie?'

'This feels right,' Abbie said. 'Doesn't it?'

Her question hung tantalisingly in the air.

Chapter Forty-eight

Louise walked out of the staffroom at the hospital ready to start her shift and was met by Julie, who rushed up to her, looking harassed.

'Oh, good, I caught you,' she said, breathlessly. 'I'm just heading off, but I wanted you to hear it from me first.'

'What is it?' Louise asked, instantly worried.

'Hazel's back.'

Louise's heart sank as Julie explained that the doctors were concerned Hazel's cancer might have returned and had brought her straight in for urgent tests. She had thought her recovery had been going so well; she'd been having regular check-ups, of course, but Alex had said how well she was the last time she had asked him. She felt incredibly sad that the little girl was back, and she ached for Alex and his sister and what they must be going through.

She thanked Julie and went to the ward, finding out where Hazel was and heading straight for her cubicle.

Louise stopped before she reached it though. Outside, Alex and his sister Sarah stood together, holding one another.

Louise backed away, not wanting to intrude on such a moment. She went to speak to the ward sister about what needed doing, but she could hardly think about anything else. She couldn't stand to think of Alex in pain like that. Seeing him holding his sister had told her what she had been trying to ignore for far too long: she had feelings for Alex. She might even be falling for him.

And she had no idea what she was going to do about it.

* * *

Later, when Alex had left, she went to see Hazel and Sarah. 'How are you guys doing?' she asked. 'Do you need anything?'

'We're fine, thank you, Louise,' Sarah said. She was sat by her daughter's bedside, worry etched all over her face.

'I brought Sam back to see you,' Hazel said, lifting up the bear. She was smiling and Louise was certain she had never in her life met anyone as brave as Hazel.

'Hello, Sam,' Louise said, trying to smile back at Hazel. It was hard when she felt so sad for her though. 'Has he been good?'

Hazel nodded. 'He helps me sleep.'

'I was sorry to hear you were back,' Louise said. 'But I'm sure the doctors are going to look after you really well.'

'I'll be okay,' Hazel said bravely.

Her mother looked away, and Louise saw her eyes brimming with tears.

'If you need anything, anything at all, just give me a shout,' Louise said. She gently touched Sarah on the shoulder and waved back to Hazel, who seemed as cheerful as ever despite the fact she was facing the prospect of her cancer returning, and hurried away before she too broke down in tears.

On her break, Louise picked up her phone wanting to say something to Alex. Something that could help. But how could anything help? So, she settled for:

So sorry to hear about Hazel. I hope you're okay.

He replied a few minutes later.

Thanks Louise. All we can do is wait and hope.

Louise put her phone down and sighed. She wanted more than anything to put her arms around him and hold him, but that was impossible.

* * *

On her way home, Louise got a text from Abbie to say that she was at Brew, so she parked her car there and found her sister at their favourite table with Eszter.

'What a day,' Louise said, sinking into the empty chair.

'What happened?'

Louise told them about Hazel reappearing on the ward. 'I

just feel so sorry for them; they've already been through so much. And Alex, too. It makes you feel so helpless. And it reminds you, doesn't it, how short and precious life is. Seeing that brave little girl in there, I don't know, it makes you not want to hold back or regret anything. Who knows how long any of us have?'

The other two looked at one another. Louise knew how grave her words sounded, but she had been thinking about it all day. She had spent two years holding back. Wasn't it time she made a change? What if she left it too late?

She looked at her sister and her friend. 'So . . .' She took a deep breath. 'I really like Alex, but I don't know what to do.'

And then, embarrassingly, she burst into tears.

Eszter and Abbie sprang into action. Eszter grabbed tissues, a coffee and a slice of cake, and Abbie wrapped her arms around her sister.

Louise wiped her eyes and tried to calm down, glancing around to see if any of the other customers were watching. Luckily, her back was to the café. 'I'm sorry,' she sniffed, taking a sip of the coffee.

'It's okay,' Abbie soothed. 'You've had a tough day. I'm so sorry about Hazel. But look, Alex likes you, I'm certain of it, so please don't worry about that.'

'But I was so firm with him that we couldn't be anything other than friends. I pushed him away. Why would he want me now?'

Eszter gently touched her arm. 'You're allowed to change your mind, Lou. You've been hurt in the past; it's

understandable you were cautious. I think Alex will get that. He obviously cares about you. Things are difficult for him right now with his niece, but I know he'll want your support. And then you can tell him how you feel.'

Louise widened her eyes. 'Tell him?' She looked at Eszter and Abbie in horror. 'But how? After everything I said to him.' She sniffed again and willed herself not to start crying all over again. 'I wouldn't be able to find the words.'

'You could show him instead,' Eszter suggested.

'I hate seeing him in pain over Hazel,' Louise said, taking a bite of her cake. It helped a little bit. Despite the fact that seeing Alex in the hospital made her realise she had fallen for him, she knew that it wasn't the right time to do anything. Not when Hazel's health hung in the balance. She was sad but in a weird way also relieved. She had been fighting how she felt for so long. She had been scared. But her heart had broken free of the cage she had locked it up in after Peter. And she knew that whatever happened with Alex, she would be okay. 'You were right,' she told Abbie. 'I had shut myself off for too long. I really like Alex, but it will be okay if he doesn't feel the same way, I'll be okay.'

'You need to tell him though,' Abbie said.

Louise nodded. 'I will. I will find a way, I promise.' She glanced at the Kindness Board behind them. It had brought her and Alex together after she had put up her plea for help in finding her earring. Alex had been kind to her ever since that day. Now she needed to show him how special he was

to her. But while she decided just how to do that, she would be there for him and his family, and she prayed that Hazel would be okay.

'We'll help you,' Eszter promised.

'The kindness pact just keeps on going,' Abbie said with a smile.

Louise smiled back. 'I still haven't quite fulfilled my part of the pact, but now I know that I want to, that I can, and I will,' Louise vowed. She had been hard on herself. She hadn't seen it until this summer, but now she knew that she did deserve to be loved. But would the man she wanted be able to love her back?

Like Alex, all Louise could do now was wait and hope.

Notes from the Brew Kindness Board:

Thank you to Littlewood college for picking up litter in the park as part of their project on the environment!

* * *

My husband for organising a surprise 40th birthday party for me. I had no idea and it was so lovely to spend the night with all our family and friends.

* * *

Jenny for bringing in doughnuts every Friday for the office. It always cheers everyone up!

* * *

Thank you to Olly, my ten year old neighbour, who offered to clean my car for me and wouldn't accept any money for it.

Part Four

New Adventures

Chapter Forty-nine

Abbie stood in the ballroom of Huntley Manor as a whirl-wind of activity happened around her. It was late in August and the French doors, which led out to the stunning grounds of the stately home, were thrown open to try to create a bit of breeze on the sticky summer afternoon. Abbie held a clipboard on which she had written an extensive list of things that needed to be done before the re-opening of the room – and hopefully the relaunch of the hotel as a destination people would flock to – which was just two weeks away. Thomas Huntley had laughed at her clipboard and told her just to use her iPhone but Abbie liked to be able to physically tick off the things that had been done, and it helped her feel more in control to carry it around with her.

Abbie was nervous. This party was pretty much the last chance for Huntley Manor but it was also her first solo PR project. Her plan to set up her own PR company meant a lot was riding on the event being a success but it wasn't the only

thing on Abbie's mind. She had offered Eszter the chance to be partners with her in her new venture, and Eszter was still thinking it over.

Last week, Abbie had brought Eszter to the hotel and shown her around and taken her up to the empty office which Thomas had kindly offered as a location for her new business, rent free. Eszter had been impressed and had talked excitedly about what they could do with the space, she had even become less nervous about the idea of working in an industry she hadn't worked in before, but she still hadn't given Abbie a 'yes'. Abbie knew it was because Eszter still didn't know whether her future lay in Littlewood or whether she and her daughter Zoe should go back to their home country of Hungary. Abbie felt in her bones that the two of them would be a great team and she hoped that Eszter would come to realise that as well, and soon.

'What do you think?' Amy, the hotel's receptionist, appeared, holding up a laminated black and white menu.

Abbie took it and looked at the 1920s cocktails listed on it. 'I love it.'

'This party is going to be amazing,' Amy said. 'I'll tell Glen we're a go then,' she added, taking it back and hurrying to find the barman. Abbie had decided that their party needed a theme and the 1920s seemed perfect – it was an era when this very ballroom would have been in its swinging heyday, and it meant they all got to look glamorous and pretend they were in *The Great Gatsby*.

Abbie went over to the florist who was sizing up how big

to make her displays. They had agreed on black and white flowers to fit the theme. 'Are you all okay if I head off?'

They agreed for Daisy to send the final ideas and quote over later in the day so Abbie headed out and towards the library, which she and Thomas were using as party planning central.

Thomas was at his desk and when she walked in, he looked up and smiled. 'How's it all going in there?'

'It's coming on perfectly.' She bit her lip.

'Why do you look worried about that?'

'It just feels as if it's all going a little *too* smoothly,' she admitted, flopping into the chair opposite him. 'I hope a disaster isn't looming.'

'I thought I was the pessimistic one in this team?'

She smiled at the idea of the two of them being a team. 'I'm sorry, I just want it all to go well.'

'You're working so hard, of course it will. And I've just ordered my suit.'

'Louise texted me earlier to say my dress has arrived. I can't wait to try it on.' Abbie had scoured the internet for a 1920s outfit and was very excited to see the cocktail dress she had ordered. She wanted to make sure she looked good enough to be on the arm of Lord Huntley.

'I can't wait to see it,' Thomas replied, holding her gaze with his own. She felt her cheeks turn warm. She liked the way he looked at her. As if she was the only woman he had eyes for. She hoped that was the case. 'But first, we have more mundane matters to deal with,' he said, moving his

gaze back to his laptop. 'One of our guests has asked if there will be canapés to meet their dietary requirements – vegan, non-dairy, gluten-free, and sugar-free.'

'I'll speak to the caterers,' Abbie replied with a laugh. Party planning was all about the details, and luckily, she loved dealing with them.

He sighed. 'Can't they just eat before they come?'

Abbie was rather glad she was the organiser, not Thomas. She told him to check on his hotel and she'd finish off checking their emails. He got up eagerly; he had far less patience with party planning than her. Abbie didn't care what the guests ate, as long as they turned up in good numbers and told everyone they knew about Huntley Manor. It really was last-chance saloon for the hotel and Abbie wanted this to be the party of the summer.

Her phone vibrated beside her and she checked the text from her sister Louise.

My dress makes me look like a sausage. A lumpy one! HELP!

Abbie sighed. She knew things had been going far too smoothly. She texted Louise back to say she would be home as soon as she could, and prayed to the party gods that her sister was exaggerating.

Chapter Fifty

Louise stood in front of the full-length mirror in her sunny bedroom, staring at herself in the sparkly dress she had ordered online for the 1920s party, and sighed, hoping her sister would be able to help salvage this disaster. Louise had never been interested in fashion really but she knew how much this event meant to Abbie so she had let her sister order her a dress along with one for herself, but it was so restrictive she could hardly breathe, and it made her look a stone heavier than she was. Why could she never look effortlessly glamorous?

She peered at her phone on the bed beside her. After she had texted Abbie for help, she had then sent a message to Alex. She had a couple of days off from the hospital and had wanted to check on Alex's niece, Hazel, who was having tests to see if her cancer had returned.

But there had been no response from him as yet.

'Where are you?' Abbie's voice called up the stairs. Louise

told her to come up and she turned around to show her the dress.

Abbie stopped in the doorway. 'Oh,' she said, taking her sister in. She looked her up and down and then to Louise's annoyance, burst out laughing.

'Hey!'

'I'm sorry,' Abbie said, trying to stop. 'But you do look like a lumpy sausage.'

'I don't know why I bother.' Louise started to take the dress off. 'I knew this was a bad idea. I'll just wear my jeans.'

'You can't wear jeans. I thought you wanted to impress Alex!'

Louise gave her a withering look. She had already begun to regret confessing her feelings for Alex to Abbie, who had developed a gung-ho attitude to how Alex and Louise could get together and be a couple. Louise kept telling her that nothing could happen while Alex had to look after his niece but Abbie had selective hearing a lot of the time. 'He won't even be there.'

'Of course he will; with everything going on, he's just forgotten to RSVP to the invitation but I'm sure he will.'

Louise spun around as she tried to pull her dress up over her head. 'What invitation?' she demanded, her voice muffled by the fabric. 'Why won't this bloody thing come off?'

'Here.' Abbie stepped forwards and helped her tug it off. Louise staggered forwards and then they watched as the dress fell to the floor. Louise stamped on it then she looked at her sister and they both started laughing. Louise folded the dress

338

up and put it on the bed ready to send back and pulled back on her beloved jeans and hoodie, and felt a hundred times more like herself.

When they had stopped laughing, Louise smoothed down her hair and faced her sister again. 'So, Alex?'

Abbie sighed. 'I've invited pretty much the whole town, Lou. And, admit it, you'd love him to come, right?'

Louise hated that Abbie was right, and had been all along about Alex being a great guy. Louise had been scared though of being hurt after what had happened to her in the past, but she knew now she wanted to fight the fear because Alex was too special for her to lose. She just had to find a way to tell him. But she couldn't while Hazel was sick. 'It would be nice to see him there but God knows what I'm going to wear.'

Abbie opened up her package and pulled out the black cocktail dress. 'This is lovely,' she said, holding it up.

'Why is the one you chose so much better than mine?' She sank onto the bed. 'I am definitely missing the how-to-shop-successfully gene.'

'Don't worry, I'm going to find you something really special. I promise.'

'That won't change the person wearing it though.' Louise hated feeling down on herself but she was constantly on edge at the thought of telling Alex how she felt, and she wasn't sure if he was still interested after she made it clear they could only be friends. She was worried she had pushed him away too often. Why would he want her now?

Abbie spun around from the mirror. 'Stop that right now.

You are gorgeous and anyone would be lucky to have you in their life, okay? What happened to being kind to yourself? I can see I'm going to have to show you how. A girly night in it is. We'd better call Eszter.'

* * *

A couple of hours later, Louise was glad Abbie had suggested a pampering session. Abbie and Louise sat on the sofa in their cottage with Eszter in the armchair opposite, all three of them in their pyjamas. On the coffee table was wine and the remnants of the pizzas they had ordered. They each had a face mask on and were painting their nails, with music playing in the background and the room lit with scented candles.

'I could get used to this,' Eszter said, taking a careful sip of wine to avoid spoiling her face mask. She had come over after leaving her daughter Zoe with her grandmother and she leaned back in the chair to smile at her two friends. 'This was such a good idea.'

'We've all been so busy lately, we definitely deserve this,' Abbie replied. She looked at Louise. 'Feeling better?'

'I'm fine. I just can't stop thinking about Alex,' she admitted, grateful that the mask covered her blush. 'He replied to my text and said they are meeting the consultant tomorrow so we should know more then. I hope he's okay.'

'It's a tough time for them,' Abbie said. 'But I'm sure he's grateful for your support.'

'Do you think he will come to the Huntley Manor re-opening?'

'It's the event of the summer,' Abbie said confidently, then groaned. 'At least I hope it will be.'

'Neither of you need to worry,' Eszter said firmly. 'It's going to be great.'

'It would be even better if I had my partner to help me navigate the inevitable dramas that will be coming up,' Abbie said.

'She's relentless, isn't she?' Louise said, with a smile at Eszter. Abbie was so determined with her ideas, she had to admire her conviction. Louise felt like she was always unsure about things. Then again, Abbie deserved this after making the wrong choice a few weeks ago about going back to London with Jack. Louise was thrilled that Abbie had decided to make her home and business in Littlewood. 'I think we need to wash these off; my face is going numb.'

'That's how you know it's working. So, Eszter, have you had any more thoughts about my offer?'

Eszter looked at Abbie. 'You know how grateful I am, and I'm excited about it but I need to feel sure that I'm making the right decision if I choose to stay in Littlewood, you know? I don't want to do the wrong thing for Zoe.'

'She loves it here, though, doesn't she?' Louise asked gently, not wanting to push her into anything, but really hoping she would decide to stay. She hadn't realised how lonely her life had been until these two – and Alex – came into it and showed her that, actually, her heart wanted to be open and full of love again.

Eszter nodded. 'She seems to have really settled in now

that she's made friends, and she and her grandmother are so close already. How do you know, though? How do you make such a big leap?'

'All you can do is follow your heart,' Abbie said. 'I know that I made the wrong decision in going back to London with Jack but if I hadn't tried it, I would never have realised that I wanted my own business or what this town, and everyone in it, really meant to me. So, I don't think you can make the wrong choice; everything you do leads you to where you need to be.'

'When did you get so wise?' Louise asked her sister.

'It's Littlewood. You showed me how wrapped up I had been in the wrong things before. Kindness, family and friendship were what I was missing. And now I have them, I want to make sure you all do too. We can be happy here, I can feel it in my bones. Can't you?'

They all looked at one another, and Louise was sure that they could all feel it; they just had to believe in it.

Chapter Fifty-one

Eszter sat in the room that had been her husband Nick's bedroom when he was growing up in Littlewood. Zoe and Anne were downstairs baking together, something that had become their favourite pastime, and Eszter had slipped in there on her way back from the bathroom. The room was just a guest room now but if they took up Anne's offer of moving in with her if they stayed in Littlewood, then it would become Zoe's room.

She tried to imagine Nick in there but it was still difficult, having only ever known him in Hungary. She hated to think he hadn't enjoyed his childhood. All she wanted was for Zoe to be happy. She knew that losing her father would leave a permanent scar but she was determined to be the best mother she could be for her. But did that mean keeping her here in Surrey or taking her back to Budapest? Eszter knew that Anne was different now. She had lost her controlling husband and had to deal with the pain of losing her only son,

from whom she had been estranged for far too long, and she knew that she wanted to be a good grandmother for Zoe, to make up for the past. But Zoe had another grandmother too.

Eszter pulled out her phone and called her parents' house in Hungary. She usually spoke to them later in the day but sitting there in Nick's room, she needed to know what they thought about Anne asking them to stay, and Abbie offering her a brand-new career. She was surrounded by people who wanted them to stay where they were but her parents were back in Hungary and might very well offer a different perspective.

When her mother answered, they exchanged pleasantries in their native language, and Eszter felt the pang she always felt when she spoke to them. She missed them and her quiet, country hometown in rural Hungary, but there was nothing there for her and Zoe so it wasn't an option to move back home. She just had to decide what other option to take up. 'Mum, I need your help,' Eszter began then and told her how Littlewood was trying to get them to stay. 'I honestly don't know what to do. Zoe seems to like it here, and I've made friends, and I've always wanted to have my own career so it's a wonderful opportunity but it would mean living so far away from home. Am I jumping into something because of losing Nick? How do I know what I should do?'

Her mother listened and waited a moment before responding. 'Darling, I think you're so worried about it because you feel like you do want to stay there, and that's a huge change to make. If you didn't want to stay you would have already

said no. Perhaps you're waiting for a sign that it's the right thing for you to do? But we don't always get a sign; we just have to weigh up the pros and cons, and follow our gut as to whether we should do it. What is your heart telling you?'

Eszter closed her eyes and thought. 'I think you're right, it's telling me to go for it but I'm scared. What if I get it wrong? What if it doesn't work out? And I'll miss home, and you and Dad too.'

'You'll still spend holidays with us. We will always miss you but you have to do what is best for you and our Zoe. You have sounded happier since going there than you have since you lost Nick.'

'I feel like he's with us in some way here. Is that crazy?'

'Of course not. He sent you there, it was his home, you're bound to feel close to him there. You'll always feel close to him. And I know he is looking down on you both. Trust yourself, Eszter. When you told me you were marrying an English man you hardly knew, I was worried, you know that, but you two were a perfect fit. You believed in your heart then, didn't you?'

Eszter felt a tear roll down her cheek, and she smiled down the phone. 'I was so sure of him.'

'And you're sure now, aren't you?'

Eszter hesitated. She had been so worried about making such a life-changing choice when she was still grieving but her mother was right: it did feel like it was the right thing to do. 'Something is holding me back.'

'Why don't you speak to Zoe? See what she thinks?'

'Shouldn't I be making our decisions?'

'Why? It's her life too. And she's your main concern, isn't she?'

'Always.'

'Well, then. Dry those tears, Eszter. You know what you need to do.'

Eszter thanked her mother and they said their goodbyes with love and when she hung up, she let the tears flow freely. She looked around the room, and pictured it filled with Zoe's things. She was sure her daughter would want the walls changed to blue, her favourite colour, and would love the view of the garden. Eszter wiped her eyes, and decided her mother was right, Zoe needed to have a say in this decision too.

* * *

Louise walked into Brew on her way to work. The weather had cooled a little and she was wearing a denim jacket for the first time in a few weeks and thought that autumn was teasing its approach. She greeted Joy at the counter. 'How are you?'

'Good. We just had Abbie in here, full of excitement for this party she's throwing at Huntley Manor. We're expecting a lot of people in town so Harry and I have been coming up with ideas for cakes and extra food we can put on in the day.'

'It's certainly going to be a big occasion. I just need to find something to wear.'

'Yes, she warned us the party is themed. But I can't see Harry dressed as a 1920s gangster, can you?' They both

laughed as Harry walked past with two plates of eggs and bacon for a couple waiting at a table. 'What can I get you?'

'Two coffees to go, please. I'm going to drop one in for Alex on my way. They are meeting the consultant today and I can only imagine how worried they all are.'

'Well, that's a lovely thought. You girls have really embraced our kindness mission. I swear half of the Kindness Board is full of things you, Abbie and Eszter do for everyone,' Joy said as she prepared the coffees for her.

Louise glanced at it and smiled. 'You inspired us at the start of the summer, and it's given all three of us a lot of pleasure. I didn't think kindness could change things so much but look at what's happened already.'

'Give Alex our best wishes, won't you? These are on us, no arguments,' Joy said, giving Louise a stern look when she tried to protest. Joy handed her the two takeaway cups.

Louise smiled. Joy was indirectly responsible for her admitting her feelings about Alex and for finally gaining the courage to decide to move on from her past romantic hurt. She had made a pact with Abbie and Eszter to be kinder to herself, and she was finally embracing the challenge. 'Thanks, Joy.' She walked out and got into her car to drive the short distance to Alex's veterinary surgery in the High Street. He lived in the flat above it. She knew it was a tiny gesture on such a difficult day but she wanted to show him she was thinking of him, and repay all the times he had cheered her up with a Brew delivery. She jumped out of her car and knocked on his door.

'Louise,' he said in surprise when he opened it up.

She could tell he hadn't slept well. 'I just wanted to drop this off on my way to work,' she said, handing him his coffee. 'I'll be thinking of you all today.'

He smiled. 'Thank you. We'll probably see you at the hospital later. I just hope it's not the news we're dreading, you know?'

'I hope so too.' She reached out and touched his arm. 'I'd better go.'

He nodded. 'Thank you again.'

'It was no trouble at all. Take care, Alex.' She walked away and got into her car, and when she looked back, Alex was watching her and lifted his hand in a wave. She waved back, wishing that the sight of him in the doorway hadn't made her heart leap. She drove to work, praying to the universe to spare Hazel and her family any more pain.

Chapter Fifty-two

Eszter, a cup of coffee in her hands, sat at the kitchen table with Zoe while her daughter was colouring, and broached the subject of staying in Littlewood with her. 'Have you been enjoying your summer here, Zo?'

'Yes,' Zoe said, looking at her picture with a critical eye. She added a smudge of blue. 'I like my friends, and Gran. Plus, we have a lot of cake here.'

Eszter smiled. 'I have something to ask you then. Your grandmother has told me that she will miss us very much when we go back to Hungary at the end of the summer, so much so, she's asked if we would like to stay longer, and if we wanted to we could go and live at her house instead of this cottage. What do you think about that?'

Zoe put down her pencil, and looked at her mother. 'That could be fun. Would I have my own room there?'

'Yes, and she's already said you can decorate it however you want. And it would mean that you'd go to school in

Littlewood; we wouldn't be going back to Hungary. Would you mind that?'

'I don't think so. I like my friends in Hungary but I've made some nice ones here, and Dad always said he liked going to school here, didn't he?'

Zoe's memory sometimes amazed her mother. Eszter smiled. 'That's right, he loved it, which is why he always wanted to be a teacher himself. He especially loved his English teacher, and all the books he loved to read and gave to you were because his teacher told him to read them.'

'I wonder if he's still there. The teacher.'

'I can ask Anne. So, you think you might like to live in Littlewood? It's very different from Budapest, isn't it?'

Zoe nodded solemnly. 'But it feels like home, doesn't it?'

Eszter smiled, and felt stupid when she started to well up again. 'It really does.' She pulled Zoe in for a hug. 'You're a very clever girl. I think we should do it. We don't need to stay any longer than what we're happy with, okay? So, you tell me if you're homesick, won't you? If you're no longer happy here?'

'I will, Mum. Can I finish my colouring now?'

Eszter laughed, and let her daughter go. She felt as if a big weight had been lifted from her. And she knew what she needed to do next.

* * *

Abbie smiled to see Kate's name flash up on her phone. 'Hello, stranger,' she answered.

'Hi, Abbie. How are you?'

'I'm good, but what's wrong?' Abbie asked, sensing a harassed edge to her friend's voice.

Kate sighed. 'I hardly slept last night and I have to rush to a meeting soon. I thought I should call you though, I didn't want you to hear it from anyone else.'

'What's happened?'

'Jack.'

Abbie sat down on her bed. Why was her ex still finding his way into her life? After she had found out he had been stealing from the company they used to work for, Abbie had left him in London and cut off all contact with him although he had texted her to say he missed her. 'What did he do now?'

'I was at a bar last night with some colleagues, and he showed up, drunk already, and came over. He just got worse and worse through the night, completely loud and obnoxious, just causing chaos really. He ended up shouting at one of the bouncers and they got into a scuffle. He was escorted out, and they called the police. I had to go to the station. They let him off with a caution and I took him back to my flat so he could sleep it off.'

'Oh my God, Kate.' Abbie couldn't believe how off the rails Jack had gone. 'What happened this morning?'

'I woke him up before I had to leave for work. He had the hangover from hell, and was sorry, but he kept asking about you, and saying that his life was in ruins. You know, real self-pitying stuff. I told him you'd moved on, and he needed to pull himself together. I told him to go and stay with his

parents for a bit, get out of London and clear his head. He kept saying he'll never get another job, and I told him he wouldn't if he kept acting like he did last night. I saw him off in a taxi. I'm exhausted.'

'I bet you are. I'm so sorry you had to deal with all of that.'

'It wasn't the best night. I mean, I do feel kind of sorry for him, but he's really not doing himself any favours. He needs to get a grip.'

Abbie felt bad for him but Kate was right: he needed to start taking responsibility for his actions, and turning things around. 'Should I ring him, do you think?'

Kate thought for a moment. 'Personally, I wouldn't. I don't think it would help. He needs to get over you, and realise that it's over for good. If he keeps relying on you, he'll never change. He's made this mess, he needs to be the one to sort it out.'

'I guess you're right. I can't help but feel bad. Everything is going so well here, you know?'

'You have nothing to feel guilty about,' Kate replied firmly. 'He'll be fine, he's a big boy. I just didn't want you to hear about this from anyone else. You concentrate on your new business, and your new man. Who I can't wait to meet at the party.'

Abbie smiled into the phone. 'I can't wait for you to meet him too. Thanks, Kate. I know you're right.'

'Yes, I am, always,' she said with a laugh. 'Everything will be okay. Right, I'd better go to this meeting, hideous.'

'Take care.' Abbie hung up and chewed her lip. She was

worried for Jack. It seemed as though losing his job, and her, had broken him, but the only person that could help him now was himself. She wanted to get in touch but she knew that it wasn't right for either of them. She just had to hope that he pulled himself out of the funk he was in and soon. She had to focus on her own life but it was hard when you cared about someone, even though they had lied to you as he had done.

Why did everything have to be so complicated?

Abbie was glad she could get up now and go to Huntley Manor and be with Thomas, who she knew would never treat her like Jack had done. That's what she would focus on.

Chapter Fifty-three

Eszter left Zoe with her grandmother and walked to Huntley Manor. If she was going to move to Littlewood, she would need a job. Brew wouldn't need extra help outside of the busier summer months, and she felt ready for a bigger challenge. She had always taken any job just for money; she had never pursued a career, never felt a passion or calling for anything in particular. Abbie was offering her the chance to build her own business, and the idea was both exciting and terrifying. She slipped into the hotel and headed upstairs to the room that Thomas Huntley had offered as their future office. Abbie had shown it to her but she wanted to see it again by herself to see if she could imagine working there.

Eszter loved the hotel. She knew it was silly to have such romantic notions of the history here in England but there was romance to thinking about everyone who had been in this house before her. Budapest was a beautiful city but she had often begged Nick to tell her more about the royal family

in England, about the history of the country he was born in, and had often pictured the two of them staying in an old house much like this very one, waking up in a four-poster bed together and taking a long walk in the beautiful grounds. She was sad that they hadn't come to the UK together before it was too late, but she was determined to make the most of being here now.

Eszter walked into the empty space and went straight to the window where she looked down at the grounds. It would be a lovely place to work, there was no argument about that.

'Ah, Eszter, it's you.'

She jumped and turned to see Thomas Huntley peer around the door. 'Is it okay? I just wanted to take another look.'

He stepped into the room. 'Of course. I hope that means you're interested in coming to work here with Abbie?'

Eszter looked around the room. She could picture how they would make it their office. She had never thought of herself as having a vivid imagination, but being in Littlewood, she seemed to have started dreaming more than she had done since she was Zoe's age. 'It would be lovely,' she admitted.

'But?'

'I've never done anything like this before,' she replied. 'What if I'm not up to it?'

'I know we don't know each other very well but your story, coming here alone with your daughter after losing your husband, it seems to me that you can do whatever you

put your mind to doing. It was very brave of you to come here this summer, and if you decide to stay then I'm sure you will be successful, because you have the courage and determination, and what more do you really need? Abbie is here to help you as well. She is sure that the two of you are meant to do this together.'

Eszter smiled. 'She's very hard to say no to.'

He chuckled. 'I have learnt that this summer. I'll leave you to your thoughts, but Huntley Manor would love to have you both.'

Eszter watched him go, pleased that he was certain she could do this. She supposed all she needed to do now was believe it herself.

Her phone rang then and she answered Anne's call, immediately worried about Zoe. 'Is everything okay?'

'Yes, but we just had the post delivered and there's a letter for you.' There was a silence before Anne continued in a shaky voice. 'And I think it's from Nick.'

Chapter Fifty-four

Louise was just finishing up her lunch in the hospital canteen when she looked up and saw Alex walking past the doors. Her heart immediately reacted to him. She wondered if they had seen the consultant yet and hastily grabbed her bag and hurried after him.

'Alex!' she called when she walked through the doors, and he stopped at the end of the corridor.

'I've been looking for you,' he said, turning to face her and then he smiled.

'It's good news?' she said, reading his expression as a positive one.

He started walking towards her. 'It's not cancer!' Alex reached for her and she found herself wrapped in his arms. He pulled back to look at her. 'It's just a nasty infection but once she has antibiotics, she'll be fine. There's no sign of any cancer cells returning so she can stay at home, and they won't

357

need to check on her for another six months; she just needs to go to the GP if the infection doesn't clear up.'

'Oh, Alex, I'm so happy for you.' Louise hugged him again and then pulled away, a little self-conscious at their sudden affection. She smiled. 'Please give Hazel and Sarah my love.'

'I will, I will. I had to find you before we went home. Hazel is going to bed, and I'm heading back to work but maybe I can see you later? We could have a celebratory drink?'

Louise wished Alex was asking her as a date but she knew that he meant just a friendly one; still, it was a chance to be with him and she wasn't going to turn that down. 'That would be great. What about Huntley Manor? My treat.'

Alex grinned. 'I'd better dig out a tie then.'

'I'm really pleased for you all, Alex.'

'I know. You've been so great with Hazel, well, with all of us. Right, see you tonight then?'

She nodded. 'You will.' She watched him head off to rejoin his family, beaming from head to toe. Hazel was okay, and he wanted to celebrate with her. Louise dared to hope that she hadn't ruined any chance of the two of them being together, and went back to finish her shift with a huge weight having been lifted from her shoulders.

* * *

Abbie loved the attics at Huntley Manor. They stretched across the top of the main building, beams high above your head, dim lighting, and so many boxes that people had

stored up there over God knows how many years. She had already found some gems to help spruce up the hotel, and even Thomas had forgotten half of what was hidden up here. While he dealt with lunch, Abbie had come up to root around for any more hidden treasures she could find.

She moved to the back where she hadn't had a good look yet. There were so many boxes; the Huntleys were most definitely hoarders but it was lucky that they were, as it meant they didn't have to spend much on extra furniture or artwork: it was all here ready and waiting.

There was something furry sticking out of one of the boxes so Abbie went to investigate and ran her hand over the soft fabric. She pulled and out of the box came a large fur coat. It smelt a little musty but it was obviously beautifully made. Abbie wasn't sure about wearing fur even if it was vintage so she laid it to one side and knelt down beside the box to see what other items might be inside. The whole box was filled with clothes.

'Ooh,' she breathed, pulling out a long, slinky dress. She stood up and held it up; the fabric was delicate silk, the colour a midnight blue, and it looked pristine. She bent over and pulled out the next dress – a shorter, fringed cocktail dress in black. She held it against her and gasped.

'Everything okay?' Thomas called, climbing up the ladder.

'Look what I've found!'

He walked over. 'I wonder who they belonged to.'

'They're perfect for the party,' she said, excitedly. 'I mean, do you think, would you mind if I borrowed them?' She

knew Louise would look stunning in the blue one, and the shorter one had stolen her heart.

Thomas smiled. 'Of course you can, take them, keep them. You have developed a real knack for unearthing treasure up here. My grandmother's fur! Wow, she wore that every winter. It used to smell of her perfume, though.'

'Some of this you might be able to sell, you know.'

'Do you think?'

'We should get an expert up here,' she said, looking around. She had picked out things to display in the hotel but hadn't thought that there could be things that were worth money up here before. 'It's worth a try, isn't it?'

'Honestly, what would I do without you?'

Abbie met his gaze and felt herself blush. 'You don't need to worry about that, I'm sticking around for a long time yet.'

'Is that a promise, Miss Morgan?' he asked, stepping closer to her.

'If you make it worth my while,' she replied with a raised eyebrow.

He chuckled softly and reached for her, pulling her towards him. 'I have a few ideas about how I can do that.'

Abbie's breath hitched. She didn't ever want to lose Thomas from her life. She leaned in, certain he was about to kiss her, and then there was a crash from behind them. She jumped and dropped his hand. 'Oh, my goodness!'

Thomas stepped back, unsteady himself. He looked behind her. 'Looks like you loosened a lamp; it's toppled over back there. Or my ancestors are making themselves known to us.'

'Ooh, you could definitely make more money if you had a ghost here.'

Thomas laughed. 'You can add it to the website. Come on, I think we need a strong cup of tea. Pass me the dresses, and I'll carry them down for you.'

Abbie was disappointed that their moment had been ruined but she knew that there would be more. There was no rush. They had the rest of the summer, and far beyond, with any luck. Abbie passed him the dresses and gingerly stepped over the boxes to follow him back down to the hotel, making a mental note to google antiques experts in the area and get someone up here to cast their eye over it all. If they only found one valuable item, it would help Thomas.

Chapter Fifty-five

Eszter arrived back at Anne's house and called out to them as she opened the door. Anne announced they were in the kitchen so she hurried through and found them at the table, tea and cake in front of them as usual.

'You might want to go into the living room,' Anne said after Eszter had kissed Zoe hello. Eszter nodded and said she'd be back in a minute. Anne obviously didn't want Zoe to know there was a letter if Eszter didn't want her to. She agreed it was best she looked at it first.

Her heart in her throat, she went into the living room and closed the door behind her. There, on the coffee table, was the envelope. She walked slowly towards it, hardly daring to believe her eyes, but Anne was right, that was Nick's writing. The letter was addressed to her at Anne's house. How?

She sat down in the armchair and sucked in a calming breath. She picked it up with shaking hands. She was terrified but desperate to read his words again. 'You can do this,' she

whispered into the empty room. She opened the envelope slowly, being careful not to rip it, and inside was a letter in Nick's hand. There was no doubt about it.

She leaned back in the chair to steady herself as she unfolded it and started to read.

Dear Eszter,

I finished writing my final letter to you and was gripped with panic that it contained the last words I'd ever get to say to you, so I immediately started to write you another one. I asked our landlord to keep it and post it to you in August when hopefully you are there in Littlewood. I have complete faith that you have got on that plane, stormed into my hometown, and transformed the place. I know that sending this to my mother's house is risky but I also know that you've never shied away from a challenge, and no one ever says no to you, so I am confident that it will reach your hand.

I can only imagine how your summer has gone. What I hope is that you have fallen in love with Littlewood.

When I walked away as a younger man than I am now, I kind of hated the place. I was angry at my father, and my mother for always sticking by him, and was desperate to change my life. I felt stifled there, I suppose. So, I left and travelled, and found you and more happiness than I could have ever expected. But as I get closer to leaving you, I keep thinking about growing up there and I realise that I was lucky. It's a small and quiet place but it was always safe and welcoming, and it is my home, no matter how far I have run from it.

I wish I could have gone back with you. Just to see it one last time. And my mother. I wish for so many things to be different but I can't change the past now. All I can do is hope that you and Zoe have enjoyed your summer there, and my mother has got a chance to know you both. I know that she will love you both as much as I do, who could not?

I bought you a return plane ticket, and the date you are due to come back to Hungary is approaching very soon. I don't know what you are planning to do next but I know that whatever you do will be a great adventure. You can't go back to our old life so you must create a new and incredible one for you and Zo. And you will. There's no doubt in my mind about that.

Please don't dwell on the past or what might have been. For whatever reason, I am not meant to go on this next adventure with you both, however much I wish to. But that's okay. You've got this.

You are a wonderful woman, Eszter, and you'll be the best mother in the world to Zoe. Don't ever worry about that. Follow your heart, and you'll be fine, and know that I'll always be watching over you both from wherever I go to next.

A love like ours never dies. It will always be with you, and it will always be with me.

Love to my mother and to Zoe and to Littlewood. And to you. Carry me with you wherever you go next, okay?

All my love, Nick

Eszter held the letter to her heart as the tears streamed down her face. What a wonderful thing for Nick to have done. Somehow, he knew that when the end of summer came she would be pining for his advice. And he had given it. It was the sign she had been looking, waiting, for. Nick seemed to have known that Littlewood would win a place in both her and Zoe's hearts and this letter seemed like his blessing to start a new life there. She knew that he would always watch over them, she could still feel him with them, and now she had the strength to make the decision she had been so nervous to make.

She allowed herself a moment of anger that Nick had been taken from them, such a wonderful man, and then she wiped away her tears and got up out of the chair, ready to start the next phase of their life.

* * *

Abbie waited in the reception of Huntley Manor for Eszter, who had rung her half an hour ago and asked to meet her there. She paced back and forth until she heard her name called. Eszter walked towards her with a warm smile on her face. Abbie pulled her in for a quick hug. 'Is everything okay?' she asked anxiously.

'Let's get a cup of tea,' Eszter said, linking her arm through Abbie's.

'You've become British this summer,' Abbie said with a laugh at Eszter's love of a good cuppa. They settled in the lounge of the hotel in two armchairs near the fireplace and

the waiter brought over a pot of tea and two scones with clotted cream and jam.

Abbie poured them both a cup and then leaned forwards in her chair to look at her friend. 'So, what did you want to talk about? You sounded serious on the phone.'

'I've made my decision,' Eszter began, taking a quick sip of her tea. She told Abbie all about the letter that had turned up at her mother-in-law's house. 'I still can't believe that he had the foresight to write it and have it sent to us here. It's just like him, though, he was always thoughtful, and it was lovely, if difficult and sad to read. It's really the last time I'll hear from him.' She took a moment to compose herself. 'But it was a perfect letter, and it gave me the sign that I was looking for. Abbie, Zoe and I would love to stay in Littlewood and I would be so excited to work with you, if you'll still have me.'

'Oh my God!' Abbie cried, hastily putting down her tea so she could jump up and squeeze Ester tightly. 'Of course I still want to! This is the best news. We really need champagne, not tea.'

'We can still toast,' Eszter replied with a relieved smile.

Abbie held up her cup and saucer. 'Here's to you staying in Littlewood, and our new business. May we have tons of success!' They clinked the china together. 'I can't believe Nick wrote to you like that but I'm so happy he did. What did he say that made you decide to say yes to my offer?'

'He told me to follow my heart, and as soon as I walked into our office I knew I wanted to do this, but I was nervous, you know? I talked to Zoe, and Anne, and we all agreed that

this is the best thing for us. We're going to move in with Anne and get Zoe enrolled in school for September. I have a couple of weeks left at Brew but I'm ready to start with you whenever you like.'

'Wow, this is going to be great. I know you've never worked in PR before but you're great with people, and that's all we need, plus we're both organised so we'll have no problem with the admin side of things. We need to think about the big stuff first, what we're going to call the company, what we want to offer people, and set up a website. It's going to be challenging but fun too, I hope.'

Eszter smiled. 'It will be. I can't thank you enough for thinking of me. I am going to work so hard.'

'We both will, but moving here has opened my eyes to see that there is so much more to life than work. I don't want this business to ever take you away from Zoe. We can be successful but also enjoy our friends and family here, can't we?'

Eszter nodded. 'Definitely. And it's so kind of Thomas to let us use the office here. It'll be a big help not having to worry about rent to start with.'

'He's so confident that we can do this.'

'Well, we'd better prove him right then, hadn't we?'

Chapter Fifty-six

Louise bumped into Abbie and Eszter as she made her way to Huntley Manor. 'What are you guys up to?' she asked, looking at their smiling faces as they walked towards her.

'We have the best news,' Abbie greeted her sister. 'Eszter has decided to stay in Littlewood, and we're going to be partners!'

'Oh, wow, that's great!' Louise replied with a smile.

'We've been plotting for hours and realised we needed to go home and eat something,' Eszter said. 'Zoe and Anne will be wondering what happened to me.'

'I'm really happy for you guys,' Louise said, excited that both of them would be staying in her town with her. She had loved having them this summer, and now it didn't have to end. 'I also have good news,' she said, telling them about Hazel being given the all-clear on cancer. 'I'm meeting Alex now actually for a celebratory drink.'

Eszter and Abbie exchanged a sly look. 'A drink? With Alex, eh?' Abbie said, nudging her sister.

Louise sighed. 'As friends,' she said slowly so her sister would grasp it clearly.

Abbie sighed. 'Surely now you have no more excuses? His niece is going to get better, and there's no need to hide how you feel anymore.'

'Shh!' Louise hissed, looking around to make sure Alex wasn't there to hear her. 'I need to do it in my own time, okay?'

'Just don't take too long,' Eszter said. 'You never know how much time you actually have.'

Louise softened. She knew how hard Eszter still found life without her husband, and she was right – Louise didn't want to miss her chance and see Alex with anyone else. She just wished she was more confident about doing it. 'I promise I am getting there. I'd better go and meet him anyway.'

'Have a lovely time, okay?' Abbie gave her a quick hug, and with a cheerful wave from Eszter, they carried on walking and Louise took off in the opposite direction towards the hotel. She was trying not to feel nervous. This was Alex, after all, and rarely had a man made her feel like she could be herself. The girls were right, the time had come to tell him that she would like to be more than friends; but when she thought about actually saying those words, aloud, to him her throat felt as if it was going to close up.

She walked into Huntley Manor and spotted Alex at the small bar in the lounge area. There were a few guests around and she could definitely see the place was becoming more of a destination again. She took a deep breath and walked up to him. 'Hi,' she said with a shy smile.

Alex turned and his face lit up. 'Louise, you made it. You look lovely,' he said, leaning in to give her a quick kiss on the cheek. 'What can I get you?'

'A glass of white wine, please.'

When they had got their drinks, Alex suggested that they took them outside as it was a clear, warm evening. They stepped out onto the terrace, finding a free table overlooking the grounds. Louise understood why Abbie had been unable to say goodbye to the place. There was a magic in the air of the late-summer evening in such a stunning location.

'To Hazel,' she said, lifting her glass.

Alex grinned. 'To good health and happiness for us all,' he added and clinked her glass with his. 'I'm so glad we decided to do this, it's been such a stressful week. Hazel and Sarah just wanted a quiet night in but I definitely needed this,' he said, taking a long sip of his cold beer.

'I'm so glad she's going to be okay, I can't imagine what you've all been through these past months; let's hope there's better things to come,' Louise replied, crossing her legs and leaning back in the chair. She was perfectly warm in her cropped jeans and white shirt and she hoped that autumn stayed away for a bit longer. 'I've had even more good news today,' she said, telling him about Eszter's plans. 'Honestly, I thought I was perfectly happy here, but this summer, having my sister around and meeting Eszter, it's been lovely. I'm so happy they'll be staying.'

'I bet you are. And I got to meet you this summer too so it's been a time to make new friends, for sure.'

Louise looked away, wishing his words didn't cause her stomach to flop. She knew it was all her fault, having set up strict boundaries with him after he asked her out for a coffee. 'I'm really glad we met,' she answered, keeping her gaze on the trees at the end of the lawn. 'And it was all thanks to the Kindness Board,' she added. Louise glanced at him then and he was looking back at her, his hand holding his beer, his expression open and unguarded as it always was, with a smile on his face. Louise wanted to take that final leap and tell Alex that she wanted to be more than just friends but the words appeared to be stuck in her throat.

'Brew has a way of bringing this community together, doesn't it? We'll have to thank Joy and Harry somehow. I have news, too, actually – I spoke to David and he and Julie are going to move in together.'

'Really? That's fast!' Louise said with a raised eyebrow. She was always shocked when she saw other people just jump in like that. And jealous of them too.

'It is but they seem really happy.'

'Well, I'm really pleased for them,' she said, taking a sip of her wine, her mind whirring. She had seen Julie and David meet and to go from that to moving in so quickly, she was stunned. 'I wonder why Julie hasn't said anything at work.'

'It's only a recent thing, I think. David was quite nervous to tell me; maybe they think people will judge them or something.'

Louise looked down at her drink. She could guess that Julie had been worried about telling her because she had

Victoria Walters

been so down on love whenever they had talked about it, and Julie thought that Louise was resolutely single. She hated to think her friend hadn't wanted to share her happy news, and resolved to tell Julie how happy she was for them when she next saw her at work. 'I admire people who can take a leap of faith like that,' Louise said quietly. 'It's so scary to take a chance on someone especially if you've been hurt before,' she said, unable to meet Alex's eyes.

'It is a leap of faith, you're right,' Alex replied gently. 'But if you meet the right person then it doesn't feel like that, does it? It should feel natural to take the next step because you've fallen in love. I think it's only scary before you actually do it, then it should feel right.'

Louise blinked back a tear. She had been so scared but he was right, now she had found Alex and fallen for him, things didn't feel as scary. She knew he was kind and thoughtful and generous and he cared about other people. She knew that he would never hurt her intentionally. They had so much in common. And she was extremely attracted to him. All she had to do was reach out and let him know how she felt and everything would be okay, she could feel it deep in her heart.

'Oh, I'm so sorry but I'd better take this,' he said then as his phone buzzed on the table. She watched him get up to answer it, and she wiped her eyes quickly. Louise hated how hard it was to speak out loud about how she felt. Alex returned with an anxious look on his face. 'Someone's cat has been run over and they need me at the surgery. I'm so sorry to run out on you like this.'

'Oh, of course you should go. Don't worry at all, I understand,' she reassured him quickly.

'Can I walk you back first?'

'No, I'll finish my drink. I'll be fine, I promise.'

'Okay, well, text me when you're home, okay?' He leaned in and kissed her cheek again. 'Thank you for this evening, I had a wonderful time and we'll do it again properly soon, okay?'

'I'd like that.' She watched him go and decided that she had to find a way to show him how she felt, otherwise she might never be able to tell him, and she wanted to take that leap with Alex. It was right. She knew it, and she hoped he would too.

Chapter Fifty-seven

'It's perfect!' Abbie said looking at her sister in her bedroom wearing the dress she'd found in Huntley Manor's attic. 'Just perfect.'

Louise looked at herself in the mirror and smiled. 'It's so lovely.' She twirled around. 'Are you sure it's okay with Thomas that we wear these?'

Abbie looked at her own reflection, and had to smile too. Her dress fit her like a glove, and it was all the more special knowing that they came from the very era of the party theme. 'Definitely. He was really excited that I found them. Louise, seriously, you are stunning. Alex won't know where to look!'

'If he comes.'

'He will if you ask him. I'm going with Thomas, you should be going with Alex. Then it really will be perfect.' Abbie really wanted to see Louise happy, and she was determined to bring her and Alex together before the end of the summer.

Louise turned to look at her sister. 'Actually, I've been thinking about that. I keep trying to tell him how I feel and the words just disappear so I was thinking that I could show him instead.'

'How would you do that?'

'Well, I thought about how we first met – because of his act of kindness in returning my earrings. If I hadn't written on the Kindness Board in Brew then we might never have become friends so I thought about using the board to tell him how I feel.'

Abbie broke into a smile. 'I love it! That's so cute. Using how you met to show him that you like him. And you know that Joy and Harry will be happy to let you use it.'

Louise nodded. 'I was going to ask them if I could open up early and invite Alex there for breakfast.'

'Perfect. And what will you write up on the board?'

Louise turned to look at herself in the dress once more. 'That's still a work in progress. You really think this dress will be okay for the party?'

'You know it will. We will be the belles of the ball, for sure.'

'And what about you? Will the party be the night that you tell Thomas how you feel?'

'How do you know how I feel?'

Louise rolled her eyes. 'Everyone knows that you two need to be a couple, you just need to get things moving.'

'Whenever we try, we're always interrupted,' Abbie said with a sigh. 'So, yes, I hope at the party . . .'

'Look at us, both hoping for summer romances like we're teenagers again.'

'Actually, I don't remember us ever having summer romances, as you were with that scumbag Peter, and I despised every boy in our town. But at least we're making up for it now, right?'

'If the boys we like actually like us back.'

They looked at one another nervously. Abbie stepped beside her sister and they looked at each other in the mirror. 'Even if they don't, we have each other, and that's more than enough this summer. I'm so glad I came to live in Littlewood, little sister.'

Louise smiled back. 'Me too. Whatever happens, we'll be okay, won't we?'

'Always.'

* * *

Eszter wiped down the counter in Brew as her shift was coming to an end. In walked Jenny who worked for Littlewood Animal Rescue. They had met briefly at the summer fete the charity had run. Eszter, Anne and Zoe had gone along and had a great time, and Jenny had since become a Brew regular. 'Hi, Jenny, what can I get you?'

'Just a latte to go, please.' She gestured towards the door. 'I'm walking Ben but needed a caffeine fix.'

Eszter looked outside at Ben, the Labrador they had seen at the fete. He was tied up outside, looking in at them, his tongue hanging out as he sat there happily. 'He's so cute.'

'I was really surprised that no one snapped him up after the fete,' Jenny said, handing over her money. 'One family wanted him but they didn't have enough space; he needs a big garden and plenty of exercise so they weren't suitable, which was a real shame. He's such a sweetheart.'

Eszter made her the latte and slid it across the counter to her. 'Can I come out and say hi to him?'

Jenny smiled. 'Of course.'

Eszter followed Jenny outside into the sunshine and was immediately greeted by a bouncing, tail-wagging Ben. 'How old is he?'

'Four, so he's trained, but his owner died suddenly and their family couldn't keep him so he came to us a couple of months ago.'

Eszter kneeled down to pet him, and was rewarded with an enthusiastic lick of her chin. She laughed as she rubbed his head, reminded of the dog her grandmother Zoe had had when she was growing up in Hungary. 'Zoe would love you,' she told Ben, thinking of her daughter's wish to have a pet. Now they were staying in Littlewood and not restricted to the no-pets rule of their city apartment, Eszter had been wondering whether to ask Anne if she would be okay with letting an animal into her home. 'Could we come and see him at the shelter?'

'Definitely. Are you thinking about getting a dog?'

Eszter stood up and Ben pressed himself against her as if he didn't want her to go. 'I might be, yes.'

Jenny beamed at her. 'Come whenever you like. He would make such a great family pet.'

377

'I can see that.'

'You two look as if you've already fallen for one another.'

Eszter patted Ben, who sat on her feet as if he belonged there, and laughed. 'We'll come tomorrow,' she promised, vowing to bring both Zoe and Anne to meet him, sure that neither of them would object to him joining their family. Eszter had been looking for some way to repay the kindness that everyone in Littlewood had shown her; maybe giving Ben a home was a good place to start.

'See you tomorrow then,' Jenny said, unhooking Ben's lead and walking off with him and her coffee. Eszter watched them go with a smile. Now that she had made the decision to stay in the small town, she felt lighter and happier than she had done since they diagnosed Nick with cancer. She knew this was just the beginning of her and Zoe's new life but she was certain it was the right one for both of them.

Chapter Fifty-eight

Abbie and Thomas stood in the ballroom of Huntley Manor with just a few days to go until the relaunch party. It was the end of a long day, and the room which had been filled with people making preparations was now empty, save for the two of them.

'I'm exhausted,' Abbie admitted as she looked around; everything was in place now. They had all worked so hard, and she was proud of what they had achieved. The room looked sparkling and transported you instantly to the 1920s – it looked grand and elegant and magical. The only thing still under wraps was the chandelier that Thomas refused to let anyone else see before the official unveiling, and Abbie could hardly wait. 'But we've done it.' She turned to smile at him. 'Everyone is going to be talking about this place, everyone will want to come and stay here just to see this room.'

'I couldn't have done this without you.'

'Lord Huntley?'

'Yes?' Thomas turned to see the man in a suit in the doorway. 'Mr Andrews, have you found something?'

Mr Andrews was the antiques expert Abbie had hired from London. He had spent the whole day up in the attics looking through all the treasures up there. 'I've found a lot,' he replied, walking into the room. 'There are quite a few items that would do well at auction, and I've made a full inventory but there is one piece that I wanted to talk to you about. Can I show you?'

They followed him into the library where he had several things laid out. He led them to the desk where, on a piece of velvet fabric, was a pocket watch. It was gold and tarnished, very old, but intricate, and as Abbie leaned over, her head close to Thomas's, she could understand why Mr Andrews was so interested in it. 'It's beautiful.'

'I remember my grandfather wearing it,' Thomas said. 'It was his father's, I believe.'

'The reason that I am excited by it,' Mr Andrews said, 'is that I believe it to have originally belonged to King George VI.'

Thomas and Abbie exchanged a look. 'Why do you think that?' Thomas said after clearing his throat and standing up straight.

'There was a pocket watch that he himself received as a gift and he was said to have passed it on to a family friend after spending a weekend at their house but it's been lost through the years, and this watch could well be the one that has been missing all this time. Did you know that he stayed here?'

'My grandfather used to tell us that but my father always passed it off as family folklore. We never really believed it, to be honest.'

'I'd like to take the watch back to London with me and have it verified. If it is that watch and you decide to sell it at auction, it will fetch a lot of money. With this, and all I've found in that treasure trove up there, you won't need to worry about money again.'

Thomas stared at him. 'I won't have to sell the house?'

Mr Andrews smiled. 'I should think not.'

'Oh, Thomas,' Abbie breathed. 'That's wonderful.'

'Think of all the improvements we could make,' he said, turning to her. He took her hand in his. 'Why did I never think of looking up there seriously? I just dismissed it all as family junk.'

'We'd all love family junk like that,' Mr Andrews replied dryly.

'I can't believe it,' Abbie said, looking at the watch in awe. She was so relieved and happy for Thomas – he could keep his family home, and see it returned to its former glory. It was all she had been hoping for all summer.

Thomas was looking at her. 'What did I do to deserve you showing up in my hotel demanding to help me save it?'

Abbie began to laugh, when Thomas wrapped his hands around her waist and pulled her in for an unexpected kiss. His lips touched hers gently and produced a sparkling fire under them. He deepened the kiss and Abbie found herself melting into him. They started to get lost in the moment

until Mr Andrews coughed and the two of them let go with a self-conscious laugh.

Thomas pulled back and gave Abbie the most smouldering look of her life; she couldn't believe that her knees actually felt a little bit like they might give way. She held onto Lord Huntley and decided that she never wanted to let him go.

* * *

After they had shown Mr Andrews out of the hotel, Thomas said he wanted to show Abbie something and led her up the grand, winding staircase to one of the suites. 'It's empty this weekend, and I want you to see this view,' Thomas explained as he opened the door. They walked through the room and out onto the small balcony.

The room was the highest level in the hotel and views of the Huntley grounds, and Littlewood beyond, stretched out as far as Abbie could see. The sun was only just starting to fade, and the sky was turning a burnt orange. She leaned on the railing and looked out over her new home. 'It's beautiful.'

'Abbie, I feel the need to apologise,' Thomas said then, beside her. He looked across at her. 'I should have kissed you a long time ago.'

Abbie turned to him and smiled. 'Well, I'm glad you finally did.'

'I suppose I've always been a bit . . . reserved. I was raised that way. Really my first girlfriend was the one I told you about at university, and she made the first move,' he said with a small smile. 'I knew as soon as I met you that everything

382

had changed. When I invited you for dinner, I wanted to tell you then how I felt but I completely messed it all up, and you left early, and then I thought I had it all wrong and you couldn't feel the same way that I felt. And then Jack came back, and I thought that was it. That there was no hope for us.'

Abbie shook her head. 'I felt it too, but after the meal, I thought that you just wanted to keep things professional. Not that it's any excuse; I was an idiot when it came to Jack, blind and stupid. I ignored everything that my heart was telling me and I'll never do that again.'

'What's your heart telling you now?' Thomas asked gently, touching her hand on the railing with his own.

'That I'm exactly where I'm supposed to be.'

'Abbie, you swept into my life when I least expected it, and frankly turned it all upside down. How will I ever manage without you?'

She laughed. 'You don't need to worry about that, I promise.'

Thomas leaned in and kissed her gently. 'You know that I've fallen head over heels for you, don't you?'

Abbie's heart soared and she kissed him again. 'Lord Huntley has fallen for a commoner,' she said with a happy smile. 'And she's fallen for him right back.'

'That is the best news I've heard today, and it's been a good news day,' he declared.

Thomas reached for her again and Abbie sank into his arms, giggling as he pulled her backwards onto the

four-poster bed behind them. 'Why, Lord Huntley, where has your reserve gone now?' Abbie said breathlessly as he trailed kisses down her neck.

'Must have left it in the attic,' he replied, brushing away a strand of hair from her face. They smiled at one another before he leaned down to kiss her again.

Chapter Fifty-nine

Abbie woke up to the smell of bacon. She opened her eyes as Thomas walked into the room carrying a large tray. 'What time is it?' she asked sleepily, struggling to sit up. Jesus, the bed was so comfortable it was obscene.

'Ten o'clock.'

'What?' She jolted up and grabbed her phone from the bedside table. 'I've slept for eleven hours, oh my God!'

'You looked so peaceful, I didn't want to wake you so I went to my apartment and showered and got dressed, checked on breakfast and then got the chef to make this up for us.' He climbed on to the bed next to her and leaned in to kiss her. 'Good morning.'

She smiled. 'Morning. I can't believe I slept for so long, this bed is amazing and I obviously had sweet dreams after last night,' she said, her cheeks turning a little pink as she thought back to the night with him. It had been perfect. Thomas slid the tray onto the bed between them. There was

a pot of tea, orange juice for two, and two plates of eggs, bacon and pancakes with a plate of pastries on the side.

'Me too,' he replied, pouring them a cup each. 'I should warn you, the whole hotel knows we spent the night in here. You can't keep anything quiet around here.'

'I wouldn't want to keep it quiet,' she replied, taking a sip of tea. 'I warn you, though, I could get used to this.' She grabbed a pastry and took a big bite.

'I'm not worried at all,' he replied, taking one of the plates and digging in. 'I seem to have worked up a good appetite this morning.' And then Lord Huntley actually winked at her.

Abbie choked a little as she laughed, a little bit in disbelief at the turn of events. But blimey, she was happy about it. She glanced at her phone and saw several messages from Louise. She would need to explain why she hadn't come home last night. First though, there was bacon, and a gorgeous man beside her. What more could you need in the morning?

* * *

Eszter, Zoe and Anne made their way to Littlewood Animal Rescue in the bright, late-morning sunshine. Eszter had decided to keep the trip as a surprise to both her daughter and mother-in-law, merely telling them that she had someone who would very much like to meet them.

'Where are we going?' Zoe wondered, as they walked to the edge of town.

'Almost there,' Eszter replied, excited to see what they

thought. They turned into the road and the large building that housed the charity stood on the edge of a field and the sign was soon visible to them.

'Animals!' Zoe cried, hurrying forwards.

'Should I be worried?' Anne asked with a smile.

'We won't do anything you're not on board with,' Eszter assured her, linking her arm through hers. They followed a bouncing Zoe inside the bright reception where Eszter went to the desk and mentioned they were here to meet Ben. The lady said Jenny had told her to expect them and called her colleague, who showed them into a small waiting room and went to collect the dog.

'Now,' Eszter said looking at them. 'I met Ben yesterday and you might remember him from the fete. He's looking for a family to take him in and I think he would be very happy with us but this is a huge decision and we must all be in agreement if we do this, okay?' Zoe nodded solemnly and Anne smiled.

'I'd like you guys to meet Ben,' the volunteer said, returning to the room with Ben on his lead.

'A dog!' Zoe cried, falling to her knees on the floor as Ben rushed up to her and started licking her. 'Hi, Ben.'

Anne looked a bit taken aback. 'He's a big dog,' she said, shooting Eszter a nervous look.

'He is, but we have a big house and garden, don't we?' Eszter said. 'I think we'd all love to have a dog and we can all look after him together.'

Ben, perhaps sensing hesitation, next went to Anne and

stuck his head on her lap, wagging his tail enthusiastically. She patted him and broke into a smile, and Eszter knew she wouldn't be able to say no. They all deserved something good after the pain of the past few months, and it really felt as if their new family had come together.

'He certainly seems to like all of you,' the shelter volunteer said, smiling as Ben went to Eszter and sat down on her feet.

'How about it, Ben? Would you like to come home with us?' Eszter asked him. He barked in reply, which was all she needed to hear.

The rescue centre needed to be sure Ben was the right dog for them so they arranged a home visit in a couple of days' time with Jenny, who would bring Ben to Anne's house to make sure it was suitable, and that they would all get on well. It was hard for the three of them to leave him there.

'I love him already,' Zoe declared as they walked back home.

'I always wanted a pet growing up, and then later on with Frank it was obviously impossible,' Anne said, referring to his allergies but also his strict control, Eszter thought. 'You two are certainly changing things around here.'

'In a good way, I hope?' Eszter asked anxiously, worried that Anne might be changing her mind about them moving in with her.

'Definitely,' Anne replied firmly. 'You know how excited I am about you staying in Littlewood; you two can have whatever you want, even if that includes a big, smelly dog,' she added with a laugh.

'He didn't smell,' Zoe told her.

'We'll give him lots of baths, won't we, Zo?' Eszter said. 'Let's hope Jenny thinks he will be happy with us.'

'I don't think there's any doubt about that,' Anne said, looking as outraged as Zoe at the very suggestion they weren't right for the dog. Eszter was sure that with Anne there, Jenny wouldn't dare to turn them down.

Chapter Sixty

Louise hurried into the hall when she heard Abbie let herself in. 'We need to talk!' she cried, pulling her sister into the living room.

'What's going on?'

Louise was crestfallen. 'I just had this text from Alex. Look!' She thrust the phone at Abbie. She had received it half an hour ago and had been pacing back and forth waiting for Abbie to come home to calm her down.

Abbie took the phone and read it. She looked up at Louise. 'He's gone away for a few days.'

'Exactly.' Louise flopped into the armchair. 'Just when I was planning to talk to him, and tell him how I feel, he's decided to bugger off on some camping trip with his cousins to Scotland. And it doesn't say how long he'll be gone, and I don't like the words he's used: "I fancy getting away". Does he mean from me?'

Abbie sat down opposite her and put the phone on the table. 'It's probably after everything with his niece, having

been so stressed, he just needs a break to relax. He didn't know you wanted to talk to him, did he?'

'What if he falls in love with someone else in Scotland?' Louise gave her sister a warning glare as it seemed as if Abbie might start laughing.

'Of course he won't. Look, if I was you, I'd reply with some kind of hint that you want to talk to him when he gets back or something. Tell him you'll miss him, maybe. I know, make sure he's going to be back for the relaunch party. Come on, Lou, don't give up without a fight, you're a Morgan, and we get what we want.'

Louise raised an eyebrow. 'We do?'

'We do from now on. I told you, I'm not watching you let things you want pass you by. You love Alex so you need to tell him.'

Louise crossed her arms. 'Just because you slept with Thomas,' she grumbled. She was genuinely worried that Alex might enjoy being away from Littlewood, and her, just too much. She wished he had given her a heads up, not just text her on the journey to Scotland so she could have put her plan into action sooner. Now, she had to sit and wait again. 'What if I've left it too long, Abs?'

'I don't think it's ever too late to tell someone what they mean to you.' She slid the phone across the table towards her. 'It took me and Thomas time to realise what we meant to one another; love isn't easy for anyone, but look how happy we are now, and I know that you and Alex will be just as happy. I knew it as soon as I saw you two together.'

Louise stared at her phone. She knew that Abbie was right. She had to give Alex some kind of hint, a sign, of what she was thinking and feeling or she'd regret it, she knew that. She nodded and started to compose a reply to him. Abbie left to make them tea and it took a good half an hour until Louise was happy with her text, and had worked up the courage to press send.

> Littlewood won't be the same without you. I hope you come back soon. I'd love to see you at the Huntley Manor relaunch party, if you can still make it? Maybe we could go together? Have a lovely trip xx

Louise hoped he knew how much he meant to her, and that he would come back for the party so she could finally tell him. But if not, Louise would just pick up the phone and tell him that way because Abbie was right, after all they had been through she couldn't let him go without trying. She did love him, and she would wait for him, however long it took.

They were drinking their tea when his reply came through. Louise crossed her fingers as she glanced down at the screen, her heart in her throat.

> Thanks, Louise. I'll have to let you know as I'm not sure exactly how long we'll be gone for. Speak soon, Alex.

'That's a brush-off, isn't it?' Louise asked after she had read it twice herself, and once aloud for Abbie's benefit. Her heart had sunk. No mention of missing her or wanting to go to the party with her, a non-committal response that didn't make any promises, and no kisses at the end. Had she completely blown it? She thought back to their drink together; they'd had a lovely time until Alex had been called away to work, hadn't they?

'Don't panic, he might just need a break and genuinely isn't sure when he'll be back,' Abbie said but even she didn't look all that convinced. 'He has to come back for work, doesn't he?'

'I don't know,' Louse replied, dully. She hoped he wasn't thinking of quitting and leaving Littlewood for good. 'This is why I didn't want to fall in love. It just makes you miserable.'

Abbie sighed. 'No, it doesn't. Look how much I smile if you say Thomas's name. It'll work out in the end, don't worry. When he sees you in that dress at our party, he won't be able to resist.'

'If he comes to it,' Louise reminded her. She shook her head. 'Well, I can't do anything right now, can I? Let's go out and take my mind off it.'

'Come on then, a curry on me, okay?'

Louise forced out a smile, she was so glad that Abbie was there with her. 'And a glass of wine, I think.'

'Definitely.'

* * *

Eszter was feeling excited about the future. She and Abbie had spent the morning working on ideas for their business. They had decided to call themselves Littlewood PR & Events because the town had united them, and they were starting to design their website and business cards. 'I think Huntley Manor should be in the logo,' Eszter said as they decided how to brief the designer they were hiring to help create it.

Abbie smiled. 'I love that idea. After all, our office is here.' They were using the library at the moment as they needed to order furniture for their office and were waiting for the party to be done with before they got cracking. She added that suggestion to the email they were sending to the designer.

'Thought we could all do with some lunch,' Thomas said, coming in with a tray filled with sandwiches and a jug of juice. 'What a morning. That annoying couple found something else to complain about, and then one of the toilets got blocked. I had to escape when I could. Is that okay? I'm not interrupting?'

'You never need to ask when you're bringing us food,' Abbie replied with a smile. 'This email is ready to send so we can have a break now, can't we?' Eszter agreed with her, and they pressed send and moved into the armchairs with Thomas, pouring drinks and filling their plates. Abbie told him about their design idea. Eszter liked how Thomas listened to Abbie with a smile, the fondness he felt for her crystal clear on his face. It made her feel a pang for Nick but she was so happy for Abbie and Thomas. She was sure they

were a strong partnership, and they'd be together for a long time. She wondered if Littlewood PR & Events might even be planning a wedding eventually, although she'd keep that idea to herself for now.

'I really like the idea of the Manor in your logo, after all, hotel events will be being run by you two,' he said, taking a bite of his sandwich. 'Can I hire you to dispose of customers we don't like, too?'

They both laughed. 'I'll remember to add that to the "about us" section as a service we offer,' Abbie told him. 'They can't be that bad, can they?'

'They actually asked me if their water could be chilled to a particular degree this morning.'

'I don't envy you,' Eszter said, shaking her head. 'I hope we don't get any difficult clients. I'm not sure I could hold my tongue,' she added to Abbie.

'You'll get used to it. I have had to deal with a few divas in my time; you just have to keep smiling and think of the money,' Abbie replied. 'You'll be fine – look how you brought your mother-in-law round.'

Eszter smiled to think of how shaky their relationship had been when she first arrived in Littlewood – now she was about to move in with Anne. 'It certainly has been a turnaround. I do wonder what Nick would make of it all.'

Abbie touched her arm. 'He'd be really happy, I'm sure.'

Eszter checked the time. 'Speaking of Anne, I'd better go because we have Littlewood Animal Rescue coming around to assess us soon.'

'Assess you?' Thomas asked.

'We want to adopt a dog. Zoe has always wanted one, and now we're here we have the space. I just hope they let us have him.'

'Of course they will,' Abbie assured her. 'Everything is changing, isn't it? When I think of where we all were at the start of this summer ...' The three of them smiled at one another, thinking about what different places they were all in now.

* * *

Eszter excused herself after lunch and walked to Anne's house, excited to see Ben again and hopeful that Jenny would let them take him. Anne and Zoe were in the living room, Zoe bouncing with excitement, and Anne obsessively cleaning so Jenny wouldn't find anything amiss.

'I don't think she'll be looking at the dust,' Eszter said, telling Anne to sit down. There was a knock at the door so Anne hurriedly put the duster away and Zoe ran to answer it, Eszter following her out into the hallway.

'Hi Jenny, and Ben,' Eszter said as Zoe flung the door open to reveal the woman and dog. Ben barked enthusiastically and ran to Zoe, who fell to her knees and lavished him with affection.

Jenny laughed as she stepped over the threshold. 'Well, he seems to like you guys already,' she said.

'I'll show you the house,' Eszter said, taking Jenny around the space downstairs and then they joined Anne in the

kitchen. Eszter opened the back door and Zoe took Ben on his lead outside.

Jenny walked to the door to look out. 'Well, you have a lovely garden,' she said with a nod. 'Let's have a chat while those two play, shall we?'

Anne and Eszter joined her at the table with tea, and Anne brought out a Victoria sponge for them as well.

'Zoe seems to have fallen in love with him already,' Eszter said, watching Zoe running around with him in the garden.

'I have no reservations,' Jenny said, sipping her tea. 'I just want to make sure you know it will be a lot of work; he's a big dog with a lot of energy. He'll need lots of walking and I would recommend taking him to some obedience classes as well.'

Eszter nodded. 'I'm sure we will cope well, Anne is obviously retired so he wouldn't be alone at all during the day, and I'll just be working nearby at Huntley Manor so can easily take him with me and he'd get lots of walks there too. And you can see that Zoe will shower him with attention.'

Jenny smiled at them. 'Don't look so worried, I want Ben to go to a loving home and I think you guys will be perfect. I just want to make sure you're prepared for everything that goes with having a dog.' They talked more about Ben's requirements and then Zoe brought him back in, a huge happy smile on her face.

'Can we keep him? Please?' she begged the adults at the table as Anne put down a bowl of water on the floor for Ben who drank greedily.

Zoe sat at the table and Eszter slid her a slice of cake and glass of juice.

'I can't imagine Ben belonging to anyone else,' Jenny told her.

'You're happy to have him, aren't you?' Eszter asked Anne anxiously.

'Anything that puts that smile on my granddaughter's face gets a yes from me,' Anne replied.

'Ben!' Zoe cried then, making them all jump and look to the edge of the table where Ben stood, paws on the wood, licking at the cake up there.

Jenny pushed him down. 'See what I mean about obedience classes?'

They all looked at one another and then burst out laughing. Ben joined in with a bark.

'What have we let ourselves in for?' Eszter said when the laughter had died down. Ben came over to sit on her feet and she shook her head. 'You won't get around me that easily,' she told him but patted his head anyway.

'I think I'd better leave before you change your mind,' Jenny said with a laugh.

Chapter Sixty-one

Louise was having lunch with Julie at work. She had invited her for a sandwich during their shift and had asked her about David. 'You're moving in with him, Alex said?' she asked her. She couldn't help but smile when she said Alex's name, although everything to do with him was making her heart hurt right now. Thinking of him away in Scotland was driving her a little bit crazy as she kept wondering what he was doing or thinking, and hoping he would be back in Littlewood again soon.

Julie beamed across at her. 'He moved his things in yesterday. Even the cats like him; they were on his lap all last night. I haven't lived with a man for a long time so it's strange but I'm so happy.'

'Oh, that's great. It's crazy to think you met him that night in the pub.'

'I know! And I thought there might be something with Alex instead. But at his party, I knew as soon as David started

talking to me that we had chemistry, you know? I don't think Alex and I would have gone well together at all. Besides, I saw the way he was looking at you at his party.'

Louise's head snapped up. 'What do you mean?'

'Come on, you must have noticed. He could barely take his eyes off you,' Julie said with a sly smile.

Louise's composure broke. 'Do you really think so?' She put her sandwich down. 'I really like him, Julie, but he's gone off to Scotland and I'm scared I've left it too late to tell him. I kept saying I just wanted to be friends but I don't!'

She shook her head. 'I don't think you've left it too late. He likes you, I'm sure of it. David even said the same, and you know how usually clueless men are about noticing things. But why did you say you just wanted to be friends if you like him? You even told me to go for it with him,' Julie asked her gently.

Louise wished she could go back and give her past self a good slap. 'Because I'm an idiot? I kept telling myself that I didn't like him. I was so closed off to any idea of romance. I was hurt, badly, by an ex and since then, I've avoided any thoughts of starting anything, with anyone. Then I met Alex, and now I can't stop thinking about him.'

'I totally understand being nervous about starting something new. Seriously, when David suggested moving in, I freaked out. I didn't return his calls for a day. Because I was scared it was too soon, but you know what? We make each other happy and that's all that matters. We can't worry about things that might happen years from now, or will never

happen, you just have to go with how you feel right now, today, in the moment.'

'I've never been very good at that.'

'But you know now how you feel. All you have to do next is to tell Alex. He'll be thrilled, I know he will.'

'If he ever comes back.'

'Well, of course he will. He loves his job, for one thing, and his family are close by. And his friends. I could ask David to talk to him?'

Louise shook her head. 'Thanks but no, it's okay. I'd rather do it myself if he does come home. If he doesn't, that's my sign, isn't it, that we're not meant to be?'

'I'm not sure I believe in signs, I think you need to make what you want happen, and not rely on fate to do the hard work for you.'

Louise absorbed her words. She liked how Julie saw life. 'I need to be more like you, Julie,' she replied with a smile.

'I don't think the world could cope with two of us,' Julie said with a laugh. 'Everything will be okay, I know it.'

Louise wished she could believe that too but the problem was, she'd been let down so badly in the past, it was hard to trust that this time it would work out.

As they left the canteen, Louise was convinced she needed to try to seize the moment more. She knew that she had already invited Alex to the Huntley Manor relaunch but she felt sure that he wasn't going to come back for it. The silence from him was driving her crazy.

Before she could talk herself out of it, she sent him a

message before re-starting her shift, and hoped it would give him the kick he seemed to need to come back home.

> Don't forget the Huntley Manor relaunch party is
> this Saturday. I really hope I'll see you there. I miss
> you, Louise xx

* * *

Abbie walked quickly into Huntley Manor, intrigued as to why Thomas had phoned her an hour ago asking her to come to the hotel as soon as she could as he had something important to show her.

'There you are!' Thomas rounded the corner and grabbed her hand, a huge smile on his face. 'I have the best news.' He steered her back out through the front door and they started walking around the house into the grounds. 'Mr Andrews called me yesterday to say the pocket watch has been verified as once belonging to King George, and he's already had an offer for it.'

'Oh my God, that's so exciting,' Abbie said, a little breathless, trying to keep up with Thomas's long strides as he led her into the grounds.

'It's a lot of money. A crazy amount. Enough to keep us going for a couple of years at least. He's arranging an auction for the other things in a few weeks' time. I got off the phone with him, and I thought finally I can breathe again. It's been such a stressful time but now we can relax, and really make this the place I've always wanted it to be.' He steered them

towards the former stables. 'We can start thinking about converting the stables, all sorts, really. And I knew as soon as I got off the phone with him, that I had to find a way to thank you for suggesting we bring him here, for everything that you've done this summer really. And it came to me in a stroke of inspiration.' They turned a corner and he stopped, making her skid a little. 'What do you think?' he asked, gesturing in front of them.

Abbie stopped and looked. In front of them was a small, shiny car. 'It's a car,' she said stupidly.

'Look at the side,' he said, pulling her with him so they could see the side of the car. Along it was written Littlewood PR & Events, with the small L logo they had had designed within a picture of Huntley Manor. He smiled at her stunned expression. 'It's for you, and Eszter too. You'll need a car around here, and you'll pass your test soon.' Then he frowned. 'You do like it, don't you?'

Abbie was thrilled. She threw her arms around him. 'Like it? I love it!' She let go and opened the car door. 'Can I sit in it?'

'Of course,' he replied, climbing in beside her.

'Thomas this is too much, you didn't need to do this,' she said, stroking the dashboard and holding the steering wheel, imagining herself driving it around Littlewood. 'Besides, you need all the money for the hotel.'

'There's plenty and this is an investment anyway, in your business, and in you. I can't think of anything better to spend the money on. It's not brand new but it's in great condition.'

'It's perfect.' She leaned over the gearstick to kiss him. 'Thank you so much.'

'I've been such a fool, worried about my business but not doing anything to shake things up. I would have lost this hotel without you.'

'You would have saved it, I know you would,' she replied, shaking her head.

'Well, I never need to know what would have happened, because you turned up and told me I needed your help, and you were right. And now I'm the luckiest guy in the world to have you by my side.'

She smiled. 'I'm lucky too.' They kissed again, and Thomas pulled her closer. As she reached for him, she leaned on the horn, blasting a loud noise which made them jump and break apart breathlessly. 'We are a disaster,' she said, laughing, thinking about how many times their romantic moments had been interrupted.

'But a beautiful one,' he told her, pulling her back to his lips again, sending a delicious shiver down her spine.

Chapter Sixty-two

The day of the Huntley Manor relaunch party dawned bright and sunny and Eszter was almost ready to head over to help Abbie with the last-minute preparations when her phone rang with a call from a frantic Joy. 'Eszter, I don't know what we're going to do!' Joy said when she had answered the phone.

Eszter stopped. 'What's wrong?'

'Both ovens have broken!' Joy cried. 'They're not working at all, and we can't find anyone to come out until later. I'm supposed to be baking and cooking; we're going to have so many people here for the party, we can't shut Brew. How would that look?'

'Don't worry, we'll think of something. I'm going to ring you back.' She hung up and called Abbie straightaway. 'We have to help Brew!'

Minutes later, Eszter was walking briskly into Huntley Manor where she was greeted by Abbie, Louise and Thomas. 'Okay, guys, I think we can do this. Anne and Zoe are

already baking at home, and you've got the ovens here on standby? Let's go and get Joy and Harry,' she said.

'I knew today wasn't going to go smoothly,' Abbie said. 'It never does on the day, but it's going to be okay. I'll come with you. You start cooking, Lou. Let's go.' Eszter and Abbie hurried over to Brew where they knocked and were let in by a worried Harry and Joy.

'You can use the ovens at Huntley Manor. Louise is already in there making a start. Anne and Zoe are baking at home too,' Eszter told them. 'There's no way Brew isn't opening today.'

'Oh, thank you,' Joy said with relief. 'Harry, you stay here and get ready to open up, I'll start cooking with Louise. Why did this have to happen today?'

'It's fine, we have caterers for the party and they're setting up in a tent outside so the kitchen can be yours completely once the breakfast is finished,' Abbie reassured her. 'Everything will be fine.'

Joy smiled. 'Huntley Manor saves the day. Right, let's carry over everything we need.'

'I'll get the coffee machine on; at least that's working,' Harry said, walking to the counter as they went into the kitchen to collect ingredients.

They made their way back to the hotel laden with food and Abbie showed Joy the kitchen. Joy got stuck in straight-away baking pastries. 'We'll have to leave cooked breakfasts today; they'll be cold by the time we get back to Brew.'

'We have lots of fruit and yogurt you could take over,' the

Huntley Manor chef offered, showing her the cute jars they put out for the breakfast buffet.

'That would be fabulous.'

'Anne is going to bring her cakes over soon,' Eszter said, checking her phone. 'So, you should all be set to open for a late breakfast.'

'Hopefully this is like a play and a disastrous morning will mean an excellent evening party,' Thomas said, running a hand through his hair. 'Right, I'll check on the caterers.'

'I'd better go to the ballroom and make sure the florist is okay,' Abbie said. 'You guys will be all right in here?' Louise and Joy didn't answer as they focused on their task so she smiled and followed Thomas out.

'What do you need me to do?' Eszter asked Abbie, leaving the kitchen behind them.

'Can you make sure that the reception looks perfect? It's the first thing everyone will see, and we need the sign up to direct everyone to the ballroom.'

'I'm on it, boss.'

'Hey, partner, you mean?'

Eszter smiled. 'I'm on it, partner.' Eszter walked to the reception, pleased she'd been able to help out with Brew's crisis. She had been nervous about working with Abbie but she knew she needed to be more confident in her ability to deal with challenges. She knew she was capable; she just needed to keep reminding herself of that. This event would be their first showcase so she was determined to make sure it was a success.

'Thank goodness,' Amy said when she saw Eszter. 'Look

at this!' She held up the calligraphy sign that had been made to welcome guests to the party. Eszter looked at it and gasped when she saw what Amy meant.

Welcome to the 1920s...
Come and celebrate with a cocktail in the
Huntley Manor ballroom, restored to its former glory.
Walk this way...

And then there was the map, which instead of sending guests to the ballroom was clearly sending them to the kitchens instead.

'Right, I need blank paper and a Sharpie,' Eszter said, walking around to the desk. There was no time for it to be re-printed; they would just have to draw their own map. 'Is there any coffee? I think we're going to need it.'

The rest of the day was spent in a similar manner. Eszter rushed to wherever Abbie sent her, making sure everything was going okay. Anne and Zoe stopped by with cakes for Brew, and Joy and Louise ran back and forth from the hotel to the café carrying food for most of the morning. Abbie was holed up in the ballroom all day making sure it was looking perfect, and Thomas strode around trying to make sure all the guests that had been invited were happy with their rooms.

Eszter walked into the ballroom at teatime utterly exhausted. She looked around in wonder. 'It looks amazing,' she told Abbie, who stood with her clipboard in the centre of the room, brow furrowed as she ticked off things.

'I think we're almost there,' Abbie said, looking up at her.

The flowers were all in place, the bar set up ready, and the wooden floor was so shiny you could almost see your face in it. Fairy lights were strung around the doors, which were open. Outside, people were setting up lanterns ready for nightfall, and servers were putting out tables and chairs. The band were setting up in the corner. And above them, the chandelier was covered ready for the unveiling later. 'Thomas is checking the caterers are on time and then I think we should all go and get ready.'

'I'll head home then to change,' Eszter said. 'If you're sure there's nothing else I can do?'

Abbie shook her head. 'No but please tell Louise to go home and get ready as well. Brew will be closing now so everyone can relax a bit. I want everyone to be ready to party in a couple of hours.'

'That goes for you too, okay?' Eszter said, firmly. 'Go and sit down for a bit before putting on your dress. Have a glass of wine too. You look nervous.'

'And you look surprisingly calm. Aren't we usually the other way around?'

Eszter smiled. 'We are, but everything is in place, we've got this. The hotel is full. The other guests will be arriving soon. There's nothing else we can do. The best thing to do is chill out before we have to put on our event faces.' She gave her a quick hug. 'See you at seven, okay?'

Abbie nodded. 'You're right. I'll head upstairs now.' She pointed to their business cards on the table by the door. 'Do you think anyone will hire us after this?'

'They won't be able to resist.'

Chapter Sixty-three

Abbie walked into Thomas's apartment in the hotel and half-fell down onto the sofa. Eszter had been right about her needing a small break before the party began, she'd been on her feet all day rushing around on pure adrenaline. She was feeling okay about things though. Brew had opened up and had been busy with hotel guests who had been milling around the hotel all day; there was a definite buzz in the atmosphere. The extra staff they had hired were all getting ready too; everyone was wearing black and white to fit with the theme.

The door opened and in came Thomas. 'Remind me why we're doing this?' he asked, flustered, and flopping down into the armchair opposite. 'I just had to tell a waiter not to smoke in the ballroom, for goodness' sake.' He looked at Abbie. 'Are you okay? You've been doing so much!'

'I'm fine, just needed a break.'

'Let me get us some refreshments before we get ready. I told

Amy that no one should bother us for an hour. I'm not hopeful they'll stick to that but we can just ignore them.' Thomas came back a few moments later with a glass of wine for them and a cheese and pickle sandwich with a bowl of crisps.

Abbie broke into a smile. 'The perfect pick-me-up.'

'Exactly.' He sat next to her and wrapped an arm around her. She leant into him gratefully. 'I was only joking before. It's looking wonderful down there, and tonight is going to be an amazing evening. I can't wait for everyone to see the chandelier.'

'I can't believe you've hidden it from me all this time.'

'Thank goodness it's high enough that you couldn't peek at it. Come on, eat up, you need it. I can't wait to see you in your dress, Abbie Morgan.'

'Why Lord Huntley, I do like it when you're in charge,' she replied, picking up one of the sandwiches.

* * *

After they had re-charged themselves, Abbie and Thomas went into his room to change. He was wearing a smart suit, this time with shiny leather shoes and not wellies, and looked every bit the Lord of the Manor when he was ready. He zipped up Abbie's dress, and she turned around to a wide smile from him. Her dress really was stunning and clung to her in all the right places. She had pinned her hair up, and with her sky-high glittering shoes and a sparkling necklace, felt like she was a million bucks, as they might have said in the era they were paying homage to.

411

'It's not fair for you to show all the other guests up like this,' Thomas murmured, kissing her gently on her neck so he didn't smudge her red lipstick. 'Can I escort you to the party, Ms Morgan?'

'As long as you promise me the first dance.'

'You can have any dance you want.'

Abbie laid her hand on his arm. 'Let's get this show on the road then.' She took a deep breath and hoped it would all go off perfectly. Thomas gave her a reassuring smile, and she was very glad that he was by her side.

They headed downstairs and immediately staff rushed up to them asking questions but Abbie extracted herself after she spotted a familiar face loitering in the hall. 'Kate!' she called to her friend who spun around and grinned at her.

'Now I understand why you've abandoned London,' Kate said, pulling her in for a hug. 'This place is gorgeous. And look at you! Wow!' she said, pulling back and taking in Abbie's outfit.

'I found this in the attic upstairs.'

'No way.' She leaned in closer. 'Now, when do I get a look at the famous Lord Huntley?' Abbie pointed him out to Kate, who whistled under her breath. 'Okay, I'm sold, I'm moving to Littlewood too.'

Abbie laughed. 'Are you all checked in okay?'

'Yep. My date is having a nap, I swear he acts older than my granddad. I wanted to find you before I get ready for the party. My dress now feels like a shabby mess but it'll have to do. I can't wait to see the ballroom but I'll wait for the full

effect later. Honestly, Abbie, you look radiant. Living here agrees with you.'

'Thanks, Kate. It really does.' Abbie lowered her voice. 'And have you heard any more from Jack?'

Kate shook her head. 'No, he's obviously been keeping his head down, I heard he might be staying with his parents, so hopefully I won't see him for a long time. You did the right thing coming here. And I'm so excited to hear all about your new business.'

Abbie was relieved there had been no more antics from Jack. 'I'm just hoping tonight goes well, we've all worked so hard.'

'Well, of course it will. I'll go and wake my date up then and try to scrub myself up a little. Good luck.' She hugged again quickly then headed for the stairs. Abbie was glad she was there. She had no desire to ever go back to London but she didn't want to lose her friendship with Kate and hoped she'd be able to persuade her friend to visit often. Abbie turned around and searched for Thomas. They needed to check on the ballroom. It was almost time.

* * *

Louise checked her phone again. There had been no response from Alex to the message she had sent him at work to remind him of the party tonight, and she was becoming more and more certain that he wouldn't come, and she was starting to worry that he was planning not to come back to Littlewood at all. She tried to tell herself that he loved his job, and he

wouldn't just leave the vets in the lurch plus he had a flat and all of his things there, but she couldn't stop her mind playing out various horrible scenarios that all ended up with her never seeing him again.

'Stop thinking about him,' she said aloud to the empty hall. Tonight was about supporting her sister and Thomas and Eszter, and having fun. She had to put Alex out of her head at least for tonight. She took a quick glance in the hall mirror. The dress really was lovely. For once she did feel glamorous. She had tried to order a taxi but everyone in Littlewood had done the same thing so she would have to walk. It was a lovely warm evening though and it really wasn't far, she just hoped her feet could stand the small-heeled shoes Abbie had made her buy. She supposed that ballet pumps wouldn't have matched the dress but the extra height felt strange to her. Grabbing the clutch bag Abbie had lent her, Louise locked up and began her solitary stroll through her town.

As she entered the High Street, Louise's eyes naturally flew straight to the vet surgery, and she stopped. Parked outside was a car, and three men were heaving things out of it. One of them was Alex. Louise had never believed your heart could actually skip a beat but it felt like something happened to it when she saw him. She took a deep breath and started walking again, and soon Alex turned and noticed her. There was a moment when they locked eyes, and her pulse started to climb rapidly, and she wasn't sure if he was pleased to see her or not but then he grinned and waved, and she sagged with relief and crossed over towards him.

Seeing someone again after a break was a good way to decide how you felt about them, and she was even more certain that she had fallen for this man. Her cheeks flushed as she walked up to him, trying to hold her smile down but was convinced she looked like the Cheshire Cat in *Alice in Wonderland*. Why was it so hard to be cool when you liked someone? 'You're back,' were her first words. Her throat felt as if something was constricting it so at least she had managed to say something, even if she felt stupid for saying it.

'It's good to see you, Louise. You look . . . wow,' he said, taking in her outfit. He leaned in and she went for a hug as he went to kiss her cheek, and they ended up awkwardly bumping each other before stepping back with nervous laughter. 'You're off to the party?' She nodded, still embarrassed. 'Well, I'm just bringing in my things, and then I'll get ready and I'll be over soon.'

'You're coming?' she said, unable to stop the smile from spreading across her face.

He smiled back. 'How could I not? And I've missed you too,' he added.

Her blush was getting out of control but she knew if she didn't say it now, she wouldn't, and she had a plan and was determined to stick to it. 'Do you fancy having breakfast tomorrow? To catch up?' she asked, feeling a bit sick at the thought of going through with it but seeing Alex had made it clear, she was in love with him and she just couldn't not tell him any longer.

'I'd love to.'

'Great. I'll see you at the party then.' She started to walk away, thinking she would need a big drink once she got there.

'How about a dance later, too?' Alex called from behind her.

She looked back at him. 'I'll check my card and get back to you,' she replied, feeling quite pleased with that comeback as she felt as if she might melt right into the pavement.

His laugh followed her as she walked to the party, smiling the whole way.

Chapter Sixty-four

Eszter arrived back at Huntley Manor wearing a chiffon knee-length silver dress and made her way to the ballroom. Waiters milled around in black and white, the barman was mixing cocktails, and the band had started playing. Abbie and Thomas stood in the room ready to welcome the guests who were starting to make their way to the party. 'Wow, I feel like I've gone back in time,' Eszter said, walking up to them. Abbie looked stunning in her dress, and Thomas was smart and handsome. They really looked like Lord and Lady of the Manor. The ballroom felt as if it was back to its 1920s' peak, and Eszter felt as if she wanted to pinch herself that she was here in England, at a stately home party, wearing a gorgeous dress, ready to start a whole new chapter of her life. She really hoped Nick was watching this.

'Here you go,' Abbie said, grabbing two cocktails from a passing tray and handing Eszter one. 'These are Bee's Knees.'

'Do we not need to be doing something?' Eszter asked, concerned, as she took the glass from Abbie.

'Everything is in place, don't worry. Now's the time to relax a bit and enjoy the party. If there are any problems you'll be the first to know.'

Eszter took a sip of the cocktail. 'I feel drunk already,' she said as the strong drink reached her throat.

'Hi, guys,' Louise said from behind her. 'Where do I get one of those?'

Abbie handed her hers. 'Take mine. I need to check on the barman anyway. You look gorgeous, Lou.'

'Guess what?' Louise hissed, smiling broadly at them. 'Alex is back, and he'll be here soon.'

'That's great,' Eszter said, pleased that things finally seemed to be working out for the two of them. British people definitely seemed to take longer to figure out what they meant to each other but she felt like Abbie and Thomas, and Louise and Alex were all for keeps. She took another gulp of cocktail, hoping she wouldn't slip into melancholy tonight. Yes, she would love to dance with Nick tonight but she had to focus on all she had achieved and how much there was to look forward to.

'I need to make sure everything is set for the chandelier unveiling,' Thomas said, excusing himself along with Abbie. Eszter and Louise moved through the room towards the French doors, stepping out into the garden. The sun was only just starting to dip but the lanterns were lit, and the atmosphere already felt romantic.

'I can't believe the transformation,' Louise said, looking around in wonder.

'Everyone is going to want to have a party here,' Eszter agreed, looking back at the ballroom. It was starting to fill with people now: men dressed in dark suits, and women wearing cocktail dresses, everyone holding a sparkling crystal glass in their hands. Eszter was sure that people would be talking about tonight for a long time, and that could only be good for their new business. 'It would be perfect for weddings too. How are you feeling about Alex being back?'

Louise took a sip of her drink. 'Relieved but scared too. I've invited him for breakfast at Brew tomorrow, and I'm going to tell him how I feel. How do people do this? I feel sick at the thought of it. But also like I can't bear not to do it.'

Eszter smiled. 'Of course you're going to be nervous but I don't think you have anything to worry about. You two belong together, I can feel it.'

'Do you mind me asking how you and Nick met? How did you two get together?'

'He came into the shop I was working in to ask for directions. He wanted to find the school he ended up working at for an interview. He was hopelessly lost, and nervous. I was due a break so I decided to show him myself as it was quite difficult to find, and I liked him instantly. After his interview, he came back to the shop and asked me out for a drink that night. We never left each other's side after that.'

'Wow,' Louise said. 'That's so romantic. And you were both so unafraid to jump in, I really admire that.'

'I knew I had met someone special. And you knew it too. You have been cautious but that's okay, it's understandable, you'll get your happy ending, I'm sure of it.'

'Thanks, Eszter.' Louise looked behind her. 'Oh, here he is,' she said somewhat breathlessly. 'Shall I go over?'

'Definitely.' Eszter smiled as Louise went to meet Alex. She looked around for Abbie and then spotted three familiar faces sneaking round the side of the hotel. 'And what do we have here?' she said, going up to Anne and Zoe, who had Ben on a lead.

'We just wanted to have a peek,' Anne explained. 'We won't stay long.'

'It's okay, I'm glad to see you all,' Eszter said. After being surrounded by happy couples, it was lovely to see her family here. 'What do you think?'

'It's like a fairy tale,' Zoe said in wonder.

'It's perfect,' Anne agreed. 'Oh, look there's Abbie.'

Abbie was walking across the lawn towards them. 'Hello, everyone. Thomas wants to do the chandelier unveiling in a few minutes,' she said to Eszter.

'Great, I'll come and help.'

'Can we stay to see it?' Zoe begged her mum.

'Okay, but then you need to go home to bed, deal?'

Zoe reluctantly agreed.

'Oh my God,' Abbie said, looking away from them, her face draining of colour. 'What is *he* doing here?'

Eszter turned to follow her gaze. 'Who . . .' she trailed off as she recognised Abbie's ex, Jack, stumbling around the side of the hotel towards them. 'Did you invite him?'

'No way,' Abbie said. 'I'd better intercept him. Try to get Thomas to hold off for a little bit, please,' she said hurriedly, leaving them to walk towards Jack.

'It was going so well,' Eszter said, shaking her head. She handed her glass to Anne who was looking confused as to what was happening. 'Hold this for me please, I'll be right back.' She hurried inside to warn Thomas and hoped that Abbie would be able to defuse the situation. There was no doubt in her mind that Jack was there to cause trouble.

Chapter Sixty-five

'Jack, what are you doing here?' Abbie said, standing in front
of him, trying to block his view of the party, and the party's
view of him. Her ex stumbled a little. He was clearly drunk.
His jeans and scruffy T-shirt complete with three-day stubble
on his chin was in stark contrast to the man she had admired.

'I saw everyone talking about coming here on Facebook.
I thought you wouldn't mind one more at the party.'

Abbie silently cursed the power of social media. 'You
should have asked me. You're not dressed for the party, for
one thing, and it's obvious you've been drinking. What are
you really doing here, Jack?'

'Kate told me you're with *him* now,' he said with a sneer.
'When I asked about you, she said you're really happy.
Lording it up out here. You think you're really something,
don't you?'

Abbie sighed. She couldn't believe that they had come to
this. 'None of this is my fault. You were the one who stole

from work, the one who lied to me; you were the one who broke us. Don't blame me for trying to rebuild my life. You need to do the same. Go home, sober up, and stop pitying yourself.' She turned to go but he grabbed her arm.

'Why are you with him? You know you should be with me.'

Abbie pulled her arm from him. 'I know nothing of the sort. Thomas respects me, he's honest with me, he loves me, we are partners. I never had that with you. You're not welcome here, Jack. Please leave.' She was pleased her voice didn't come out as shaky as she felt. She turned before he could see the tears in her eyes and she hurried back to the party.

'Abbie,' Thomas rushed up to her. 'Eszter said Jack is here. Are you okay? You look shaken up.'

'I'm okay.' She grabbed a passing drink from the waiter's tray and took a gulp. 'I just can't believe he would show up.'

'Has he gone?' Thomas asked, looking behind her.

'I think so. I'm sorry, he almost ruined everything.'

'You have nothing to be sorry for.' He gave her a quick kiss. 'Do you need to go home?'

She shook her head. There was no way she was letting Jack ruin the night. 'Let's do the unveiling.'

'Are you sure?'

'Positive.' She drained her glass dry and wrapped her arm through his. 'Lead the way.' She looked worriedly over her shoulder as they walked into the ballroom but there was no sign of Jack. She hoped he would get a taxi home and start to move on as she had done.

Thomas led her to the centre of the room. The party was in full swing now, everyone oblivious to any drama, just enjoying themselves, which was what she had wanted. She smiled to see the room just how she had pictured it when she first walked in weeks ago. It had been neglected for years but now it was as it was supposed to be.

'Eszter said Jack is here,' Louise said, coming over with Kate. 'What happened?'

'He just showed up drunk. He was angry that I'm with Thomas now,' she said in a low voice, not wanting to upset Thomas when he was about to have his big moment. He was talking to the man who was going to take the cover off the chandelier. 'I can't believe I ever thought he was the man for me.' Louise gave her a quick hug.

'I'm sorry, Abs,' Kate said. 'When I last saw him, he kept asking about you so I told him you were happy now. I thought it would mean he'd leave you alone, not that he'd come here.'

'It's not your fault,' Abbie reassured her. 'He's gone. Let's try to enjoy ourselves. I saw you talking to Alex,' she said to her sister, who was clearly glowing.

Louise's face lit up. 'We're having breakfast tomorrow. I'm going to use the Kindness Board, like we said.'

'That's great!' Abbie was thrilled her sister had finally opened up her heart and she was certain that she and Alex would be as happy as she was with Thomas.

A clinking glass stopped their conversation, and the whole room turned to look at Thomas who stood holding a glass

underneath the chandelier. 'Good evening, ladies and gen-tlemen,' he said in his clear, cultured voice when the room fell silent. Abbie wanted to tell them all that he was hers. 'Welcome to Huntley Manor,' he said to a ripple of applause. 'I am so proud to welcome you all here tonight in our newly restored ballroom. This room was once the pride and joy of the hotel but it fell into disrepair and hasn't been used for years until tonight. I think we can all agree that was a real shame. Seeing it back to its former glory has been a labour of love. I want to thank all the Huntley Manor staff and everyone who's helped make tonight possible.'

Thomas turned to Abbie then. 'I'd like to add a special thanks to the wonderful Littlewood PR & Events, who have put this event together. This room would have stayed disused if it wasn't for Abbie Morgan telling me to open it up again. Thank you, Abbie, and Eszter for all your hard work.' Abbie beamed at him. She found Eszter in the crowd and raised a glass to her. Thomas turned back to the room. 'The one part of the room that needed special care was the chandelier that has hung from the ceiling for many years. We had it restored and tonight I'm delighted to show you all the finished result.' He gestured to the side and in one fluid sweep, the covering was pulled off to reveal the sparkling, lit chandelier. Everyone gasped. It really was stunning. Abbie looked up at it in wonder. It had been worth the wait. It was the perfect centrepiece for the room. Everyone broke into applause.

'Here's to Huntley Manor,' Abbie cried over the noise.

Everyone repeated her toast and raised their glasses. She went over to Thomas and he wrapped his arms around her. 'It's perfect,' she told him.

'So are you,' he said, leaning down to kiss her.

A loud bark made them draw apart. They looked at one another confused. The barking continued, making the room fall silent again as everyone looked around confused.

'Oh, no, is that Ben?' Eszter said in horror, turning around to see Anne and Zoe in the doorway, evidently having misplaced Ben. She followed them out of the ballroom towards the noise, with Abbie, Louise and Thomas and a lot of the guests behind them, everyone curious to see what the dog was so upset about.

'Oh my God,' Abbie said when she had stopped. She looked at the scene in front of her in disbelief. Jack was in the lounge of the hotel, holding a painting, with Ben in front of him, barking and blocking his exit from the room. 'What the hell is going on?'

Jack turned and saw everyone staring at him. 'This dog tried to attack me,' he said, trying to sound indignant, even though he had been caught red-handed.

Thomas strode forwards then and grabbed the painting from him. 'To stop you stealing, it looks like. You have already been asked to leave my premises,' he told him coldly. 'If you don't do so in the next five seconds, I will call the police. In fact, I think we even have an officer with us tonight, if you'd like to wait for me to find him.'

Jack looked at him with pure hatred. He threw his arms

up in the air. 'Fine, okay, I'm going.' He turned to Abbie. 'Darling, I . . .'

'I don't want to hear from you ever again,' she told him. She walked up to Thomas and took his hand in hers, so grateful that he was there. 'Goodbye, Jack.'

Jack slumped, as if in defeat, and shook his head, giving the now quiet Ben a glare before marching through the door of the hotel. A few people clapped his exit and Abbie leaned against Thomas, relieved that he had gone.

Eszter took Ben's lead and ruffled the dog's head. 'Well done, Ben,' she told the dog who wagged his tail happily. 'We did what we set out to do at least,' she said to Abbie. 'Everyone is going to be talking about this party,' she said, nodding to the crowd heading back to the ballroom chattering excitedly.

Abbie wasn't sure whether to laugh or cry.

'Don't worry,' Thomas assured her, seeing her concerned face. 'Let's go back in and enjoy ourselves. We won't be seeing him again. We shouldn't let him spoil our night. How about that dance?'

Abbie smiled at him. 'I'd love that,' she said, taking his hand and letting him lead her back to the ballroom, closing the door firmly on the past behind her.

Chapter Sixty-six

Louise let herself into Brew just after dawn the following day. She had begged Joy and Harry to let her have the place for a couple of hours before they opened and when she explained why, they had been happy to hand their keys over. After turning on the lights, she pulled a table out in the centre of the room and set two chairs down on the floor. She laid it for two, complete with fresh flowers in a vase she had brought with her.

Then, Louise walked over to the Kindness Board and wiped it clean. She hoped the people who had written up there wouldn't mind starting again. Picking up the chalk, she took a deep breath and started to write.

After she had written what she wanted to say, she went into the kitchen and set about making breakfast.

Half an hour later, Alex called out her name and she went out into the café to greet him. 'Good morning,' he said with a smile. 'This looks lovely,' he said, looking at the table.

'Sit down, I'll be back in a minute with breakfast,' she said, wishing she didn't feel quite so nervous. She hurried back into the kitchen and plated up their breakfast of pancakes and berries drizzled with syrup, scrambled eggs, bacon and toast, and brought them out. She added freshly brewed coffee to the table and a plate of croissants: all the best that Brew had to offer, although she was sure that Harry would have made it even better.

'Wow, this is a treat,' Alex said, helping her to put everything down onto the table. 'Beats my usual cereal, for sure.' He looked at her as she sat down. 'What's all this in aid of?'

'The Kindness Board will explain all,' Louise replied, her voice shaking a little. Her palms were clammy as she watched him turn to the board. She felt a little sick, which was a shame as the food looked amazing, but she really wasn't sure how he would react to all of this. What if she had got it all wrong and he wasn't at all interested? She glanced at the door, planning a quick escape route.

Alex got up to read the board properly and it seemed as if time stood still as he read what she had written up there just for him.

Alex, for bringing so much kindness into my life this summer. For finding my earrings and for finding my heart. I didn't realise how trapped my heart was until you set it free. You have bought me my favourite flowers, delivered me my favourite coffee, cheered me up when I was sick, looked after me when I drank way too much, and

brightened up so many days with a kind word and a smile. You understood that I'd been hurt before and I was scared. You showed me that I do need people. That I do deserve love. And how much love I have to give. Alex, you've changed everything this summer. I wanted you to know that. My heart is yours, if you'll still have me?

Louise bit her lip as silence hung heavily around them. His back was still turned to her as he read the board so she had no idea of how he was reacting to it. Finally, she couldn't take it anymore, and cleared her throat.

Alex turned around slowly to face her, and his eyes were brimming with tears. 'Louise, you wrote this for me? You did all this for me?'

She got up. 'All summer you've looked after everyone. Me, your sister and your niece, all the animals, you are always helping other people and I just wanted to do something for you. I wanted you to know how much you mean to us all. To me,' she said, her words choking up at the end. 'I understand if you don't feel the same way but I had to tell you. I have run from love for the past two years but I don't want to run anymore, because of you.'

'Of course I feel the same way!' Alex walked over to her and wiped away the tear that had rolled down her cheek. 'I was convinced that you would never want me, kept telling myself to walk away from you, but I always had this hope that you would. One day.'

She nodded. 'I want to be with you,' she said, the tears flowing freely now.

'Is it okay to kiss you even though you're crying?'

Louise wrapped her arms around his neck and felt his hands on her waist, anchoring her in a way she could never have believed someone's touch could, and when their lips finally met she knew that she had nothing to be scared about anymore. Alex was what she hadn't realised she had been looking for.

'Shall we eat?' Alex asked with a laugh when they parted.

'My appetite is back, so yes.' Louise sat down and took a sip of juice. She was relieved, and happy, and a little bit giddy from their kiss. 'I was so worried you wouldn't come back to Littlewood, and that I'd missed my chance to tell you how I felt. I was considering coming up to Scotland and beating down your tent.'

'I must admit I did go away because of you,' he began, taking a quick bite of eggs. He saw her face and shook his head. 'I mean that when we went for that drink at Huntley Manor, I really wanted to kiss you. So much. But I was so worried you still just wanted to be friends, and I was too scared to ask you in case I got rejected again. So, when my cousins suggested a camping trip, I jumped at the idea. I thought if I could get away for a while, get some distance from you, I'd realise that I wasn't really in love with you at all and I could get over you, once and for all.'

'It worked well then?' Louise said, smiling across at him. His leg touched hers and neither of them moved.

'It was a disaster. I saw your face in every view. There was so much peace and quiet, I thought of you even more than I

had done here. I missed you a lot. But it did help in one way. It made me see that I had to try one last time or I'd always regret it. I had to come back and see if there was any hope that you might feel the same way about me one day.'

'I was so happy when you came to the party.'

'When I saw you in that dress, I knew I'd done the right thing.' He winked. 'When we danced, I knew I couldn't be anywhere but right here, with you.'

'Why didn't you say anything last night?'

'You have no idea how badly I wanted to. When you invited me for breakfast, I dared to hope but I could never have expected any of this.' He glanced at the board again and smiled. 'I'm very glad I came back.' He reached for her hand across the table and squeezed it.

'Me too. I'm sorry I pushed you away so much.'

'You needed time, I understood that. I would never hurt you intentionally, I hope you know that.'

Louise nodded. 'I do.'

They finished their breakfast with Alex telling her about his trip, and Louise telling him about the drama at Brew and at the party. When they had finished, Alex pushed his chair back and asked her to come over. He pulled her down onto his lap when she did. 'I can't quite believe this has happened finally,' he said, kissing her softly on the lips.

She smiled, amazed how good it felt to kiss him. 'I'm sorry it took me so long,' she said, pulling him in for a deeper, lingering kiss.

A knock behind them at the door made them both

turn in surprise. Outside were Joy and Harry, smiling and waving at them.

'I think we'd better let them open Brew,' Louise said, laughing at how happy they were seeing her draped over his lap.

'I don't want to let you go.'

'Come back to the cottage with me,' she suggested boldly, climbing off him reluctantly. The look he gave her made her pulse quicken, and she hurried to let them in, keen to get Alex back to hers as soon as she could. She was so relieved that it had gone so well, and was certain as she could be that their future together was going to be a happy one.

Chapter Sixty-seven

Abbie and Eszter stood in the centre of their new office at Huntley Manor a few weeks later and watched as Louise walked around, taking it all in. Summer had faded into autumn and the trees in the grounds of the hotel were starting to turn a burnt orange, making the view from their window even more stunning.

'It's perfect,' Louise declared enthusiastically. They had finally moved in to the space now. There were two desks and chairs, a large plant in the corner, two paintings from the attic treasure trove hanging on the wall, and a sofa at one end for visitors. The walls were cream, the floor polished wood, and light blinds had been fitted at the window. It felt airy and bright, and the views over Huntley Manor and beyond were bound to stun even the most cold-hearted of clients. 'This calls for a toast.' She picked up the champagne she had brought for both of them to celebrate the official launch of Littlewood PR & Events. It opened with a bang, making

them jump and laugh, and she poured out three glasses. They were having lunch with Thomas, Alex, Joy, Harry, Anne and Zoe later downstairs but they had wanted just a moment with the three of them to mark the start of their new business.

Louise cleared her throat and the three of them stood together, glasses poised. 'Okay, I just wanted to say that I'm really proud of both of you. I know this business is going to be a big success, and I'm so happy that you have both stayed in Littlewood with me. I also wanted to say thank you. At the start of the summer, I was lonely but I didn't want to admit it and you not only brought friendship and family back into my life, but you helped me open up again and I found Alex. If it hadn't been for our kindness pact, I might have always been scared to take a leap and I would have missed out on so much. I'm really happy and I know you both are too, so I think we should raise our glasses to Littlewood PR, and to kindness!'

They clinked glasses and took a sip, all three of them trying not to cry.

'I can't believe we've actually done it,' Abbie said, looking around the room. 'This could have all turned out so differently.' She gave a little shudder at the thought of that.

'It's all happened so fast,' Eszter agreed. 'Zoe starts school here next week and we're all moved in to Anne's. I never thought I'd be moving to the UK permanently. Honestly, what is it about this place?'

'Littlewood gets under your skin,' Abbie said.

'It's because there's a community here, and we look out

for one another,' Louise said. 'And it's just a lovely place to live. I can't imagine living anywhere else now.' She was very much still in the honeymoon stage of love with Alex, and felt as if she had a smile on her face most of the time. 'And you were right – kindness is good for you. And not just helping others but looking after yourself too.' Louise would always love caring for other people and reading the Kindness Board in Brew but she now also made sure that she didn't lose sight of what she wanted. Following her heart was something she had been running from for a long time. She now knew that being kind to yourself was important if you were going to be happy. And she deserved to be happy.

'Hear hear,' Abbie said, wrapping an arm around her sister's waist. 'What's that?' she asked, hearing a noise outside. A dog barked and they looked at one another with a smile. Soon after, the door burst open and in ran Zoe with Ben at her heels as usual. They were followed by Alex who was carrying a bunch of balloons, Thomas who had two bouquets of flowers and was stumbling under their weight, and behind them Anne, Joy and Harry were carrying wrapped-up presents.

'We couldn't wait any longer to see it,' Zoe explained, rushing over to look out of the window, Ben scampering after her and almost knocking over the champagne. Eszter grabbed it just in time; she was getting used to looking out for Ben chaos, and even though he could be naughty they had all fallen head over heels for the gentle, soppy dog.

'That's okay,' Abbie said. 'What do you think?'

'I like it,' Zoe declared.

'You've done a great job,' Alex agreed, looking around. He tied the balloons to the desk. 'Congratulations.'

They piled the gifts up on the desk, and then everyone took a drop of champagne and another toast was ordered.

Thomas cleared his throat. 'I just wanted to say that Huntley Manor is very pleased to welcome Littlewood PR to its fold. At the start of the summer, I thought that I would have to sell my family home, but thanks to everyone in this room, it's still here and bookings are full for the first time in years. And, thanks to the auction, we are starting an improvements programme to make sure this house stands for years and years to come. I hope we'll all be here to enjoy it for years and years to come too,' he said, holding up his glass. They all cheered the sentiment and drank their champagne. Zoe, annoyed that she wasn't allowed any, took a sip of her orange juice. Even Ben joined in with an enthusiastic bark.

'Are you okay?' Louise asked, noticing Eszter looking out of the window as they got ready to go down for lunch.

'I'm fine. I just wish Nick was here to see all of this,' she admitted.

'I think he is. That letter he wrote, it's like he knew this place would claim you and he gave it his blessing. He'll always be looking down on both of you, I'm sure of it.'

Eszter nodded, her eyes welling up. 'I know one day I'll move on but right now, I still miss him so much.'

'Of course you do. There's no rush to move on. You have family and friends and a new home here, and look at what

437

you're starting with Abbie. It's just the beginning of your new adventure. And I think Nick is coming along right beside you.'

'Thanks, Louise.' Eszter gave her a quick hug. 'Can you imagine if I hadn't run into you and Abbie on my first day here?'

'I'm very glad my sister was so careless and dropped her bag, and even more so that you were kind enough to chase after her with it,' Louise replied, thinking that it must have been fate that brought them all together. She looked around the room. She was sure that there were still ups and downs to come, that was life after all, but they would get through it because they had each other.

'Are you ready?' Alex asked her, taking hold of her hand in his. She smiled. She was.

Notes from the Brew Kindness Board:

The compliment card that a shop assistant handed me really brightened up my day!

* * * *

Thank you to everyone who donated items to our local food bank, I was really struggling and am beyond grateful for the help.

* * * *

A lovely patient brought in cupcakes for all the nurses on the ward they had been on to say thank you – what a treat!

* * * *

Thank you to the lady who spotted my son had wandered away from me in the supermarket. She brought him back to me before I could panic and I am so grateful.

A Note from the Author

Dear reader,

Thank you for choosing to read *Summer at the Kindness Café*. I loved creating the town of Littlewood, and its inhabitants, and thinking about how kindness has the power to change lives. I really hope that you enjoyed reading it, and it inspires you to add some kindness to your own life.

I love talking to readers, so please do let me know what you thought of the book. Leaving a review online really helps other readers to find the book, so please pop your thoughts up on Amazon, iBooks, Kobo and Goodreads.

You can also let me know if you're a fan of the story by following me on Twitter (@Vicky_Walters), on Instagram (vickyjwalters) and by liking my Facebook page (VictoriaWaltersAuthor).

I am looking forward to hearing from you!

Much love,

Victoria x

FIRST CLASS
HOLIDAYS

Booking your dream holiday is not a decision to be taken lightly, whether that be a touring holiday, a luxury honeymoon or a holiday to celebrate a special occasion.

That's where award-winning First Class Holidays come in. Specialising in tailor-made holidays to Canada & Alaska, America, Australia, New Zealand, South Africa and the Pacific Islands, they take away the hard work when it comes to planning the trip you've always imagined and provide an outstanding level of service while doing so, and with over 750 years' experience between the team, over 100,000 satisfied customers and 23 years delivering exceptional service, they'll plan your journey to absolute perfection, offering first-hand advice with the knowledge they've garnered throughout their own travels.

Victoria Walters writes uplifting and inspiring stories. Her moving debut novel, *The Second Love of My Life*, was chosen for WHSmith Fresh Talent and shortlisted for an RNA award. Victoria was also picked as an Amazon Rising Star.

As well as being an author, Victoria works as a Waterstones bookseller and buys far too many books there. She lives in Surrey with her cat Harry (named after Harry Potter). Victoria is not only obsessed with books, but loves buying slogan tops, mugs and notebooks, and posting them all on Instagram.

You can discover more about Victoria – and find pictures of Harry the cat – by following her on Instagram at @vickyjwalters, on Twitter at @Vicky_Walters or by visiting her blog at victoria-writes.com

'A really lovely story – heart-warming and life-affirming'
Jo Thomas, author of *The Honey Farm on the Hill*

'An entertaining and timely reminder that a
random act of kindness can change not only
someone's day, but also someone's life'
Penny Parkes, author of *Practice Makes Perfect*

'A beautiful story – full of heart'
Giovanna Fletcher

'Such an uplifting, warm story, with characters I
already feel like I know. I loved every minute of it!'
Cressida McLaughlin, author of *The Canal Boat Café series*

'A heart-warming read – cosy and comforting. I loved it!'
**Heidi Swain, author of *Sleigh Rides and
Silver Bells at the Christmas Fair***

'Victoria Walters has such a wonderful, fresh voice and
the characters really do leap off the page. The perfect
pick-me-up for those long winter nights, and a timely
reminder of the importance of kindness in every part of life'
Phoebe Morgan, author of *The Doll House*

'Brilliant and superior women's fiction'
Heat

'Perfect holiday read . . . Just darn brilliant'
Look

'A powerful tale of love, loss and courage'
My Weekly